# TOWARDS THE
# SUNSET

Also by Muriel Elwood
*Heritage of the River*
*Deeper the Heritage*
*Towards the Sunset*
*Web of Destiny*

# TOWARDS THE SUNSET

MURIEL ELWOOD

CUTTING EDGE

ISBN-13: 978-1-957868-32-5

Published by
Cutting Edge Books
PO Box 8212
Calabasas, CA 91372
www.cuttingedgebooks.com

# TOWARDS THE SUNSET

# CHAPTER ONE

H E THREW back his head and laughed like a man who enjoyed laughter. The green-blue eyes beneath his flaming red hair were dancing and eager as he skilfully maneuvered the canoe over the dangerous waters that tried by every trick of nature to overturn them and send him and his three companions to certain death. The men turned quickly at the sound of his sudden laughter, and then looked away again without comment. It was not that it was an unusual sound to them, because formerly he had laughed all the time, but in these last few weeks he had scarcely spoken, let alone laughed. Normally the thunder of the fierce rushing waters of the Lachine Rapids would have been in competition with their voices raised in familiar boat songs but these, too, were silent on this return journey.

"Le Roux", as the men called him because of the rare shade of his thick curly hair, could not repress that one outburst as he manipulated the canoe. This swift, dashing descent over the treacherous rapids always thrilled him. It was something of which *coureurs de bois* boasted, for only the skilled dared attempt it. Step by step the waters fell, bubbling and boiling, swirling and spraying, thundering and murmuring, hiding beneath their swift moving surface jagged rocks that seemed to leap out and try to catch the sides of the birch-bark canoe or failing that to crush its frailty against their strong, sharp crags. It took a deft hand to twist and turn a canoe to avoid these dangers and not until they reached the place where the waters stretched out beyond in a steadier but still strong current, did the boatman dare to take

1

his attention for one instant off the task before him. It was at that moment that "Le Roux" Boissart or André de Courville-Boissart as everyone but the *coureurs de bois* called him, had let out the laugh that would not be repressed. It lingered for a moment or two in a smile about his lips and then faded quickly. The strong chin, covered for the present with a short red beard, was thrust out as once more the thought of the difficult task awaiting him at Montreal bore down upon him. The men felt the weight of it too, and in silence they sped along with the current, dipping a paddle here and there, now and then, to guide the canoe past the islands in the St. Lawrence River.

About two miles west of Montreal they came to the de Brievaux and de Courville Seigneuries, joint seigneuries owned by members of the same family. All day flotillas of canoes had been coming down the river and at their approach children shouted, while from every door habitants ran down to the shore to greet them. But the greetings died on their lips as they realized that the boatmen in this canoe were not singing, and that could mean only one thing. As André's smile had faded a while back, so their smiles now faded to expressions of anxiety and in silence they watched the canoe draw nearer. The crowd along the shore increased, and anxious eyes searched the faces of the four men.

The men jumped out and wading in the water drew the canoe up on to the shore.

"I'll go and see my aunt. You see the families of the other three," André said in a low voice.

The men nodded.

Aunt Marie, summoned by her children as they had sighted the canoe, watched in silence. Her tall son, Philip, with his wife holding the baby in her arms and a small boy of two clinging to her skirts, stood beside her.

André came towards them, his face solemn and his eyes betraying the anxiety he felt. For a moment he saw an expression of terror and dread upon his aunt's face but when he came up to her the expression had gone and she met his glance calmly.

"Philip?" she queried and there was resignation in her tone. For the quarter of a century that her husband had been a fur trader, she had known that some day this moment must come.

André nodded. "Yes, Aunt Marie," he said gently.

She raised her black, sad eyes to his. "Indians?" she asked.

André nodded again.

She turned away, facing the river, her broad shoulders bowed. Her throat ached but no tears would come. The rest of the family—Paul, Charles and Elise had arrived and all stood for a moment or two stunned. Then with their elder brother they went to their mother. Elise was crying—the boys could not, too many people were watching in respectful silence. Marie held out her strong arms and drew her children to her, uttering no word, merely trying to draw strength from their presence about her.

A similar scene was taking place in three other parts of the Seigneury for three other husbands had been captured with Philip Boissart, their leader for so many years. Some of the women like Marie Boissart, took it grimly and silently until they could be alone with their grief; others were more fortunate and could give way and relieve their tension with tears.

It was only a matter of minutes that Marie stood there with her back towards him, but it seemed endless to André, who, like many who bring sad news, had the feeling that somehow he was the cause of the grief. When he saw a redheaded girl running towards him, the tension eased and he enveloped his twin sister in his arms.

"André, darling!" she exclaimed as she kissed him several times on both cheeks, giving way for a moment to the joy of seeing her brother again. "What has happened?" she asked and then before he replied, answered her own question. "Uncle Philip has not returned?"

He nodded.

The crowd that had gathered parted to let the Seigneur and his wife come through. It was the Sieur's youngest brother over whom they mourned. For a brief, but poignant moment, André's father and mother clasped him to them and then his mother went quickly to Marie and put her arms around her, while Paul talked to André.

"How did it happen?" he asked.

"Ambushed, father," André replied.

"Tortured?" the Sieur inquired sharply.

André nodded. Paul bowed his head. This youngest brother had been his favorite. Without Philip's jolly, blustering good humor, the Seigneury would never seem the same.

"I was afraid this would happen one day," he said speaking almost to himself. "Poor Philip. Did he suffer much?"

"I'll tell you all about it later," André replied. "It was ghastly. Should I tell Aunt Marie the details or would it be all right if I just told her the Indians killed him?"

His father was thoughtful for a moment. "Wait and see if she questions you. Spare her all you can."

With her arm around her sister-in-law, Madame de Courville-Boissart led her toward her house. Marie stopped as she saw André looking anxiously at her and came over to him. "Thank God you were spared, André," she said. Relieved, André put his arms around her wide, short body and held her tightly to him. Between aunt and nephew there had always been affection and those few words meant much to him.

Two-thirds of the habitants on the Seigneury were related to the Seigneur and they now gathered around André to hear what had happened. Briefly he gave them the news. They did not ask questions. Later they would be able to learn the full story.

"We also lost Henri Boissart, Duval and Bouton," André informed them. Two of those named were his cousins.

When they had heard the news, most of them returned to their work. It was dinnertime and the women hastened back to their bake-ovens.

"Come up to the house, son," the Sieur said quietly. "Your mother will take care of things."

André glanced anxiously towards Aunt Marie's house, silent in grief when it had always been such a happy place.

"Could you come over and see the children?" Elise asked. Her house was nearby. "They're having their dinner now. Antoine's in Montreal."

"I'm so anxious to see them all," André said. "But I think I had better go along to Montreal first with the furs."

"Why don't you have supper with us then? You and mother wouldn't mind if we steal him, would you?" she asked her father.

"Of course not, dear," her father replied.

"I don't know whether I can keep the children quiet till then," she said and smiled. André was a great favorite with her family.

"I'll come over the moment I get back from town," André told her and kissed her affectionately. There was a warm understanding between these twins.

As Elise watched them for a moment as they walked away together she thought how alike they looked. Both were the same height and had the same stocky build. The Sieur's hair had originally been the same red-gold but now it was streaked with grey and had faded to a sandy color. It seemed to Elise as she looked after them that her father's limp was more pronounced—a limp caused many years ago when he had been wounded in the wars against the Iroquois.

"Indians!" she thought and sighed. What a toll they took of men's lives in this rugged country.

Paul de Courville-Boissart had once been a *coureur de bois* himself and still retained his interest in the fur trade as partner with his son and the brother just killed. He understood the natures of these intrepid men of the forest and knew that hardened though they were to hardship, the loss of any of their company was something that went very deep.

5

"How was the trip otherwise?" he asked his son. "Were you able to bring back many pelts?"

"We are laden," André replied and pointed to the banked canoe in which bales of furs were piled in all the available space. Paul studied them thoughtfully. It was a heavy price to pay for men's lives, yet without the fur trade Montreal could not survive.

As they walked up the steps of the Manor House, André's grief was superseded, momentarily at least, by the joy of once more being back in this home that he loved so dearly. He paused on the steps to look over the Seigneury—the immense acreage that over half a century ago had begun as one small homestead. As he did so, an intense feeling of nostalgia came over him. He had been away nearly two years and now he wondered why he had given up all this comfort for the hardships of forest life. Always when he came back he felt this way but after an interval, wanderlust returned. This time he did not believe he would want to go away again very soon. The sight of Uncle Philip and his companions being slowly tortured to death had sickened him.

"How do you think it looks, son?" his father's voice interrupted his thoughts. There was pride in the Seigneur's tone and it was justifiable.

"Wonderful, father. I was just thinking what a fool I am ever to leave it."

Paul's green-blue eyes showed the pleasure he felt at the words.

"It's good to come back to then?" he asked and as André turned to him he saw the faint smile on his father's face.

"Very good. I shan't leave it again for some time."

"Had enough of fur trading?"

André hesitated a moment and then said: "Yes, I believe so. I want to take my place here."

Paul's arm went across his son's shoulders. "I'm glad to hear you say that, André. You will make a good seigneur," he said as they entered the house.

The Manor House, as all the seigneurial houses were styled, stood upon a knoll commanding a fine view of the St. Lawrence River. It had stood there for sixty-four years dominating the lives and activities of the many families who were part of the de Courville Seigneury. About two miles west of the struggling town of Montreal, the Seigneury had been granted in 1656 to the Sieur de Courville, whose memory would always be revered, especially by the older members of the five families who had pioneered with him. Now in this year of 1720, these families had increased to over one hundred and fifty souls and with the French-Canadian's prolificacy would go on increasing, provided that wars with the Indians and the English did not wipe them out.

Paul de Courville-Boissart was not a direct descendant of the Sieur de Courville, but had acquired the Seigneury by adoption and had carried out the old Sieur's dreams and hopes by making it a model for all who had the courage and the endurance of the pioneer. Now, stretching far along the banks of the river and straggling back for miles to the rising hills, all was cultivated and prosperous. Where there had originally been five shacks and the Manor House, now there were many houses, as each son in accordance with feudal law had taken his own portion and had built his own home and had begun to rear a family.

Antoine de Brievaux had married the Sieur de Courville-Boissart's only daughter, Elise, and the two men had combined their fortunes and interests to create communal advantages. Within the last few years a large granary had been erected on the boundaries of the two seigneuries, to which the habitants brought their grain. Paul de Courville-Boissart's cherished hope was that sometime in the near future they would be able to build their own church and perhaps their own school.

The de Brievaux Manor House was one of the few that could qualify for the title. Built more recently, it had been able to reap several advantages over its predecessors. In the first place Antoine de Brievaux had a fair fortune of his own and had been able to expend money which most of the older seigneurs had lacked. He and his wife had spent their honeymoon in France and had brought back numerous tapestries and furnishings which gave the interior an elegant appearance. Furthermore, Elise's artistic sense had added not only to the interior but to the exterior. She had conceived the idea which, without her knowing it, had already become a part of homes in the south of the American continent and had suggested that they build a porch or *galerie* where during the warm evenings they could sit and enjoy the view of the river.

The joint arrangement was a good one. The de Courville-Seigneury produced more wheat and vegetables than was required and these products were supplied to the de Brievaux Seigneury, while the latter had a large orchard and in return supplied fruit and nuts. When the de Courville Seigneury had been developing, almost every tree had been cut down, because of the Iroquois wars and the danger that a tree could hide a threatening savage. But with this danger past, Antoine had been able to preserve his precious trees. Maples for sugar; cherry, apple and walnut trees for their fruit; pines, firs and cedars for medicinal use and for their rosin; birches for making canoes; and ash as well as oak, maples, and pines for their precious wood, with beeches and elms for shade—all these he had preserved and used.

Elise had also exercised her artistic taste by planting flowers all around her house and though her father's Seigneury provided for their table, she had nevertheless planted her own kitchen garden. The orchard running off from one side of the house was her especial joy and during the picking season she and her children had merry parties. Hers was a happy nature, made the more so because there had been a period when her happiness had been threatened and she had feared she would never be able to marry the man she loved. This threat had made their marriage more precious and they knew the joy that can only come when two people are perfectly mated. Even Antoine did not fully know the joy it had given her to see him develop into a good seigneur because this had been the one thing she had feared would not happen. Reared in Paris, a gentleman of leisure until he was twenty-one, she had been afraid that with this easy way of living, he would never be able to accustom himself to the hard life of farming, for in this new continent seigneurs and habitants alike worked in the fields. She had feared that because of his love for her he was only pretending to like the new life, but the fear had faded with the years. Though they had visited France several times during these years, he had always been delighted to return to the Seigneury and had left France with no regrets.

# CHAPTER TWO

THE sun was beginning to set as Elise de Brievaux left her Aunt Marie's house hard by the boundary of the two Seigneuries. Her eyes were glistening with tears for she had had a deep affection for her Uncle Philip and was more devoted to Aunt Marie than to any of her numerous relations. She had tried to bring comfort to her but felt her effort had been inadequate. By the river she paused and stood looking out over its calm waters, marshalling her thoughts before returning to her house. This was the time of evening she loved, when the hills turned to mauve as the sun reflected on them and activity on the farm began to subside. The lowing and bleating of the animals as they went to the barns were music to her ears. A gentle breeze ruffled through the luxurious waves of her red-gold hair, now seemingly afire as the setting rays of the sun touched it. She lifted her face to the breeze, enjoying its soft caress on her cheek. She was a beautiful woman, with delicately carved features. It was necessary to look closely to detect the fading marks of smallpox that had once threatened to ravage her beauty. Life had been kind to her and she had never known the hardships of the pioneers for these had been mostly overcome prior to her birth twenty-eight years ago. When sorrow and separation came to families as it had this day, she was grateful for the happiness and security that were hers.

She turned and looked towards her home, beautiful now as the sun touched some of the windows making them shine with golden light. On the steps to the *galerie* she could see her youngest son straining to the full height of his five years and watching anxiously for the first glimpse of his Uncle André. Ever since she had told him at noon that his uncle had returned, he had been waiting and watching. Paul-André had been named after his grandfather and his uncle and he had all the merriment that characterized his uncle and all the spirit of both uncle and grandfather.

As she looked at him, her eyes deepening with the warmth of her love, he suddenly bounded down the steps and rushed towards her shouting at the top of his lusty little voice: "Uncle André's coming! Uncle André's coming!" His reddish-brown eyes were shining with excitement as he looked up at her. She smoothed back the wavy auburn hair which his nervous little hands had disarranged as he had waited impatiently.

"Where, darling?" she asked and her voice was as eager as his. She turned and gazed into the distance but could see no one.

"I saw him from the *galerie,* really I did," he insisted and grabbing her hand, hurried her up the porch steps. "There—he's coming along the riverbank. May I go and meet him? Please maman."

The eager eyes of the little boy had not deceived him and she could now see André striding along the riverbank.

"Yes, hurry along," she said and watched him as he scrambled down the steps and ran so fast that several times he stumbled but picked himself up again and ran on, not stopping until he had been swept up onto his uncle's shoulder and was borne triumphantly home.

Elise went to the door and called inside that André was coming. There was a scrambling of feet as her other three children came hurrying out and were joined in a moment by their father. Antoine put his arm around his wife and smiled understandingly at her. He shared with her a fondness for this twin brother of hers. Antoine de Brievaux was a tall man, with dark wavy hair and a cheerful, good-natured face. Though he wore homespuns, there was an air about him that reflected his aristocratic birth.

André waved to them gaily. "He's been waiting hours for you!" Elise said laughing as he lowered his nephew and embraced her. Paul-André held securely to his uncle's hand, having no intention of being superseded by his brother and sisters who now crowded around their uncle. With difficulty André extricated a hand and over the heads of the children, gave Antoine a warm handclasp. There was little chance for any conversation as the children clamored for recognition. André surveyed his nephews and nieces with affection.

Elise had given all her children double names to distinguish them more easily from the numerous relatives on the seigneuries. So many of the others had the same names that it was necessary always to refer to them as "Georges' Pierre" or "Etienne's Pierre" and "Henri's Marie" or "Philip's Marie." Thus, as Paul-André was named after her father and brother, so Jean-Baptiste was named after her older brother who had died and the two girls were called Ann-Marie, after her mother and Aunt Marie and Charlotte-Marguerite after an old friend and her father's twin sister, Marguerite.

Jean-Baptiste, the eldest, though not yet eleven years old was nearly as tall as his uncle, for André was only five feet six. Jean-Baptiste was as serious as his younger brother was irresponsible, yet he idolized this younger brother and was always ready to protect him or shield him when he was in trouble. Like his father he had black wavy hair but instead of Antoine's deep black eyes, his were hazel, softening the sharp lines of the rest of his features.

André shook hands with him and commented upon how he had grown. "He's going to be as tall as his father," Elise remarked and smiled with maternal pride at the son who soon would look down at her from his greater height.

"And is already learning to manage the Seigneury," Antoine commented proudly.

"Fine," André said and added, "It's a grand life."

Elise shot him a quick glance at this remark but he was already greeting his nieces. He gave each of them a resounding kiss which was accepted by Ann-Marie, the elder, with coyness and Charlotte-Marguerite with simplicity. No two sisters could have presented a greater contrast. Ann-Marie had combined the red-headed tradition of the family with that of the dark hair on her father's side, so that instead of the red-gold of the two previous generations, she had rich auburn hair which fell in long wavy tresses that were her particular pride and of which she was rather conceited. With less red in her hair, her complexion had less of the yellowish pigment and freckles of her mother and her pink and white skin gave promise that she was going to develop into a beautiful woman. Her eyes were the color of dark amber instead of the green-blue of other red-headed members of the family. Even at nine her appearance was a matter of importance to her and she showed signs of maturing early as she centered her interest more on the boys of the Seigneury than on her schoolmates.

Charlotte-Marguerite stood shyly by as André teased Ann-Marie. When he turned to her he was struck by the deep somberness of the large black eyes which looked at him. Without this dominating feature she would have been a plain child, for her straight black hair was devoid of any suggestion of curl. Among the rest of the curly headed members of the family, she stood out almost freakishly and immediately André realized, as others had done, that this child was different. When there was laughter she only smiled deeply and despite all her mother's efforts, she remained a serious child who played quietly and often alone. As André talked to her he was conscious of a spiritual quality about her which made the flippant conversation he had used with the others die on his lips. Instead he cupped her chin in his hand and kissed her again, putting his arm around her and going into the house with her on one side and Paul-André clinging doggedly to the other.

During supper the conversation remained general as all the children had been allowed to stay up for this special occasion. There was no denying them attention as they pestered André with eager questions about the trip. He told them stories of his experiences in the woods, avoiding any reference to the tragedy that had overtaken them. They had all been told earlier in the day that their great-uncle Philip had been killed and Elise had emphasized the danger of Indians hoping that this might depreciate Paul-André's interest in them. But all through André's narrative the little boy's eyes were wide with interest and no amount of prompting would make him eat his supper. Over and over again he kept saying to his uncle: "Tell me more about the Indians," and André would describe some of the more friendly savages who frequented the forts. At the end of each story the same request would be repeated until André asked him with a smile:

"Why are you so interested in Indians, Paul-André?"

"I like them. I want to be an Indian," he said and small as the chin was it had a stubborn look.

"But you've hardly seen any Indians," his mother protested. "How can you know whether you like them?"

"I've seen them in Montreal. I like them. I want to be an Indian," he repeated. Laughing, they left the matter there, his mother knowing full well that all the morrow the air would resound with warwhoops as he played his favorite game.

Supper over, the children were sent to bed, Paul-André stubbornly refusing to obey unless his uncle carried him up and put him to bed. This done, André returned and joined Elise and Antoine in the parlor. While Elise embroidered, the two men sipped their brandy and the conversation remained general in the way that people will talk of everything but that which is unpleasant and close to their minds.

As Elise looked at her brother, she thought as she had often thought before, that there was no denying the attraction of these men who risked their lives and endured hardships in order to bring the valuable pelts to the Montreal market. They had about them an air of adventure and a strength of personality that often remained undeveloped in those who remained on the farms. André's eyes were keen and bright and he seemed so vital even as he lounged in his chair sipping his brandy. The deerskin jacket and leggings with their fringed seams and the bright sash about the waist gave him a daring look. The red beard on his chin made him look rather fierce and detracted somewhat from his good looks. She commented upon it and he laughed merrily.

"Don't you like it?" he asked and fingered the stiff, strong hairs.

"No." She shook her head vehemently. "You don't look like my twin brother."

"Well, you can hardly grow a beard so that we can look alike, so I suppose I'll have to shave it off." He laughed and fingered the beard again. "I have grown rather used to it and a little fond of it, but, to please you I'll take it off tomorrow."

"I'm glad," she said and smiled fondly at him.

"I had meant to take it off today but Father and I sat talking and the time went by."

The conversation lagged for a short space and knowing by the heavy look that had now come into his face, what her brother was thinking, Elise opened the way by saying.

"The trip was very hard this time, André?"

He looked at her and then at Antoine. "It was a wonderful trip until we fell foul of the Indians. They were Foxes..."

"I hear they're giving a lot of trouble," Antoine commented.

"Yes. Presumably Uncle Philip thought they were friendly. He had always been able to get along well with all the tribes. He spoke their language and knew their ways and even when their approach at first was hostile, he was always able to make them understand that he came as a friend." He paused to relight his pipe and puffed at it in silence for a few minutes. "I don't understand it. I have been trying ever since to figure it out." An anxious frown rumpled his forehead.

"Were you ambushed?" Antoine asked. He had never been into the woods but the lives of these men fascinated him and he admired them.

"We were out hunting," André went on. "We had separated into two groups and had arranged to meet at a certain place to camp that night. We arrived first and made camp and prepared supper. We were not unduly alarmed when the others did not come and we rolled into our blankets for the night. The next morning we waited and still they did not come. Then we became a little alarmed and retraced our steps to pick up their trail. We followed it for two days and then came upon traces of an ambush. We found Henri Boissart—he was the more fortunate, he had been scalped. We buried him and then went on until we came to a small Indian village. Before we saw, we knew. We could hear by the sounds what was going on. It was these sounds that perhaps saved us from being caught too. By that time the savages were all too drunk to notice the barking of their curs and we remained in hiding hoping up to the last that we could do something to rescue our men. But it was hopeless. We were four men against some twenty or thirty and anyway …" He stopped as the horror of what he had seen came back to him. He had heard all his life of these Indian tortures. His own great-grandfather and his father's twin sister had both been caught by the savages but had lived to tell of the horror. It was the first time that André had had to witness it.

"I'll spare you the details. They were too horrible," he said.

"Try to forget it, dear," Elise said gently.

"I have tried to but I can't. I can't lose the feeling that somehow I failed Uncle Philip. If the position had been reversed he would have thought of a way. I have gone over it all so many times. We should not have waited until the next morning. When they didn't reach camp we should have gone to look for them and then as I think that, reason tells me that in the dark we couldn't have found their trail and I would have risked the lives of the men with me by moving at night. I don't know, I just don't know."

"Uncle Philip would understand, dear. He knew that you would do anything that was possible."

André still looked unconvinced. "I hope Aunt Marie doesn't question me. I can't tell her the details…"

"I doubt whether she will ask you for details," Elise said. "Hers is not a morbidly curious nature. She has always known there was danger and that probably one day he would not return. In fact, I believe she had a premonition that this was his last journey. One afternoon I was visiting with her and we were talking about Uncle Philip. Very quietly she said: 'One day he will not return.' I think she knew."

"Probably," André said and then added: "She is wonderfully brave."

"She is," Elise agreed, "but I wish she could let go of her grief. She suffers so much inside. I was with her this afternoon. One thing she kept saying and it's how I feel, too, André, that she hoped you would give up fur trading now. We can't lose you, André. I know it's hard for you to settle down, but Father and Mother have already lost Jean-Baptiste and if they lost you too, who would carry on the Seigneury?"

"I know. Mother talked to me this afternoon."

He sat thinking of the conversation he had had earlier with his mother. It was seldom that Ann de Courville-Boissart lost her quiet poise but when he had told them the details of what had happened to Uncle Philip, her composure had broken and for the first time she had pleaded with him to give up the fur trade. There had never been any comment upon his pursuit of the profession he loved, not even after his elder brother Jean-Baptiste had died. Since his father had been a *coureur de bois* before he had married, he knew and understood the life. Because Paul's own father had been so much against it, he had determined that his son should not have the same prejudice to combat. But all the time André was away, Paul worried about him, though he would not have let his wife know it, for he knew that she also worried. But this afternoon Ann had given way to her feelings and had pleaded with her son to remain at home.

"Your father and I are both getting older, André, and we need you," she had told him.

He had readily acquiesced to their request for he had had enough of roving and a shock that would take time to get over.

Rousing from his reverie he said: "No. I shall not go away again, Elise. I told Mother and Father that this afternoon and I mean it. It is time I devoted myself to the Seigneury. Father's nearly fifty now and it is only right that I should be here to help him. He has been very good in letting me have all these years of freedom—not that being home curtails my freedom."

"And you will think about getting married?" Elise urged.

André directed a thoughtful smile to her.

"That seems to be a very urgent question since my return," he said.

"But don't you want to get married, André? You like women, don't you?"

"Of course."

"And wouldn't you like to have a family of your own? You seem to enjoy my children."

"You think I'd make a good father, then?" he bantered.

"Yes, I do. You have such a way with children. Paul-André adores you."

"The little rogue!"

"Yes he is. He takes a lot of managing."

"I'll spend more time with him now."

"But you should have children of your own to spend time with. They should be sons and daughters—not nieces and nephews."

He grinned at her and as she returned the smile, they looked very much alike.

"I promise to give it very serious consideration, my dear sister," he said and stood up. "And now, it is time we all went to bed."

As he kissed his sister goodnight she clung to him for a moment. She and Antoine watched him as he walked away and the hunch of his shoulders told them that his thoughts were deep.

"I'm glad you never became a fur trader, Antoine," she said quietly. The arm around her tightened and she was glad of the strength and comfort.

# CHAPTER THREE

A MONTH after André's return it was the Feast of the Nativity of St. Jean-Baptiste—a festival celebrated every June 24th throughout the colony. It was only a minor feast day but it meant a holiday and a respite from the heavy labors of the summer season.

At the river's edge could be seen the mound of ashes which had not yet been cleared away since the previous night—the remains of the huge bonfire that was a traditional part of the Eve of St. Jean-Baptiste, when the habitants held an impressive ceremony handed down from their Norman ancestors. Every year the boys and girls collected quantities of wood and piled it high on the riverbank before the Seigneur's house. Six to ten feet high it rose, with branches of fir and strips of cedar intertwined to give it a solid foundation. Nor was it just piled in haphazard manner, but into a definite formation, shaped like an octagon, with little piles of straw at each of the eight corners. On every seigneury there was the same arrangement and also in Montreal before the Church where the priest offered prayers and blessings before the pile was ignited. An hour after sunset was the signal. Then the Sieur de Courville-Boissart and the other seigneurs on their land took a torch and started the bonfire. The whole pile burst into flames amid shouts and gun-firing from the crowd. It had a definite purpose, for this was their way of signalling to friends all along the shore. Many of them had prearranged signals and as the fires flamed along the darkened shore, eyes were strained to watch those of intimate friends. From these they could tell whether all was well or whether there had been death or illness. If the fire burned steadily, then it was good news and hearts rejoiced. But if it was made to sink gradually, it indicated sickness and if it was extinguished suddenly it meant death. If it appeared to be extinguished more than once then it signified several deaths. The deaths of Philip Boissart and his three companions were signalled across the river but not until the fire had burned steadily for a while to indicate that otherwise all was well. Laughter and songs filled the air on most of the seigneuries, for this traditional method of conveying news had lost some of its significance since the savages had been kept from the shores.

To Ann de Courville-Boissart the day was more important than many of the larger festivals ordained by the Church. It was the day dedicated to the memory of her elder son, Jean-Baptiste, who had died at the age of twenty. As the Seigneur's wife it was incumbent upon her to attend the celebrations on the Seigneury but she always retired early to be alone with her thoughts and prayers. Her husband respected her feelings for he knew how much Jean-Baptiste had meant to her. Though Paul had loved this elder son he had never understood him as Ann had done.

Ann de Courville-Boissart was an aristocrat—the only daughter of the Chevalier de Luc, Minister of France. From her Jean-Baptiste had developed a sensitivity that had made it difficult for him to apply himself to the rough, simple life on an early Canadian seigneury. He had preferred the glitter of Versailles, the shallowness of Parisian society and the leisurely life of a gentleman. He had been born of the first passion of Paul and Ann, when she was trying to adapt herself to pioneer life. As the years went on she had been able to succeed but had not been able to transmit her adaptability to her son. She alone had understood the two sides that pulled constantly at his nature and his death had left a gap in her life. It was not that she did not love André—few could help loving him, but he had been away from home so much. Also he had a self-sufficiency that did not need her help as had the sensitive Jean-Baptiste who had never been sure of himself and had needed her to lean on.

As that morning she knelt for a long time at the *prie-dieu* in her bedroom she dwelt on the memory of these things and prayed that at last her bewildered son had found peace and happiness. She prayed for a long while and when she rose to meet her family and friends, she was poised and gracious, with her personal loss well hidden in her heart. Aristocratic lineage had not stood in the way of Ann's understanding of the people surrounding her. Into every habitant's home she was welcomed and it was always to her that they turned freely in time of trouble or need, whether it be to assume control at the birthing of their children, to administer medicine when any of them were sick or bring consolation at the passing of loved ones. Born though she had been to a life of luxury, she was efficient in her own kitchen and could bake as well as any woman on the Seigneury, though this skill had been acquired in the thirty years that she had been the wife of Paul de Courville-Boissart. She was a woman who despised idleness or laziness; one who was strangely endowed with a fierce pioneer spirit.

Though it was a holiday, the habitants had been astir shortly after dawn, for there were chores to be attended to before the families could go into town to watch the procession and attend Mass. Also there was much preparation for the feast that would follow.

From early morning the aroma of roasting pigs and sheep filled the air, as every outdoor bake-oven was tended so that the dinner should be ready on time. Returning after Mass, the men gathered around the tables, smoking their pipes and gossiping about their farms until the women should call them to carry over the roasted meat. Then with their hatchets they carved the sheep and pigs, severing the joints and splitting the backbones, so that every man had a healthy portion. Appetites were large and they laughed and talked as strong teeth crunched into the crisp crackling of roasted pig or tore away the meat from a leg of lamb. They licked the grease from their fingers and smacked their lips as they washed down the food with quantities of spruce beer.

It was a merry gathering and when all had eaten well, pipes were filled with homegrown *tabac*. As the smoke rose into the air, the inevitable songs burst from all throats. The fiddlers were called upon and played vigorously, while the children scampered about laughing and shouting and occasionally fighting and quarreling. As the men and women thumped the table in accompaniment to their songs, childish voices also joined in, for from the time the children could utter words they began to learn the songs.

Sitting at the head of the first table, Paul sang lustily and at the same time thought, as he always did on these occasions, how proud he was. These sturdy people, mostly all originally of Norman stock, could not fail to build a strong inheritance. They were light-hearted and careless, yet staunch and loyal, with a simplicity of nature that was at times surprising. They had no ambition; they asked for nothing but what they had; knew very little of what went on outside of their farms and didn't want to know. So many of them were his relatives, the offspring of Old Pierre, his grandfather, the progenitor of the family.

Paul had decided to take this opportunity of talking to the men about the proposed church. He had asked them to gather together after dinner so that he could talk with them, before they departed for the wood-pigeon hunt that was a tradition of this day. While the women cleared up after dinner, the men gathered around one of the tables. Paul and Antoine sat at the head with André beside his father.

"I have asked you men to meet with me today," Paul began, "because I have a proposition to make to you, which I hope you will like and which you will think is an improvement for the Seigneury. With my son-in-law here I have long been contemplating the building of our own church." He paused a moment to let the statement sink in and while he puffed on his pipe he quickly appraised the expressions on the men's faces. They all showed keen interest. Eyebrows were raised in surprise and several heads nodded with approval.

"The Sieur de Brievaux and I would bear the expense," he continued, pausing again briefly after this important statement. "We will hire men to get the wood, if you men will undertake the building. We do not contemplate anything elaborate—just a simple structure. We will undertake to procure a bell for the church and also some sacred relics. We will, of course, have to obtain a curé. It is my hope that we can acquire the services of a priest who will also teach our smaller children." Heads were nodding all around and he stopped and asked: "What do you think of the idea?"

There was a general murmur of voices as they talked with each other and Paul was pleased to note the animation with which they discussed the idea.

"Good. Good." The word was uttered by several voices.

"Where would you build it, Monsieur Paul?" an older man asked.

"Over towards the granary. Partly on this Seigneury and partly on the de Brievaux Seigneury, in the same manner as the granary. You all know the uncleared part of the land belonging to my late brother Philip." He paused and when they indicated they understood he resumed: "His widow and family are quite willing that we should use that land. It will have to be cleared and we can all help with that. It would not take long. I would like to clear enough so that we can eventually have our own cemetery and perhaps later our own school."

The men sat thoughtfully and some discussed it with each other.

"What do you say, Georges Benoit? You are the senior habitant. Let us have your opinion," Paul said.

The man addressed stood up. There was respect in his attitude and yet at the same time pride in his seniority. He was a man nearly sixty and the son of one of the original habitants.

"I'm an old man, Seigneur, and I would welcome not having to go all the way into Montreal for Mass. There are oftentimes in the winter when I can't make it and I don't like to miss Mass."

Several of the older men voiced the same opinion.

"And you, Pierre?" Paul addressed his nephew, the eldest son of his oldest brother. "What do you have to say?" Pierre was about thirty-five and he had the tall, upright build of this oldest branch of the family. Paul had always liked him the least of the family, for he was taciturn and narrow in his viewpoint. He had inherited this from Paul's father, Jacques, who had been a rigid disciplinarian, hardworking but bigoted.

"I think there are several points that we should discuss, Uncle Paul. There is no question in my mind that it would be a grand thing to have our own church but, for one thing, how are we going to get the news? We all look forward to the announcements made by the militia captain..."

"And to visit with our friends in Montreal..." another younger man interpolated.

"And what about our women?" another remarked. "It's the only chance they get to go into town and visit."

"Yes, we have thought of all these things," Paul answered, "and they must be weighed against the difficulties of travel in wintertime, and the advantage of having our own curé. We are steadily growing in size and there would be distinct advantages in having our own priest."

"There would be nothing to prevent any family going into Montreal for Mass whenever they wanted to, would there?" Georges Benoit asked.

"Nothing at all that I can see, so long as they attended their own church most of the time."

The arguments went back and forth and when Paul finally ended the discussion, most of the men were in favor of it. But all agreed they would like to discuss it with their womenfolk.

"You can be thinking about it, men. There's no hurry. Weigh the idea carefully and then we will discuss it again. Now let us get to our shooting."

The meeting broke up and the men scattered to their own homes to get their muskets and to meet later at the appointed place. Paul went inside for a few moments to speak to Ann and then he and André walked over together to the de Brievaux Seigneury. Antoine was standing outside, involved in an argument with Paul-André.

"But why can't I go, Father?" Paul-André was repeating persistently.

"I have already told you that you are too young. Next year perhaps you can," his father said firmly.

"But Jean-Baptiste is going. I want to go, too," he said, his face long and disgruntled.

"I have just explained to you that Jean-Baptiste is several years older. When you are his age you can do the things he does. He is old enough now to reload muskets."

"I can do that, too," the boy grumbled. Then he saw André and his face lit up. "Uncle André let me go with you," he said and ran over to him.

"Not if your father says you can't, Paul-André," André replied kindly.

"But I can keep with you, Uncle André. I won't be in the way."

Antoine's patience was short and he said sharply: "That's enough, Paul-André. You heard what I said. Now go inside and see what your mother has for you to do."

Elise came to the door and asked what was the matter as she saw her young son's face so long and his eyes ready to release their tears. Paul-André voiced his complaint to her. She bent down and looked into his little face, smiling. "I have things I want you to do for me, dear. Next year you can go," she said quietly.

"I want to go this year." His lower lip stuck out and the corners of his mouth drooped.

"May he walk as far as the palisades with us, Antoine?" André asked hoping that this conciliatory measure might solve the problem.

"Yes, as long as he comes right back," Antoine conceded. "Now, come along, we can't waste any more time. The men are already way ahead of us." He stopped to kiss his wife and then went on, followed by Jean-Baptiste who during the altercation with his brother had said nothing. But as they walked along he put his arm across the little boy's shoulder and said in a whisper: "I'll bring you back a pigeon all for yourself." The reward was not enough and Paul-André did not reply.

Antoine had made a gate through the palisades for the benefit of the hunters. It was by the last farm and to his surprise as they approached he saw ex-sergeant Ménard sitting outside smoking. He remembered now that he had not seen him at the feast.

"Why, Ménard, aren't you joining in the festivities today?" he asked cordially.

"No," the man replied. He had a hard, swarthy face with sharp lines and dark eyes that shifted as he talked.

"Where is Madame? I didn't see her at dinner either did I?"

"No. She's in Montreal." The remark was made in the same terse tone.

Antoine looked surprised but as no further information was forthcoming he asked no questions. Elise had mentioned to him that she had not seen Madame Ménard for several days and that she had heard from one of the other women that she had gone back to her parents in Montreal.

"Won't you come shooting with us?" Antoine said trying to hide his dislike of the man behind an assumed cordiality.

"Thank you, no, Seigneur," the man replied a little more graciously. "I prefer to sit and smoke."

"As you wish," Antoine said and joined the others who were waiting. Paul-André looked as though he were about to open up the argument again but the frown on his father's face deterred him.

"Go along back home now, son," Antoine said kindly and closed the gate behind him.

Paul-André lingered, pressing his face between the logs of the palisades in an effort to see beyond. Because it was forbidden, this wild forest had an insatiable fascination for him. He stayed there a while and perhaps would have remained longer had not Georges Ménard called to him.

"Wouldn't they let you go?" he asked.

Paul-André turned a disgruntled countenance to him and shook his head.

"I'm too young," he said.

"That's too bad. Come over here and let me see you."

Short legs brought him slowly over. Curiosity for the moment made him forget about the forest.

"Who are you?" the boy asked.

"You know who I am." Paul-André shook his head in denial. "I've seen you around several times. You're the Seigneur's youngest son. Isn't that right?"

"I'm Paul-André de Brievaux," he said in a small voice that was proud.

"That's right. And I'm Georges Ménard, ex-sergeant of His Majesty's garrison."

The small mouth formed into a round as he looked at the exsoldier. "Oo, a soldier! Where's your uniform?"

"I took it off when I left the army."

"You're not a soldier any more? Why not?"

"Had enough. Wanted to have a home of my own."

"You live here? Alone?"

Ménard laughed with a smirk that was lost on his young friend. "So it seems."

Paul-André wrinkled his forehead. He did not understand the reply. "Why do you live alone?" he asked.

"Because my wife doesn't love me any more."

"Don't you have children?"

"Can't have children without women, son, though you're too young to know that. Come here, How old are you?"

"I'm five years and nine and a half months," Paul-André told him with head up.

The ex-sergeant took the small body between his large horny hands and as he held him his expression became lascivious. "Too bad you're so young," he said slowly.

Paul-André pulled away crossly. "That's what they're always telling me. But I'll be growing up and then I'll do as I like. I'll go into that forest and stay for days and days."

The unpleasant expression on Ménard's face had been only fleeting. "Why do you want to go into the forest?" he asked. "What do you think you'll find there?"

"Everything. Indians and rabbits and bears and snakes and ..."

"Wouldn't they frighten you?" Ménard asked with an amused smile.

"I'm not afraid of anything! I may be little but I'm brave and I'm strong." He doubled up his small fist and extended his arm back and forth.

"Want to take a look at the forest?" Ménard asked.

"Oh could I?" he asked eagerly. Then his face dropped. "But I promised to go back at once."

"Oh, there's plenty of time. I'll open the gate and you can just have a look outside."

The boy's face was alight with eagerness as Ménard lazily pulled himself up from his chair and drew back the bar which closed the gate. Paul-André was almost breathless with excitement as the gate opened and the wonders of the forest, which were so exaggerated in his mind, lay before him.

"Oo!" he exclaimed and ran forward along a narrow path trampled by the feet of many men. Ménard puffed on his pipe and did not restrain him. Then Paul-André disappeared behind a tree, and he was about to follow him when a voice behind him said:

"Excuse me, but have you seen a small boy—my son?" He turned to face Elise. He took his pipe from his mouth and as he looked at her radiant hair and delicate features, his mouth went dry.

"I'm Madame de Brievaux," she said as the man did not speak.

"Of course, Madame. I'm Georges Ménard."

"Yes, I know." Then Paul-André darted from behind the tree and she saw him. "Paul-André come here!" she called sharply.

Guiltily the boy came towards her.

"I thought you promised your father that you would return immediately," she said severely.

"He was coming right back, Madame. He just wanted to see the forest and I opened the gate. I wasn't going to let him go far," Ménard said.

"It was very kind of you but we don't want him running in the forest. Now that he knows how to get out it will be difficult to stop him." Her tone was cold. "Thank you," she said as she took Paul-André's hand firmly in hers and walked away.

Georges Ménard looked after them but he was not thinking of the little boy. His black eyes bulged as he watched Elise's graceful figure retreating. He licked his sensual lips and swallowed hard.

# CHAPTER FOUR

THE men returned home shortly before sunset laden with wood-pigeons which at this time of the year perched so thickly on the branches of the trees that even the worst marksman could knock them down. Some were roasted and eaten for supper that night and the remainder the women laid aside. On the morrow they would prepare them and lay them in melted lard, then to be packed into stone jars so that throughout the winter months there would be a plentiful supply for every family.

The desire to dance and sing was the very soul of these people and no festive occasion was complete without it. Despite the fact that the night was warm, fires were lit all along the riverbank. In the glowing light, groups danced and frolicked to the tunes of the fiddlers. They had their own traditional dances in which old and young joined. Flagons of wine were brought out and passed around freely.

Paul and Ann retired, leaving the seigneurial honors to André who went from group to group, chatting and dancing. His cousins were so numerous that often he did not know them from those on the seigneury who were unrelated to him. He was popular with all and there was not a girl of sixteen or older who did not angle for him to dance with her. Had they known his thoughts, the competition would have been even keener, for he was taking this opportunity of looking them over with a view to marrying. He had long been a topic of conversation among the younger women of the Seigneury and the news of his return had made many a heart flutter, for not only would they have liked to be the future lady of the Seigneurial mansion, but André with his charm, looks and warm-hearted manner was so much more attractive than most of the men who were prospective husbands.

Most of the men in the colony married when they were sixteen and upon those who did not marry when they reached the age of twenty a fine was imposed. André had paid the fine some eight years ago and had still not found the woman he wanted to make his wife. Many pondered the matter and wondered at the reason. It was not that André disliked women nor was he celibate; in fact quite to the contrary. He often felt rather guilty as he thought of the crudity of his association with women, all of whom had been Indian squaws. He wondered whether his yielding to this temptation which came into the lives of all *coureurs de bois,* had not perhaps spoiled his regard for women. Yet he knew that no man could consider an Indian squaw in the same way that he thought of a white woman.

Despite his having taken himself to task over the matter, he found himself treating all the girls in the same lighthearted way, with a chuck under the chin or a sly kiss. None of them interested him beyond that. As he sat by the riverbank with a pretty girl whose dark eyes watched him eagerly, he tried to overcome his nonchalance. He put his arm around her waist. She needed no second invitation and edged nearer to him. He could feel the warmth of her plump body beneath her thin dress and knew that the slightest movement of his hand would have produced a ripple through her body.

She was the youngest granddaughter of Georges Benoit and as a member of one of the oldest families on the Seigneury would have been suitable as a wife. The dark eyes she turned to him held an invitation as she asked coyly:

"And are you going away again soon, monsieur?"

"No, Marie, I believe I shall remain at home now. I have had enough of the woods."

She edged a little closer as he said this and there was a depth of meaning in her remark as she murmured: "I'm so glad."

"Why are you glad?" he asked looking into her face with a smile that made his eyes dance roguishly.

"Need you ask such a question?" she said, letting her voice drop to a seductive note.

"But I'm a stranger to most of you."

"Not in the least. You have been away a lot but…perhaps that makes you all the more interesting to us." "And whom do you mean by us?"

"I did not like to say *to me.*"

"Yet that is what you meant?"

"Yes," she answered and looked down into her lap with feigned modesty.

The moon was practically full and cast a silvery streak on the water which was reflected in her face as she looked up at him again. The air was filled with the laughter and murmurings of lovers and the background of music and song stirred the blood.

"You're very pretty, Marie," he said, and the softness of his tone was encouraging. What difference does it make, he was saying to himself. She's attractive and desirable and would no doubt make as good a wife as any. It was not a very flattering thought, but at his compliment her head had come nearer to his shoulder until it now rested there with her eyes reflecting the depth of the emotion that she would have liked to have released.

André put his hand under her chin and turned her face to him. Then he lowered his head until their mouths touched. He kissed her lightly and it only served to increase her dissatisfaction. She had wanted him to put both his arms around her and kiss her longingly. She was about to urge him to hold her tighter when a figure appeared out of the shadows and a voice said:

"I'm so sorry, André. Please excuse me. I don't want to bother you, but have you seen Paul-André?"

André jumped up, rather relieved with the interruption which had prevented his being carried away by the excitement of the moment which might have brought regrets later.

"Why no, Elise. Isn't he around?"

"No, that's the trouble," she said, and smiled at his obvious question. "He should have been in bed hours ago. I sent him home with Jean-Baptiste and the girls but they stopped to visit on the way and then missed him. They thought he might have gone looking for you."

"He can't be far away. I'll come and look with you."

"Please excuse us," Elise said to Marie who was looking very displeased at the interruption. "André'll be back in a few minutes."

"Sorry, my dear," André said lightly. "Run and join the dancing." And with that he dismissed the matter and left with his sister, while poor Marie sat disconsolately looking at the water, angry with Elise for interrupting what had seemed to be such a promising start.

"What worries me, André," Elise said as they walked away, "is that he was naughty this afternoon and I haven't told Antoine about it. I suppose I shall have to …"

"What did he do?" André asked and his smile was broad. Paul-André was always in trouble of some kind, but small trouble.

"He did not come back right away. I had to go looking for him. And where do you think he was?"

"Somewhere he had been forbidden to go, I'm sure."

"He was out in the forest."

"The forest!"

"Yes, that strange man who has the last portion of land on Antoine's Seigneury had opened the gate …"

"Ménard?"

She nodded. "He's very odd, André. He looked at me so peculiarly. He's not in the least like the others. Frankly I don't like him. But that's not the point. He had let Paul-André through the gate and casually said he was doing no harm."

André frowned. "Perhaps I had better go and have a look and see if he's done the same thing again. Where's Antoine?"

"In the house. He was dozing in his chair. I haven't told him."

"Well, wait a while. I'll go over to Ménard's and see what I can find out."

The gate in the palisades was closed with the bar in place. André lifted it and opening the gate looked outside, but it was a futile gesture as without a torch he could see nothing in the impenetrable blackness before him. He hesitated and then banged on Ménard's door. There was no answer and he rapped again.

"Who is it?" a voice shouted from inside.

"Sorry to bother you, Monsieur Ménard," André called "but have you by any chance seen Paul-André? This is André Boissart."

Ménard opened the door a little way. His hair was disheveled and his chin unshaven. Furthermore he was completely naked and seemed quite unconcerned about it. Possibly he slept like that on hot nights, was André's thought. In the faint light beyond, André noticed the disorder of the room and also that a large flagon of brandy stood on the table.

"And why should I know where the young man is?" Ménard asked in a disgruntled tone.

"I'm sorry to disturb you. But we can't find him and my sister said he was with you this afternoon."

"He was not with me. He was looking through the palisades and I merely opened the gate and let him see outside. Is that such a crime?"

André could smell the man's breath even though he was not standing very near. He could tell he was far from sober. "Again I'm sorry. Please excuse me for disturbing you," he said coldly and walked away.

An ugly grin spread over Ménard's features as he watched him go and as he closed the door he chuckled to himself. Paul-André scrambled from the corner where he had been hiding and rushed for the door. Ménard swung round and grabbed him by the arm.

"Wait a minute!" he said sharply. "Why such a hurry?"

"They're looking for me. I'll get into trouble. I must go." The boy's voice was frightened.

"I thought you told me this morning you weren't afraid of anything?"

"I'm not." Tears welled up to join Paul-André's fright. "Let me go, please," he pleaded as the grip on his arm tightened. This man terrified him as in the flickering light of the candle he leered at him. Ménard's laugh that followed was even more frightening.

"If they see you coming out of here what are you going to say, my brave little man?" he jeered. "They may be still outside looking for you."

"Let me go," was all Paul-André could say.

"Didn't your parents ever tell you to say thank you after a visit?"

"I don't like you," Paul-André said vehemently.

Ménard laughed again. "Not many people do like me," he said. "But you see I like myself and I don't care."

"Let me go," Paul-André reiterated.

"Very well," Ménard said. "But you'd better let me see if it's clear outside."

He thrust the boy back into the room as he opened the door and looked out. The music and songs from the other Seigneury floated to him in the darkness. Unconcerned over his lack of attire he leaned against the door portal and memory of the boy's mother as he had seen her that morning returned to him. What a wench and how he could use her just now! Or any woman for that matter. He looked down at himself and wondered whether he should dress and wander over to the other Seigneury. He could probably pick himself up a woman. There were a lot of young ones around and on a night like this they were looking for a man.

A small figure darted past him and ran as fast as little legs would carry him. Ménard let him go and returning inside lifted the brandy flagon to his lips.

Paul-André raced up the steps of the watch-tower and crouched in one corner. He was still shaking with fright. The man had been so horrible and that morning he had seemed so nice. He had only wanted to see what the forest looked like at night—just for a moment before going to bed. But the man had acted so funny, taking him on his knee and …

Footsteps on the tower steps made his heart beat faster and he crouched back into the corner hoping Ménard would not see him. Then he saw that it was Uncle André and wanted to rush to him and tell him what had happened.

"Paul-André! What are you doing here? We have been looking everywhere for you." His uncle's voice was stern and he was afraid to tell him.

"I … I was only looking for Indians," Paul-André faltered.

"If you don't stop looking for Indians they'll get you one day, young man. Your father's very angry," André continued sternly.

"Oh." The word had a wealth of meaning in it. He knew that he was in for trouble now.

After leaving Ménard's, André had searched everywhere and had finally returned to Elise's house. She had wakened Antoine from his doze and had told him Paul-André was missing. Antoine had been angry and together he and André had continued the search, each going in a different direction. Then the idea of the watch-tower had occurred to André.

He picked up Paul-André and carried him back on his shoulder to the house. The boy was silent. He turned him over to Elise and then went in search of Antoine. Antoine's face was set as André bid him goodnight. He felt glad at that moment that he wasn't a little boy whose father was certainly going to be very cross with him the next day.

# CHAPTER FIVE

I N NEW FRANCE the seasons practically divided into two—the summer months when everyone worked from dawn to dusk and the five long months of winter when all communication with the outside world was cut off. During these months even communication with Quebec, one hundred and eighty miles away, was restricted and those within Montreal and its vicinity, lived in a snow-bound world of their own. When first the river froze over in December, it brought a welcome respite from the hard labors in the fields and men and women were glad of the opportunity to relax and attend to the many things in the house that had been neglected during the busy months. For the men there was the repairing and making of furniture, shoes, and many other things and for the women the spinning and weaving of clothes for all the family. There were sleighing parties and hunting when the weather was not too severe and much visiting from house to house.

That winter was especially severe and in March there was a blizzard that kept everyone in their homes for several weeks. The snow piled high against the houses so that the two Manor Houses were as isolated as though they had been miles apart. For days and nights the wind howled and many a habitant found cracks in his house that he had failed to seal in the autumn checking. Fires were kept lighted all day and all night so that families were warm and comfortable. For the grown-ups the confinement was tiresome—for the children it was tedious and boring. Small faces were pressed against panes that were too clouded for them to see through. They became restless and quarrelled with each other and nerves became strained.

In the de Brievaux Manor House with its several rooms life was not so confining but the children with their conflicting temperaments were frequently at cross-purposes.

Jean-Baptiste had a contented disposition and asked nothing more than the mode of life he had inherited. The Seigneury was his ideal and he eagerly learned all that his father taught him. He disliked the thought of ever having to leave it and often wished that his father was not so insistent upon his going into the army for a few years. Antoine had himself been an officer in the French army and had expected to make it his career, since in France this was the only field open to a gentleman of modest income. What he had inherited from his mother would have been a trifle in France even though considered ample in the colony. Coming to Montreal for a visit had changed this and he had resigned his commission in order to marry Elise and become a seigneur.

Unlike his younger brother, Jean-Baptiste could always find plenty to keep him occupied and when the weather kept them in the house, he amused himself with his wood-carving which was his hobby. Not so Paul-André whose restless nature prevented his staying amused with any one thing for long. He would wander from room to room getting in everybody's way and when reprimanded tried rushing up and downstairs, letting out blood-curdling yells as he pretended to be an Indian.

Usually the two girls were able to amuse themselves tranquilly but there were days when they did not get along. It was almost always Ann-Marie who became provoked with Charlotte-Marguerite. Such as one morning when she was in one of her superior moods and became exasperated because Charlotte-Marguerite ignored the mood and remained unimpressed.

"Oh, you don't know anything!" she exclaimed. "You're only two years younger than I and yet you always act as though men did not exist."

There was no answer from Charlotte-Marguerite and glancing covertly into the room, Elise saw that the younger girl continued quietly reading a religious book and ignoring her sister's conversation.

"I tell you Catherine said it was so. She has an older sister who is going to be married and she told her and Catherine told me that when men touch you here it gives you tingles all down your spine."

Elise stopped abruptly when she heard the trend of the conversation. She waited quietly just beyond the open door and heard Ann-Marie's low voice continuing.

"Oh can't you stop reading and join in the conversation!" Ann-Marie said with exasperation.

"I have already told you I am not interested, Ann-Marie," Charlotte-Marguerite replied firmly.

"Surely you want to know about men?"

"No I don't. I don't intend ever to get married."

"Oh that's stupid. You're plain but some men like plain girls," Ann-Marie continued. Charlotte-Marguerite ignored the remark and showed no sign of annoyance. "I intend to have lots of lovers before I get married. Catherine says that in Quebec girls aren't considered anybody unless they have at least six or seven lovers. Men are going to be easy for me to get because I am beautiful."

Elise listened outside the door with alarm. Her first thought was to enter the room abruptly and reprimand Ann-Marie for her remarks. But wisdom came to her aid and she realized that to make an issue of the matter would only impress it upon a mind such as Ann-Marie's. She waited a moment and then came into the room without a word, leaving her daughter to wonder how much of the conversation she had heard. Because she was feeling guilty, Ann-Marie tossed back her luxuriant wavy tresses, a gesture which had long annoyed her mother and of which she was trying to break her.

"Ann-Marie," she said quietly, "I have told you not to throw your hair about in that fashion."

"But it is so heavy, maman, and gets in my way. I have to push it aside," she replied petulantly.

"Then if it's too heavy we shall have to cut it off," Elise replied promptly.

There was a look of alarm which Elise did not miss. "Maman! You wouldn't do that!" she exclaimed.

"If it's in your way I shall and particularly if you are going to be so conceited about it. I'll not deny you have beautiful hair but there are many in our family who have beautiful hair and they don't behave like you."

"Charlotte-Marguerite hasn't," came the cross reply.

"But she has many other qualities to make up for it. Beauty of character is more important, Ann-Marie."

Charlotte-Marguerite looked up at the remark and smiled sweetly at her mother. She saw that Ann-Marie was pouting at the reprimand and said quietly: "Her hair is very wonderful, maman. She has reason to be proud of it."

"Proud, yes, but not conceited. It is well for us all to remember that what fine looks and attributes we have were given to us by God and therefore we should be grateful not arrogant about them. We can take no credit to ourselves for them."

With that remark she left them but not to put them out of her mind. The comments upon men that she had overheard from Ann-Marie's lips alarmed her. There was no doubt that her daughter was maturing fast and she would take careful watching. She was not so foolish as not to realize that any growing girl is curious about men but she did not like the trend of the conversation and wondered who the Catherine was who apparently had undertaken to provide Ann-Marie with knowledge that was rather premature. Elise had several times had to admonish Ann-Marie for her behavior. She had one day heard her being very patronizing to several of the boys on the Seigneury and when Elise had reproved her for her manner, she had said with a surprise that was not feigned: "But, maman, why shouldn't I? You wouldn't want me to encourage them? I shall not marry a habitant!"

Here was going to be another problem. She and Antoine had tried to bring up their children with an understanding of the cross elements that prevailed in the colony, wanting them to have the advantage of the finer cultural things yet endeavoring to keep them to a level of understanding of the people with whom they were surrounded. Elise had seen this same difficulty in her own family and had profited by her mother's sound advice upon the matter. She thought often of her brother, Jean-Baptiste. Undoubtedly the same thing would arise with their four children and of all of them Ann-Marie was going to be the most difficult. Elise's father had talked to her not long ago upon this subject. He was the only one who had known Antoine's mother, who had died at his birth. She had been a beautiful and exotic creature, loving many men. He had warned Elise that Ann-Marie had inherited many qualities from this grandmother whom she had never known. She was even now exhibiting many of the qualities of Hélène de Matier and with each year her laugh deepened until Paul could often hear an echo of the quality of her grandmother's voice and it made him uneasy.

That night Elise told Antoine of the conversation she had overheard and spoke of her misgivings. Antoine listened, his face serious, and then he echoed Paul's statements about his mother.

"It is inevitable I'm afraid, my dear, that some of my mother's characteristics should evince themselves in our children. Though I never knew my mother, I know many things about her and what your father says is true. Ann-Marie, unfortunately, has inherited some of those characteristics, even to the looks, as I understand from your father." He puffed a while on his pipe and then added: "We can only hope that by guidance we may be able to control these tendencies. Perhaps you should have a talk with her."

"It seems so early to talk about things to her. She is only a baby..."

"In years, perhaps, but boys and girls mature early here. And if she is discussing these things with her schoolmates then it would be better for her to learn them from you in the right way."

"I suppose so. I must give it some thought," Elise replied and continued to brood over it through most of the night.

Some days later she tried to talk to Ann-Marie but with little success. The child looked rather embarrassed but nevertheless pretended to be very grown-up and when Elise tried to explain certain things to her she merely replied, "Of course," as though she already knew all about them and thought her mother was being superfluous. She also indicated that she thought her mother's ideas were old-fashioned and, as children will, looked upon her mother as quite old and past all emotional feelings.

Fortunately the blizzard ceased and a hard winter sun came out to give sparkle to the white world. What had threatened to be a serious matter passed into relative unimportance as all the family helped in clearing away the snow. It made grand fun, especially as father and mother joined in the snow-balling that relieved the work from time to time.

It took several days of hard work before the men could make a path through the two Seigneuries and the de Brievaux were still clearing the heaped snow from their *galerie* when André greeted them with a shout. Paul-André had been provided with a small shovel and the moment he espied his uncle he shouted gleefully: "Look what I'm doing, Uncle André!" and bent his sturdy little back, shovelling energetically—so energetically in fact that he sprayed snow all over the steps which his father had cleared. Antoine was about to reprove him, and then realized the excitement back of it and merely said with a laugh:

"You'd better clear the steps now, Paul-André."

"Come on, I'll help you," André said and together they worked.

"How is everyone at home, André?" Elise asked.

"All well. Mother's busy dispensing Barbados tar ..."

"What's that?" Ann-Marie asked and was echoed by the others.

"Oh, it's a tar that is used for the eyes when the glare of the white snow affects them," André told them.

Paul-André immediately rubbed his eyes and declared that he needed some.

"Oh no you don't, young man! Your eyes are young and strong," André told him.

"Come in and have some refreshment," Antoine said and they all trooped into the house.

"Father wants to know if you're going to Mass tomorrow," André said as they went in.

"Is the road clear?" Antoine asked.

"Yes."

"Then we shall."

"Father's hoping that this blizzard will make them realize how much better it would be if we had our own church. We've had to miss three weeks."

"Yes, I was thinking that, too. In fact, Elise and I were only talking about it last night. It's the women of course who have raised the objections. That's the trouble with women, they must gossip!" Antoine said and laughed at Elise.

"We don't gossip any more than you men do," Elise came to the defense, although she knew her husband was right. Ever since June when Paul had broached the plan for a church, there had been a great deal of controversy over the matter. It had since stalemated and Paul had held his disappointment in check, hoping that by the time the winter was over, the general feeling would have changed to a more favorable one.

# CHAPTER SIX

I N 1721 Montreal was still a small struggling town that belied its eighty years of existence, having been retarded so frequently in its youth by the devastating Indian raids. When in 1642 Father Vimont had blessed the first settlers who arrived under the leadership of the Sieur de Maisonneuve, he had uttered the memorable words: *"You are a grain of mustard seed that shall rise and grow, till its branches overshadow the earth. You are few, but your work is the work of God, His smile is on you and your children shall fill the land."* Their children did now "fill the land" but it had been a bitter struggle for existence in which the most common expression was: "In the midst of life we are in death." Despite the doubling of the population when the Iroquois had been subdued, it still did not exceed four thousand including the garrison at the fort.

On every Sunday morning the entire population streamed towards the many churches which dominated the town. From the outlying seigneuries the people came in carrioles and carts or on horseback, giving the town an unusually crowded appearance. The narrow streets became a jumbled confusion as the miscellaneous conveyances jostled along in general disorder.

The town was rectangular in shape, with two long main streets running from east to west. Along these the people streamed, some making their way to the smaller church of Notre Dame de Bonsecours founded by the saintly Sister Marguerite Bourgeoys, and situated at the north end of the Rue St. Paul which was the business street of the town. But the larger and more fashionable section of the people crowded along the Rue Notre Dame to attend the parish church of the same name. The church of Notre Dame occupied the center of the street blocking traffic,—a constant reminder to the populace that they should pause and consider before they passed on. This fine edifice, enlarged from time to time and still inadequate to accommodate all the worshippers in Montreal, gave dignity to the street and stood amidst the residential area of the town.

It was to this church that the Seigneurs de Courville-Boissart and de Brievaux conducted their families. The Sieur de Courville-Boissart and his wife arrived first and paused to greet acquaintances while they waited for Antoine and Elise. When all were assembled they walked with dignity down the aisle to the pews reserved for them. Hardly had they settled themselves when the Governor and his family entered, causing a slight stir which immediately settled as the congregation turned its attention to devotion.

During Mass there was scarcely a person to be seen upon the streets for there were few, no matter how dissolute they might be, who would miss these devotions. But immediately the service was finished, the people poured again into the streets, eager now for the exchange of news and gossip. Outside every church they gathered in groups, drawing their beaver coats tightly around them, braving the cold wind rather than miss the cherished opportunity to visit with friends and neighbors whom they had not seen all the week and often, when the weather was bad, for several weeks. Later there would be the weekly gatherings in homes as the social courtesies were exchanged.

It was a crowd that exhibited strange contrasts as the heterogeneity that composed Montreal mixed freely with each other. The well-born were distinguishable to some extent by their clothes and the privilege of wearing a sword, but, particularly on Sundays and special occasions, this distinction became confused as many of the rich merchants aped the noblesse in this matter of dress. The wearing of the wig which had never become universal in the colony and had been confined mainly to the Government officials and noblemen, was now frequently adopted by those of the lesser classes who wished to appear important; while to the contrary, many of the seigneurs of noble birth disdained the custom and rigidly adhered to the wearing of their own hair dressed in the prevailing style.

Mingling with the crowd were officers and soldiers of the garrison and also many *coureurs de bois,* distinctive in their deerskin jackets with fringed seams and the colorful blanket coats. About each of them there was a defiant air, daring even the priests to belittle them. This question of the legality of the *coureurs de bois* was one that had been argued and fought over ever since the founding of New France. The Church was against these fur traders because they went off into the woods where there were no churches or priests and often all thought of religion was forgotten. The government was against them because it took the young men who were the strength of the colony away from the farms and prevented the development of the land. Both were against them because away from all law and restriction, the men led wild lives, consorting with Indian women and consuming brandy in large quantities and also trading the brandy to the Indians, who unable to stand the effects of the *eau-de-vie* became uncontrollable and went on the war path. But the young men had equally strong arguments. They argued that with the present feudal laws pertaining to the division and sub-division of land within each family, there were too many of them to live off the land. Furthermore, the only way they could make any money was in the fur trade and, the strongest of all the arguments, it was by the fur trade that Montreal survived. So despite edicts and laws and the curbing of the issuance of licenses, men in increasing numbers went into the woods—and the Governors did not enforce the laws because they and their officials profited by the fur trade.

On the outskirts of the crowd stood several Indians watching these white people with inscrutable and suspicious eyes and an air of wondering what it was all about. Wrapped in their blankets and standing erect, they appeared shorn of their glory. They had made a pitiable exchange when they gave up the freedom of the forest to work in the warehouses and trading centers. Even the acceptance of Christianity in place of their simple belief in the Great Spirit, seemed a poor exchange. They had now become outcasts in a land over which they had once roamed so freely and happily.

The first to emerge from the church was the Governor of Montreal, with his wife on his arm. Their carriage waited at the foot of the steps but they always lingered a while to greet their many friends. Claude de Ramezay had been Governor of Montreal for eighteen years and his administration had been very popular. For two years, during the absence in France of the Governor-General, the Marquis de Vaudreuil, he had been Administrator of the colony. It was his cherished ambition to become Governor-General of New France but de Vaudreuil showed no inclination to retire, nor, despite his years, to die. De Ramezay and de Vaudreuil had arrived in the colony together thirty-six years before, and had been close friends until their nominations had caused rivalry and jealously between them, but officially they managed to agree quite well.

Among those who waited to greet the Governor were Paul and his family. The two families had long been staunch friends. Paul and the Governor, as well as the Marquis de Vaudreuil, had all married in Quebec during the winter of 1691. The three ladies had been acquainted with each other, but with Ann de Courville-Boissart and Marie-Charlotte de Ramezay the friendship had ripened with the years. Of the three, Ann was the most distinguished by birth, the other two ladies being from Colonial families, though nevertheless highly distinguished in Canada.

It had always been Claude de Ramezay's regret that Paul had not become an official part of the government. But Paul had no official ambition; also he understood the reason why he was debarred but held no resentment. His twin sister had many years ago eloped with an Englishman and Paul's acquiescence to the marriage and his tolerance of the hated English had frequently placed him, erroneously, under the suspicion of siding with the enemy. But he and the Governor understood each other and de Ramezay knew that there was no more loyal Frenchman than Paul de Courville-Boissart and though Paul held no official position, the Governor often discussed colonial business with him and appreciated his advice.

While the two families exchanged news, André wandered off to greet a group of his friends who stood talking with each other. They greeted him warmly but berated and teased him because he had discarded his deerskins. Actually André hated these formal clothes he was wearing and was much more at ease with a gun in his hand than with a sword at his side.

"Out of deference to my father I usually dress for Mass," he replied accepting their chaff with good humor. "And anyway I'm giving up trading," he added.

Most of them laughed. They had heard men many times say this but knew that it never lasted. "You'll never settle down," one of them remarked. "It's impossible after the free life."

"What soured you, Le Roux?" another asked rather caustically. "Weren't the squaws good to you last time?"

André grinned at the remark and did not reply to it. "My uncle was killed and three of the other men," he said.

One of the men snorted. He had a hard-bitten expression on his face—the face of one who had seen the crude, rough side of life so long that he liked no other. "What if they were," he replied. "Surely you're not so soft that you can't stand to see a few men killed? That's what we expect when we go to the woods. Can't have good luck all the time."

"That's just the point," André retorted. "I don't want to tempt my luck too far."

"That still shows you're soft," the man snapped.

"That's a matter of opinion," André replied and his voice was hard. He had never liked this man, who was the type of *coureur de bois* who had given the profession such a bad name.

"I was very sorry to hear of the loss of Philip Boissart," another said steering the conversation into a more amiable channel. "He was one of the finest *coureurs de bois* we ever had. He traded for many years."

"Twenty-five," André added.

"Well, we'll be seeing you at Michilimackinac next year," one of them added and slapped André on the back in good-natured comradeship.

As he rejoined the family circle, he heard the Governor say: "I am anxious to have you meet him, Paul. He is a very learned man, a professor of *belles-lettres* and he has also written several books. He has been sent here by our government to tour the colony and I understand to write an account of it." Then he lowered his voice. "I know that he sends letters every few days to the Duchesse de Lesdiguières whom I haven't the honor of knowing but whose noble family of course we all know."

Paul nodded though he did not know the family mentioned but was flattered by the Governor's tact. He must ask his wife later about this Duchesse whom "we all know."

"If he's going to write about us I am anxious that he shall receive a good impression," the Governor continued, his face wreathed in a mischievous smile. "Who knows, perhaps his report may succeed in our getting some of the things we need."

"If you and the Governor-General have failed, why should a Jesuit priest succeed, Excellency?" Paul remarked.

"A very fine formal statement for the public, Paul. But you forget the power of the Church as against the State." He made the remark in a lowered voice and they all smiled. Everyone knew only too well the constant friction there was between the two factions and there was no question that this friction often retarded the progress of the colony.

André wondered whom they were discussing but before he could inquire Elise touched his arm and asked if he had seen Paul-André.

"You don't mean he's off again!" he said and could not help laughing.

"He was here a minute ago," Elise said anxiously and then saw Antoine looking at her.

"Where's Paul-André?" he asked.

"That is just what André and I were discussing. He was with me only a minute ago."

Antoine's expression was hard. "I am going to have to give that young man a lesson he won't forget," he said.

"Now don't get angry, Antoine…" Elise urged.

"I'll look for him. I have an idea where he might be," André said.

But Antoine had already left to look for his son and Elise silently prayed that it might be André who would find him. It was only a few minutes before her prayer was answered and André returned firmly gripping the little boy by the hand.

"That was very naughty of you Paul-André," Elise scolded. "Your father is very angry."

"But I only went to speak to the Indians."

As André had expected, he had found Paul-André standing before one of the Indians and looking up at him with an absorbed expression which had no effect whatsoever upon the stoical red man.

"Haven't I told you many times, over and over again, that you are not to go off by yourself?" Elise was saying as Antoine returned.

"We'll take this matter up when we get home," he said sternly, taking Paul-André by the hand in a grasp that would certainly not permit any escape.

Elise looked at André. "That means another thrashing. I do wish Antoine would not adopt such stern measures. It has absolutely no effect," she said anxiously.

"I'll have to think of something that will cure him of this habit," André said and tried to sound comforting.

"Something will have to be done," Elise remarked hopelessly.

When the Governor's carriage departed, the *capitaine de milice* mounted the church steps and conversations gradually ceased as all turned to listen to the announcements that would now be made. In latter years, the position of *capitaine de milice* had increased in importance. Originally he was only a musketry instructor, whose task it was to keep the militia in training. But now he was considered the general factotum of the government. Every Sunday it was his duty after Mass to read to the people the various orders and edicts that had been issued and later to post them on the door of the church. As a large majority of the people could not read, the custom was a necessity. The position of *capitaine* was a coveted one for he became the representative of the people, being chosen by them from their own ranks, and never from the seigneurial ranks.

The matter of importance today was an order to strengthen the town fortifications which were rapidly falling into decay. A look at most of the faces provided the answer, for it was the same answer they had voiced every time the subject had been brought up. The order informed them that a generous government would pay part of it but that the colonists would have to pay the remainder over a period of years. There was a murmur among the men and Paul glanced at Antoine.

"Try to get it carried out!" he whispered to his son-in-law.

The Militia Captain ignored the murmuring, although he noticed it and it would be his task to try to get the order enforced. He went on to the next announcement knowing that this one would please them better.

"His Excellency, the Governor-General of Canada, the Marquis Philippe de Vaudreuil, has granted to one, Thomas de la Naudière, the privilege of establishing a postal system between the town of Quebec and Montreal, on condition of observing certain tariffs according to the distance. This same monopoly to be in effect for a period of twenty years. The service will be begun in the spring and will make only one stop on the way, that is to say, at the town of Three Rivers."

The moment the Captain had finished, a buzz of conversation started, some voicing their delight at the establishment of this first postal system and others arguing with each other about the fortification of the town. The groups began to move away, eager now to get home to their Sunday dinners.

As they drove back, André asked his father about whom the Governor had been conversing.

"A Father Pierre Charlevoix is coming to Montreal," Paul told him. "It seems he is a learned gentleman, a member of the College of Jesuits, who has been commissioned to study the colony and write a report on it. Also, to find out something about the passage to the Western Ocean."

"Oh?" Andre's tone was interested, particularly about the last statement, for he was one of those who was keenly interested in this rumor that a large ocean lay beyond their western boundary.

"The Governor has extended an invitation to all of us and to Antoine and Elise, to attend a party he is giving for Father Charlevoix next Saturday. He is due to arrive the middle of the week."

"It should be very interesting," Ann remarked.

"Very," André agreed and his eyes had a faraway expression in them as he looked out across the river. He knew the course of that river thoroughly and what lay beyond as far as the western boundaries of Lac Huron but he longed to traverse Lac Superior and find out whether, as many declared, that lake disclosed the route to the great and enigmatic Western Ocean.

# CHAPTER SEVEN

THE visit of Father Pierre François Xavier de Charlevoix to New France on such an important mission provided an outstanding event that was to grow in magnitude when later his book on Canada appeared and constituted the first reliable account of people and affairs in the colony.

The reception given by Governor de Ramezay at his Chateau afforded a brilliant spectable and represented a side of Colonial life that contrasted with the simplicity that was the general rule. The Chateau was one of the outstanding residences in the town and stood on a hill overlooking the Jesuits' garden on the opposite side of the Rue Notre Dame. The Montrealers were proud of the Chateau and of their Governor and, despite the cold, gathered outside to watch the arrival of the elegantly attired guests. There was no bitterness or resentment in those who watched, as there would have been on similar occasions in France. The lights from the many windows of the Chateau glistened upon the crisp white snow and between the opening and shutting of the huge door, the spectators could catch a glimpse of the brilliance within.

The *petit salon* where the guests gathered was ablaze with light from hundreds of candles shining from crystal chandeliers. From behind a mound of shrubbery came the soft notes of the fiddlers. The occasion was not as brilliant as many given at the Chateau for visitors from France of greater magnitude, but all of the nobility wintering in Montreal and all the officials as well as many of the merchants had been invited. They had been informed that Father Charlevoix would give a report to the

Regent on conditions in the colony and they were determined that that report should be flattering. They set out to impress him not only with the hospitality of Montreal but with their own importance.

The Governor and Madame, with Father Charlevoix between them, stood to receive their guests. Governor de Ramezay was in his sixty-third year and growing rather obese now that he could no longer take part in the military campaigns that had brought him renown. He was a large, well-built man with a florid complexion, deep-set eyes placed wide apart, a long straight nose and full mouth. Beside him Madame looked short. Hers was a gentle, kind disposition and it showed in the soft lines of her face. The Governor owed much of his popularity to his wife, for every Montrealer knew that whatever their rank, or whether Indian or aristocrat, they were free to come to the Chateau whenever they needed help.

For the most part the women and also the men who now thronged into the salon were dressed as stylishly as at any comparable gathering in France. They welcomed the diversion afforded by these entertainments given by the nobility, and every summer the ships that came from France were laden with silks and satins and other precious materials to be made up fashionably for the coming winter season. Letters were eagerly awaited that would inform them of any change in mode and while some would jealously guard the information received, others would share it, so that ultimately it became universally adopted, though often not until the first ball of the season had given away the secret. The tailor who revealed it before that first ball, knew that it would lose him the trade that he prized.

As Elise followed her father and mother down the receiving line and then walked across the room to join friends, there were many comments, though those by the men were flattering. Her gown was of luxurious green brocade, trimmed with gold lace, and the tiny shoes that peeped beneath the wide hoop of her skirt were of the same color. Her gowns were invariably of some shade of green to complement her hair. Around her throat she wore four strands of pearls intermingled with diamonds—part of the exquisite collection that had belonged to Antoine's notorious mother. Who had been the donor of this magnificent piece or of any of the other beautiful jewels that Antoine had given her when she became his wife, no one would ever know, for Hélène de Matier had distributed her favors liberally and those who might have blushed in recognition of the jewels were now all dead.

While almost all the guests wore their hair powdered, there were a few exceptions, in all cases among the younger men or women. Though this was the leisure time of the year, there were always many chores to be done on the seigneuries and once hair had been powdered it could not be changed without considerable bother. Few men or women in the colony had the time to spare for hours of brushing and as wigs were an expensive luxury, many disdained the custom.

Among those who were conspicuous by wearing their hair unpowdered was Elise de Brievaux. Antoine revelled in the glory of her red-gold tresses and had playfully threatened to send her back home if she dared to spoil them with powder. As this coincided with her own desires, there was never any argument about it. But not all in the colony shared the opinion that red hair was beautiful. It was extremely rare to find a French woman or man with this colored hair and all their lives André and Elise—and Paul and his sister before them—had been subjected to some derision. But they all ignored it, for they enjoyed the phenomenon.

There were some comments now about Elise and André as they stood conversing with their friends. Antoine resented these remarks on Elise's account, but André merely smiled. He had won his way with his mother in refusing to put on a wig, though he had consented to have his hair dressed in the prevailing style. In a light blue coat with gold embroidery and a long flowered waistcoat that extended almost to the knee-breeches, he looked very handsome—and felt most uncomfortable.

Antoine enjoyed these intervals of returning to the sophisticated atmosphere in which he had been born. His enjoyment of these occasions was, he knew, shared by his mother-in-law. There were times when he and she would be together and reminisce about the Paris where they had both been born. It made a strong bond between them. Antoine had a genuine admiration for his mother-in-law and on occasions such as this the admiration increased. She was so very much within her correct element and though she had been many years in the colony she still retained about her an air of Versailles. Her presence seemed to dominate the room. At forty-eight she had lost none of the magnetic quality that had distinguished her in younger years. The sharp lines of her face had softened and beneath the white powder her hair was grey. Her dark eyes were animated and her mood gay as she and Paul chatted with their many friends. Years ago Paul had been as rebellious as his son on these dress occasions but he had mellowed with age and now was completely at ease in formal clothes and wig. He had first met Ann at a ball given by her father and had immediately fallen in love with her. On that occasion he had been wearing his first dress clothes and had felt very uncomfortable. He seldom dressed for a ball without remembering it or referring to it as Ann adjusted his cravat or arranged some part of his attire. He had acquired a natural dignity which he frankly ascribed to his wife's teaching. "She has made a Seigneur out of a farmer boy," he would frequently remark.

Father Charlevoix in his sombre black clothes presented a sharp contrast among the colorfully dressed guests. The distinguished priest was a surprise to all, for they had expected to see a somewhat venerable gentleman instead of a man who was little more than middle-aged. His life of intensive study had deepened the lines on his scholarly face, and the keenness of his eyes testified to the astuteness of his mind. As he stood with the Governor and his lady receiving the guests there was little opportunity for any to converse with him, and so they stood in groups and conversed *about* him. How was it that the Regent of France, the wily Duc d'Orléans who ran the country with a sharp but dissipated mind until the young King should come of age, had selected this Jesuit to study conditions in the colony? Would it do any good to the colony? Would it bring them more advantages? And what would his observations be? "He is a shrewd observer," several commented as from time to time Charlevoix's sharp eyes moved from group to group, making mental observations that later would be reproduced in words upon paper.

There was a stir as the Baron de Longueil entered accompanied by his eldest son, Captain Charles le Moyne on whose arm leaned his young and beautiful wife. Also with the Baron was another man whose arrival turned the conversation into new and inquisitive channels. The Sieur de la Vérendrye had been the name announced and there was a momentary hush as the newcomer was presented to Father Charlevoix and they saw the latter's face light up in an expression of keen interest as the Baron explained that La Vérendrye was a man who knew a great deal about this search for the Western Ocean.

"Undoubtedly we shall have an opportunity to talk in more detail later," they heard the Baron say. "La Vérendrye can be of great help to you I am sure."

As they passed on to allow further arrivals to be presented, the Sieur de la Vérendrye paused a moment to let his alert eyes rove appraisingly over the company. He was a man of magnetic personality, with deep-set steel-blue eyes, a mobile mouth and a long, thin face ending in a sharp-pointed beard. He was of powerful stature and had about him an air of daring and fearlessness, causing many a feminine heart to flutter. Such men were the backbone of the colony and women adored them.

That he had a nonchalant disregard for conventions was immediately obvious as he caught sight of André. He regarded him intently for a moment, a look of incredulity on his face and then as André came forward with a broad smile, he strode towards him and in a loud voice exclaimed: "Le Roux! You rogue! I wasn't sure at first that it was you. You look so different!"

"Pierre!" André exclaimed with equal warmth and the two men thumped each other on the back. When they had met on previous occasions both had been dressed as *coureurs de bois* and they laughed loudly as they examined each other's clothes.

"And what brings *you* to such a gathering?" André asked laughing.

"Intrigue, my boy," La Vérendrye replied lowering his voice. "The Baron's aiding and abetting me ..."

"Western Ocean?" André inquired, also lowering his voice.

La Vérendrye nodded.

"What have you been doing all these years?" André asked. "I've inquired for you every time I've stopped at Michilimackinac but could get no news ..."

"Why didn't you inquire nearer home?"

"You mean you've been here?"

"Vegetating in Three Rivers. I'm a married man now with a family." Aspiring hearts of many women around sank as they overheard this remark.

"I heard that you had married. Congratulations. But what are you doing in Three Rivers?"

La Vérendrye grimaced. "Running a small trading post on my property at La Gabelle." He looked round quickly and then said in a lower voice, "But I am hoping that this Father Charlevoix may be able to do something about renewing the search for *La Mer de l'Ouest*. I understand from the Baron that that is part of the commission. I hope to be able to have a talk with him and see if he won't persuade the authorities to commission me to carry out the project."

"I'll come with you if you do," André said and his tone was also lowered.

"That's what you've always said and I shall keep you to it."

"You'll have no difficulty in persuading me," André said. "It's been my lifelong dream."

Whenever the de Longueil's arrived at any reception in Montreal, the conversation always became more animated for they represented the oldest family in the colony and many thought that the Baron should have been Governor-General long before this. But one thing had stood in his way. He had been born in the colony and the French Ministry would not appoint anyone to that high position who was native born. It was rumored that the Baron was writing long epistles to France trying to get this changed. The people loved him not only for the fine service he had rendered to the colony but for the warmth of his nature. As he stood now talking to his many friends, his empty right sleeve was a reminder of this service. His arm had been shot off at the bloody massacre of Lachine. Despite his title, he was descended from a humble innkeeper in Dieppe but he and his brothers had made history. These brothers were the renowned Sieur d'Iberville and the Sieur de Bienville, now Governor of Louisiana.

The Baron was holding a small court and answering questions about the guest he had brought. As the newly appointed Governor of Three Rivers, he had become keenly interested in this young explorer who because of a country that all too frequently ignored those who served it valiantly, had been forced to bury himself in this intermediate town of his birth and make a bare living as a fur trader.

"Where did you discover him, Baron?" several asked.

"He's a native of Three Rivers and a very fine fellow. I hope to be able to do something for him through this Father Charlevoix."

"It seems to me I have heard something about him," Paul de Courville-Boissart remarked, wondering the while how it was that André knew him so well, yet had not mentioned his name.

"Everyone should know his name for what he has done for France. He served in three campaigns over there and was wounded at the Battle of Malplaquet. Had no less than four sabre wounds and several bullet wounds and was left on the field for dead. Because of that he was made a prisoner of war for fifteen months. And when it was all over, he was ignored. The best we could do for him was to secure him an ensigncy—that was thanks to Governor de Vaudreuil or," he added with a smile, "to the Marquise de Vaudreuil."

The words were hardly out of his mouth than like an echo came the ringing voice of the *laquais* announcing: "His Excellency the Governor and Lieutenant-General of Canada, Acadie … and Madame la Marquise de Vaudreuil."

Immediately all conversation ceased and everyone turned to face the door, the ladies dropping deep curtseys and the men bowing, presenting a picture reminiscent of the Court of Versailles as they paid homage to this supreme representative of the King. The Marquis Philippe de Rigaud de Vaudreuil and his wife acknowledged the greeting with graciousness yet with a manner that indicated that they felt it due to them. As a pair they presented a contrast for de Vaudreuil was now nearly eighty, while the Marquise was not yet fifty. Though the Governor-General's manner was proud and a little arrogant, he was well-liked and revered for the tireless energy which he had devoted to the colony for thirty-four years.

After Governor de Ramezay had presented his superior to the guest of honor the receiving line broke up and they joined the Governor-General as he made the rounds of the guests. Conversation became general again. There was much comment among the groups as they waited to be presented.

"He's getting very old."

"Well, yes, he's nearly eighty."

"She looks so much younger."

"She is. They say she is only half his age."

"She's the Comte de Frontenac's goddaughter."

"But a native of the colony. She was born in Acadie."

"So much more to her credit." The last remark produced some discussion and would have led to argument as it always did only someone else remarked:

"She was at the Court of Versailles for seven years."

"Some said she had left her husband."

"Not officially any way, but I understand she was tremendously popular with the King."

"Probably helped her husband."

"Not much good now. That was in Louis XIV's day."

"I understand the Court is terribly dissipated under the Regent's régime."

"Oh yes, more so than ever."

"She's very beautiful isn't she?"

"They say she is the power behind his government."

"Due to her experience at Versailles, no doubt."

"How old would you say she is?"

"Might be forty, might be fifty."

"Oh I'm sure she's more than forty. Nearer fifty."

"She has preserved her figure well. Must take a lot of trouble over herself," remarked another woman.

"Who was she before her marriage?"

"I don't know. Do you?"

"Yes. She was Louise Elizabeth Joybert de Soulange."

"The name isn't familiar to me."

"A very wealthy and prominent family I believe."

"How long have they been married?"

"Married after Phips' siege of Quebec. That would be 1691."

"Then they have been married thirty years. He must have been past middle-age when he married her. Had he been married before?"

"I don't believe so. They say he was severely censured in France for marrying a colonial."

"So was our own Governor…"

"Haw! Why shouldn't they!"

"The Ministry doesn't like its officials to marry natives of the colony."

And the gossip continued so that few perhaps noticed a change that had come over the guest who had been the previous topic of discussion. When the Governor-General and his wife were announced, the Sieur de la Vérendrye was still talking to André. At the announcement of the de Vaudreuils, he swung round and stared at the arrivals. André heard him mutter under his breath: "I didn't know they were to be here!"

"Have you met the Governor-General before?" André asked.

"Oh yes, yes. In France."

"Not since then?"

"You forget I have been buried in Three Rivers my friend."

He continued to stare at the Marquise de la Vaudreuil. his jaw set hard and his eyes penetrating. Then realizing where he was, he assumed a set smile that was still on his face as the Governmental party approached. Curious André watched Madame la Marquise's face and noticed her expression change when she saw La Vérendrye. It was a fleeting expression, quickly controlled and when Governor de Ramezay said:

"You know the Sieur de la Vérendrye, I believe, Excellency?" it was Madame who answered:

"Why yes, of course. We are so glad to see you again, monsieur."

La Vérendrye bowed low over the hand she extended and placed his lips to it. Only she felt the pressure of those lips and returned it with a quick contraction of the fingers.

The Marquis was assisting his short-sightedness through a quizzing glass and was saying:

"Ah, La Vérendrye. We have rather lost sight of you since your return."

"All France has, apparently, your Excellency," La Vérendrye replied and his tone was dry and hard.

"Yes, yes, too bad. You served so valiantly. Something should have been done."

"I am hoping it still can be, Excellency."

"Probably. I shall do my best," he said and passed on.

# CHAPTER EIGHT

THE banqueting hall of the Chateau was a majestic room, heavily panelled in dark wood with huge fires burning at either end. The long table was set with the choicest linens and silver brought long ago from France. As Father Charlevoix took the seat next to his hostess, he observed the exquisite taste with which the table was set and noted the details so that that night he could write in his journalistic letter to his patroness the Duchesse de Lesdiguiéres: "The dinner served to me was charming and most delectable, not only from the excellence of the food itself but from its appointments and service. I had furnished myself with my own knife, as is the custom, but it was unnecessary to use it, since the table was set with the finest silverware, as well as china and glass set upon a tablecloth of exquisite workmanship."

The "delectable" food took hours to consume, as changing dishes passed in succession, each change being brought in by a parade of liveried servants and presented first to the Governor for his approval. Suckling pigs and sheep had been roasted whole, as well as hinds of beef and venison, fowls and the more delicate partridge—all consumed in a manner and quantity that has long passed.

André found himself far down the table, seated between two pretty young ladies whom he had never met before. He listened sharply for whatever La Vérendrye might say but as the conversation stayed upon general topics and not upon the Western Ocean project, he turned his attention to the ladies and endeavored to comport himself more charmingly. Among those at his end of the table were several members of the de Ramezay family, including the Governor's youngest son, Jean-Baptiste-Nicholas-Roch, who was seated next to the lady on André's right. Though only twelve years old, Jean-Baptiste was considered to have reached his majority and had just received his commission as Ensign in the Colonial troops. This was his first official reception and he was nervous.

André knew him only slightly, as one does the youngest child of a large family. Realizing the boy's nervousness, he tried to help him by including him in the conversation.

"Charles-Hector still in France?" he asked, more as a statement than as a question for he was quite well aware that this eldest son of the de Ramezays was still away.

"Yes, monsieur. He's a Captain now," Jean-Baptiste replied and one could sense the pride and perhaps envy that he had of his brother's superior rank.

"Excellent. He'll be proud of you when he returns."

Jean-Baptiste made a wry face. This brother was fourteen years his senior, a gap which had prevented any great companionship between them. There had been other brothers in between but now there were only sisters.

"You know my nephew, Jean-Baptiste de Brievaux?' André inquired.

"Oh yes, well."

"He is going into the army next year."

"So he told me the other day. I hope he can be stationed with me."

"It would be a nice companionship for both of you," André agreed.

At the top of the table the conversation had begun with Madame de Ramezay politely inviting the guest of honor to talk of himself.

"This is not your first visit to Montreal, is it, Father?" she inquired.

"No, madame," the priest replied. "I was here several years ago, but in the summer, and I find it looks very different now with the snow everywhere."

"Ah yes, we wear our winter shroud for many months," Governor de Ramezay commented.

"You came over the ice from Quebec?" Madame la Marquise inquired.

"Yes, madame. A very easy way of travelling and swift..."

"But very cold." She shivered.

"I, fortunately, do not mind the cold," the Father remarked.

"I am sorry I was not at Three Rivers when you stopped there," Baron de Longueil apologized.

"But I have the pleasure now of meeting you," Charlevoix replied politely. "A visit would hardly have been complete without my having met the representative of the famous le Moynes."

"Thank you, Father. I hope I can be of service to you," the Baron replied showing his pleasure at the compliment paid to his family.

"Tell us, Father, how did you leave our beloved France? What are conditions there now?" Madame la Marquise asked.

Father Charlevoix did not reply at once. These were questions that had to be weighed carefully before answering. He mentally passed his host and the guests in review before he said with a smile: "Rather disturbing from marry points of view..."

"And the point of view is very important." It was Madame de Courville-Boissart who made the comment and followed it with a laugh. There were few present who knew the French Court as well as she, though it was thirty years since she had been intimately connected with it.

"Indeed it is!" Madame la Marquise took up the remark. "Has it changed much, Father, since the days of our illustrious King Louis?"

"Yes, but not for the better," Charlevoix commented. And then to safeguard himself said, directing his gaze to the

Governor-General and to de Ramezay: "But you gentlemen here know as much as I would know." He did not wish to be quoted as having made any remarks about the Regent.

"Haw!" de Vaudreuil threw back his head as he made the guffaw. "We know it only too well. Without being indiscreet and speaking among friends, I am afraid we can all agree that His Grace the Duc d'Orléans is hardly leading the country to prosperity; at least, every time I ask for funds with which to run this colony, I am informed the coffers are empty."

"He has many qualities that are brilliant and some of his reforms have been very commendable," Father Charlevoix remarked tactfully.

"Yes, but we hear that matters are becoming more corrupt and dissolute than ever before," de Vaudreuil remarked boldly.

"Of that I can only speak from hearsay," Charlevoix replied. "I do not attend the Court."

"What is more important to us, Father," Governor de Ramezay said, "is whether this peace that now exists between our country and England is going to last."

"It has lasted since the Treaty of Utrecht," Charlevoix replied.

"All the more reason why we should be wary, is it not?" de Ramezay asked.

"Would you really call our present conditions peace?" the Marquis interrupted.

"Well…" de Ramezay smiled and let his superior continue. He knew only too well that de Vaudreuil preferred to be listened to rather than have to listen.

"I should rather call it a cessation of hostilities. There are no feelings of peace here between us and the English. We each watch the other and from time to time take a step forward and each step is nearer to a renewal of the fight." De Vaudreuil stopped to drain his glass and de Ramezay immediately signalled to a lackey to fill it. "To my mind this so-called peace has always been rather like two very fierce dogs who have been chained up by order of their masters and are straining with all their might to break those chains. We and the English are those dogs. Some day a link will wear and break in one of the chains and then we had better watch out. Each of those fierce dogs has a number of ragged and uncontrollable curs at its heels, curs which go over and nip at the heels of the opposing dog and make him more angry. Those curs are the Indian tribes who are forever being egged on by one side or the other to carry out raids that are devastating. We all know the tragedies that have occurred and continue to occur."

"But aren't these just minor tragedies?" Father Charlevoix asked.

"It can hardly be called minor to have a home which you have striven to build, burned to the ground and all those you love massacred," de Vaudreuil replied.

"But don't we do the same thing to the English settlements?" Charlevoix asked.

"Yes, but it is our only means of reprisal."

"And then the English make another reprisal and so it goes on."

"Exactly."

"And what is the solution, Your Excellency?" the wily Jesuit asked.

"Haw!" de Vaudreuil guffawed again. "If I could answer that question I would be a more successful administrator than I am. It is the survival of the fittest or the strongest, and the English are getting far too strong for our comfort. They have convinced the Iroquois that they are English subjects and under their protection and it is only by threats that we are able to keep those warlike savages from descending upon us. And, you can quote me in this, Father, and make it as emphatic as possible, unless they send me more trained soldiers there will come a day when we can no longer hold this colony. I have done everything that I can think of to convince them of this but have been unable to get results. While I was in France a few years ago, I talked and talked about it and received only promises. All they do is to write me that I must keep peace with the tribes and then in another letter they order me to subdue the trouble makers among the red men. How can I send out an expedition when I have only a handful of soldiers? We have already had very unpleasant reminders of what happens when these campaigns fail. We sent out an expedition against the Foxes not so many years ago but all we did was to cripple them and a crippled tribe breeds revenge. We think we are safe because we have subdued the Iroquois, but be warned, the Foxes are every bit as dangerous."

"But aren't they an inferior tribe compared with the Iroquois?" was the question asked.

"Inferior in number but not in war-like tendencies. They seem now to have been seized with homicidal fury so that no white man is safe near them."

"And this is what we have to look forward to in the spring?" Madame de Courville-Boissart asked ruefully. "Does it mean that again our men are going to have to leave their fields and their homes unprotected and go to fight this Indian menace?"

"I hope not, madame, and, please forgive me for having introduced such an unpleasant and serious note on an occasion when we should be light and gay. It was only that I wished to give Father Charlevoix a true picture that he could take back with him."

"And that I shall do, Excellency. It is part of my commission to study these Indian tribes ..."

"But be warned to steer clear of the dangerous ones and particularly of the Foxes I have mentioned."

"My cloth should be my protection ..."

"Don't rely on it though." It was La Vérendrye who spoke. He had said little as yet, disturbed as he was by the woman across the table and by the glances which she had been directing at him while her husband was absorbed in conversation. "We here have had much experience with these red men and you yourself must know how many of the Jesuit Fathers suffered unspeakably at the hands of the savages."

"I am cognizant of that, monsieur, and respect your warning."

"Where do you plan to go after you leave Montreal?" Madame de Ramezay asked.

"By easy stages to Michilimackinac..."

"Ah! On that I can help you, Father, if you will permit me, that is, if you have not already received all the help you require," La Vérendrye said eagerly.

"Indeed I shall appreciate your advice, monsieur. I understand you have travelled much in those parts."

"Yes, though for that matter so have many of the gentlemen here," La Vérendrye replied modestly.

"But you know the situation more recently than many of us," the Baron remarked.

"Possibly, monsieur," La Vérendrye agreed. "I know Michilimackinac very well for I have been there for long periods at a time."

"That will be helpful," Charlevoix said. "I wish to study the various tribes who inhabit the country along the way. Later, perhaps, I can consult with you on the subject."

"And about the other part of your commission—the search for the Western Ocean?" La Vérendrye asked.

"And that too..." Father Charlevoix said.

"Then we ladies will adjourn while you gentlemen have your discussion," Madame de Ramezay remarked rising. "But don't remain too long," she added and smiled pointedly at her husband.

The other ladies observed the signal and when they had all retired there was a general shuffling of places as the men drew more closely together. André had been watching for this moment hoping that he would be able to get a seat nearer to La Vérendrye so that he could hear the details of the discussion. He had no difficulty for La Vérendrye called to him:

"Come over here, Le Roux."

"You have met my father, the Sieur de Courville-Boissart and my brother-in-law, the Sieur de Brievaux," André said, introducing them.

"You two appear to be old friends," Paul remarked with a smile as he shook hands with La Vérendrye.

"We have met many times at Michilimackinac," André informed him.

"I gathered that it must be something of that kind by the name he uses."

"Le Roux? They all call me that out in the woods."

The men had now all reseated themselves and the brandy was passed among them.

"Now, Father Charlevoix, tell us what we can do for you and what your plans are," the Marquis de Vaudreuil said. His face, like that of several of the other men, was flushed with the wine and his conversation was interspersed with several loud belches.

"My orders are quite wide in scope and rather far-reaching, too far-reaching to be accomplished in one visit I am afraid." The well-modulated voice of Father Charlevoix was easy to listen to. "I have already indicated to you that I am making a study of conditions in the colony and also of the various tribes here. My commission also reads that I am to make inquiries regarding the best route to the Western Ocean."

"How is it that this subject has been revived?" de Ramezay asked. "Ever since this colony was founded interest in the matter has waxed and waned."

"I am not in a position to know how the revival of interest occurred," Father Charlevoix replied. "But His Grace seems to be keenly interested."

"La Vérendrye, you seem to know more about it than many of us," de Vaudreuil said. "What is your idea?"

"I have talked with many Indians who tell me that they have met and conversed with white men to the far west, men of fine stature, bearded and well armed."

"They would be Spaniards," Father Charlevoix commented.

"Spaniards!" several exclaimed. "Then we would have opposition?"

Father Charlevoix smiled. "If we approach in a hostile manner, but we are not talking yet of taking the land but only discovering how to reach it and to find out what exists between here and that coast. Probably we shall find it is only a short distance away..."

"That I doubt, Father," La Vérendrye remarked quickly.

"So do I," the priest agreed.

"If we knew or had even some inkling, it would be much easier to equip an expedition," the Marquis said.

"It is my belief that any expedition would have to be equipped for a very long trek," La Vérendrye said.

"And that would be very expensive and who would bear the cost?"

"Perhaps some of the merchants here in Montreal could be persuaded to bear the expense on a share basis." It was Joseph le Ber who made the suggestion. He was one of the most prosperous of the Montreal merchants.

"Perhaps," Governor de Ramezay replied. "But first let us hear what these learned gentlemen think is the route to the west. What are your theories, Father Charlevoix?"

"I have none as yet."

"How much truth do you think there is in the theory that Lac Superior empties into this far ocean?" someone asked. Several of them began to answer at once including André. They gave way in deference to Governor de Ramezay who had begun to speak.

"The Sieur de Lhut explored as far as the western tip of the Lac but found land beyond it that had not yet been penetrated."

"Then it is your belief, gentlemen, that we would have to traverse a great deal more land before we reached this ocean?" the Marquis asked.

"Undoubtedly." The Baron de Longueil took up the discussion. "I have explored much of that region myself and have also, like our friend here, talked with the Indians. I agree with La Vérendrye that this Western Ocean is undoubtedly a long way off."

"Unquestionably," La Vérendrye said. "But it would not necessarily mean crossing by land. I believe we would make great discoveries if we traced the Missouri River to its source..."

"The Missouri River? Where's that?" was the question.

"It is a tributary of the Mississippi River or at least so I have been told," La Vérendrye replied. "Anyway it joins the Mississippi and I believe flows west. If we could follow it, then we might find that it empties into the Ocean."

"It would be necessary to establish posts along the way for the continuance of supplies."

"Wouldn't it be possible to finance the project in this way?" Joseph le Ber asked. "I mean, if it was taken step by step and a fort established at each important point, then it would be possible to trade in furs at each of those forts and so reimburse some of the expense."

"It would be possible, of course," La Vérendrye agreed reluctantly, "but that would be a very lengthy method and would necessitate leaving men at each fort to trade. Would we be able to get enough men to carry out such an idea? Surely it would be better to get together a picked band of men and carry out my first suggestion of an expedition up the Missouri and perhaps beyond."

A heated discussion followed. All were agreed that to know what lay beyond the present western boundaries and how far was the distance to this large ocean, would mean much to the colony and to its expansion. Yet all realized that little could be done without the permission of the authorities in France and without their active cooperation. It was not a matter in which any concrete conclusion could be reached. It would be a year, perhaps two, before Charlevoix reached France and certainly some long time after that before the authorities acted. There was nothing to do but hope that Father Charlevoix's report would be well considered.

To some of the ladies waiting for the gentlemen to return, the interval was long and tedious. It was noticed that Madame la Marquise was restless and not as vivacious as usual. Instead of dominating the conversation as was her custom, she listened rather abstractly to what was being said.

Elise took the opportunity to become better acquainted with young Madame le Moyne. She had been at the magnificent reception which Baron de Longueil had given to welcome his son's wife but had seen little of them since, as Captain Charles le Moyne had been away on duty and his wife had accompanied him. Elise had a particular interest in Charles' wife because he had at one time been one of her suitors. Whether it was his disappointment over her marrying another, or whether he had not found another woman who appealed to him, he had remained single for all these years and had only married the previous April. She now learned from his wife that an heir was expected shortly. Thanks to the innovation of hoops her condition was concealed and she had been able to attend the reception. Catherine-Charlotte was a beautiful girl and was to mother sixteen children, but only two of them were to survive to carry on the famous de Longueil name.

When the men returned to the drawing room, the ladies broke up their conversation. Father Charlevoix asked that he might be excused as he had much work to do and Governor de Ramezay sent his young son to escort the priest back to the Jesuit College across the way.

While card tables were being prepared, the guests talked in groups and Madame la Marquise beckoned discreetly to La Vérendrye. Standing a little apart in a recess made by the windows, they conversed in an undertone, the Marquise being careful to cover her expression to give the appearance of a polite conversation. La Vérendrye's eyes were alight with suppressed desire, not however, for a woman but for a project that was even dearer to him. Louise de Vaudreuil saw the brightness of his blue eyes that could also be so steely, and misread their expression. She was disappointed when he began to talk animately over the renewal of the Western project. She listened patiently hoping that others would hear his words so that there should seem to be a good reason for their talking together. Then she broke into the conversation and in a low tone asked:

"And how have you been all these years, Pierre?"

He shrugged his shoulders. "Physically fit of course, I always am, but restless, so restless."

"Despite your marriage?" she asked and her tone was brittle.

"There are two sides to men, Louise. Surely you know that. My wife and children satisfy one part but—a man must have work to satisfy him too."

"Perhaps I can help you. I will speak to my husband. You know that I will do all that I can for you. I did before, didn't I?"

He met her eyes and his softened slightly. He had first met Louise de Vaudreuil during the years she had resided at Versailles. The rumors that had spread through the colony over her long absence in France away from her elderly husband, had not been unfounded. She was a beautiful woman and ambitious and the Court of Versailles had offered many opportunities for her. After his recovery from his wounds, Pierre de la Vérendrye had gone to Versailles somewhat of a hero and had for a time been much feted. He had been unmarried then and a woman with influence at the Court, served his purpose admirably. That they had been lovers had been a secret well-guarded. Unfortunately that had been all the advantage gained, for in the wake of the rumors the Marquis had arrived in France and Louis XIV had died, before Louise could get a hearing for La Vérendrye.

"Come and see me, Pierre. Why not after the reception? Philippe will retire immediately we get home."

"This is not Versailles, Louise," La Vérendrye answered. "And, too, I am now a married man..."

"I was a married woman when we met in Versailles. That did not deter you."

La Vérendrye's handsome face broke into a smile in which there was mischief.

"Of course I was ten years younger then..." Louise went on.

"And you want me to reply that you are still beautiful."

"If you mean it."

"I do."

"And you will come afterwards...?"

Before he could reply the room broke into a hubbub. Jean-Baptiste de Ramezay had returned and was talking excitedly to his father. At the same time the bells of the churches all began to ring. The guests rushed to the windows, unceremoniously pushing the Marquise and La Vérendrye aside. Everyone began talking at once and pointing towards the west where flames could be seen leaping to the sky. The older ones immediately thought of Indian raids. With difficulty the Governor was able to obtain silence. Then in an excited voice that he tried to make sound calm he said:

"Ladies and gentlemen, I have just been informed that the Hôtel Dieu is afire and that it is spreading rapidly. Some of your homes may be in danger, I have ordered your carriages."

There was a general rush for the door. Those who lived outside the town, made way for those who must reach their homes quickly. Madame de Ramezay gathered together the women whose houses were outside of Montreal and asked them to remain and help her.

"If it spreads there will be homeless people who must come here and injured to be attended to," she said quietly.

Ann and Elise immediately volunteered to remain and also Catherine le Moyne and many others. Madame la Marquise was biting her lips. Without a word, La Vérendrye had rushed off at the announcement, eager to help but also sensing adventure. With him had gone André and Antoine and many of the other younger men.

The Marquis offered his arm to his wife. "Come, my dear, we must return home immediately. I may be needed there," he said.

# CHAPTER NINE

THE crowd along the Rue St. Paul was so dense that at first it was impossible for those from the Chateau to get through, until their fine clothes being observed, way was made for them.

It was a scene of panic. The Hôtel Dieu was not only entirely ablaze, but fanned by the wind, the flames had already gutted many of the houses around. The frail wooden structures easily fed the flames, despite the fact that in some instances the roofs still held patches of snow. The flames danced like witches, gleefully flinging themselves into the air, springing back from the patches of snow that retarded their progress and then tripping lightly to other parts that welcomed them. The crackling of the wood was like the brittle laughter of an old hag.

The town possessed no fire-fighting equipment beyond a brigade armed with wooden buckets. These and others furnished with every available receptacle, formed lines from the river's edge to the burning structures. Tirelessly they worked but their efforts were so inadequate, impeded by the frantic people who were striving to rescue their furniture and belongings from their houses. These they piled haphazard in the middle of the street—furniture, bedding, household pots, clothes—all heaped in confusion so that no one knew his own possessions.

The Sisters of the Congregation had worked frantically to get the patients out of the hospital and these lay in rows, many of them with only a single blanket to protect them from the bitter cold. They groaned and cried out in fear, while the priests passed among them trying to give assurance and succor.

Those from the Chateau surveyed the confusion in horror and bewilderment. Some seized large pots from the household possessions in the streets and joined the bucketlines, while others relieved those whose arms had grown limp and weary from their exertions. Smoke and grime covered faces and made eyes water and parched throats. But there was no stemming the progress of the flames. The fire pursued its way relentlessly until the number of houses burning exceeded a hundred. The people stared stupefied and helpless, fearful that the whole town was going to burn up.

"We must get some help for these people," Antoine said. "They can't lie here in the road. Surely there is some building left where they can be taken."

"What about the Chateau?" André suggested. "They have plenty of room there. I'll go back and speak to the Governor."

People were sobbing as they saw everything they possessed consumed by flames. Some knelt in the streets impeding the progress of those who were trying to help, yet no one had the heart to tell them to get up. Twice Antoine grabbed women who driven frantic with grief, attempted to enter the burning buildings to rescue some valued possession. In their satin coats and breeches, the men looked rather absurd especially as their wigs were knocked awry and their swords frequently got in their way, but they ignored these things and took no notice when their elegant clothes became grimed with soot and the lace at their wrists was scorched by the flames.

Then above the screams of the women and the agonized cries of those who had lost their homes, there came a terrific shout. The crowd fell back in confusion, as with a roar and a rush of flames the roof of the Hôtel Dieu fell in, scattering burning wood everywhere and searing many of those who watched. Suddenly the noise of the people ceased as two soldiers pushed their way through the crowd dragging a large negro slave woman. Where they had found her or how they had discovered that she was responsible no one as yet knew but soon the word spread that she had started the fire as an act of revenge. The crowd surged around her and the two soldiers, and it looked for a moment or two as though they would tear her from them. Undoubtedly this might have happened for the frenzy of the people quickly turned to ugliness. But at that moment the Governor arrived and took charge of the situation.

"What is this?" he asked sternly as he stepped from his carriage.

The woman was writhing and struggling so that neither of the soldiers dared loosen his grasp to salute.

"We found her, your Excellency. She started the fire," one of them stated.

Governor de Ramezay looked at the pathetic figure of the slave woman who, whether she knew who he was or not, knew that he was someone of importance and began to whimper.

"Is this true?" the Governor asked and his tone was not unkind, though he was fully conscious of the ugly looks on the faces of those around.

The woman did not reply but fell to her knees trembling.

"Lock her up securely. I'll attend to the matter tomorrow," the Governor said. He called sharply to other soldiers in the crowd and ordered them to assist in escorting the prisoner. André had come back with the Governor and de Ramezay turned to him: "Would you take charge of this matter, André? These men may need help."

"Certainly, Excellency," André replied. It was one of the first times he remembered drawing his sword with a possibility of having to use it. He cleared the way and as they passed, the crowd murmured angrily at the wretched woman.

It was not possible to get much attention except from those immediately around him, but to them the Governor spoke decisively and his calmness helped to quell some of the riotous atmosphere.

"I want all these sick people carried up to the Chateau. Also there is room there for all of you who have lost your homes. Volunteers among you men will please take charge and see that these orders are carried out at once." There were officers who had been at the party among the crowd and they immediately came forward. Young Jean-Baptiste in his very new uniform proudly stepped forward with them and was rewarded by a quick approving glance from his father. Governor de Ramezay gave them orders to organize the people.

With something to do, the atmosphere became less chaotic and soon a long line of people were wending their way to the Chateau carrying the sick from the Hôtel Dieu. It was more difficult to get the homeless to leave the scene of desolation but Paul de Courville-Boissart, who had now arrived, limped among them and with kind words and gentle persuasion he and others gradually were able to get them headed towards the hospitable Chateau.

"Wooden houses and no means of fighting a fire!" the Governor muttered. "And hundreds of homeless!" He walked among the people, making suggestions, but there was nothing he could do to stop the fire.

Inside the Chateau the scene of gaiety and entertainment had changed to one of distress. Madame de Ramezay, immediately André had brought his message, had issued orders for the reception of the sick and injured. The servants, tired from the banquet had at first been inclined to mutter, but, when required, Madame de Ramezay had a sharp tongue and under its lashing they moved quickly to obey her orders. Closed rooms were opened up and fires lighted in the grates. Every spare blanket was brought down and that which so short a time ago had been a festive banquet hall, was cleared to receive the sick. As they began to arrive, aided by Ann and Elise and the other ladies, she directed the bearers where to lay them. She went from patient to patient and tended to their needs. Some had received minor burns but most of them had been removed before the danger of the fire had reached them. To these injuries she and Ann attended, while Elise went to see about procuring something hot for them to drink. Fortunately the amount of the food left over from the banquet was abundant and the ladies forgot their beautiful dresses as they passed out hot broth and food.

No one slept in Montreal that night. Many from homes on the opposite side of the river, seeing the flames, had crossed in their sleds and offered homes to friends who had been left destitute. It was past midnight when the men returned to the Chateau, hardly recognizable as the immaculate gentlemen who had left it some hours ago. André had torn the sleeve of his coat and his hair was singed; Antoine had a bad burn across the back of one hand and all of them were begrimed and bedraggled, with eyes bloodshot and watering from the smoke. They gratefully accepted the offer of wine with which to ease their parched throats.

The Sisters of the Congregation had come up to the Chateau and took over the care of the sick. Not until she was certain that everything had been done that could relieve their distress, would Madame consent to rest. Ann offered to remain all night but Madame would not hear of it. She then left with the rest of the family, but promised to be back early the next day. Actually the next day had already arrived and dawn broke before they reached home.

With a last tour through the house, Marie-Charlotte de Ramezay went to her room. It was empty and she went in search of her husband. She found him in his study, slumped wearily over his desk, his wig thrown in a heap on the floor. Though he snored loudly, it was evident from his position that he had fallen asleep from utter weariness and dejection. The fire had died in the grate and the room was icy cold. Madame took a shawl from a chair and laid it gently over his shoulders and then quickly stooped to replenish the fire. She was encouraging it with the bellows when her husband awakened.

"Marie, you shouldn't be doing that!" he exclaimed and jumped up to take them from her. "Where are the servants?" he asked. Then recollection returned to him and rather apologetically he said. "I had forgotten for the moment. I had meant to return and help you."

"You have enough to do, dear," she said quietly. "You must come to bed."

"Yes," he answered abstractly. He walked to the windows and pulled back the curtains. "Why, it's morning!" he exclaimed as the light of early day greeted him. His wife stood beside him. From where they stood they could see the smouldering ruins.

"How did it happen, Claude?" she asked.

"That is what is worrying me. They say a negro slave woman started it..."

"Negro slave woman!"

"The soldiers found her. I have to go and find out what made her do it. Revenge no doubt. If only they would not bring negroes here!"

"What will you do with her?" Marie-Charlotte asked.

"She'll be tried and undoubtedly hanged, presuming she is guilty and I expect she is."

"Horrible!"

"Yes, too horrible," Claude said and turned away from the window and went to the fire. "Years of work undone in one night..."

"And hundreds homeless. What shall we do about them?"

"They must be housed here until we can make some arrangement. I must go down to the Court House."

"Can't you sleep first... Just for a few hours?"

He shook his head and then a half-smile crossed his drawn face. "I have already slept," he said. "But you must rest, my dear."

"I shall for a little while. If you're not going to bed then I will get you some breakfast."

Still in her party finery, Madame went into the kitchen to prepare her husband's breakfast.

# CHAPTER TEN

JUSTICE was swift and reconstruction slow. The negro woman who had taken her revenge by setting fire to the Hôtel Dieu was tried and condemned to be burned alive. There were many who felt sorry for the poor woman who had been torn from her native land and brought to an alien country as a slave. This question of importing black slave help to Canada had caused a great deal of controversy and condemnation. Some, like the Baron de Longueil approved of it and had several negro slaves, but most of the seigneurs were definitely opposed to it. The negro could not withstand the intense cold of the winter and few survived. The negro woman in question had been torn from her family in Africa and bought by a merchant in Montreal who traded with the West Indies. Now she had had her revenge. There would have been considerably more sympathy for her had it not been that so much sympathy was required for the one hundred and twenty-six families who had been left homeless by her action.

Those who gathered in the Market Place to see the sentence carried out were largely from the families who had suffered and their faces were grim and set as they watched the prisoner dragged from the jail towards the pyre set up near the gallows. It was a long time since anyone had been burned alive in Montreal. In earlier days many an Iroquois prisoner had been disposed of in this way. There was a murmur among the crowd but it was not all vengeful and there were tones of pity as they saw the pathetic creature who was too terrified to walk, dragged along with her feet bouncing over the rough cobbled stones. But it was not to the pyre that the soldiers escorted her. The people watched with puzzled expressions while the *capitaine de milice* mounted the steps of the scaffold and read from a paper that the Governor had changed the sentence from being burned alive, to hanging and being burned dead. Most of the onlookers, except the most vindictive, approved of this change of sentence.

The poor creature sank in a heap upon the platform, beating the wooden floor with her hands and crying out. A priest stood by her murmuring words that did not penetrate to her terrified mind. Action was swift, for the authorities were afraid of the effect upon the people. Two soldiers lifted the heavy woman by the armpits and held her up while the noose was adjusted. There was a bloodcurdling scream and then a swift jerk of the rope and the body slumped upon the broken neck. A deadly hush had fallen over the crowd and continued as they removed the body and carried it to the pyre, fastening it to the stake and setting light to the faggots. Quickly the wood ignited and the flames licked around the inert body on which the head sagged and the tongue lolled out of the mouth. Many of the crowd had begun to disperse but some stood watching, their faces blank and stunned. Some were thinking that this was justice yet the taking of this life did not restore to them their homes and possessions. Most of them felt depressed and nauseated by the sight and smell of the burning body.

One result of the fire was an edict from the Governor which the *capitaine de milice* read to the people after Mass on the following Sunday. It was an order that houses should not in the future be built of wood but should be built of stone, of which there was a plentiful supply within the neighborhood. It was an order that could not be enforced effectively and despite it, there were many who rebuilt their houses in wood. But the Governor hoped that it would be largely considered and offered to give help in collecting the necessary stone to any man who needed such help.

The edict had an important effect upon the de Courville-Boissart and the de Brievaux Seigneuries. A few weeks earlier the habitants had come to Paul to inform him that there had been a decision in favor of building their own church. The hard winter with its blizzards had forced them to a realization of what an advantage this would be, not only for uninterrupted attendance at Mass, but for the teaching of the children who so frequently had to miss school during the winter. Paul had discussed with them the construction of the church but now he realized that the original intention of building this of timber should be discarded and it should be built of stone. He talked to the men about it and they agreed with him. Instead of going into the forest to cut down trees, they would now have to go into the hills to gather stone. Furthermore, it would not be possible for them to build it entirely themselves. Some of them knew how to work with stone but a stone-mason would have to be hired and with so much building going on in Montreal after the fire, it would be difficult to obtain one. Still they agreed that this should be done, but it would mean that in all probability it would not be completed until the following year.

Since their decision, Paul had been thinking of the procuring of a curé and had gone to see Father Bellemont, Superior of the Seminary with a suggestion which had been made by André. André knew of a priest up at Michilimackinac who greatly desired to be transferred to Montreal. He was an aging man yet still with sufficient energy to carry out the less arduous duties of curé on a seigneury. Paul had discussed the subject with Father Bellemont, who had promised to consider the matter. If he should approve, then André would go to Michilimackinac and bring the priest back. But this, too, would have to be delayed, though Paul was in favor of securing the curé and letting him live at the Manor House where he could conduct Mass for the people during the coming winter.

It would be another two weeks or more yet before they could expect the ice to break, heralding the start of the new season. Everyone was restless and impatient, bored with the long idle months and anxious to get back to work in the fields. Antoine stood looking over his land and thinking what would have to be done during the coming season. Stretching away from the house were large meadows where soon the cattle, horses and sheep would be put out to graze. His barns were large and well-kept. The fields now lying fallow would soon be bright with waving golden wheat, as well as peas, oats, rye and barley and in some places the maize which the Indian had introduced to the white man. His orchard was his particular pride and though the avenues of trees through which he walked were now bare, they would soon be a glory of pastel shades and deeper pinks.

He walked out to his tobacco fields and inspected the drying sheds. He grew a larger quantity of tobacco than any of the seigneuries, excepting the de Longueil, and some of the larger ones across the river.

Antoine was restless to begin work. He loved these fields and meadows in the spring and summer when everything seemed so alive. He was immensely proud of what he had been able to do in so few years. He knew now the satisfaction that comes from healthy physical labor and he enjoyed it.

The tobacco field lay on the farthest boundary of the seigneurial tract and as he stood there meditating on the coming season, he saw a group passing along the riverbank and heading towards Ménard's house. It brought to his mind the only disagreeable element on the Seigneury. During the winter, gestures of friendliness had been made towards Ménard by the other habitants but to these he had hardly responded. They had invited him to their neighborhood parties but he seldom came and if he did it was to stay only a few moments and then leave. Antoine could not understand him and several times wished that he had never let him have the land. But the Governor was anxious to keep these ex-soldiers in the colony. They were trained men and with the garrison always inadequate, it was useful to have retired soldiers who could be called upon in times of emergency. When their time of duty expired they were given the choice of returning to France or settling down on the land and many had taken advantage of the latter offer. Ménard had had no intention of remaining in New France, for he hated colonial life but an incident had occurred which had forced him to change his mind. It was not until some time after he had occupied the land that Antoine had heard the true story. Ménard was a man of fierce animal passion and while stationed at the fort had made sport with many women. This, however, was expected of the soldiers and little notice taken of it. But Ménard had miscalculated when he had taken Louise Bernaise and she had become pregnant. She was a homely peasant woman who had not been able to find a husband because of her bad temper and ugly disposition. She had threatened to tell her father unless Ménard married her. The child had died and for this she blamed her husband. The few years that they lived together were one continual stormy session. She had returned to her parents and Ménard had remained alone, neglecting his land and drinking continuously.

It was not until the following day that Antoine found out the meaning of Louise's return and then he heard it from his own son. They were having dinner when Jean-Baptiste remarked:

"Ménard's wife has come back and her parents with her."

"I saw them arrive yesterday," Antoine said.

"Their house was destroyed in the fire and they've come to live with her and her husband," Jean-Baptiste further informed them.

"How did you hear that?" Antoine asked, curious.

"Pierre Demuzet told me." This was the oldest son of the family who lived next to the Ménards.

Little more was said upon the subject then, but Antoine learned a few days later that Louise and her parents had left again. The habitants spoke of hearing angry words and even screams.

Antoine did not go near Ménard. There was little a seigneur could do in such matters, so long as the habitant kept his land in order. Ménard could not be given much credit for this, but he did clear enough to prevent Antoine being able to take the land from him. Antoine had more than once spoken to the Governor about the matter. It riled him to have this unpleasant element on a seigneury that was otherwise so well ordered.

# CHAPTER ELEVEN

THE *ice shove* came on the 10th of April. Once the shove started, the change was rapid as the imprisoned waters threw off the icy coat they had worn all the winter and great blocks of ice began piling on top of each other, pushing and grinding and thundering as they strove for release. Along the banks men with long poles guided the great jagged blocks away from the houses, their feet slithering and slipping in the slush and mud that turned every hole into a lake and every ridge in the road into a small river. Then the rains came, the melted snow rushing in great streams from the hills, until all signs of winter were washed away and there were alternate days of sun and warm rain. The earth awoke and the sowing of grain began. Narcissus and violets poked up their delicate heads and the trees began to bud. The first of May was celebrated with the traditional Maypole ceremony before every seigneurial mansion. By the fifteenth of the month all sowing was finished. The first ships began to arrive bringing needed supplies from France and perhaps a new emigrant or two. The *coureurs de bois* returned from their winter trading and the town resounded with their boisterous celebrations.

The de Brievaux children continued to present their various problems. The two girls pursued their diverse ways and Ann-Marie needed very careful watching. It was Paul-André who presented the greatest problem, for no sooner had spring arrived than he continued to thwart parental control and to wander away whenever the desire came. Three times they had found him in the forest and for this Antoine blamed Ménard. Paul-André could not himself have lifted the bar to the gate. On the third occasion Antoine had angry words with Ménard, which however, produced little satisfaction.

"Don't blame me, seigneur, if you can't keep your son in order," Ménard had said with a sneer and when Antoine threatened to have him dispossessed of his land, the man looked at him with defiance.

This question of Paul-André's disobedience had now reached its zenith. Thrashings, arguments, locking him up in his room without food, produced no effect. The boy took the punishment and stubbornly went his own way. Finally André voiced the idea which he had been conning over during the winter. Perhaps if Paul-André met some Indians he would get over this insatiable desire. André was going on business to Caughnawaga, an Indian settlement some ten miles outside Montreal, and he suggested that they let him take Paul-André with him. They agreed and when André told his nephew about it he whooped with glee.

"But there is one condition, Paul-André," André said and there was sternness in his voice. "You must give me your word that you will not run away again. If you do, then you cannot go on the trip with me. It that understood?"

Paul-André nodded. "I promise," he said.

"Good. Then we can think of the trip. It won't be for several weeks as I have to make a new canoe. You can help me with that. You can never be a *coureur de bois* unless you know how to make a good, sturdy canoe. And, if you want to know about Indians, there are many things you will have to learn first. I will teach you."

The days of preparation that followed were a source of endless delight to the small boy. The hardest thing of all was the patience required each day waiting for Uncle André to come, because he was so busy on the Seigneury and had to make the canoe in his spare moments. The greatest adventure of all was going into the forbidden forest with his uncle to select a tree with the right bark to make the canoe. This it appeared was a matter of great importance and Uncle André explained it all very carefully as they trudged through the forest.

"There is nothing so important to a voyageur, Paul-André, as knowing how to make a good canoe. It may mean the difference between life and death, escape or capture. The best time to select bark for a canoe is in August, this month..."

"Then if your canoe is wrecked some other time of the year, you have to wait until it is August before you can make another one..."

"No. August is the *best* month. The bark comes off more easily then... It is more trouble in other months. Also there are many ways of making a canoe. Most Canadians make them of birch-bark..."

"Are Canadians us?"

"Why yes!"

"Aren't we French?"

"Yes but we live in Canada..."

"Why is it called Canada?"

"Well, that's what the Indians named it. At least more or less. When our people first arrived here they asked the Indians what was the name of the place and they said *Cannata* which is the Iroquois word meaning "collection of dwellings or houses" and from that we derived the word *Canada*. Is that clear?"

Paul-André nodded.

André stopped abruptly and tapped a birch, then looked up and examined the tree critically. "This looks like a good one. You see how straight it is and about the right size around. We'll only make a small canoe." Paul-André swelled with pride when his uncle said, "*We'll* make it" and not "I'll make it."

"Are you going to cut the tree down?" Paul-André inquired.

"No. Some do, but there is always the danger that as it falls the bark will be injured and if you have holes in it, the canoe is spoiled. No. I'm going to climb up about half way. Watch now."

With the agility of a monkey, André climbed the tree, paused and judged his distance, climbed a little higher until he was about fourteen feet from the ground. Then he drew his knife from his belt and made a circular cut around the tree. As he did so he examined the trunk critically and then with an experienced hand, he descended making a straight perpendicular line with his knife as he came down. At the same time he very carefully loosened the bark on each side of the slit. When he reached the ground, he made another circular cut shortly above the base of the tree.

Paul-André watched with eyes wide with admiration. André paused to wipe his forehead with a large handkerchief, smiling at his admiring nephew.

"What do we do now?" Paul-André asked.

"Now we take the bark off. Very carefully, for if we split it, then we'd have to patch those splits and that means weak spots in the canoe. You can help me, but do *only* what I tell you."

Paul-André watched and never had he obeyed instructions more carefully. He was surprised how easily the bark peeled from the tree. When they had finished they had a large wide funnel-shaped piece, which they carried home between them. Paul-André on one end stumbled several times because he had not the practised tread of his uncle.

"You'll have to learn how to walk in a forest," André said after the first stumble. He never scolded only smiled at his nephew's awkwardness. "Not only will it save you turning an ankle, but if you step on a twig and hostile Indians should be around, then it would give you away." When they paused to rest he demonstrated what he meant and Paul-André walked up and down practising what he had been shown, until André told him to rest or he would not make the remainder of the long journey home.

"Why are some Indians hostile, uncle?" he asked.

"Well, because we came and took their land. They were here before us you know."

"Why did we do that?"

"Because France is crowded and we needed more room to live." It was a rather broad explanation but André considered his nephew too young to go into the question of oppression and taxation.

"And the Indians don't like having their land taken from them?"

"If we give them things in return it's all right. You will have to learn to understand Indians…"

"Oh yes." The words came eagerly.

"You must learn to treat them fairly. Many white men are bad and don't treat the Indian right. They take his pelts and don't pay him for them. Always be fair with the Indian and he will be fair with you—most of the time anyway."

The making of the canoe due to the sporadic intervals which André could devote to it, took many days. While Paul-André waited for him, he would sit by the canoe, not touching anything but regarding it almost as though it were sacred. There were small things that he could do to help in the making and then he was very proud, but sometimes it took someone with more strength than he, and then Antoine would give a hand.

As the boat began to take shape, Paul-André's eagerness grew and he talked of nothing else. He found too that his father was intensely interested, for as a landsman Antoine knew little of canoes, and those he owned had all been made for him by someone else.

It was a small light canoe that one man could carry and as André lifted it and put it into the water, Paul-André could not contain his excitement. With bated breath he stepped in beside his uncle and took the smaller paddle that André had made for him. That first trip up and down about a mile of the river, was a memorable occasion. He quickly caught on to the rhythm of handling his paddle and mentally he had grown inches in stature when he returned home and recounted the adventure.

# CHAPTER TWELVE

CAUGHNAWAGA was an Iroquois settlement about ten miles above Montreal and situated on the south shore of the St. Lawrence across from the Lachine Village. It was, in effect, a seigneury or concession granted to the Jesuit Fathers for the protection of the Iroquois whom they had converted to Christianity. It had from time to time been moved from different positions along the south shore of the river, beginning at La Prairie and finally being settled in 1716 at Caughnawaga. It was a typical settlement with the longhouses of the Iroquois arranged around a square and dominated by the mission church and school and at one time protected by a small fort that was now falling into ruin. Palisades enclosed and protected the area. Government was by Indian chief who not only kept a firm hand over his own people but as the importance of the settlement grew, played an essential part in the affairs of the rival French and English colonies.

To reach the village, voyageurs had to paddle up the St. Lawrence against the tide and then portage over the Lachine Rapids. A well-worn path marked the route over which canoe and supplies had to be carried. André knew it well for he had traversed it on every voyage to the trading posts. But never before had he had so much enjoyment from it as he watched the delight of his young nephew for whom everything was such a new experience. They camped the first night at the foot of the rapids, cooking their supper and then rolling into their blanket to sleep beneath the stars. Elise had made Paul-André a deerskin suit like his uncle's and in the little boy's estimation he was already a *coureur de bois.* As they lay that night huddled in the same blanket, André thought of the day and of the tired little boy who now lay sleeping beside him. He wished that he were his own son and wondered why he did not devote more serious attention to finding a wife. Never before had he realized how much it would have meant to him to have a son like Paul-André, whom he loved for the very things that caused his parents so much trouble. There was absolutely no fear in him, nor did he ever cry out when he was hurt. Already the intrepid spirit of adventure was stirring within him and some day he would make a courageous voyageur.

The portage took three days and two nights, for although they had little beside the canoe to carry, they had to rest frequently because Paul-André's little legs could not travel very far at a time. They took it slowly enjoying the quiet freedom of this primeval world. When André had said he would give up going into the woods he knew that what he would miss the most would be these days and nights far away in a quiet world where nature held sway. It was a world of beauty, with tall majestic trees that had been there since time immemorial, stretching forth their long wide arms to embrace the blue sky. Some of them were gnarled and grisly with decrepit age. When travellers rested they sat on fallen trunks which had been hurled down by a storm or perhaps rotted away when life became impotent. Beneath their moccasined feet green moss carpeted the rough ground and through the trees the noonday sun sent keen rays that cast entrancing shadows into the impenetrable forest on the one side and the fierce dashing waters on the other.

"These are the most treacherous rapids there are," André said. "When we come back we shall come down them in the canoe."

"Down these in the canoe! Oooo! That will be exciting!" Paul-André exclaimed.

They went to sleep at night to the song of these rapids as they burbled and thundered without ceasing.

On the morning of the fifth day they arrived at Caughnawaga. As they approached André tried to give Paul-André some idea and outline of the people who inhabited the village.

"We, the French, called them the Iroquois. The English call them the Five Nations because the tribe is made up of five different tribes—the Mohawks, Oneidas, Onondagas, Cayuga and Senecas. They call themselves the *Hodeno-saunee* which means *longhouse* and that is because of the way they build their dwellings. As you someday visit other tribes you will find that some live in birch-bark huts and others in houses of different shapes. It is important to know this because then from a distance you can tell what tribe you may be approaching. As you will presently see, these Iroquois have longhouses with several families dwelling in each. These people are the most powerful of the tribes and the most warlike, only the ones here have become Christians."

Paul-André was listening intently unable yet to understand all his uncle was saying. "Do these people scalp?" he asked.

"Er, yes. When they go to war they do. But they don't attack us. They are our allies, that is our friends. They are friendly with some tribes and enemies of others."

André ran the canoe up on to the shore and jumping out pulled it out of the water. Paul-André scrambled out and stood by his uncle. His large dark-amber eyes were shining with excitement and he watched eagerly.

Their arrival had been noted and the villagers flocked to meet them, recognizing André by his red hair and giving him a warm welcome. He spoke to them in their own language, and introduced Paul-André who was immediately the center of attraction. They fondled his auburn hair and commented on it to André. He explained to them that this was Paul-André's first visit to an Indian village and that, of course, he did not understand their language. Most of them, however, had learned French and they asked him questions which he answered eagerly and without shyness.

"Are the Williams' at home?" André asked and when he received a reply in the affirmative, went towards the house where they lived. As they approached, a young woman came to the door and her face broke into a smile when she saw André. Paul-André gazed at her in amazement for although she was dressed as an Indian, her skin was white. When she spoke to André she used the Indian language. She looked from André to the small boy with him and asked in the dialect.

"He is your son?"

André laughed. "No, Margaret. I'm still unmarried. This is my sister's youngest child." Then turning to Paul-André he said: "This is Mrs. Williams, Paul-André."

Paul-André hesitated as to what he should do, but when the lady held out her hand he put his into it. She was a tall woman about twenty-five. Paul-André had to look a long way up to her.

"Are you Indian?" he asked.

Before she could reply a tall man came out of the house accompanied by a young boy and André turned to greet them.

"Ah, Amrusus, how are you?" he said in the dialect. The man addressed was a fine looking Iroquois, with the massive build of his tribe. He wore only a breechclout as the day was warm and the boy with him was dressed the same. Paul-André and the boy eyed each other with keen observation. The boy was much taller than Paul-André and though he had Indian features and build, his skin was tawny. Two little girls joined the group and eyed Paul-André curiously.

André spoke to the Indian boy. "Oure, this is my nephew Paul-André. Would you look after him for me while I attend to some business in the village?" When he spoke to the boy he spoke in French and Paul-André's face lit up when he heard the boy reply in the same language.

"Oui, monsieur," Oure replied politely. Then turning to Paul-André said simply: "Come."

Paul-André looked at his uncle and then at the boy.

"Run along with him, Paul-André. Have a good visit and ask him about Indians. I'll be back for you in a little while."

Paul-André went gladly, following Oure in silence. The boy led him down to the water's edge and then sat down. Paul-André did likewise and they fell into awkward silence. He was fascinated by his companion, the first Indian boy he had ever seen. He wanted to ask a lot of questions but did not like to begin. Oure turned his liquid brown eyes and they met Paul-André's. Then Oure shifted his gaze to Paul-André's red hair and he smiled.

"You have hair like your uncle's only darker," he said.

"My mother and uncle are twins. They have hair alike. My father's though is black like yours."

"Is he Indian?"

Paul-André shook his head and said: "How could he be? I'm not Indian …"

"Nor's my mother …"

"Is she French?"

"No, English."

"She dresses like an Indian."

"She was adopted."

"By the Indians!" Paul-André's eyes lit up with interest. "How did she get adopted?"

"She was captured by my grandfather."

"Captured!" Paul-André looked alarmed. "And they made her become an Indian?"

"She wanted to. She refused to go back to her own people. They have tried to get her to several times but she won't."

"How was she captured?"

"In a raid on the village where she lived …"

"An Indian raid?"

"Us and the French …"

"Where was it?"

"Deerfield."

"Where's that?"

"In a place called Massachusetts."

"Massach … Where's that?"

"A long way off."

"Have you been there?"

"Once."

"You have!" Paul-André was all admiration for his travelled companion.

The conversation lagged as Paul-André thought over what Oure had said. He had never expected that white people became Indians.

"How old are you?" he asked Oure, breaking the silence.

"Nine. How old are you?"

"Nearly seven. Do you go to school?"

"The priest teaches us."

"Are Indians Catholics?"

"We are. Most Indians aren't."

"Why are you?"

Oure looked a little puzzled and then said: "Grandfather says the priest knows best. He became a Catholic. He's the Chief."

"Will you be a Chief when you grow up?"

"Maybe. You have to be very brave to be made a Chief."

"Then your grandfather must be brave."

"Of course."

"Have you older brothers?"

Oure shook his head. "Only two sisters."

"Then won't you become chief after your father?"

"My father isn't a chief."

"But he will be when his father dies, won't he?"

Oure looked puzzled. "I don't understand," he said.

"Well, my father is a seigneur and when he dies my older brother will become seigneur. It is the same kind of thing, isn't it? Father is head man of our village."

For the first time Oure appeared to be a little impressed. Then he shook his head. "It isn't that way with us. Descent does not come from our fathers but from our mothers …"

Paul-André became thoughtful again. Then he asked: "You're an Iroquois aren't you?"

"Yes, but we are Mohawks," Oure said with much pride. "Mohawks are the most important."

Paul-André remembered his uncle telling him of the different divisions of the Iroquois and wished he could remember the difficult names so that he could have mentioned them and perhaps impressed Oure.

The conversation lagged again. Oure looked out over the water, his strong features set. Except for the lightness of his skin he had all the characteristics of his Indian father—high cheek bones, long straight nose and greasy, straight black hair.

"What do you do all day?" Paul-André asked.

"Fish and hunt when I don't have to go to school..."

"Fish and hunt! They let you?"

Oure's brown eyes were rather scornful. These white people knew nothing! Yet he quite liked this white boy even if he seemed so ignorant.

"Of course they let me. Father insists upon it. Only I like it. Don't you?"

"They won't let me. They say I'm too young," Paul-André admitted reluctantly.

"I learned long before I was your age."

"It must be fine to be an Indian," Paul-André said enviously. "Aren't you glad?"

"Of course. Only... I wish I were all Indian instead of part. I would never marry a white woman."

"Don't you like white people?" Paul-André asked rather despondently.

"Some."

"Couldn't you like me?"

"I don't know you."

"Perhaps Uncle André will bring me again, many times, and we could get to know each other and you could teach me to hunt and fish." Paul-André's voice became eager. "I know how to make a birch-bark canoe," he added proudly.

"How?" came the skeptical reply.

"Uncle André taught me. Of course," he admitted, "I'm not good at it yet but I shall be. My Uncle André knows everything. He's the best *coureur de bois* in Montreal."

"I know," Oure agreed and Paul-André liked him very much then. "Father has been on several trips with him…"

Paul-André considered a very important decision. He took from his pocket a long narrow, wooden whistle. He contemplated it for some time and rubbed its smooth surface lovingly. Then he held it out to Oure.

"You can have this."

Oure took it and studied it with a puzzled expression. "What is it?" he asked.

"A whistle. Put the end with the hole in it to your mouth and blow."

Oure put the end in his mouth and blew hard but nothing happened. He looked at Paul-André inquiringly.

"No, this way," Paul-André said, happy that at last he had found something he could teach the Indian boy. He held out his hand for it and puckering up his lips tight, extended the upper one slightly over the lower and blew gently. A high shrill sound came out. For the first time Oure's serious face broke into a smile and he took the whistle again. Paul-André showed him how to form his mouth.

"Don't blow too hard, just gently," he instructed him.

This time it was successful and Oure looked very pleased with the gift.

"My Uncle André made it for me. But he will make me another. You keep it," Paul-André said magnanimously.

"Merci," Oure said and after trying it several times stuck it into the top of his breachclout.

Paul-André waited, hoping that he would receive something in return but no gesture was made. Oure stood up.

"Come up to the house," he said and without waiting for any agreement, walked away. Paul-André followed him. As they neared the house, Oure's mother called:

"Come and eat."

"Dinner," Oure shouted and began to run, for red boy or white was the same when it came to eating.

Paul-André ran with him asking: "Do I eat with you or am I to find my uncle?"

"I don't know. Ask mother."

Margaret Williams' stern, hard expression relaxed as she saw them. *"Mangez,"* she said to Paul-André.

"Am I to eat with you, madame?" he asked politely.

She nodded and motioned to him to sit on the ground next to Oure. The two little girls sat on the other side of the fire and peered at him curiously. Oure's father came and sat down without saying a word. Paul-André was very nervous. The tall woman with the white skin who had become Indian was stirring a huge pot that hung over a fire outside the house. Her hair was black and straight and covered with bear grease, as was that of all the others. Paul-André with his curly hair waving in the breeze looked as though his head was on fire. He wished his had been black like theirs. If only he had had the black hair instead of his brother, then he would not have felt so conspicuous. He noticed that all the others had bowls and large wooden spoons. He leaned over and whispered to Oure: "I have a bowl in the canoe and a spoon. Shouldn't I get it?"

Oure turned to his mother and spoke in the dialect. Again Paul-André was impressed. Only two years older than he yet he could speak two languages!

Margaret answered in the dialect and Oure said to Paul-André: "She says she will find you one."

Paul-André waited. Mrs. Williams had taken her husband's bowl and ladled thick soup into it. Then she put her fingers into the pot and fished out several large lumps of meat and put these into the bowl. Silently she handed the bowl to her husband and he began to eat. Then she went away and came back with a bowl and spoon. The rim of the bowl was incrusted with food from another meal, in fact by the look of it, from several other meals. It made Paul-André feel a little sick. Margaret filled Oure's bowl and then Paul-André's. The brown liquid was thick and greasy and a scum had begun to form. Paul-André glanced covertly at Oure, but he was eating hungrily and so he took a mouthful. The half warm liquid was not appetizing. Oure got up and dipped his hand into the pot and brought out a large piece of meat which he handed to Paul-André. He had no alternative but to take it. He hesitated about eating it, for clinging to it were several black hairs. He looked quickly at Mrs. Williams. Strands of her hair were hanging about her face. He knew he would be sick if he tried to eat it. He had always hated fat and this was mostly fat. The question was, however, decided for him, for one of the many curs jumped up and snatched it from his fingers. In his surprise he jumped and upset his bowl of soup over his short deerskin trousers of which he was so proud. No one took any notice of the incident, except Oure who fished out another piece of meat and handed it to him, with the comment: "Watch the dogs."

This piece wasn't so fat but it still looked unappetizing. He looked to see if any of them were watching and as they were all occupied, he tried to pull off a black hair that was around it. In doing so, he dropped it. He stooped to pick it up from the ground but Oure quickly stopped him. "No!" he said sharply. "Leave that for the dead."

Paul-André looked puzzled, especially as one of the curs was busily eating the meat. Did they call these dogs the dead? Perhaps the meat would soon make him dead, for it certainly had looked horrible enough to kill anyone.

"You'll have to go without meat now. That's all there is," Oure said, his face expressionless.

Paul-André felt most relieved.

A pudding made of corn followed and this was not too unappetizing and hungry as he was, Paul-André ate it all up.

When the meal was finished, Oure stood up, wiping his greasy fingers upon his breech clout.

"Come," he said and Paul-André followed him. They entered a long wooden building and he followed Oure about half way down. On each side of the interior of the building there were partitions about every twelve feet. In the center were the ashes of many fires and Paul-André counted ten of these. Oure was standing on one of the lower benches between two partitions and rummaging for something in the upper bench.

"Is this your house?" Paul-André asked.

"Ours and others."

"You mean others live here too?"

"Of course. This is our section. Twenty families live here."

"Twenty!" Paul-André's voice went up with surprise. "Where do you sleep?"

Oure pointed to the upper shelf where he had been rummaging. "We sleep here. Father and mother there," he pointed to the lower shelf. "We sleep here in the summer to avoid the fleas. In the winter we sleep around the fire." He pointed to the cold ashes in the center of the floor.

"Don't you have bedclothes?"

"We have blankets when we need them."

"Oh." Paul-André's reply was flat and puzzled.

Oure was holding out something to him. "For you," he said.

Paul-André took it, his pleasure at the gift making him forget the more disquieting details of Indian life. He examined the article given to him.

"It's a rabbit's skull," Oure said. "I found it in the forest."

Paul-André examined it more closely. It was a small bone with two hollows where the eyes had been and tinier ones at the end of the snout.

"Merci," he said. "But don't you want it?"

"I'll get another."

As they came out of the door they saw Uncle André and the priest talking to Amrusus. Uncle André hailed his nephew. "Been having a good time?" he asked.

Paul-André nodded. He did not seem as excited as he had been on arrival and André noted it with satisfaction. Perhaps his interest in Indians would now wane.

Paul-André showed him the rabbit's skull. "Oure gave this to me. I gave him the whistle you made me, do you mind?"

"Not at all. I will make you another one."

"Are we going now?"

"Yes, in a few minutes. Have you enjoyed it?"

"Very much. Will you bring me again? I like Oure."

André smiled at Oure and put his arm across his shoulders. "Thank you, Oure, for looking after him. Did you teach him a lot about Indians?"

"Some things. He doesn't know much."

André laughed at the remark. "He's only young yet. When he's as old as you he will know more."

Oure seemed pleased with this. They all walked down to the canoe and Amrusus and André shook hands warmly. "I'll let you know any further developments, Amrusus," André said.

Amrusus nodded.

"Say goodbye to Oure now, Paul-André," André said.

The two boys eyed each other rather shyly and then Oure held out his hand as his father had done to André. They shook hands.

"Come back again," Oure said and turned away.

André helped his nephew into the canoe and jumped in himself. Paul-André sat silently watching the two Indian figures on the shore, watching them until they were out of sight. Then he settled down thoughtfully.

# CHAPTER THIRTEEN

WHAT had taken several days and nights on the outward journey, took only a few hours on the return, as they did not have to make portage over the rapids. The journey by canoe over the Lachine Rapids was thrilling and exciting for Paul-André, yet a little frightening, though he tried to conceal this as Oure had said that chiefs must be brave and as Oure might some day be a chief, Paul-André wanted to be as brave as he.

As they sat eating their supper that night, Paul-André was still thoughtful. André watched him and smiled, knowing that many thoughts and ideas were crowding his young mind.

"Did you like the Indians?" he asked.

"I liked Oure…"

"I thought you would."

"He hunts and fishes. He has done it for many years—when he was younger than me. Will you teach me to hunt and fish?"

"We'll have to talk to your father about it."

"He'll say I'm too young," Paul-André said despondently.

"To hunt perhaps. Guns are dangerous things…"

"Doesn't Oure use a gun?"

"Probably. Or maybe he uses a bow and arrow. But I don't see why you shouldn't learn to fish. I'll talk to your father."

"Will you, Uncle André! Oure does so many things." He was silent again. Then after a long pause said: "Uncle André, why do so many Indian families live together?"

"It is their custom."

"But Oure said there were more than twenty families in that longhouse. Why don't they live as we do?"

"White people and red people have different ideas. Even white people don't all live in the same kind of houses."

"Don't they?"

"No. Different nationalities have different kinds of houses. The English houses are different from ours."

"Oh." There was another pause while this statement was given thought and then he asked. "Is the Mohawk language hard?"

"No harder than any other …"

"Would you teach me that first?"

"Why?"

"Oure speaks it and French too."

"Yes, that's so."

"And when I go to Caughnawaga again I could talk to Oure in his own language."

André smiled and left the subject where it was. Paul-André was thoughtful for several more minutes, then asked: "Why do they call dogs dead?"

André looked puzzled. "What do you mean?" he asked.

"Well, while we were eating dinner I dropped a piece of meat on the ground and when I went to pick it up, Oure said quickly, leave that for the dead, and then one of the dogs ate it."

André laughed. "The two things don't really have any connection. The Indians believe that people need food even after they're dead, and so if anything is dropped it is left there for them. It is just a superstition …"

"What's a supersti … The word you just said?"

"Superstition? Well, belief in good and bad luck. Sort of fairy stories."

"Then the dogs didn't have anything to do with it?"

"No. The dog just grabbed it and didn't leave it for the dead people."

"Oh." A pause. "Will you take me there again, Uncle André? *Soon.*"

"Well, we shall have to see what your mother and father have to say about it. Perhaps some day I shall be able to."

"But I want to go again soon."

"We shall see," André said in a noncommittal way.

It was a very tired little boy and a hungry one who reached home the following evening. He was proud to be able to tell his brother and sisters of his adventures and all through supper babbled about what he had seen. His grandfather and grandmother were having supper with them and listened with interested smiles as he chattered.

"Oure's mother is a white woman," he told them. "She was captured and became an Indian. She was English but doesn't like to be reminded of it. Her people wanted her to return but she wouldn't. Once they went back to the place where she used to live but she and her husband camped out in the orchard. Her husband is a great big Indian and may some day be a chief. Oure may be a chief too." The words came out rapidly and rather breathlessly. Paul-André looked round the table as he chattered, happy to be someone of importance for the first time.

"Eat your supper, dear," Elise said softly.

"What does he mean, the Indian boy's mother is a white woman?" Ann asked.

"It's quite a story," André replied. "You remember the raid on Deerfield?"

"Yes, another of those vile massacres like Schenectady," Paul answered. He had been on the expedition that many years ago had attacked Schenectady. Half of the people had been murdered and the rest taken prisoners, and he had never been able to forget it. He was much against these raids on innocent settlements even if they were English and in the manner of reprisals. "I believe it was even worse than Schenectady," he added.

"Yes," André agreed. "Well, this woman, mother of the Indian boy Paul-André mentioned, was Eunice Williams and was captured and taken to Caughnawaga when she was a little girl. Her father was the minister at Deerfield. He was captured too and his wife and the rest of his children. The wife was too weak to continue the journey and was killed by her Indian captor. But the rest were distributed among the Indians and sent to different places. Poor Williams had a dreadful time. Governor de Vaudreuil arranged his ransom and even allowed him to go to Caughnawaga to try to get his daughter. But the chief would not let him see her …"

"Why not?" Elise asked.

André shrugged his shoulders. "She was his captive …"

"Yes, but not to permit a father to see his own child …"

"The story is that the chief had grown very fond of her and was afraid the father would persuade her to return. Williams came again some time later and was allowed to see her. Then strangely enough she refused to return with him. There were several attempts made later to persuade her to return home but she married the son of her captor and now has three children. She won't even speak the English language. Says she has forgotten it. She changed her name to Margaret."

"What a strange story," Elise said.

"There have, however, been several like it," Paul said. "I have heard of other captives who have refused to return home."

Paul-André tried again to monopolize the conversation but tiredness overcame him and he stumbled over what he started to tell them.

"You had better get ready for bed now, dear," his mother said kindly. "You're very tired."

He tried to rally and said stubbornly. "No, I'm not tired. I …"

Charlotte-Marguerite was sitting next to him and putting her hand into his said gently: "Will you tell me everything tomorrow, Paul-André? I want to hear *everything,* every detail."

Paul-André nodded, pleased with her interest.

Elise excused herself from the table. "I'll have Madeleine carry up some water," she said. "Come, Paul-André, I must give you a bath."

"I can bathe myself!" he remonstrated indignantly.

And with that he stalked from the room, clutching his rabbit skull and feeling very much the adventurer.

# CHAPTER FOURTEEN

SUMMER was to fade into winter and two more complete seasons to pass before the church on the joint Seigneuries was finished. Work on it could only be intermittent as in the summer months the men were so busy on their land and in the winter the heavy snows retarded progress. During those years the tenure of life passed smoothly in the colony, with nothing more than threats of danger to disturb the people.

A fine plan was drawn up for the building of new fortifications around the town and the work progressed as far as the demolition of the old palisades but there it ceased, for the colonists were opposed to paying six thousand livres towards the cost. Two thousand of this was to be contributed by the seigneurs and few had anything to spare, as most of them had little beyond the *cens et rentes* paid annually by their habitants, and this amount was negligible. The balance was to come from the religious orders and the habitants, and while the former might have been able to pay, the latter certainly could not. It was easy for the Regent of France to issue such an order—another thing for the colonial authorities to get it carried out. And the majority of the people thought it an entirely unnecessary precaution, insisting that in the past they had been able by personal valor to quell their enemies and that they could do so again without the town being fortified.

On the Seigneuries, the children grew with the rapidity of childhood. Jean-Baptiste reached maturity and entered the army, was commissioned an ensign and attached to the

Montreal garrison. Ann-Marie's early beauty developed and matured dangerously. Charlotte-Marguerite asked her parents permission to become a nun and enter the Ursuline Convent in Quebec. And Paul-André went to school every day in Montreal, starting as most children did at the mixed school for boys and girls established by Sister Marguerite Bourgeoys and when he was ten years old going to one of the schools under the guidance of the priests and clerks of St. Sulpice. Education was free, though each year a collection for their support was made from those able to contribute and the balance made up by the Seminary.

When Paul-André began school soon after his return from Caughnawaga, he felt very important as he talked of his visit to the Indian village, but this importance was soon lessened when he found that there were boys at school who had been to Quebec and some even to France. What he learned at school seemed insignificant to him compared with what he was learning from Uncle André who was instructing him in the Mohawk language and also the sign language. On some days he exasperated his father because he would speak only in Indian dialect, pretending he did not understand his native language. André was also teaching him many details of Indian character and the zenith of his joy was reached when together they made a small canoe that was his own possession. Now there was no desire to run away because there was so much at home to interest him. The possession of the canoe, however, occasioned many an argument because his father would not let him go out in it without permission and this permission was not always forthcoming when desired. In this respect André agreed, for he knew that with Paul-André's adventurous nature, each journey would have been longer than the previous one. To compensate, André taught him to fish and these hours were memorable. But on the subject of hunting, Antoine remained adamant, insisting that Paul-André was still too young to handle a gun. André did not agree with this but could hardly argue with father about son.

The church was finally completed in the spring of 1724. The day of dedication was paramount in the history of the two Seigneuries. The story was to be told and retold afterwards on many a winter's night. Excepting for the de Longueil seigneury, this was the only outlying seigneury in the Montreal colony to have a church of its own and the pride of the habitants grew as those from miles around came to view it.

It was a simple construction of stone with a belfry containing a bell which Paul had obtained from France. Though it had taken so long to complete, the habitants had not been idle in their contributions. Once the idea had gained favor with them they vied with each other in making things for the interior and the exterior. They grouped together and decided between themselves what each of them should contribute. One group undertook to make the pews, with two specially carved ones—one on each side of the aisle—for the two Seigneurs and their families. Another group, composed largely of the older men, had obtained the Seigneurs' permission to construct a large cross over twelve feet high, which would be placed outside. At the foot of the cross were carved in wood the instruments which the Jews had employed in crucifying Jesus—hammer, tongs, nails, sponge and a flask of vinegar. All during the long winters the men worked on these carvings, putting into them all their skill and reverencing the work.

The Bishop of Quebec, the aging Jean-Baptiste de Saint-Vallier journeyed to Montreal especially to perform the ceremony of dedication, and Governor de Vaudreuil timed one of his visits to Montreal to coincide with the ceremony, bringing Madame with him. Governor de Ramezay and all the notables and merchants of the town also attended and in all its years the Seigneury had never presented such a resplendent appearance.

Every habitant was garbed in his Sunday best, with the children's faces shining brightly with excitement and a good scrubbing.

The sun shone throughout the day, adding the warmth of its blessing. When the bell pealed out for the first time every heart overflowed with pride and thanksgiving, but none more than Paul, who though he shared the pride of Antoine, nevertheless felt that it was his own particular dream that was being fulfilled. It was named the Church of St. Jean-Baptiste in memory of the Sieur Jean-Baptiste de Courville and also in memory of the deceased son, Jean-Baptiste de Courville-Boissart.

Late on the night of the dedication day, when all their guests had departed, Paul and Ann went together to the church. They had entertained their distinguished guests with a sumptuous feast, with long tables set outside for the habitants. They had been proud of the compliments paid to them by the visitors who looked over the seigneuries. But no moment of pride equalled that when they stood hand in hand inside the church still and peaceful in its emptiness. They lighted candles and prayed— prayers of thanksgiving and of hope for the future. Then quietly they talked together.

"We have a magnificent heritage, Ann," Paul said.

"Indeed we have, Paul. And, you know, dear, I believe Father Xavier is going to be a valuable addition to the Seigneury."

"I do, too. I like him and apparently so does everyone else."

Father Xavier François Messein had arrived a few weeks before to take up his duties as curé. He had made the journey from Michilimackinac in company with some of the returning *coureurs de bois*. Though past his middle fifties, he was still a man of robust activity. His rumpled features were good humored and there was always laughter in his eyes as he talked. It particularly pleased them to see his manner with the children, the youngest of whom he would begin to teach as soon as he was settled. He had spent a quarter of a century in the colony and understood its people. He had known the savage life among the

Indian tribes and the roughness of a town like Michilimackinac, where the *coureurs de bois* and the traders were so difficult to handle when it came to matters of religion. He had also known life in France, and Ann and Paul found him an agreeable addition to their household, where he would live until time could be found to build him a little house near the church.

On the day of the dedication, Governor de Ramezay had discussed with Paul the appointment of their own *Capitaine de milice* and the next day Paul spoke to the senior habitants in regard to the matter. Many of them would have liked André to take the appointment, but it was customary to make the selection from the habitants and not among the seigneurs. The choice, therefore, fell upon Pierre, the son of Paul's eldest brother. Pierre was now thirty-eight and the father of many children. It was one of the few times that Paul had ever seen his nephew's habitually solemn face light up with pleasure as he was informed of the selection. This now made him the most important of all the habitants and it would be his responsibility to gather all the news and read it to the people every Sunday from outside the church, as well as seeing that the men received their militia training.

The first hesitation, particularly among the women, about having their own church seemed now to have been forgotten, and every Sunday they attended regularly and none went into Montreal. It thrilled every heart when the bell sounded for Mass and also when the Angelus rang out clearly at morning, noon and night. Paul noticed, too, that the pride in this new addition extended also to the individual farms and that the new season began with a spurt of energy that exceeded that of any other year.

It spurred Paul and Antoine to make further improvements and, towards the end of May, Antoine and André left for the forest on a new project which they anticipated would bring additional revenue to the Seigneuries. Their quest was in the nature of an experiment which Antoine was anxious to try and with which Paul and André were much in accord. The suggestion had in fact come from André. While at Caughnawaga, Father Lafitau had spoken to André of a plant by the name of *ginseng*. The Jesuit priest had discovered it growing wild and had found out that it was a plant much valued by the Chinese. André had brought back a specimen and the information from Father Lafitau that it would undoubtedly be found in the forests around them.

Paul had no space in which to plant it but Antoine had and if the experiment proved satisfactory they intended to plant whole fields of it. They had made further inquiries in Montreal and Quebec and had learned that the Chinese market would take all they could obtain. As yet they knew very little about it. Father Lafitau had told André that the Chinese used it for medicinal purposes. Further inquiry had elicited the information that it was good for colds and stomach disorders, while others claimed it promoted fertility particularly in women. Some scoffed at this last, maintaining that the idea had originated in some obscene mind because of the peculiar shape of the root, which was forked and resembled the legs of a man. But whatever powers it might have there was a continual demand for it in China, the only other market being Tartary and Korea. Since its discovery in the Canadian forests the price had been steadily soaring. It would require a concentrated search, for it did not grow everywhere and some who had set out with high hopes had returned without a single plant.

Antoine had demurred a little about going because Elise was again pregnant but she and her mother had quickly reassured him and because of his excitement over the new idea, he was not difficult to persuade. The child was not due until about the end of September and he would be away only a few weeks.

He did not leave, however, without one altercation and that was with Paul-André who the moment he heard of the expedition clamored to go with them. He spoke first to Uncle André who could see no objection; in fact, he thought it would be a good experience for the boy. He spoke, however, from his own opinion and without reckoning with that of Antoine and thereby added to the difficulty. Antoine thought the idea ridiculous and would not consider it. André could not very well argue with him about it but he did speak to Elise. She thought the matter over carefully.

"I think we had better let Antoine decide, Andre," she said. "It isn't that he doesn't want the boy along but naturally he can't walk as far as you men in a day and Antoine doesn't want to be away longer than necessary at this time of the season."

She repeated the argument to Paul-André. His mouth was set in a stubborn line and his freckled face was angry.

"Father never lets me do anything I want. He just doesn't like me," he said sullenly.

"Oh, Paul-André, how absurd!" his mother exclaimed. "Of course he likes you. But you're not eleven yet, in fact only just turned ten and you surely realize that he knows better than you do."

"Knows what?" was the disconcerting question.

"Knows what is best for you, of course."

He stared out of the window, mouth pursed and eyes looking straight before him. Thoughts were racing through his mind and his mother tried to find out what they were. But he would not answer. Presently he turned abruptly and left the room. Elise saw him walking towards the orchard where he would thrash out the problem.

When later he returned he ran into his father.

"Well, Paul-André, been busy?" Antoine asked and put his arm across the boy's shoulders. "What have you been doing?"

"Thinking," came the terse reply.

"Oh! That does sound important," Antoine said and laughed.

But Paul-André did not smile. He stopped suddenly and looked up at his father with a direct gaze.

"Father, why don't you like me?" he asked and the tawny eyes held a challenge.

"Don't be absurd, Paul-André! Of course I like you. Whatever put that foolish notion into your head?"

"It isn't foolish," Paul-André snapped. "Anything Jean-Baptiste wants you let him do. But when I ask, you always refuse."

"Jean-Baptiste doesn't ask the kind of things you do. What's all this about? Because I won't let you go with us?"

"Yes."

"I have already told you many times that when you are older you can do these things but not yet."

"That's only an excuse. You don't want to bother with a boy, that's all."

Antoine's face clouded and there was anger in his expression as he said. "I'm beginning to think, Paul-André that the position is reversed and that it's you who dislike me."

"I don't understand you, that's all," Paul-André replied.

"I don't think we understand each other," Antoine said slowly.

"Oure's father lets him go with him …"

"Who's Oure?"

"Indian boy I met at Caughnawaga."

"Indian boys are different. They are brought up in an uncivilized way and most of the time they have to go along because they can't be left."

"Yes, Indian boys are different," Paul-André said slowly and his chin was thrust out stubbornly.

"I'm glad you agree," his father said.

"They're not made to feel they are little boys; they're made to feel they are men." The last part of the sentence was said in a hard tone. With it Paul-André turned on his heel and walked away.

# CHAPTER FIFTEEN

THE widening rift between Paul-André and his father worried Elise, particularly as she felt Antoine was largely to blame. She could not understand his attitude. Until recent years his had been such an even disposition and his manner light-hearted. Was he, as he grew older, going to develop into a moody man with a stubbornness that would be difficult to handle? Was his success as a seigneur going to change him and make him self-centered and narrow?

She talked it over with her mother one afternoon as they sat on the *galerie*. Ann listened quietly and then said:

"Men are strange creatures sometimes, darling. I had the same trouble with your father over your brother, Jean-Baptiste. He could not understand him though for the reverse reason. As you will remember, Jean-Baptiste did not want to be a farmer, he preferred the more sophisticated life he had lived in France. He angered your father just as Paul André angers Antoine." Elise had known this about her brother but it was the first time her mother had mentioned it.

"Perhaps it is their individual backgrounds," Ann went on. "Your father was born a farmer and had been a *coureur de bois* so he understood André much better than Jean-Baptiste. Antoine was born in France, so he understands your Jean-Baptiste better and does not understand Paul-André."

"But he doesn't oppose his becoming a *coureur de bois*."

"No, though really I don't think he likes the idea."

"Possibly not. Perhaps that is why he keeps telling him he must wait."

"Perhaps it is," Ann agreed. "Does he miss Jean-Baptiste much?"

"To some extent, no doubt. They are all such individualists and have always had their own interests apart from each other. Jean-Baptiste has always been tolerant of Paul-André and they are devoted to each other. Their lives will undoubtedly go separate ways."

"Jean-Baptiste seems to be very happy over his commission."

"Yes, and that rather surprises me because he didn't want to go into the army, he wanted to stay and work the Seigneury."

"It is better he should have a few years of it. It will broaden him."

"That was Antoine's argument and I think he's right. Jean-Baptiste has an easy, contented disposition and remaining here he would have sunk into a rut. He doesn't have the ambition of Paul-André, nor the spirit."

"That has always been the way with our men," Ann said.

"And with our women too, it would seem. At least it is with the two girls. They're as different as any two girls could be."

Ann held out her hand to Elise and said fondly. "I only had the one and she was never any trouble."

"Oh yes, I was!" Elise said and laughed. Then she looked at her mother keenly and asked: "Maman, is it more difficult to have twins?"

Ann looked at her sharply and there was some concern in her tone as she asked: "Do you think you are going to, dear?"

"If thinking has anything to do with it, I shall. I have thought of nothing else since I knew I was pregnant."

"Keeping up the family tradition?" her mother asked with a smile.

"Perhaps. I think it would be so wonderful to have two alike..."

"You and André were wonderful..."

"And you had no more difficulties than with Jean-Baptiste?"

Her mother hesitated and then said: "Unfortunately I did. And—I couldn't have any more afterwards, though I had always hoped for a large family."

"I wouldn't want any more if I had twins..."

Ann smiled wisely at the statement but held her counsel.

"I have always wanted it so much, maman," Elise continued, "and with the children growing up, well, it would be lovely to have two more just alike. Charlotte-Marguerite will be leaving us soon, Paul-André will undoubtedly be away years at a time and Ann-Marie and Jean-Baptiste will marry." She clasped her hands together ecstatically. "I do so want more babies."

"You had a difficult time with your last baby," Ann warned.

"That perhaps was my own fault. I didn't take enough care of myself..."

"Then we must see that you do this time. You're so energetic..." Ann smiled fondly at her.

"But I'm being very good this time. Especially good. I want them to be wonderful babies."

For the rest of the afternoon they talked of the children and when Ann left she took with her worried thoughts about Elise and her family. As with most grandmothers they were of prime importance to her and their problems became hers.

Halfway across the Seigneury she met Paul-André hurrying home from school. He paused politely to talk to her and she thought how like André he was at the same age. He had the same freckled face, the same keen eyes and the same red hair, except that his was darker. There was the same fascination about him and Ann wondered why it was that Antoine could not understand him when he seemed so lovable and so full of spirit.

The delay occasioned by his having to stop to talk to his grandmother made Paul-André hurry all the more. It was only recently that he had hurried home from school. Hitherto he had always dawdled on the way, the slightest pretext being an excuse to delay. But now there was a definite reason for this hurry. He had discovered that he had an ally in his mother. For the first two days after his father's departure he had remained sullenly alone, nursing his disappointment. Then on the third day, his mother had surprised him by asking: "Don't you want to go out in your canoe?" His large eyes had become larger with amazement and as he had looked questioningly into those of his mother, he had seen a look there that he had never before discovered.

"You mean I may—alone?" he had asked.

"As long as you keep near the shore and don't go beyond the boundaries of the Seigneuries."

"I won't," he had readily agreed.

"You won't forget, will you?" she had emphasized.

"No, maman," he had said and felt a new comradeship with his mother. "Thank you for letting me go," he had added and again had seen that new expression on his mother's face.

Every day after school he had been allowed to go out in his canoe, paddling along the shore and letting his imagination run freely as he pretended to be a *coureur de bois* and played exciting games.

The legs that hurried him home were no longer fat and stubby but had lengthened out sturdily. He was only about four and half feet tall and since his Uncle André had told him *coureurs de bois* should not be too tall as tall men were awkward in a canoe, he had ceased to be envious of his tall brother and father. When other boys measured their height and remarked gleefully that they had grown so many inches, Paul-André's reaction was to the contrary and he regarded any growth with trepidation. Five feet six was the limit he wished to attain.

After her mother had left, Elise stood for a while upon the steps looking out over the Seigneury and thinking of her children. The two girls had come in from school and Ann-Marie had said she was going over to visit with one of her cousins. Charlotte-Marguerite was somewhere in the house, no doubt reading.

When the days came to a close Elise always missed Antoine. They had so seldom been parted. She started to go into the house and then turned back, poised on the edge of the top step. She thought she saw Ann-Marie on the far boundary and wondered what she was doing there when she had said she was going to her cousin, Jeanne's. She strained her eyes but could now see no one. She decided she must be mistaken for the children never went to Ménard's and that was where she had thought she had seen Ann-Marie in her light dress.

That pause proved fatal. The next moment she was rolling down the steps with Paul-André frantically clutching at her. He had rushed out of the house with his head down as he fastened his shirt and had dashed headlong into her, throwing her off balance and himself with her.

Paul-André scrambled to his feet and then knelt by the inert figure of his mother.

"Maman, are you hurt?" he asked frantically. There was no answer. "Maman!" he called again and then repeated it in a voice that rose to hysteria.

Madeleine, the woman who cooked for them, came running out and saw Elise crumpled at the bottom of the steps.

"Mother of God!" she exclaimed and knelt down, cradling Elise's head in her arm. There was a long graze across the side of her face where she had hit the ground and Madeleine wiped the blood away with her apron. Paul-André watched, rooted to the spot with horror that showed on his scared face. Charlotte-Marguerite hurried out of the house asking: "What has happened?" and then rushed down the steps and also knelt by her mother.

"I knocked her down the steps," Paul-André said in a tense voice.

"Run and get Aunt Marie—quickly," Charlotte-Marguerite said, and spurred to action Paul-André raced across the Seigneury shouting for his Aunt Marie. She came running out of the house wiping her hands on her apron.

"What is it, Paul-André?" she asked and seeing from his face that something must have happened at the Manor House, hurried along with him. On the way she learned what had happened. She hurried into the house and to the couch where they had carried Elise. Immediately she took charge. Elise had recovered consciousness and was moaning.

"The baby…" Madeleine whispered.

Aunt Marie nodded. "Get hot water ready. This is serious. Send for her mother."

Charlotte-Marguerite hurried out and found Paul-André standing staring in a dazed way at the house but not daring to go in.

"Run for grandmother," she told him and then added, *"vite! vite!"*

He ran, ran with all the swiftness he could.

The hours that followed were tense and harrowing. The news spread fast over the two Seigneuries and the women hurried over to see what they could do. That the fall would induce a miscarriage there was no doubt. The parlor downstairs was soon crowded with women, ready to help though there was little they could do. They had carried Elise up to her room and Ann and Marie watched and waited unable to do more than apply cold cloths to the head of the suffering girl. Experienced as they were in child birthing and even with premature births, they knew that they must wait upon nature.

Ann-Marie returned home. When she saw the crowd gathered outside, she broke into a run, inquiring of the first bystander what had happened. She flushed guiltily as she realized that tragedy was being enacted in her own home while she had been misbehaving. She rushed into the house and upstairs to her mother's room. She looked at her mother's face drawn in agony and then to her grandmother.

"What is it? Where is she hurt?" she asked in a whisper.

"We'll tell you later, dear," her grandmother said quietly.

"Isn't there something I can do?"

"Pray, dear. She will need all our prayers," Ann answered.

"She isn't going to die?" Ann-Marie asked, and her voice shook.

"She is very ill," Ann answered and turned to change the cold cloth on Elise's head.

Ann-Marie left the room and sought her sister. She was kneeling before the *prie-dieu* in their bedroom. Ann-Marie knelt down beside her and began to sob, mostly for her mother and partly because of her own conscience.

Paul-André could not go into the house. His castle of happiness had crashed. The joy of the past few weeks was wiped out. His agonized fear increased as he heard those standing around talking as though his mother were dying.

The six o'clock Angelus sounded and all dropped to their knees murmuring fervent prayers. Never had the Angelus been so timely. Paul-André dropped to his knees but he could not pray. No words of prayer would come to his mind. He got up and ran towards the church. Father Xavier came out of the church half an hour later. Dusk had fallen and the land would soon be enveloped in darkness. As he passed the large wooden cross outside he saw a figure at its foot. He waited a moment. Dry hard sobs came from the boy kneeling there. Gently Father Xavier placed his hand on Paul-André's shoulder.

"Can I help, son," he said softly.

Paul-André shook his head.

"If you're in trouble maybe it would help to tell me," Father Xavier's soft voice comforted.

Paul-André raised his tear-stained face. "I've killed my mother," he said.

Immediately the priest was galvanized into action. "What are you saying! You're the Sieur de Brievaux's son aren't you?"

He had thought that the boy's grief was through some childish misdemeanor but this was different. He pulled Paul-André to his feet. "Tell me what it is? Maybe I am needed." His voice had a note of command. Haltingly Paul-André told him what had happened. Even before he had finished Father Xavier was hastening with him towards the Manor House. He had time to give the boy some advice.

"You must get control of yourself, son. You may be needed to help and you can't do that if you give way to hysterics. Do you understand?"

"Yes, Father."

And as they neared the house he said. "Go to your room and wash your face. Then, if there's nothing for you to do, pray."

The approach of Father Xavier brought both relief and alarm. They did not know whether or not Paul-André had been sent to fetch him. If he had, it might mean that Elise was nearing the end. A dead silence fell. Father Xavier mounted the steps and then turned to raise his hand in blessing. Again the people fell upon their knees. As he entered the house Aunt Marie's son, Philip, met him.

"I'm going to get Jean-Baptiste," he told him.

"It's serious?" the priest asked.

Philip nodded. "Jean-Baptiste should be here."

Paul-André heard and hurried to his room. What would his brother say when he heard what he had done?

Father Xavier went up to the bedroom. A piercing scream met him. "It's coming," he heard Ann say. He stood there for a few moments unnoticed. He did not at first comprehend what was happening. As soon as he realized it, he tiptoed downstairs again.

"Let us pray," he said to those assembled. He continued to pray while the screams of the suffering woman upstairs pierced the air. The women assembled, all relatives, sobbed as they prayed and the faces of the men were set as they controlled their feelings.

Presently Jean-Baptiste arrived and hurried upstairs.

The beauty of the starry night with moon full gave way to dawn—not a cold grey dawn indicative of despair but a beauty that heralded the coming of a fine June day. Ann went to the window and the golden light shone on her haggard face. An hour ago she and Aunt Marie had delivered Elise of two children—twin boys who did not live.

# CHAPTER SIXTEEN

AUNT MARIE plodded across the Seigneury on her way back to her own house. The July sun was sweltering and the perspiration poured down her large, red face. She stopped for a moment at the water's edge where the air was cooler, and breathed deeply. She was dreadfully exhausted and it showed in the dark circles beneath her eyes. For two weeks she and Ann had not left Elise and even now they were not sure that she would completely recover. But for the first time there was hope. Last night the crisis had passed and with the coming of the morning there had been the first indication that she was conscious of what was going on around her. Aunt Marie thought of another occasion when they had watched through another crisis with Elise, when it had seemed that she would succumb to the scourge of smallpox. They had won the fight against death then, and now she believed they would win this second fight.

They had not realized how soon having their own church and curé would be a boon. Every day Father Xavier had conducted a special Mass for the suffering woman and there was not a man or woman on the two Seigneuries who did not at some time during each day, go into the church to offer up prayers for her.

As Aunt Marie was turning away from her moment of relaxation beside the river, she noticed the little canoe tied up against the bank. Then it was that she saw Paul-André lying face downwards—lying so still that she thought he was sleeping. No one had given a thought to him during these two weeks of anxiety and now with a rush it dawned upon her how much the boy must have been suffering as he undoubtedly heard the discussions as to whether his mother would survive.

She went to the edge of the water and, with difficulty because of her bulk, crouched down and called to him. The face raised to hers shocked her. It was drawn and tense and the eyes were dulled with anguish.

"Darling, I'm going back to my house. Will you come and help me?" she asked.

He struggled to his feet slowly and stepped on to the bank. "Yes, of course, if you want me," he said in a flat voice. She noticed then how thin he looked and it occurred to her that probably he hadn't been eating during these past weeks. They had left the children's food entirely to Madeleine and had seen very little of them except as they crept in each day to look at their mother and now she remembered that not once had Paul-André been with them.

She put her arm around his shoulders. "Your mother is going to be all right, Paul-André," she said kindly. She felt his shoulders stiffen. He did not reply. She looked down at the deerskin suit that he was wearing—the new one his mother had made for him only a few weeks ago. Every day he put it on even though it was much too warm for this time of the year.

"You look like a real *coureur de bois* in that suit," Aunt Marie said and tried to make her voice sound cheerful. "It won't be long now before you'll be going into the woods." Still there was no reply. "You'll like that, won't you?" she asked. He nodded his head but there was no enthusiasm in the action.

As they entered the house she realized that the kindest thing was to talk to him about what was troubling him. "I'm going to have something to eat and you must be hungry too," she said and bustled over to the cupboard and produced a large cake and some milk. She cut a piece of the cake and gave him some milk but he did not touch it.

"I'm sorry but I'm not hungry," he said.

"Try and eat it, dear," she urged. "You know, you won't want your mother to see you looking thin and hungry. She'll think we haven't been taking care of you."

"She won't mind any more," he said and she saw his lips compress together tightly as he tried to hold back the tears that filled his eyes.

Aunt Marie pushed her chair over closer to his and put her arm across his shoulders. "You mustn't take this so hard, dear. It was an accident and your mother will understand. She won't blame you."

"Does she know about the children?" he asked.

"What children?"

"Those who died. She wanted twins so much."

Aunt Marie was a little startled. She had forgotten how gossip went around the Seigneury and evidently he had heard the discussions over the loss of the twin children.

"She will understand that, too," she said rather lamely.

"But my father won't. He'll be very angry. I wish I could go away. I would run away but it would be cowardly."

"Yes, it would. Besides that would only add to your mother's suffering and you wouldn't want that."

He shook his head quickly.

"We must do all we can to help her and you can best help by doing everything that she likes."

"We were so happy those weeks before this happened. She let me go out in the canoe every day after school," he said sadly.

"I used to see you paddling by. You enjoy that, don't you?"

"I did. I don't any more."

"Why not?"

"I was rushing out to the canoe when I knocked her down the steps. If I hadn't been so excited I ..." he broke off and buried his head in his arms. Aunt Marie's own eyes filled with tears. She could not seem to think of anything to say that would alleviate the suffering inside the boy. All she could do was to gather him to her ample bosom and let him cry himself out.

"I'm sorry," he said presently and smeared a grubby hand across his eyes.

"You'll feel better now, dear, that you have cried it out."

"Men shouldn't cry," he said sheepishly.

"But they often do. Do you remember your Uncle Philip?"

"A little."

"I've seen him cry and he was a big burly man."

"What did he cry about?"

This question was rather difficult to answer for truthfully she could not remember any particular time that Philip had given way to tears.

"Oh, when something hurt him very much. Men don't cry often, but there are times when they have to. But I don't want you to have to cry. Now I tell you what. In a few days you will be able to see your mother and then you tell her just how it happened and you will find that she understands perfectly and doesn't blame you. But she won't be happy if she sees you looking thin and unhappy. So suppose you eat that cake now and let's you and I keep together and we'll help each other. And then when your father returns I'll tell him all about it and see that he understands." The brighter look that had come into his face faded again at the mention of his father, but he did eat the cake and once he had started ate ravenously, so that she cut him a second piece.

By the end of the week Elise was sufficiently recovered to hear the whole story. At first her anguish and disappointment over the loss of the twins was uppermost. Then she realized how much Paul-André must be suffering.

"Poor little Paul-André, he's always in the wrong. Send him to me, will you?" she asked her mother.

There was no scampering of feet up the staircase. He came so quietly that he had been standing in the doorway for a while before she saw him. He was staring at her with his tawny eyes wide with fear, afraid to cross the threshold. There was no one to him as beautiful as his mother. She lay against the pillows with her red hair spread out and her face thin and white. He could not move.

"Darling!" she called to him and held out her arms. There was a moment's hesitation and then he ran to her, kicking over a chair as he came. She hugged him tight and smoothed back the untidy hair while he struggled to keep back tears that he was determined she should not see. "I've missed my baby so much," she said soothingly.

It was the wrong expression to have used and she did not realize it until he said: "Can you have more babies?"

"What dear? Oh, I meant *you,* darling. You're my baby you know."

"Yes, but those others, you wanted twins so much."

Her expression was one of astonishment. "Why, darling, who has been talking to you?"

"And now you can't have any more and it's all because of me."

"Who told you these things, dear," she asked gently.

"I heard them talking. Can't you have more twins?"

"Don't bother your head about that, dear."

"But it was my fault and if you don't, then I shall always be to blame."

She took his face between both her hands and looked into his eyes, so deep with sadness now—too much sadness for a little boy. "Darling, I want you to forget all about it. It was an accident. Maman doesn't blame you. I was standing right on the edge of the step and ... and anyway I'm going to get better now and soon we'll have good times together again. You mustn't think so much about it. Things like this happen in life and we must be strong and courageous about them."

"And father?" he asked.

"I'll speak to your father and he will understand. I'm sure he did a lot of things when he was a little boy that he was sorry about. Now you can make up for it by being a good boy and helping him with the Seigneury. And you can help me by being happy and smiling. Will you do that?"

"I'll try, maman."

"And I want you to come in and see me several times each day. Have you been out in your canoe?" He shook his head. "Then, why don't you, dear? Now run along and have a good time. Don't be late for dinner though. It will soon be time but you can go for a little while and I'll watch you from the window."

She watched him walk down to the river but he did not scamper as he usually did. He walked slowly and she knew that she had not succeeded in making him forget. It was also going to be difficult to make Antoine understand. She lay back thinking what she should say.

The following week Antoine and André returned. Paul-André saw them coming and something inside him froze. Every day he had watched from a high knoll, for he wanted to be prepared and not run into the house one day and find that his father had returned. The two men were in high spirits and were singing a canoe song as they strode along. On their backs they carried huge sacks which evidently contained the roots of the ginseng plant. He saw them wave to the habitants who had come to their doors at the sound of the singing and he saw his father pat several of the children on the head. Such a gesture would have meant so much to him just then.

He watched them as they paused by the steps, talking, and then Uncle André went on his way. His father ran quickly up the steps and into the house. Paul-André came closer and sat down quietly on the top step. From inside the house he could hear the murmur of voices. Aunt Marie was keeping her promise and he heard her explaining why his mother was in bed. He listened and heard his father's footsteps hurrying up the stairs and heard his mother's delighted exclamation as she saw him. Then there were a few minutes of silence as they greeted each other and then the murmur of voices. He could not hear the words, only the tone of their voices. He heard his father's raised angrily, his mother's arguing and rather pleading; then a steady flow of words from his father in a firm tone and then the voice came clearly as his father was evidently standing near the window.

"That's asking me to do a great deal, Elise. The boy should be punished." Paul-André's heart stood still for a moment.

The further murmur of words was indistinguishable. Then he heard his father's footsteps on the stairs and crossing the hall with a firm, quick tread. Now would be the moment. If his father thrashed him, he would not mind. He would take it without a sound. He braced himself against the post beside which he sat. Already he could feel the sting of the lash on his bare back. If only he would let him talk it over with him, explain it to him and let him give him his assurances that from now on he would do everything that his father wanted. He would even give up being a *coureur de bois* if his father wanted him to and this would be giving up the thing dearest to his heart. Through him his mother had lost something that was dearest to her heart and he was willing to make this sacrifice to recompense her for what he had done.

His father came out on to the *galerie.* His step faltered a moment as he saw Paul-André who was not looking at him but out to the river. He came to the top step and Paul-André looked up. His father looked straight at him,—then strode down the steps and towards the barn. That hard look without a word of recognition cut deep into Paul-André's heart. He gathered up his legs and ran towards the orchard and buried his face in the warm earth.

# CHAPTER SEVENTEEN

ON AUGUST 1, 1724 Governor de Ramezay suddenly died. The moment the news was brought to the Seigneury, Paul and Ann hurried into Montreal. Madame was prostrated and no one could bring her more comfort than Ann. Fortunately the eldest son, Charles Hector, had returned recently from France and could take charge of family affairs. The Baron de Longueil, who would succeed Governor de Ramezay, hastened back from Three Rivers and superintended official matters.

The Governor had been much loved and on the day of his funeral all work in and around Montreal ceased. Everyone on the seigneuries attended the funeral. Although she was still weak, Elise insisted upon going. Since the days when she had been engaged to Claude de Ramezay, she had retained a deep affection for Madame de Ramezay. Of the children, only Jean-Baptiste was considered old enough to attend and especially since he and Jean-Baptiste de Ramezay had now developed a close friendship.

The other three children watched their parents depart and then went their separate ways. Charlotte-Marguerite, after a few gentle words to Paul-André, went up to her room and Ann-Marie departed on some mysterious business of her own.

Paul-André went down to the river and sat in his canoe. He did not untie it because he had promised his mother that he would not go out in it while they were away. The August day was hot and he took off his shirt, letting the sun beat down on his tanned back. Dejectedly he thought over all that had happened in the past weeks and tried to find a solution. His brother and sisters had been kind and had tried to help him. During the interval before his father's return, Jean-Baptiste had remained at home on leave and had helped him by giving him chores to do. They had talked over the accident and Jean-Baptiste had been big-brotherly and understanding. It was not his place to reprimand. But the day after Antoine's return he had gone back to duty in Montreal and so knew nothing of his father's attitude to Paul-André. Probably he had noticed it that first morning at breakfast and would have thought it only natural then. Paul-André thought of that breakfast the first morning after his father's return and felt desperately miserable. He had ventured to ask his father a question about the trip. Antoine had glanced at him coldly and had then answered the question generally, as though one of the others had made the inquiry. After that Paul-André had remained silent. It had seemed to him that his father had been especially enthusiastic in his praise of Jean-Baptiste who now looked so very grown up in his uniform. He had joked and patted Jean-Baptiste on the back as he departed for Montreal and Paul-André had heard him say: "I'm proud of you, son." At any other time the words would have meant nothing but at that particular moment they had cut like a knife. Perhaps he had only imagined that his father gave him a significant glance as he said them.

Ann-Marie had been kind in her way, but that was always casual and lately she had been more restless and aloof than usual. The greatest kindness to him had come from Charlotte-Marguerite. She alone appeared to have noticed her father's attitude at breakfast that day. She had seen Paul-André bite his lip and go silent and when she had finished her household duties, had wandered down to the canoe where he was sitting. He saw her coming arid was not surprised when she said sweetly:

"May I come and sit in your canoe with you for a little while, Paul-André? Is there room?"

"Oh yes. You're only little," he had replied.

At first they had sat silent and then she had slipped her small hand in his and had said: "Father doesn't mean to be unkind, Paul-André. He is trying to understand."

"How do you know?" he had asked dubiously.

"Because he is a kind man and wouldn't hurt any of us. He is upset now but it will be all right."

"It will never be all right, Charl," he had said using the name which he alone used to her. "I can't give maman back the babies..."

"She will have more..."

He had shaken his head violently. "She can't. I heard them talking. I wish I knew what to do. I want to go away."

"You mustn't do that."

"No, it would be cowardly. But I don't belong here."

"Have you prayed, Paul-André?"

"Yes, every day but I think God is angry with me."

"God is never angry with children, Paul-André," she had said quietly.

He had tried to believe this in the days that followed but when his father's attitude did not change, he knew that Charlotte-Marguerite could not be right. He avoided seeing his father except at meal times and those became agony so that he could not eat.

He had talked it over with Uncle André. At first he had hidden from him because he was ashamed but after a few days Uncle André had come in search of him and they had talked it over. His uncle was also sure that his father would get over it in a few days and had tried to assure him that accidents happened to everyone. He kept telling him that he must forget it, but Paul-André could not. He did forget it for a little while when he and his Uncle fished but this was only occasionally. He could tell that Uncle André was doing everything he could to help him. There had been the day when the men started out to plant the ginseng roots. As they started Uncle André had turned to him and said: "Coming along, Paul-André?" He had looked quickly at his father but he had turned away without any comment.

"I think I had better not," Paul-André had said, but Uncle André treated it lightly.

"Come along by all means. You can help us," he had said.

Paul-André seemed so pathetic that André had decided to take matters in his own hands. Perhaps if the boy worked with them, Antoine would forget his anger. "It will be all right," he had said and had given Paul-André a friendly pat on the back.

All the morning Paul-André had worked with them, keeping close to his uncle and making himself very useful by separating the roots and handing them to them. Though his back ached, he would not stop until they did. It would have been such a wonderful day under other circumstances, but not once did his father speak to him. When they returned, he had gone to see his mother, trying to pretend that he had had a good time. But when he left her he had gone into the orchard and lay there under his favorite tree, crying.

When Antoine and Elise returned from the funeral she went straight to bed, exhausted from the trip and the emotional upset. Antoine changed his clothes and went out to check things on the Seigneury. Paul-André saw them return, but he did not go up to the house. Antoine was worried and unhappy and also very restless. He walked over to where they had planted the ginseng and inspected it. Some of the plants had died but most of them looked healthy. He tried to concentrate on them and to lose himself in thoughts of the Seigneury. His enthusiasm over this new project was growing and as soon as Elise was well again, he planned to make another trip to the forest, taking several men with him so that they could obtain a large supply of the roots. The price of ginseng was steadily rising and the return would be very gratifying. The habitants on his Seigneury were also enthusiastic about it and were clearing all their land so that they could plant the product.

Only Ménard continued to take no interest. Antoine wished he knew what he could do about him, but as long as the man kept within the law, he was helpless. Then a thought occurred to him. Perhaps he could persuade Ménard to let him have half of his allotment for a consideration. This would give him additional space to plant ginseng. The thought grew and he decided to go at once and speak to Ménard. As he approached the place, he noticed that Ménard had been doing some cultivating, though it still looked unkempt beside the other prosperous farms.

Ménard was not outside and he went round to the back of the house to see if he were there. Returning to the front he peered into one of the windows to see if he were inside. He stiffened as he looked inside and then unable to believe the evidence of his eyes he looked again more closely. There was no mistaking what he saw. Ann-Marie was sitting on Ménard's knee, her head on his shoulder and her mouth half open. The front of her dress was open exposing her breast over which Ménard had his hand as at the same time his coarse mouth closed over hers in a long ardent kiss. Antoine remained frozen to the spot as he saw him run his hand up under her dress and her back suddenly arch in a convulsive movement.

Blind with rage he rushed into the house, pulling Ann-Marie off Ménard's knee with such force that she landed heavily on the floor. Then his fist shot out and connected with Ménard's chin before he had time to get up from the chair. He and the chair went over backwards but in a moment he was up on his feet. The two men faced each other. Ménard was as tall as Antoine but much heavier in build. His breath stank of brandy and he was dazed by the blow. They closed together, landing heavy blows and as Antoine felled Ménard again he went down with him, and they rolled from one side of the room to the other smashing at each other.

Ann-Marie quickly picked herself up from the floor and when she saw that it was her father, she stifled a scream. For a moment she watched the two men fighting and then terrified rushed from the house. She ran home by the back way and tore up to her room where she was so afraid that she hid in the closet. She was trembling all over with fear of what her father would do and from the emotional experience through which she had passed. She had known it was wrong to go to Ménard's and that she should not have listened to his flatteries and his subtle suggestions that he could teach her a lot. She had even found him repulsive with his foul breath and his sweaty hands that clawed at her. Yet something she could not control had urged her on and now she would have to face her father's wrath and account for her actions.

Elise heard the running footsteps and when they did not come to her door, sat up listening. Silence followed and she waited a while wondering. Then puzzled, she got up and putting on a *peignoir* went to Ann-Marie's room but found it empty. She looked into Paul-André's room and found it also empty, as she had expected, for from her window she had seen him sitting in his canoe.

She returned to bed and closed her eyes but opened them again almost immediately as she heard her door open stealthily. Ann-Marie looked in and Elise called to her. With a rush Ann-Marie came to the bed and threw herself on it, sobbing. Elise put her hand on the luxurious hair stroking it, sensing that the outburst came from some emotional upset and with difficulty controlled her anxiety as she wondered what it was.

"Oh maman, maman, I've been so bad," the girl cried, her voice half-stifled as her face remained buried in the bedclothes.

"What have you done, dear?" Elise said gently though her alarm increased. The sobbing continued and she let her relieve herself of it and then said: "Try to tell me, dear."

"I can't, maman, it's too awful."

"You'll feel better if you do."

"You'll never understand."

Elise waited a moment and then said: "I was a young girl once, dear."

"It was different then ..."

"Was it?" Elise said and as Ann-Marie looked up at her mother she saw a half-smile on her face.

"You never did wrong things, maman ..."

"Didn't I?"

"Not with men."

"Suppose you tell me what has happened," she said kindly.

"I didn't mean to do wrong, maman. Really I didn't. I ..." the head went down again in shame and she sobbed more.

Elise's arm drew her daughter to her. She cradled the head against her breast, thinking of her own emotional upsets when she was young. She remembered Gaston Renault, her father's bonded servant, whom she had allowed to make love to her, with results that were later tragic.

"Who is the man, Ann-Marie?" she asked gently.

She did not answer at once and then ashamed murmured the name of Ménard.

"Ménard!" Elise could not control the sharpness with which the word came out. Then rather sternly she said: "You had better tell me from the beginning, Ann-Marie."

"I didn't realize that I was doing wrong ..."

"That is understood. Tell me what has happened."

"I was restless and one day while walking around that way he spoke to me."

Then it *had* been Ann-Marie she had seen in that direction the day of her accident, Elise thought.

"When did you first go there?" Elise asked.

"I don't remember ..."

"Was it the day I fell?"

"I'm not sure. Why?" Ann-Marie asked guiltily.

"Never mind. Go on." While she was talking Elise was remembering that if she had not turned back to look that day, she wouldn't have been standing on the edge of the *galerie*. She kept her counsel.

"He flattered me and…" Ann-Marie stopped. "I can't tell you, maman."

"Perhaps I can tell you…"

"How? You mean you have known?"

"I know from experience, Ann-Marie. He flattered you, told you you were beautiful and kissed you. Isn't that right?"

"Yes."

"Anything more?"

Ann-Marie hesitated.

"Ann-Marie, you must tell me. Did this go any further than a kiss?" Elise's voice was insistent.

"He touched me here and here," she indicated. The expression on her mother's face scared her.

"You were in his house?"

"Yes."

"On the bed?"

"Oh no! I was sitting on his knee when father came in."

"Your father!"

"He caught us. He and Ménard were fighting when I ran away."

Abruptly Elise pushed her away and started to get out of bed.

"What are you going to do, maman?" she asked tearfully.

Elise had hurried to the window. She did not know what to do. There was no man in the house. She must go herself.

"Maman, what are you going to do?" Ann-Marie's voice was frightened.

"Ménard is a powerful man. Your father may get hurt. Help me to dress."

Ann-Marie quickly handed her mother her clothes and Elise slipped them on without any regard for appearance. When she was dressed she took Ann-Marie by the shoulders and looked deep into her face. "Ann-Marie you are telling me the truth? Ménard did not seduce you?"

"No, maman, it was not as bad as that."

"That is the absolute truth?"

"Absolutely."

"You had better go to your room. I will talk with you again later."

Elise's legs shook as she went downstairs. She stood for a moment mustering her strength, afraid that she would not have sufficient to reach Ménard's. In fact she knew she had not. She must call to one of the men outside.

Then Antoine came in, his forehead bloodied from an ugly gash and his clothes torn.

Paul-André that afternoon came to a decision. First there had been despair and humiliation at his father's attitude and then periods of resentment and bitterness. During these periods he told himself it was his mother who had experienced the accident and who had suffered, yet she had not blamed him. Why then should his father act this way, when his mother was all kindness? His father had not suffered. But with this thought came another that perhaps his father had also suffered over the loss of the twin boys. Was this why he could not bear to speak to him? Paul-André knew so little about this matter of having children. The boys at school talked and some were very horrid, but Paul-André had never bothered about such things. In his dreams of the future, girls did not enter. The future? Was he going to go on always like this with the gap widening between him and his father? Then he asked himself why he was so afraid of his father. He had never been afraid of anything. More than once he had heard his mother say: "Paul-André isn't afraid of anything," and that had been his pride. It had almost become his creed.

Then it was that he formed his resolution. He would go to his father and have this matter out with him. They would never come to an understanding by avoiding each other.

Resolutely he stepped out of the canoe and walked with a determined air to the house. He heard voices in the parlor. He had thought at first of speaking to his father alone, but if his mother were there, he would still speak because she might be able to help him. He went to the parlor door but there he paused. His father and mother were deep in conversation and his mother was crying. His father's head was swathed in bandages. That made him stop short. His father must have been hurt somehow. They did not see him. He stood there for a moment more and then turned on his heel and walked quietly away.

# CHAPTER EIGHTEEN

PAUL-ANDRÉ pulled Brun under the blanket and wound it around both of them. The warmth of the dog's body was very comforting on this bitter cold night. Brun lifted her head and licked his face, then with a shuddering sigh settled down and was asleep. Paul-André wished he could go to sleep that easily; he usually did but not tonight. Every movement of the trees above him; the scurrying of the furred inhabitants of the forest beyond and many other eerie sounds kept him awake. He tried not to be frightened but it took a lot of courage to feel at ease lying alone for the first time in his life on the shore of the river. He was glad that Brun had come with him. As early that morning he had sat waiting for the dawn to break, the dog had climbed into the canoe. He did not know her name and had called her Brun because of the color of her coat and she answered to any sound of his voice. She was a large, nondescript animal, with a rough, brown coat—a conglomeration of breeds. He pulled her closer now, holding on to her very tight and trying to feel she was a protection. He had no other protection, because he did not know how to handle a gun and was not very familiar with the knife in his belt. He put his hand into his belt now and felt the knife. It took his mind back to the day before when Jean-Baptiste had given it to him. It was a real *coureur de bois'* knife and Paul-André had long coveted it. It had made him happy that Jean-Baptiste had given it to him before his departure. It had formed a closer bond between them. He thought of this tall brother who had sailed the day before with Jean-Baptiste de Ramezay. Both of them had been transferred to duty in Acadie and it would be some years before Paul-André would see him again. "I want you to have the knife," Jean-Baptiste had said and his voice had been gruff.

They had all gone away the day before. Charlotte-Marguerite had been very gentle as she had said goodbye to him. Probably he would never see her again. She was on her way to enter the Ursuline Convent in Quebec and Ann-Marie was going with her, but not to become a nun. Paul-André knew nothing of the reason that made his parents decide that Ann-Marie should remain for two years in the convent and receive instruction there, instruction that while it would be mainly cultural, was also hoped would keep her from getting into further mischief.

His parents had gone with the two girls and again, as he lay there sleepless, he tried to tell himself that there was no reason why they should have taken him. Yet he still could not help feeling resentful that he had been left behind. It was not as though his father could not have afforded it. He had heard them talking enthusiastically over the profits they would make out of the experimental crop of ginseng. No, it was not a matter of expense. It was, he was convinced, his father's intention to punish him; yet even as he thought of this he remembered the pat on the back which his father had given him just before they had boarded the ship. It was the first caress that he had received from his father since he had learned of the accident. He had wondered about it and wondered again now. He could not know that the disconsolate look on his face had suddenly given Antoine a twinge of conscience and at the last moment he had realized that his stubbornness in refusing to let Paul-André go with them was very severe on the boy. Paul-André could not know that his father and mother had very nearly had a serious quarrel over the matter. He had seen tears in his mother's eyes as she had said goodbye to him. At any other time he would not have minded being left behind for he was to stay with his grandparents, and Uncle André had promised to teach him to hunt. His mother had made him a heavy blanket-coat—an exact copy of the one Uncle André wore when he went into the woods. Still these things did not compensate and he felt unwanted.

Lying there, cold and very lonely, he began to regret that he had decided to run away from them all. His arms ached terribly. Paddling his canoe all day, moving as fast as he could so that they should not catch up with him, he had realized how much more difficult it was to handle a canoe alone. Unaccustomed to paddling for hours at a time, the muscles of his arms had protested and were still protesting. Furthermore, he had not been able to get nearly as far on this first day as he and Uncle André had when they had gone to Caughnawaga before. He knew he could not be more than halfway to the portage, if that far, and if Uncle André came after him, it was likely that he would overtake him before he reached the foot of the rapids. He wondered at what time Uncle André had received his note. He had thought it all out carefully and had given his young cousin, Pierre, his old blunt knife as a present if he would promise not to deliver the note before afternoon. Pierre had promised readily enough but suppose when they discovered he had gone, Pierre had felt he should give the note then, or suppose Uncle André had not waited for any word but had guessed he had gone to Caughnawaga and had started at once? He did not know when he fell asleep.

He was wakened by a violent licking of his face and opened his eyes to see that dawn was breaking through the trees. He caressed Brun and wondered how her canine mind had known that he wanted to get started as soon as it was daylight. Had she sensed it the day before as he sat in the canoe in the darkness, afraid to start off before he could see ahead? He threw off the blanket, talking to the dog, whose tail, half as long as her body, kept wagging back and forth every time she heard the sound of his voice. The October morning was bitterly cold and he rubbed his hands together to try to get them warm. He went to the canoe and took out the food he had concealed. It did not look very appetizing and again he thought of breakfast at home. He tried resolutely to put these thoughts behind him as with his knife he cut off a chunk of bread and a piece of the ham he had brought. He threw a piece to Brun who gobbled it hungrily but when he tried to chew it, he found that uncooked ham was hard to eat and even harder to swallow.

Back in Montreal they did not become alarmed at his absence until dinnertime. He had not appeared at breakfast and though his grandmother had at first shown concern when it was found he was not in his room, André had lessened her anxiety when he had said laughing:

"He'll be over at their own Seigneury; probably sitting in his canoe. Poor little chap, he was very much upset when they all went away yesterday. And when he's upset he always goes off on his own. I'm going over there shortly and I will find him."

But several hours elapsed, because there was so much to do with the closing season and when André reached the de Brievaux Seigneury which he would look after in Antoine's absence, there were many things claiming his attention. He forgot about Paul-André until he went to the storehouse to seal it up for the winter and then something brought him to his mind. He went down to the river's edge but the canoe wasn't there. He frowned as he strained his eyes to see whether there was any sight of the canoe on the river. He went into the orchard and called Paul-André and then decided that probably the boy had paddled his canoe to his grandfather's Seigneury as he would now be living there. It was dinnertime before he had finished his tasks and his parents were already at table when he came in.

"Haven't you found Paul-André?" his mother asked anxiously.

"No, isn't he back?" André asked.

"I thought you were looking for him, André," his mother said and there was a slight reproof in her tone.

"I did, but he wasn't on the Seigneury." He got up and went to the window. "I thought probably he had brought his canoe down here." But there was no canoe at the bank. When André came back to the table his face was worried.

"You don't think he has run away again, do you André?" his father asked.

"Oh no. He's around somewhere. He gave me his promise, you know, that he would never run away again." André ate his dinner but not with his usual hearty appetite. The absence of the canoe worried him but he did not want to say anything yet. He hurried through his dinner and got up. "I'll go and make a search," he said.

"Perhaps I'd better come with you," Paul said. "You go over the de Brievaux Seigneury and I'll make inquiries on this one."

The two men went out, André hurrying along the riverbank and scanning the water as he went. He thought of the watch-towers where once before he had found Paul-André. He searched each one of them and then went through every room in the house. He scoured the orchard again and went through all the fields. He inquired of the habitants if they had seen the boy and finished up at Ménard's. The house was locked up and empty, for Ménard had left some time ago presumably to go hunting. The shutters on the windows were closed so that André could not see inside and the door was locked.

He returned home, his concern deepening as he met his father. "You didn't find him?" he asked anxiously.

"No, and no one seems to have seen him today. His canoe's gone, hasn't it?" Paul asked.

André looked out over the river and said slowly: "Yes."

Then it was that he saw young Pierre standing by him. "Hello, Pierre, have you seen Paul-André?" he asked. The boy thrust a note into his hand and ran away as fast as his legs would take him. "Well, what's this?" André exclaimed as he watched the boy's rapid departure. He unfolded the dirty piece of paper. The writing on it was scrawled and hardly legible. "*Sacré dieu!*" he exclaimed. "He *has* run away." He handed the note to his father but his eyesight wasn't very good and he handed it back and asked:

"What does it say?"

" 'Dear Uncle André, I'm sorry to break my word but I had to go away. I don't ...' "I think the word is *belong*, it's hard to read," André said and continued: 'I don't belong any more. I shall ...' André held the note nearer to decipher the words. 'I shall be all right. Don't follow me.' "*Sacré diable,* father, what are we going to do? I'll have to go after him."

"Where do you think he's gone?"

"Caughnawaga, undoubtedly. What time is it? It's hours since the Angelus rang. The afternoon's half gone. I can't get very far tonight." As he spoke he was already hurrying towards the house. "I'd better tell mother," he said.

"I'll tell her," his father said. "You get ready."

Paul found Ann in the kitchen and he told her what had happened. She hurried upstairs to André. "Oh, André, this is dreadful. Suppose something should happen to him while they are away? And going on that journey all alone. Anything might happen."

"I know, mother, that's why I'm leaving at once. *Diable,* why did I ever make him that canoe! I'll give him a good thrashing."

Ann laid her hand quickly on his arm. "No, André. Don't be angry. The boy has been so unhappy of late and it isn't all his fault. He must have been very distressed to go away like this. Show me the note."

André handed it to her and she went to the window to read it. "Yes, he is very unhappy, poor little fellow," she said. "They should never have left him behind. It was most unfair."

"I'd better take some provisions, maman. Can you get them for me?" André asked.

"Oh yes, of course. Forgive me."

"Just anything. I don't want to waste any more time than I have already. I'll have to take your canoe, father. Mine's in need of repair. I already have it in the workshop. Didn't think I would be needing it any more. Is yours alright?"

"I believe so, André. Frankly I haven't looked at it lately."

"I'll go and see. Would you bring down the things when they are ready?"

"You'd better take a musket."

"Oh yes..."

"I'll get it and some powder."

"I never started on a trip in such a haphazard way."

"I wonder if Paul-André took any food." Ann said anxiously as she came out with the supplies.

André shook his head. He knew that journey well and with Indians on the roam at this time of the year, he feared for the boy.

André and his father went down to the shore to examine the canoe. "I think it is all right," André said, but did not sound too sure.

And his doubt increased as before nightfall the canoe began to ship water. He swore lustily and turning into the bank pulled the canoe ashore. He turned it over and felt along the bottom until he found the weak place. Besides this, there were several small holes that would get larger and larger. The light was failing and though he began the repairs he soon had to give up. He swore again. As he ate his supper he thought anxiously of Paul-André and wondered how far ahead he was. With his knowledge of the river he had thought to travel even after the light had gone and so catch up with him. He turned over in his mind the idea of abandoning the canoe and taking the path along the shore but this would save little time in the end so he rolled in his blanket and slept till dawn.

At the same time Paul-André reached the foot of the rapids, so exhausted that he could not climb out of the canoe for a while. Every bone in his body ached and his hands were blistered. He gave way to tears until Brun came and licked them away.

"We must camp for the night, Brun," he said and the dog wagged a furious tail. Exerting himself he climbed out of the canoe while Brun tried frantically to grab the edge and help. This gave Paul-André an idea and taking a rope from the canoe he fastened one end to the canoe and looped the other around the dog's neck. He picked up the demi-john that contained his small supply of water and the package of food, lest the canoe should overturn and then ordered the dog ahead.

Immediately Brun began to pull while Paul-André pushed at the other end and easily they got the canoe up the bank. But there Brun did not stop. With excited barks she ran along, the canoe bumping behind her and before Paul-André could scramble up the bank, the dog had entered the forest. He shouted to her to stop but the dog took no notice, except to reply in quick staccato barks. He followed along the narrow path the dog had chosen, still calling sharply to her. The canoe bumped and bounced along the hard ground and Paul-André shouted more frantically, fearful of the damage that would be done to it. Suddenly Brun turned off to the right where the branches were so low that Paul-André had to bend down. When lie reached the dog, she was panting and wagging her tail. Only then did he understand that Brun had been on this voyage before, probably many times and had led him to an ideal camping spot. Before him was a huge live-oak whose branches spread out about four feet from the ground, with a bed of thick leaves and bracken beneath. He unlooped the canoe and patted the dog who licked his face.

It was very cold but he was afraid to make a fire for fear that it would be detected. He and Brun crawled under the protecting tree and rolled together into the blanket. Exhaustion closed his eyes immediately.

When he awakened the next morning, the sun was already high and he scolded Brun for not having wakened him. While he was giving his lecture, the dog's ears suddenly shot up sharply. A low growl came from her. Tense, Paul-André listened but could hear nothing. He waited without making a movement, taking his cue from the dog who growled a second time, and then after a moment that seemed very long, she relaxed and her tail wagged again. Evidently the danger, whatever it had been, had passed.

André reached Caughnawaga on the fourth day. He had decided to leave his canoe at the foot of the rapids and have Amrusus bring him back later. It lightened the portage and he stopped only long enough to rest at short intervals. Day and night he tramped, eating as he went along. Continually his eyes searched ahead for the sight of a young boy and more than once his eyes deceived him so that he called Paul-André's name, only to find it was an illusion.

He was exhausted when he reached Caughnawaga and the more so when he learned that they had neither heard nor seen anything of the boy. Amrusus was away hunting but Oure was there, an injured hand having prevented his going.

"You would surely have passed him on the way," Oure said. "He couldn't travel as fast as you."

"That's what I expected, Oure. I scanned the forests all the way. I was certain I would pick up his trail at least over the portage, but there were no signs."

"You should have been able to see where he pulled his canoe ashore at the beginning of the portage."

"I looked..." Then he stopped suddenly. "It was nearly dark when I reached there, of course. Perhaps I shouldn't have been in such a hurry and should have waited until morning. That may have been where I missed him. There certainly wasn't a sign beyond there, not a footprint..."

"The ground's hard at this time of the year..." Oure remarked.

"I had hoped to be able to tell by the bushes—a recently broken twig and so on..."

"That might have been someone else."

"I'd better start back early in the morning. I'll probably meet him on the way back. I don't know where else he would have gone."

"Into the forests around the Seigneury, perhaps," Oure suggested.

"But he wouldn't then have taken his canoe..."

"No, that's true. You say he left you a note. He evidently thought it out very carefully and knew that you would pick on Caughnawaga."

"That's so," André said despondently. "I was so alarmed I didn't think beyond Caughnawaga. I should have sent search parties in other directions. Maybe my father will, though I doubt it. He was as sure as I that I would overtake him."

As they shot the Rapids the next day they watched for a small figure on the bank but saw no one. With experienced eyes Oure and André examined the ground at the foot of the rapids and found the trail where Paul-André had dragged the canoe ashore.

"Does he have a dog?" he asked.

"No," André said.

"There's been a canoe brought ashore here and there are dog's hairs on these bushes."

"Must have been an Indian. Can't you find any footprints?"

Oure carefully examined the path into the forest but the ground was too hard.

"I'll get back," André said. "Let's hope he has returned." Thanking Oure he went on his way.

# CHAPTER NINETEEN

QUEBEC, or Kebec in the language of the Algonquin, *the place where the waters narrow,* in 1724 was a town with a population approximately double that of Montreal. Founded in 1608 by Samuel de Champlain, it had for one hundred and sixteen years struggled for existence, as had the other settlements along the St. Lawrence, though by its strategic position at the entrance of the Gulf it had been less subject to attack by Indian tribes than Montreal and Three Rivers which formed an intermediary protection from the savages. But, for the same reason, it was more open to attack from the sea, and twice the English had attempted to storm it and twice had failed, giving to the settlers a false sense of security. When rumors were abroad of threatened attacks by their perpetual enemies settled in the North American continent, they scoffed at them and argued that their position was impregnable. That impregnability was the rock upon which the town was built, dividing it into a Lower and Upper Town. The latter was peopled by the government officials, residents of quality, priests, nuns and the soldiers of the fort. The Lower Town, straggling along the river front, was the home of commerce, sailors off the ships and the fur traders bringing their skins to the magazine to be sorted and shipped to France. From the strategic position above, the Governor-General could gaze across a magnificent panorama of waters, forest and mountain, and watch all ships that came in from France. The Chateau St. Louis that was his home, flanked one side of the fort built flush with the edge of the rock, with a gallery around it running the whole length of the building, where the people of quality who were entertained by His Excellency would promenade and impress the hardworking colonists with their elegance. When Louis XIV had taken New France under his fatherly care and had proclaimed it a Royal province, members of the nobility and their families had begun to emigrate to Canada and had established at Quebec, a miniature court in imitation of Versailles.

Sharing the dignity of the Upper Town were the various churches, all Catholic, for no Protestant was permitted in the colony. It was these ardent Catholics who, inspired with religious zeal, had sacrificed everything to come to a strange and unrelenting country and convert the savage to a belief in the white man's God. Near the Fort stood the Church of the Recollects, those barefooted monks of the Franciscian order, who in accordance with their vows of poverty had given up all earthly possessions and lived chiefly by alms from the people. Beyond this was the College of the Jesuits, who had brought their learning to the colony and had sacrificed so many of their order in the missionary field. This faced the Cathedral which served as Parish Church to all the city, and before it, lower down, was the magnificent Bishop's Palace built by Monseigneur de Saint-Vallier. The Seminary and the Hôtel Dieu completed the picture.

The Ursuline Convent stood upon the heights of the Upper Town with the Recollects, Jesuits and Cathedral as its more pretentious neighbors. Twice it had been burned down and rebuilt again with courage and confidence. Those brave souls who by Divine direction had come to the colony in its early days, brought with them a determination to succeed at whatever cost and none more so than Marie de l'Incarnation who had founded the Ursuline Convent in Quebec in 1639. After the death of her husband she had joined the cloistered order, giving up her son, Claude, to whom she was devoted. Like many others who followed her a few years later, Mère Marie de l'Incarnation had heard the call to come and teach the savage, and with her devoutness had combined practical ability and good common sense. Kind-hearted and understanding she soon became the idol of the dirty, wild little Indian girls, whom she and her associates strove to convert and teach. From a bare two-roomed hut they had pro-gressed against almost insurmountable odds, until in 1724 they had a fine building in which to carry on their noble work. It was not only the dark-skinned Indian girls whom they now taught, but the daughters of the French settlers who came to them as day pupils and as boarders.

Two days after their arrival, Elise went with her two daugh-ters to the Convent, accompanied by Madame de Ramezay and Marie-Catherine. Marie-Catherine was twenty-eight years old and was the second of Madame's daughters to enter a convent. The other, Marie-Charlotte, had entered the Hôpital-Général de Quebec several years earlier and had already taken her vows. Despite the disparity in their ages, Charlotte-Marguerite de Brievaux and Marie-Catherine de Ramezay had always been close friends, the former having a deep admiration for the latter with whom she had in recent years found so much in common. They walked along together now, talking, both their faces alight with anticipation and eagerness to start in the profession they had chosen.

Ann-Marie walked between her mother and Madame and she appeared much more reconciled than heretofore. The rea-son was an unexpected development that had occurred on the journey to Quebec. Jean-Baptiste de Ramezay, as well as Jean-Baptiste de Brievaux had accompanied them. During the trip, de Ramezay had evinced a sudden interest in Ann-Marie, an interest which had deepened with each day on the ship. They had grown up together as children and had hitherto taken little notice of each other. Now there came about a subtle change as they regarded one another in the light of approaching maturity. De Ramezay had become conscious of Ann-Marie's beauty and, as though seeing him for the first time, she was surprised to find that during his few years in the army he had grown into a very personable young man who looked handsome in the uniform of an ensign. During the voyage they had been constantly together and their mothers had exchanged glances filled with satisfaction. It had always been Marie-Charlotte de Ramezay's greatest hope that the two families would be united. This had almost been realized when Elise had been engaged to Madame's oldest son who had died of smallpox. And now it seemed that her hopes might be fulfilled by Elise's daughter marrying her youngest son. For a while Antoine and Elise had been tempted to alter their decision to send Ann-Marie to the convent but in talking it over they had decided to abide by it. Ann-Marie was only thirteen years old and Jean-Baptiste sixteen and though many married at these early ages, it was thought better that Jean-Baptiste should finish his duty at Acadie and the marriage take place two years hence. With Ann-Marie's combustible temperament, those two years might be dangerous and under the careful supervision of the Ursuline nuns she would be out of the way of temptation.

By the end of the voyage, nothing definite was settled except in the minds of the two mothers, who laughed together over their schemes. During the voyage, Elise kept a strict chaperonage over Ann-Marie. De Ramezay's attraction was mirrored in his face whenever he was with Ann-Marie and several times Elise had intercepted glances flashed from Ann-Marie's dark-amber eyes to his blue ones. It was de Ramezay who had persuaded her to allow Ann-Marie to enjoy some of Quebec's society before going to the Convent. Though she had pretended to be rather stubborn over the matter and to need a lot of persuading, she had thought of the idea several days before they reached their destination.

At the Convent they were cordially welcomed by the Reverend Mother Marie de la Conception. Her soft black veil framed a face that showed the serenity of a woman who had found inner contentment in the profession she had chosen and in the joy of devoting her life to others. Her voice was gentle and well-modulated as she greeted Madame de Ramezay, whom she had met before. She expressed pleasure at the prospect of welcoming the daughter of the late Governor as one of their sisterhood and spoke a few words to Marie-Catherine.

Then Madame de Ramezay turned to present Elise. "This is my very good friend, Madame de Brievaux," she said.

Elise acknowledged the Mother Superior's greeting and said: "This is my elder daughter, Ann-Marie, and my younger daughter, Charlotte-Marguerite."

The two girls curtseyed as they were introduced and Mère de la Conception's discerning eyes appraised the two different girls before her.

"Both will be pupils, Reverend Mother," Elise said, "but Ann-Marie for only two years. She is to be married to Madame de Ramezay's son. Charlotte-Marguerite wishes to remain and enter the sisterhood."

Mère de la Conception turned to look at the eager young face watching her. "How old are you, Charlotte-Marguerite?" she asked kindly.

"Nearly twelve, Reverend Mother," she answered quietly.

"You cannot enter the novitiate until you are sixteen, you know that?"

"Yes, Mother. But I have much to learn and would like to enter the school now and then when I am old enough I can take my vows."

"We are much in need of teachers. You also wish to become a teacher, Marie-Catherine?" she asked.

"Yes, Mother."

"My daughter is twenty-eight, Mother," Madame de Ramezay remarked.

Mère de la Conception inclined her head in acknowledgment. "We require a three months probationary period for those who will become teachers. If at the end of that time you are still of the same mind, you can then become a novice. You will have two years as a novitiate before you take your final vows." She paused a moment and then added: "There are sometimes those who come as postulants who later find they do not wish to continue."

"I shall not be among those, Mother," Charlotte-Marguerite said quickly. "It has been my dearest wish for a long time."

"That is true, Mother," Elise added.

"I also, Mother," Marie-Catherine remarked.

"I am pleased to hear it," the Reverend Mother said but there was reservation in her tone. She had known those who had come to her with this burning desire, particularly young girls, but they had later found the life too rigid. Studying the two girls before her she felt their earnestness, particularly the younger one whose large black eyes were fixed earnestly upon her face as she talked to them. Of the older one she could not be as sure, for Marie-Catherine was very reserved. At her age her wish to enter the convent might indicate failure to find a husband or some other worldly disappointment.

She turned to regard Ann-Marie who sat demurely with her hands in her lap, taking only a cursory interest in the conversation. Mère de la Conception noted the girl's beauty and felt the restlessness that was there.

"Ann-Marie will not enter as a pupil for about a month, Mother," Elise said.

Again the Reverend Mother inclined her head in acknowledgment and made no comment.

Elise had suggested to Charlotte-Marguerite that she, too, enjoy Quebec before entering the Convent but even before the girl spoke she could detect the disappointment in her face. She had hastily assured her that she could make her own choice and Charlotte-Marguerite had chosen to enter at once. Worldly entertainments held no interest for her.

"We shall welcome you both," Mère de la Conception said. "You understand, of course, that in accordance with the plan laid down by our beloved founder, Mère de l'Incarnation, we have Indian as well as French pupils. We make no discrimination." As she made the statement her wise eyes covertly watched Ann-Marie and noted the expression of distaste that quickly crossed her face. She would not be an easy pupil, particularly as she was already engaged to be married and would have her thoughts constantly on outside interests. These pupils were difficult and often influenced postulants to change their minds. Yet she could not refuse to accept them, for they brought much needed revenue to the Convent. She would have to be carefully watched. This became even more apparent as while the girls were being shown over the Convent, Elise remained to talk with the Reverend Mother and without condemning Ann-Marie, nevertheless felt that she should explain her daughter's emotional nature and ask that she be rigidly disciplined.

Ann-Marie viewed the Convent in a much different light from her sister and Marie-Catherine de Ramezay. It had troubled her a little that she did not feel the same piety as her younger sister, for whom she now had the most profound respect and admiration. But hers was not a saintly nature; life and romance beckoned too strongly. She was going to hate the rigidity and discipline of the Convent, though the thought of a month's gaiety helped to soothe her rebellious feelings. She hoped against hope that something would happen to shorten the period of two years. She hoped, too, that her parents would let her come home between school sessions or at least let her spend holidays with friends in Quebec. She had mentioned it to her mother whose only reply had been: "It depends how you behave."

As she later walked back with her mother and Madame, Ann-Marie was very thoughtful but her cloudy face cleared when she remembered that she would see Jean-Baptiste at supper that night. In an onrush of fervor she thanked God that she had fallen in love and would soon be married. The thought of it would sustain her through the school period, which she knew was virtually a period of probation because of her misbehavior with Ménard. She wondered what Jean-Baptiste would be like as a lover. From the look in his eyes she thought he was going to be exciting but she was too inexperienced to know and her mother watched her so closely that she did not even know what his kisses were like. She had bragged to her friends that she was going to run away from the convent and have lovers. But it would be better to be able to write to them and brag that she was going to marry the son of the late Governor. She tossed back her auburn curls and thought of the many times that Jean-Baptiste had whispered to her that she was very beautiful. She was glad he was handsome but having to wait so long was going to be very difficult.

Antoine and Elise plunged into the gaiety of a winter in Quebec. Antoine was generous and insisted upon her buying many new gowns. They attended balls at the Chateau and were cordially welcomed by the Governor-General and his wife. It was flattering to be received as old friends and to be urged to stay at the Chateau as the Governor's guests, since Madame de Ramezay was also staying there.

Governor de Vaudreuil had become much more feeble since his last visit to Montreal and his eighty-four years weighed heavily upon him. He had just recovered from a severe attack of the gout and walked with a cane. Madame de Vaudreuil, on the other hand, appeared more handsome than ever and was a scintillating hostess.

It was not until the time came for their departure that Elise fully realized what it was going to mean to leave her girls behind. As long as they remained in Quebec the thought of separation had not been so pronounced. Now, though she was prepared for it, it was hard, particularly with Charlotte-Marguerite who would never again be part of the household. She tried to be controlled as she kissed them goodbye but the tears would not be restrained and in a sudden paroxysm she hugged Charlotte-Marguerite to her. Both the girls cried with her and that night when she lay in bed, Charlotte-Marguerite for the first time felt pangs of homesickness. An inner zeal had kept her buoyed up, yet she was still only a little girl and was going to miss the mother she adored.

# CHAPTER TWENTY

THE days and nights of the remainder of Paul-André's journey were an ordeal for the boy, with waverings of doubt as to whether he had not better turn back and go home. This was particularly so on the day when he saw Oure and his Uncle André shooting the rapids and knew that they were searching for him. Brun warned him of their approach and he scurried into the woods so that he would not be seen. Yet even while he waited, he wanted to rush out and shout to them. He had had to leave his canoe behind because Brun's sudden dash into the woods with it had damaged it badly and also because he became too weak to carry it.

Without the canoe, he was not able to cross the river to Caughnawaga and it was hours before he could attract the attention of anyone in the village. The light had begun to fade when he saw a canoe put out from the shore, and then all went black. He knew nothing more until later he wakened to find Oure's mother sitting by him watching. Dazed and weak he looked at her and then drifted off into unconsciousness again. When later he wakened, his mind still befuddled, Margaret Williams gave him some hot soup. When his mind cleared she told him that his Uncle André had been there looking for him.

"I know. I saw him and Oure going over the rapids. Was my uncle worried?" he asked.

"Very," she replied.

"You won't send me back?"

"Why did you run away?' she asked. He told his story. Her many years of adoption had taught her Indian stoicism and he could not tell from her face whether she was approving or disapproving. "They will try to persuade you to return. My people came many times and they sent other people to me…many times."

"But you haven't wanted to go back?"

"Why should I? This is the better life."

"Will you let me stay with you then?" he asked anxiously.

She did not answer for a while. "Monsieur André asked that we send you back if you came."

"And will you?" he asked anxiously.

"My husband is away in the woods, hunting. The river will be frozen by the time he returns," she said flatly. It took Paul-André a moment or two to understand her meaning.

"And you won't send word that I am here?" he asked.

"My husband makes those decisions," she replied.

Paul-André felt happy for several days but then it began to worry him that his uncle and grandparents would be so concerned over his disappearance. So eventually an Indian who was going to Montreal took a message.

He felt strange at first with Oure. He hardly knew his friend who in the three years that had elapsed had grown tall and lithe, and had matured so much more than he. Oure was now treated as a man and did a man's work and knew so much that Paul-André felt a little boy beside him. He had much to learn and Oure taught him. Though few words passed between them and sentiment was something unknown to the Indian temperament, yet there developed a warm, loyal friendship that had begun during their first meeting. Oure's opinion became paramount in Paul-André's life. Sometimes Oure expected him to do things that were very hard and took a lot of endurance, and when Paul-André failed he felt Oure's scorn. He kept at it until he succeeded and then, though his only reward was a grunt or a nod, he knew that Oure approved. He became Oure's shadow just as Brun was his shadow.

Winter life in an Indian village proved to be dull yet interesting. The most difficult thing for Paul-André to get accustomed to was the community living. At night the entire family rolled in their blankets and slept around the fire with the door of the longhouse tightly closed. Twenty families inside one house, all sleeping and snoring and reeking with bear grease and human dirt, was sickening. With the coming of the warm weather the situation improved somewhat since he could sleep outside, but this also brought another difficulty for with sleeping on the ground he became covered with fleas and lice. He began to long for his bedroom at home, with his soft bed and clean sheets.

The food, too, was nauseating, but like the sleeping there came exceptions. Oure responded to his request that he teach him to shoot and he did so both with bow and arrow and with musket. When Amrusus returned, he accepted Paul-André's presence in silence and on the next trip took both the boys hunting with him. Then Indian life took on a glow. The days in the forests were thrilling and sleeping in the cold, fresh air under the sky was much more acceptable than the nauseating stuffiness of the hut. Paul-André was an apt pupil and followed carefully and obediently as they tracked moose and deer and trapped beaver. He learned how to skin animals so that the pelts were not injured and sitting around the camp fires with the men, he hungrily devoured moose steaks and venison. This food tasted so much better than the nauseating concoctions that came out of the family stewpot.

Confidence grew as Paul-André found himself treated as a man though he had not yet reached the twelve years of maturity.

Winter was the time for story-telling and at night around the fire, Paul-André listened quietly while one of the older men of the tribe, related one of their legends. He was grateful that Uncle André had taught him the rudiments of the language and with his sojourn among them he soon became proficient. He found that though these people had accepted the white man's God, they still retained their superstitions and belief in various spirits. Conversion had been easy for the people of this tribe because many of their beliefs coincided with those of the Catholic faith. The Iroquois did not, like many of the other tribes, believe that heaven was a *happy hunting ground* but "a happy home beyond the setting sun." They believed that the wicked passed info the dark realm of purgatory, and also in the confession of sins, though absolution and forgiveness of sins formed no part of the motive or object of confession. Yet with all this they had a deep-seated belief in witches and witchcraft that no amount of conversion ever entirely dissipated. From infancy they knew the fables, legends, and traditions connected with these witches and spirits. In winter, when the water was frozen, the spirits lapsed into a torpid state and then tales could be related with perfect freedom. But the relation of such stories must be hushed as soon as the ice broke on the river, for they believed that all spirits lived in the vicinity of the water and could hear every word spoken. Spring was indicated by the first croak of a frog and with that croak the story-tellers must become silent, lest the spirits hear them and become offended.

Paul-André loved these stories, and nature took on an added interest as he learned that the sun, the clouds, the winds, the rains and the thunderstorms, all were the whims and fancies of the spirits who ruled them. He heard the story of He-no, the Thunderer, who was the finest specimen of man and wore the costume of a warrior. On his head was a magical feather that rendered him invulnerable against the attacks of the evil-minded. On his back he carried a basket filled with fragments of rock— the thunderbolts which he hurled at evil spirits and witches as he rode the clouds. His voice was the rumble of thunder and the instrument of vengeance. To him was attributed the formation of the clouds and the gift of rain. He was the avenger of all deeds of evil.

With the coming of spring, Paul-André witnessed his first Indian ceremony, as with the sowing of the grain they invoked He-no to water and nourish the seeds and bring them to full fruition.

When the wind blew in his face, he no longer thought of it as something that stirred the trees and rippled the water, but knew that Ga-oh, the Spirit of the Winds, was restless. For this spirit he felt sorry, for he was an old man sitting in solitary confinement surrounded by a tangle of discordant winds from which he would have liked to escape. He lived in the "Great House of the Winds" stationed in the western heavens. From time to time he struggled to free himself and then the winds became violent. Only when he ceased his struggles did the trees cease to stir and the waves become calm.

He learned, too, to smoke a pipe and though he did not at first enjoy the taste, he persisted because Oure smoked and the pipe was of such prime importance. Oure told him that tobacco had been given to them as a means of communication with the spirit world and that through its ascending smoke petitions could be sent to the Great Spirit. Impressed with the seriousness of it, Paul-André persevered and as clouds of smoke rose he sent up a petition to the Great Spirit that he might become a good Indian. He learned the rituals of the calumet, so sacred to every red man. Oure had told him it was a present made to them by the Sun and that whenever he should be called upon to smoke the calumet, he must never fail to blow the smoke towards the planet that had bestowed the gift upon them. He had not yet learned the meanings of the different kinds of calumets, though Oure said there were different kinds for every treaty and that when any agreement was made it was confirmed by the presentation of a calumet and on no account could such an agreement be broken.

It seemed to him that there was an endless amount to learn and that it would take him years to absorb it all and still more years to become proficient in the different ways and customs.

Because he was afraid of his own vacillation, he was anxious to be adopted, believing that with this he would no longer be tempted to return home.

Uncle André came again in the spring but he refused to go back with him. The visit exposed to him his own weakness. There would be other visits he was sure, and he wanted to be able to say with stolidity: "I have been adopted; I cannot return."

One afternoon as he sat fishing with Oure, he broke the silence by asking: "When can I be adopted?"

Oure's reply was slow in coming and he spoke without turning his head. "I don't know. Have you spoken to my mother?"

"Not since I first arrived. Does the decision rest with her or your father?"

"Her, if you want to belong to the same tribe as I."

There was another long silence, broken again by Paul-André who asked: "Is there a ceremony of adoption?"

"Yes, for captives … but you're not a captive."

"What is the ceremony?"

"Running the gantlet …"

"And that is?"

"Running between two lines of men armed with sticks and clubs. If you fall you are beaten to death."

Six months before Paul-André might have been affected by this statement but now he showed no emotion. "And if you don't fall?" he asked.

"Adopted."

"I shall ask to be allowed to run the gantlet," he said with bravado.

Before he could speak to Mrs. Williams, however, he found that there was another power in the village with whom he had to reckon. Though the temporal power of the village rested with the Chief, it was the priest who exercised the spiritual power and this was by far the greater influence. Father Lafitau had been away during the winter and returned a few days after André's second visit. He had met André in Montreal and had heard the story of his runaway nephew and had undertaken to use his influence. He let a while elapse and then sent for Paul-André. Father Lafitau had spent a lifetime among the savages and understood them. Paul-André had suspected what was coming when he was summoned to the priest's house but he felt no misgivings or fear as he faced the venerable priest across his desk. The face was deep and wrinkled and like all Jesuits he was a scholar. The grey eyes were gentle and there was a smile on his face as he received Paul-André. He took a quick appraisal of the boy before him, noted the stubborn chin and the air of determination.

"Sit down, Paul-André," he said and indicated the chair opposite. "How long have you been here with us?"

"Since last October, Father," he replied.

"I see. And suppose you tell me in your own words why you came here."

There was a pause and then Paul-André began rather haltingly to tell his story. The priest listened quietly to the account of the accident and his father's attitude afterwards, and he changed his tactics half way through the recital. When Paul-André concluded he was silent and thoughtful for a while.

"Resentment, unfortunately, has a way of increasing as time goes on," he said softly. "It's rather like a snowball."

"You're not going to insist that I go back, Father, are you? I should only run away again."

The priest studied him intently for a moment and said: "I'm not going to *insist* that you do anything. But if you remain here you must follow certain rules that we have for all. Have you been attending school?"

"No, Father, I am nearly twelve years old. I have had enough schooling."

"Oh?" the priest smiled. "That we shall see." He pushed a piece of paper and a quill towards Paul-André and said: "Write down what I dictate."

Paul-André obeyed and when he had finished the priest took the paper, read it and smiled again. "As I thought. You have made three spelling mistakes. Now take down these figures." This result was better. "Apparently you can do figures but can't spell. I think you had better attend school for a little while longer." Paul-André began to protest but the priest went on ignoring the interruption. "You can attend in the mornings."

"But what about fishing and hunting?"

"Afternoons will do for that unless it is something important. And, oh yes, Paul-André, I want you to wait another six months before you become adopted."

"Oh no, Father! I want it sooner than that."

"No, son. Wait another six months. I have my reasons. Have you been attending Mass regularly?"

"Yes, Father."

"Good."

Paul-André walked from the priest's house down to the river's edge. It seemed that in this world one always had to do what other people told you and he longed for the day when he would be sufficiently grown-up to do as he pleased. It seemed to him then a matter of great importance. He stood by the water's edge and suddenly the blood froze in his veins. Coming towards him in a canoe were two redheaded people and a priest. He turned quickly wanting to run somewhere but not knowing where. He saw Oure sitting on the ground whittling sticks for spearing fish. Oure looked up and Paul-André jerked his head towards the river.

"My mother and uncle are in that canoe," he said and despite the effort he made, his voice shook.

Oure gave him one of his rare smiles. "Another test for you," he said and went on whittling.

Paul-André remained where he was, watching the canoe come in to the shore. He saw his Uncle André jump out and pull the canoe on to the bank. He watched Father Xavier climb out and both of them help his mother. He wanted to rush down to them and feel his mother's arms around him. He dug his fingers into the palms of his hands and stood rigidly where he was. They were coming towards him, talking as they came. Then they were before him and Uncle André was saying: "Hello, Paul-André," and, "How are you, Oure?" Oure stood up and remained beside Paul-André.

He replied: "Hello, Uncle,"—then looked at his mother. Her tired face expressed all the horror she felt as she looked at his auburn hair now thickly daubed with bear grease. It was long, down to his shoulders and looked black, giving a peculiar expression to his red-brown eyes.

"Oh no? Oh, Paul-André, what have these savages done to you!" she cried and continued to stare at him. He could not move and he kept the muscles of his face rigid. His mother turned away and walked a few steps towards the river. She was trying hard to control herself. She couldn't believe that in eight months her freckled faced boy with the dancing eyes could be changed into this solemn statuesque person with black greasy hair.

For the first time that he could remember André lost his temper with Paul-André. He took him by the shoulders and shook him and said sharply: "How dare you behave like that to your mother! She has come all this way to see you and you don't even have the decency to greet her. This nonsense has to stop. Do you hear me?" and again he shook him. He wanted to slap him and perhaps would have but a hand was laid on his arm and Father Xavier said:

"Let me have a visit with the boy. I haven't seen him for a long time. Take Madame up to Father Lafitau's house. I will join you there shortly."

André turned away and went to Elise.

"How are you, son?" Father Xavier asked. "You remember me, I hope."

"Yes, Father," Paul-André replied. His voice seemed far away.

Father Xavier looked up at Oure. "And this is your friend?" he asked.

"Pardon me, Father. This is Oure—Father Xavier, our curé," Paul-André managed to say.

Father Xavier spoke to Oure in his own language, words of formal greeting and then said: "Shall we walk by the river for a little, Paul-André."

He put his arm across the boy's shoulders as they strolled along. He looked around with feigned interest and said: "This is my first visit to Caughnawaga, although I know Father Lafitau. How do you like it here?"

"Very well, thank you."

"You like living with the Indians?"

"Yes," Paul-André's reply was guarded.

"I've lived among them for many years. Interesting people. Have you learned any of their legends and customs?"

"Yes. And I can also hunt and fish now."

"That's very good."

"When did you live among the Indians, Father?" Paul-André asked, unable to control his curiosity.

"Oh, most of my life, son. I have lived with the Assinboines and the Sioux and also some time with the Iroquois. These people are Iroquois are they not?"

"Mohawks."

"Same family. And you want to become a Mohawk? Do you know the language?"

Paul-André replied in the dialect and there was pride in his voice.

"Splendid," Father Xavier said continuing in the dialect. "And how do you like their food?"

Paul-André was ready for the question. "It is wonderful when we catch it ourselves and eat it fresh."

"Yes, particularly the fish. But the stewpot isn't so good is it? Nor the sagamité?"

"No, it's rather dirty."

"And where do you live?"

Paul-André pointed to one of the longhouses.

"Fleas, lice, smells, dirt and mangy dogs," Father Xavier said and smiled. "Rather hard to get used to isn't it?"

"Yes," Paul-André admitted.

"And you sometimes long for the cleanliness of your own home and the delicious food your mother used to put before you…"

Paul-André gave no answer.

"Don't hold resentment against your father, Paul-André. He will understand you better when you return…" Father Xavier said quietly.

"I'm not returning, Father. I enjoy being an Indian. They understand me here and I'm treated as a man."

"Of course, yes, you're growing up. Your mother just wants you to know how much she misses you. Your brother and sisters are all away, you know. Pretty lonely in the house. And when you get tired of this, you can always come back. They will always want you."

He did not say any more then.

Up at the priest's house, Father Lafitau was talking earnestly to Elise. "I believe you will find I am right," he was saying. "He will tire of it in time. Try to force him and he will get more stubborn and go farther away from you. The novelty hasn't yet worn off, but I believe it will. Human nature is such that when once we get a thing we have longed for, it soon begins to pall. I will watch over him. I may be wrong, but it is my feeling that he will return to you of his own free will one of these days."

Paul-André did not go up to Father Lafitau's house with Father Xavier. He could not trust himself. Instead he ran into the forest and lay face down, battling with himself the desire to go back home, yet knowing that if he did he could never return here because Oure would deride his weakness. He lay there for a long time until a rough brown form found him and licked his face joyously.

"Oh Brun," the boy said and hugged the dog to him and let the tears come. The dog licked them away.

# CHAPTER TWENTY-ONE

TRAGEDY again struck the de Ramezay family when in August of 1725 the eldest son, Charles-Hector, was drowned on his way to France when the *Chameau* was sunk. His death left Jean-Baptiste the only surviving son. Out of a family of sixteen there now remained only this one son and six daughters, two of whom were nuns and one married. Governor de Longueil arranged for Jean-Baptiste's return to the Montreal garrison until the affairs of the family could be settled.

There was not time for recovery from Charles-Hector's death, when the whole colony was plunged into mourning with the passing of the eighty-five year old Marquis de Vaudreuil on October 10th. He had governed the colony with vigilance and firmness for twenty-one years. The Baron de Longueil became Administrator for the colony and hastened to Quebec, sending off by the last ship to France an urgent request that he be appointed Governor-General. He had served the colony well for over half a century, and his father before him, and except for the prejudice in France against native-born officials in Canada, his would have been the logical succession. He hoped to be able to overcome this prejudice but was to be disappointed. The people of the colony wanted him, but the officials of State and Church were against the appointment, adhering to France's policy. All through the winter the Baron tentatively held the position he coveted but with the arrival of the first ship from France in the spring came the news that the new Governor-General would be the Marquis de Beauharnois. Immediately rumor and conjecture became rife. Some said that the Marquis was a natural son of Louis XIV and this rumor spread until for many years afterwards it was believed to be the truth, though actually without any foundation. Charles de Beauharnois was a naval officer of fifty-five years of age. His family was known in the colony, as his brother, François, had been Intendant from 1702-1705.

By the same ship had come other news which interested the entire colony. Louis XV had been married at the age of fifteen to Maria Leczcynska, daughter of the exiled King of Poland. Since the death of Louis XIV, France's interest in the colony had not been the same. The former King had fathered their interests; young Louis XV was the tool of wily ministers, especially Cardinal Fleury who exercised absolute power.

The changes in the government at home and the changes in the government in the colony, brought about a new order of things, though, as it was to prove, the selection of the Marquis de Beauharnois as Governor-General was a very satisfactory one.

During this year from August 1725 to August 1726, several developments took place on the Seigneuries. All through the summer of '25 Elise waited and hoped for Paul-André's return. When she and Antoine had returned from Quebec and had learned that Paul-André had run away, they had had the first real quarrel since their marriage. Elise had turned furiously upon Antoine upbraiding him for his treatment of his son. With all the force of her redheaded temper she had uttered words that had been too long pent-up. She had left for Caughnawaga without speaking to him again and it had taken many months for the rift to heal.

It was to Father Xavier that the credit went for finally bringing them together again. After the trip to Caughnawaga with Elise, he had grown closer to them and his nightly visits to their house lessened the restraint between them. He talked to each of them individually both through the confessional and privately. He was too wise to try to force them together and he took time to plot his campaign well. Elise was ill for several weeks after her return from Caughnawaga, due to the shock she had sustained, and during the long evenings Father Xavier played cards with Antoine and talked to him. The love between Elise and Antoine was too deeply rooted to allow a complete break. Father Xavier gradually lowered the barrier between them and when reconciliation finally came it was without words—the rush of two lonely souls aching to become united again.

Before winter again set in, André prepared to go once more to Caughnawaga. As he was leaving, Antoine said to him: "Give him a message from me, André," and then hesitated. "You can tell him in your own words how I feel. Er... tell him... I'm sorry for the way I acted. Ask him to forgive me." Armed with this message, André hoped for success and his hopes rose, as he saw a change of expression come over Paul-André's face. He thought seriously before answering his uncle and then said. "Thank him, Uncle André, but I have now made up my mind. I have been adopted into the tribe. I shall remain."

By his own insistence, Paul-André had run the gantlet before adoption, though this was usually only for captives. Because he was so insistent, the Indian braves had not held back but had struck at him fiercely as he had run between their lines. Twice he had gone down but had recovered himself and when he reached the end of the line was bleeding from several wounds. But he had proven his courage to them and to himself and had become a man among them as he reached the age of maturity.

Elise went away to be by herself when André brought them the disheartening news. Antoine and he sat and talked of the matter. Antoine was fearful that the rift between him and Elise would now be re-opened. But she thought it out for several hours and shortly after André had left, came to Antoine, kissing him tenderly and making no further comment.

In August of the following year, 1726, Ann-Marie and Jean-Baptiste de Ramezay were married. Jean-Baptiste de Brievaux was also home, having now completed his military training and ready to resume his work beside his father. Not since Elise's own marriage had there been such a celebration on the Seigneuries, though Ann-Marie's wedding brought the added joy of being celebrated in their own church. It was the first celebration to take place there. Between lines of habitants who had known her all her life, Ann-Marie walked from the Manor House to the church, leaning on the arm of her father. For days the pathway had been swept and beaten down so that it should not be rough to walk on. She had just passed her sixteenth birthday and with the freshness of her beauty there was a maturity beyond her years. Her sojourn at the Convent had given her a veneer of quietness and gentility but the same fire burned inside, as anyone could have realized who cared to look into her flashing eyes. Her Titian hair beneath her white veil caught the rays of the sun as she walked along, proud in her bearing and smiling at those who had come to pay her homage. After the ceremony as she walked back on the arm of her husband, resplendent in his Lieutenant's uniform, the hearts of everyone on the Seigneuries swelled with pride and their voices rang out in greeting.

Jean-Baptiste de Ramezay felt that he was the luckiest of men. There had been little entertainment during the past winter because of the mourning but the families had visited with each other and he had come to know his future wife better. Elise had maintained her strict chaperonage but there had been opportunities that could be snatched and with the first ardent kiss, Jean-Baptiste had realized the strong emotions of the woman he was to marry. The months of courtship had been irksome and now as he sat beside her at the wedding feast, he was impatient for the moment when after such long waiting he could claim her for his own.

They spent the night at the Chateau and sailed the next morning to honeymoon in Quebec. That night two natures so long restrained gave way to their emotions. It had seemed to

Ann-Marie that the day would never come when she could break the dam by which she had had to control herself. Inexperienced as she was, she had reason to be glad that her young husband had been well-guided in his education. As she lay in his arms all the passion that she had inherited from her grandmother raced through her body and they were two young souls united in supreme delight.

Their arrival in Quebec coincided with the arrival of the new Governor-General and they immediately plunged into the gaiety. The Marquis de Beauharnois arrived on August 15th, which was also the Assumption of the Blessed Virgin Mary-one of the most important of religious festivals. With this double event all Quebec wore its most festive air.

The night before, Jean-Baptiste and Ann-Marie had been welcomed by the Baron de Longueil with whom they had been invited to stay. They formed part of the official party which gathered at the wharf at half past eight on the following morning. Promptly at that time a signal from the cannon on the ramparts started all the bells in the town ringing. The Marquis de Beauharnois, dressed in a suit of red with an abundance of gold lace, then stepped into a barge covered with red cloth and was rowed to the wharf. All eyes were strained for a first glimpse of the man who would now be their ruler. With him was also a new Intendant, Claude Thomas Dupuy, who had replaced Michel Bégon. The two officials were eyed keenly by the other officials of the colony and almost immediately they placed them in two categories. The Marquis had an easy and friendly manner and Dupuy gave himself airs. Dupuy had held a high position in the Conseil de Roi and, it was said, was a man well-versed in public affairs. Some said that he had reason to feel important; others, and these were the majority, remarked that they were going to have trouble with him.

As the new Governor-General stepped ashore he was welcomed by the Baron de Longueil who addressed him in a very elegant speech, which all knew were the words demanded by the occasion but which could have had little sincerity in de Longueil's heart. The cannon on the ramparts gave a general salute and while the bells of the town continued to peal a loud welcome, the Governor made his way to the Cathedral. The whole street up to the Cathedral was lined with men-at-arms, drawn chiefly from the habitants. Behind the Governor-General walked his servants dressed in green and carrying firearms on their shoulders. On arrival at the Cathedral, de Beauharnois was received by the venerable Bishop de Saint-Vallier arrayed in his pontifical robes, with a gold mitre on his head and a great crozier of silver in his hand. In a brief speech the Bishop welcomed the new Governor-General, while they both undoubtedly appraised each other, since harmony between the Church and State within the colony was something that could not always be maintained with ease.

The reception and ball that night were Ann-Marie's first venture into public life and the many compliments which her beauty called forth were very gratifying to her. As her husband hoped one day to hold an official position, perhaps even to be Governor, to have a charming and gracious woman beside him would always be an advantage. She was radiant with happiness and her early restlessness had now begun to give way to poise. Jean-Baptiste was very proud as he presented her and enjoyed her success.

During their stay in Quebec they had further cause for delight in Ann-Marie's receiving an unexpected inheritance. Shortly before her wedding day, her father had received a letter from the man who was the only relative who acknowledged him. This General François de Truite was the brother of the man who had fathered Antoine out of wedlock. Antoine had never cared for his uncle, though at the same time he was immensely grateful to him, for it was through him that he had been able to trace his parentage and thus marry Elise. When he had told

Elise the story, after their marriage, she had insisted that they call upon General de Truite during their first visit to Quebec. She had not found him as repulsive as Antoine had and because she showed the aging man some kindness and consideration he had become very fond of her. During subsequent visits, she had always called on him and had on one occasion taken the children with her. François de Truite was very wealthy, yet one of the loneliest men in Quebec, for his repulsive appearance and mean disposition, excluded him from making friends. He was also extremely bitter. Though once married, he had no children of his own and when Antoine's children had sat on his knee and had not shown any repulsion when he fondled them, his parched soul had responded. From then on he had showered them with devotion and now at past eighty his unhappy life was drawing to a close. He had written Antoine a rather pathetic letter that was practically pleading in its tone, asking that before he died he might see some of them again.

Ann-Marie had promised to respond to his request and she and Jean-Baptiste called upon the General. They found him in bed, propped up with pillows and looking more like a gargoyle than ever.

"Uncle François, don't look startled," she said. "It is Ann-Marie. Don't you recognize me?"

He continued to stare and then said in a voice that was hardly intelligible: "Ann-Marie? You're not Hélène de Matier?"

"She was my grandmother. My father's mother."

"Your father's mother?" The claw-like hands shook as they fumbled at the sheet. "You're Hélène de Matier come back to scoff at me."

Ann-Marie glanced quickly at her husband who had remained standing by the door. He smiled sympathetically and nodded to her to humor the old man.

"No, dear. I haven't come to scoff at you. I've come to visit with you. I have been told I look very much like my grandmother."

"You are she returned to earth. She never liked me. She…"

"But I like you, Uncle," Ann-Marie humored, and took one of the shaking hands. "I've just been married and I have brought my husband to meet you." She signalled to Jean-Baptiste to come forward. "This is my husband, Uncle—Lieutenant de Ramezay."

The General studied him and said: "You're a lieutenant. Remaining in the army?"

"Yes, monsieur, for a time at least."

"See that you get recognition." Then de Truite turned again to Ann-Marie and studied her. "You're a beautiful girl. Have I seen you before?"

"Yes, Uncle, when I was a little girl. Mother brought us all to see you."

"Where are the others?"

"My elder brother is in Montreal helping father, and my other brother … er … he is at Caughnawaga at present. My sister has just entered the Ursuline convent."

"A nun? That is good for your family."

"She is going to become one. We are very happy."

"There are four of you?" He was lost in reverie for a little while and then said: "I am dying. Tell your father I …" he seemed to be searching for words and they waited in silence as he tried to remember what he had started to say. He began a different sentence. "My brother was your father's father. Tell your father …" he looked at her again and paused. "He's a fine man your father …"

"Wonderful," Ann-Marie replied.

"Tell him I'm grateful to him. You children have made me very happy." Ann-Marie could not fully understand this for she did not know the full details of the old man's lonely life and his longing for children who might have loved him. "I am leaving all my fortune to you, to be divided among the four of you. You won't have to wait long. I shall be dead soon."

Ann-Marie started conventionally to protest but he stopped her. "No one will be sorry when I'm gone," he said and feeling that words would be superfluous, Ann-Marie simply touched her lips lightly to the emaciated hand that she held. She was surprised and a little embarrassed to see tears in his eyes. He passed his hand lightly over her luxuriant hair and said: "Hélène's hair, only hers was black."

He turned suddenly to de Ramezay and asked abruptly: "Have you a fortune?"

Jean-Baptiste looked embarrassed. "Not very much at present, monsieur. My father was not a rich man and his expenses exceeded his governmental income."

"Fools! It always does. The government expect its officials to keep up the dignity of France and never provides for them to do so." He turned now abruptly to Ann-Marie and said: "Did you bring him a good dowry?"

Ann-Marie smiled, trying to understand that his abruptness was old age and not rudeness. "Fairly good, uncle. Father is ... er ... quite successful." The discussion was embarrassing in view of the shortness of the time they had been married.

"And do you intend to live off your wife's inheritance?" de Truite snapped at de Ramezay.

Ann-Marie saw her young husband's face flush and felt sorry for him. "Indeed not, monsieur," Jean-Baptiste said sharply. "I have not lived long enough yet to have had many opportunities but I intend to find them or make them. There are many opportunities for young men in the colony."

De Truite nodded, evidently satisfied with the reply. "I was in command of the troops here for many years until I became too old. I shall write to the Commandant and tell him about you."

When they rose to leave, Ann-Marie bent over the bed and pressed a kiss to the bony forehead. The claw-like hands clutched at her arm and held her there for a moment, then relaxed as he lay back on the pillows exhausted.

"Thank you," he murmured.

"Thank you, Uncle dear," she said and patted his cheek. "We'll come and see you again."

But they did not see him again. He passed away the following day and there was a smile on his face.

And in Montreal on the same day there came another echo from the past. Paul de Courville-Boissart received a letter brought by messenger from town and the letter was signed: *Renée de Renault.*

# CHAPTER TWENTY-TWO

WHILE Paul and Ann talked with their guest, André had time to study her. Upon receipt of the letter from her, they had sent the carriage into town to bring her to the Seigneury and now were the recipients of some quite surprising news. Renée de Renault was the niece of a man who many years ago had been a bondsman employed by Paul. He had been a loyal worker and Paul had given him his freedom a few years before it was due. Then suddenly Gaston Renault had been found in the woods shot through the head. It had been thought an accident, though the family had considered it suicide and only André and Elise could have given the explanation.

The woman talking to them was about thirty or perhaps a year or two younger. There was nothing particularly striking about her features which, however, were aided by her vivaciousness which gave them a mobility that was charming. This changed the rather hard line of her mouth which set straight and narrow when she was not talking. Her eyes predominated and in them André could see the likeness to her uncle, whose large black eyes had been so unusual.

Paul was talking. "I am so sorry, Mlle. de Renault, that you have had this long and arduous journey without knowing that your uncle was dead."

"How many years ago did you say it was, monsieur?" she asked. André liked her voice. It had a purring quality.

"It was about fifteen years ago, wasn't it?"

"Yes, about that," Ann replied.

Mlle. de Renault turned her gaze to André and smiled. She held his gaze for a moment and then turned to listen to what Paul was saying.

"We were very attached to Gaston. He was a fine man, though not altogether a happy one. You knew, of course, that he had been sent out of France...?"

"That, monsieur, is, or was the object of my visit. I don't know whether you knew the story behind my uncle's disgrace?"

"No, at least not all. He told me that he and his half-brother did not agree and he intimated..." Paul stopped abruptly. "The half-brother he mentioned would be your father?"

"Yes, monsieur. He probably told you that it was my father's fault that he had been sent out of France." She smiled frankly.

"Yes, he did tell me that."

"It was true. My father died a few years ago and on his death-bed signed a confession. He seemed very anxious to clear himself. Unfortunately, my father and my uncle both loved the same woman. My father was a ruthless man. He contrived to make it appear that his brother was concerned with salt smuggling and had him sent out of France so that he could marry my mother." There was silence in the room as they heard the truth that verified statements that Gaston had made. "My mother died soon after I was born. I have here the statement that clears my uncle of the charge of salt smuggling." She handed the paper to Paul.

"I was shocked, as anyone would be," Mlle. de Renault continued. "I did not like to think that my father would so injure his own brother, even though he was only a half-brother. There was nothing I could do but try to find him. I had thought at first that I would write you and then..." she paused as though undecided as to what explanation to make, "and then I decided I would come to the colony myself as some acquaintances were coming here and I was able to travel with them. It was rather stupid, since it proves to be a fruitless journey."

"Oh, but you will stay a while now you are here," Ann said cordially.

"I don't believe so, madame."

"But you had thought of remaining here a while after so long a journey?" Ann asked.

"To be quite frank, madame, I had in mind staying with my uncle. I ... er ... I found France very lonely since my father's death."

"Of course, my dear. We can understand that," Ann said solicitously. "I hope you will look upon us as your friends and accept our hospitality. We have a large house here and plenty of room. My daughter and her family have the next Seigneury. The season is getting late and we wouldn't want you to take the risk of returning to France at this time of the year. The winters here are quite gay and we would enjoy having you as our guest."

"You are very kind, madame," Mlle. replied. She had looked directly at Ann while she spoke, but seemed to be calculating something.

"May I add my few words to those of my wife and repeat we should be delighted to have you as our guest," Paul said.

"And I, too," André added.

"You are too kind," Renée said and after a quick glance at André lowered her eyes, dabbing them lightly with a fine lace handkerchief. "Forgive me," she said, "but your kindness touches me. When you have felt so alone and then people who are strangers offer you hospitality and kindness, well ..." the rest of the sentence ended in a touching gesture.

"We know what loneliness is, my dear," Ann said kindly. "We used to be quite a large family. Then our elder son died and our daughter married. For many years, André was away in the woods as a fur trader and my husband and I were alone. Now we are happier because André is here with us again." She smiled at him and said: "Why don't you take Mademoiselle de Renault over the Seigneury, André, while we send into Montreal for her things?"

André turned his green-blue eyes to the guest and said: "Would you care to?"

"I should be delighted, if it is not too much trouble."

"Trouble? It would be a pleasure." André's smile was always infectious and Renée's darting black eyes quickly appraised him as with a bow that had a surprising flourish he stood back to let her precede him.

The late September air was a little chilly and she drew her cloak tightly around her.

"Would you like a warmer coat?" André asked. "I would be glad to fetch you one."

"Oh no. This one is warm enough. It was the change from the warmer air inside." She glanced out over the Seigneury and said: "What a charming place!"

"You think so? Do you think you would like it in the colony?"

The question seemed direct and she flashed a quick look at him as she said: "It is a little early to say, but..." she held his eyes and added: "I might grow to like it very much."

André was surprised to find that his blood ran swiftly through his veins and made his heart pump. He began talking, quickly explaining the set-up of the Seigneury to her. She was quite petite and only came up to his shoulder so that he felt tall standing beside her.

"You must meet my twin sister..."

"Twin? How interesting! And does she have fascinating hair like yours?"

He unconsciously bent slightly towards her as he said with a broad smile: "Do you find it fascinating?"

"I have so seldom seen red hair."

"It runs in our family. My father's was red and so was his twin sister's..."

"More twins!"

"They run in the family too! That is," he felt a twinge as he thought of Elise, "they did. We don't have any more now. But the red hair continues. My sister has four children and two of them have the red hair, though theirs is more auburn because their father has black hair."

"But your mother had black hair, didn't she?"

"Yes, that is true, but all the same my sister and I have this color…"

"Burnished gold," she said looking up at his hair and thinking she would like to run her hands through it.

"That sounds very complimentary."

"It was meant to be."

"Thank you. And may I give you one?" She waited for him to continue. "You have the same eyes as your uncle's and his were large and dominating. In a woman it is beauty."

"Thank you, monsieur." She dropped him a small curtsey and they both began to laugh. André found he was enjoying himself and in a way that was exciting.

"I was telling you about my sister, Elise. You will like her. When she and I were children we adored Gaston. He taught us to ride, to canoe, skate, everything. Do you like to skate?"

"I'm afraid I must confess I don't know how."

"Then may I have the pleasure of teaching you?"

"Thank you."

"And you will like sleighing. We have so much fun in the winter when the river is frozen over. Then we can cross from one side to the other."

"When does it freeze?"

"It starts about November usually and by the end of December it is frozen solid. Then we are practically cut-off from the outside world…"

"How nice!" There was a strange note in her voice that prompted him to say:

"You sound as though you would be glad."

"I would. I have been very unhappy these last two years."

"Because of the loss of your father?"

She hesitated slightly and answered. "Yes, chiefly."

"We shall help you to forget."

There was a pause as they looked across the Seigneuries. Harvesting was in full swing and it was a picturesque sight to watch so much activity in the fields.

"What do you grow here?"

"Practically everything. Corn, wheat, barley, oats and all kinds of vegetables and fruit. My brother-in-law also grows quantities of tobacco and ginseng..."

"Ginseng? What is that?"

André explained.

"And what is it good for?"

"Medicinal purposes." He paused and decided he had better not mention stomach disorders and the other things that the plant was good for.

"And you will one day own this Seigneury?" she asked and her tone was rather quiet.

"Oh yes, eventually. Though father has many years ahead of him yet, I hope."

"Of course. But I suppose you take the most active part, I mean as he gets older."

"Not exactly. He has the strength of an ox. He has always lived an outdoor life."

"He came from France, of course. All seigneurs do, don't they?"

"Oh no, not all. Most do, though. No, my father was born here. His grandfather came here as a pioneer. He was just a humble habitant."

"Oh!" There was disappointment in the tone but André was not discerning enough to notice it.

"We are real pioneers. And we are proud of it."

"Of course," she replied conventionally.

"My mother came from France, though. She was born and brought up in Paris. Her father was a Minister, the Chevalier de Luc."

"Oh indeed." Interest had returned. "Was it through her that your father became a Seigneur?"

"Oh no, not at all." André then explained about the Sieur de Courville and his interest and subsequent adoption of his father.

"Very interesting," she said at the end of the recital.

"You will find us a strange mixture here. You see, in the colony, gentlemen are permitted to work. Of course, this did not apply to my father because he wasn't a nobleman, but it did in the case of the Sieur de Courville and of many others. You will see it everywhere here. A man will be in homespuns during the day and in the evening—that is in the winter, in the summer there isn't time—but in the evenings during the winter he will change the homespuns for silks and satins and all those things."

"And do you wear a wig then?"

"If I have to. I hate the things."

She was silent for a moment and then said: "I would like to see you in a brocaded coat and satin breeches and powdered hair." She studied him as she spoke and again their eyes held.

"Perhaps you will. I'll dress up especially for your benefit. The Governor will undoubtedly give some balls and *soupers* and then I can perform, though confidentially I am much more comfortable in these." He indicated his homespun trousers and shirt.

"Are the balls and such elaborate here?" she asked.

"Very. Just the same as in France. You will be at home then," he said graciously, forgetting that she was a Breton and had made no mention of ever having been in Paris.

Ann came out and suggested that Mademoiselle would probably like to go to her room. With the previous conversation in mind, André swept her a bow and taking the hand she extended put his lips to it.

After she had gone he stood for a while deep in thought, a strange excitement encompassing him. Then he walked over to the de Brievaux Seigneury thinking how he should break the news to Elise. No one but he and Elise knew of Gaston's love for her and that it had been because of her rejection of him that Gaston had burned down his house and gone to the woods to end his life with a musket shot. Elise was upstairs when he went into the house but at his call came down.

"Why, André, what brings you here in the middle of the afternoon?" she asked and kissed him.

"News, my dear. Sit down and I'll tell you what has happened."

"Good news, I hope?"

"Oh yes, I think so. Still it may disturb you for a moment."

Her eyes looked anxious but she listened without further comment. André hesitated for a moment and then said: "A Mademoiselle de Renault came to call on us today."

He saw Elise start as he had anticipated and her eyes glazed anxiously. "Relation of Gaston's?"

"His niece. Daughter of the half-brother he sometimes mentioned."

Quickly he hold her the story that Renée had told them.

"Poor Gaston! I'm sorry he never knew."

She sat looking troubled as she thought of that day many years ago when Gaston had attacked her in the storeroom out of revenge for her having slighted his love. She had always had a guilty conscience over it, feeling that she had sent him to his death. "What is she like, André?"

"Oh, quite attractive," he replied trying to make his voice sound nonchalant. "She has eyes like Gaston ..."

"Oh dear!" Elise remembered those dark burning orbs of Gaston's only too well. "What did you say her name was, I mean her first name?"

"Renée de Renault. Rather euphonious don't you think?"

"*De* Renault? Gaston was just Gaston Renault. How does she happen to have a *de* in her name?"

"Oh, I don't know. The half-brother I suppose was entitled to it."

"Perhaps," Elise said doubtfully. "And you say mother has invited her to stay the winter?"

"Yes, it will be nice, won't it?" André said naively. Elise looked at him quickly but made no comment. "You and Antoine must come over this evening and meet her."

"Perhaps we will," she answered.

"And have you any news?"

"Ann-Marie and Jean-Baptiste will be back any day now. I am so glad they will be here for the winter. I was afraid Jean-Baptiste might be sent to some outlandish fort. But Governor de Longueil arranged it so that they could be here. It will be lovely. And, I told you a notary had arrived from Quebec about General de Truite's will."

"Yes. That is great for the children. What are you going to do about Paul-André's share?"

"We don't quite know, André. We talked about it with Father Xavier last night and he suggested he go to Caughnawaga and see Paul-André and tell him. It might make a difference, though I doubt it."

"I do, too. Still it would be a good idea. Perhaps I'll go with him."

"I wish you would. If only he would come back," she sighed. "It's nearly two years now. Sometimes I despair that he will ever return."

"I have a feeling he will, Elise. I can't tell you why I have the feeling but I do."

"I hope you're right," she said despondently.

"How about Charlotte-Marguerite's share of the inheritance?" he asked changing the subject. "That will go to the Convent of course."

"Yes, we had a letter from her today by the new postal service. I was going to bring it over later for you all to read. Wait a moment, I'll get it." She went up to her room and returned with the letter. André read it carefully.

"She sounds very happy," he remarked as he handed it back to her.

"A little homesick, though I think. Ann-Marie will have seen her ..."

"Yes, she mentions it."

"Oh yes, of course. I wish she would have come back for the winter. Ann-Marie was going to try to persuade her. Still I suppose she is right in what she says. Now that she has become used to convent life, I suppose it is best for her not to return home. I had hoped though that until she becomes a novitiate she would spend a holiday here."

"How many years is it before she enters the profession?"

"She'll be sixteen in the January of '29."

"Over two years yet."

"Yes." Again a sigh escaped her. "I suppose having given her to God I must not give way to motherly regrets. It's not easy to give up a child, even in so lovely a way. I'm so lonely for my children, André."

"I can understand that, dear," he said and laid his hand on hers. "At least now you have Jean-Baptiste home."

"Thank God for that."

"And Ann-Marie will soon be here and she'll be giving you grandchildren," he said cheerfully.

"I know, I shouldn't be depressed."

As he was leaving he said: "And you'll come over this evening and meet our guest?"

"If Antoine isn't too tired," she replied guardedly.

She watched her brother as he strode back, her thoughts dwelling on the news he had brought. Gaston Renault's niece! She wondered if she had the fire and fascination that had made Gaston so attractive.

# CHAPTER TWENTY-THREE

THAT winter was one of the gayest in which André had ever participated. He, who had hitherto spent the winter months hunting with the men and only occasionally joining in the more frivolous pursuits, now went to a tailor in Montreal and had several fine suits made. He attended *soirées* and *petits soupers,* balls and masquerades, as escort of Mademoiselle de Renault and instead of spending his time in the card-room with the men, he danced and played the cavalier.

Paul and Ann were delighted with his interest in their guest; Elise was not. From the first meeting she had instinctively felt an antagonism towards Renée. She had tried to analyse her feelings, thinking that she was prejudiced because every time she met Renée's glance, the eyes reminded her uncomfortably of Gaston. That Renée had from the first intended to enslave André was to her quite obvious. She doubted the woman's sincerity, was concerned over her ambiguous replies regarding her life in France and did not like the change she so soon wrought in André. That she was attractive no one could deny, but there was something brittle about her and Elise did not like the way in which more than once she had referred to the fact that André would ultimately become Seigneur. Though she was ingratiating to Paul and Ann, there was something feline about it, with a purring that would perhaps later change to scratching.

Ann reserved her judgment. When Elise mentioned these things to her she merely replied:

"We are so glad to see André thinking of marriage at last."

"Yes," Elise agreed, "but I would like to feel that it is for his happiness."

"Of course, dear. But he is so much in love that it cannot help bring him happiness."

Elise searched her mother's face at this remark, knowing full well that Ann was not speaking from her heart. She, too, then reserved her judgment.

Nor were these doubts confined merely to the immediate family. As might be expected Aunt Marie was tremendously interested. In the first few days of Renée's visit, André took her to see his aunt, giving her a vivid account of the blunt, warm-hearted woman who was regarded so affectionately by all of them.

"You'll like her," he said with almost boyish eagerness. "She's frank and rather brusque at times, but has a wonderful humor."

As the two women were presented to each other there was an instant appraisal and instead of the rough, jolly greeting that André had expected, Aunt Marie became quite formal and during the visit sat with her hands folded in her lap, conversing politely. She had not liked the keen look which she had received from Renée's onyx eyes nor the quick disdainful glance around her humble home. Sincerity and deception do not mix and though outwardly cordial, there was restraint which both instantly felt. André felt it too.

She and Aunt Marie met frequently at the Manor House and elsewhere but the initial dislike never changed. When Aunt Marie heard that André was courting the lady, she was intensely worried but kept her thoughts to herself. At the same time she decided on a plan of procedure and whenever they were together purposely referred to the rough life André had led in the woods; how this was what he really enjoyed; and how he loved the simple things in life.

Renée would smile, an enigmatical smile in which there was no warmth. On one occasion she looked coldly at Aunt Marie and remarked: "Men change."

"Indeed they do," Aunt Marie agreed heartily. "But what's deep down in their hearts does not change. André will never be anything but a wanderer at heart."

Again an enigmatical smile hovered on her lips as she replied: "Perhaps."

Whatever might be the opinion of his family, André had no doubts in his own mind. From his first impression, his interest had grown until his world had entirely changed. No young man in the flush of his first love was ever so deeply engrossed and when he had taken his first kiss and sensed the depth of her passion, his love was aflame. That first kiss was delayed, for Renée de Renault knew how to be provocative and enjoyed adding one small piece of fuel at a time to the fire of his love. She led him along, not gently but firmly, enjoying his discomfort which gave her a feeling of power. She noticed that during the winter evenings he now discarded his homespuns for broadcloth and when he conducted her to the entertainments given by the nobility in Montreal, he was as elegant in his dress as any man and wore his hair powdered! She was a woman of excellent taste in dress and her poise and quick repartee drew the men to her, so that André did not by any means have the field to himself. Never having courted a woman before, he was uncertain of himself and when she danced and flirted with other men, it produced a fever of nervousness within him. Having for nearly twenty years avoided marriage, he was not going to be thwarted now that he had met the one woman he desired.

He was determined to make his proposal at the first opportunity and searched frantically to find this opportunity. Blizzards came and confined them to the house and her nearness tortured him. At home she was a model of propriety, playing picquet in the evenings with him and his parents and giving him no chance to be with her alone. Yet at the same time she would torment him with a glance, a provocative remark or gesture.

The moment the blizzard ceased, André suggested a sleighing party, knowing that there was nothing so conducive to romance. It was a large party but though all the sleighers started out together, as always the distance between each vehicle lengthened as they proceeded on their journey. André employed every ruse he knew. They must of course stop to rest the horse and he took advantage of it. The air was brisk with the coldness of the snow all around them and naturally he must tuck the fur rugs snugly around her. The cold air had whipped her cheeks to a rosy hue and beneath her round beaver hat her black eyes were dancing merrily. He leaned over and looked into them and seeing her with the eyes of a lover said in a tense voice:

"You are beautiful, Renée."

"You find me so?" she answered provocatively.

"You know I do," he answered and brought his face closer to hers. He moved carefully, not yet sure whether she would reprimand him. But the reprimand did not come and when he impulsively drew her to him and implanted his lips on hers, she lay there with her head against his shoulder. Encouraged he drew closer to her and slipped his hand beneath the fur rug. He put his lips to hers again and his blood raced as he felt them part in response to desire. He went further and placed his hand where he could feel the curve of her breast beneath her dress. He touched her lightly at first, felt her tremble but not resist, and his passion flamed. His active fingers stirred her and he thrilled as he felt the motion, while his hungry lips drank deep in a long kiss that threatened to overthrow all the barriers of convention. When at last he could regain his control he asked in a voice that shook: "Renée when will you marry me?"

She laughed, a teasing laugh that she knew would upset him. "I haven't said I would marry you!"

"I know you haven't, but you will, won't you? You know I love you, have loved you since first you came. Don't torment me longer. I want you. Don't you love me?"

"I don't know. Perhaps."

"Don't say *perhaps* in that tone," he said roughly. "You *must* love me." And he drew her rather brusquely to him but this time she decided to play the tormenter. She turned her face away from him quickly. His hand came up sharply and then he steadied himself and instead of the intended rough movement, he gently put his hand to her cheek and turned her face to him. He looked deep into her eyes and though they were rather mocking, he continued to drink from their depths. With studied gentleness he kissed first one and then the other and feeling her resistance slacken, then put his lips to her mouth, trying to make it a tender kiss.

"Say that you love me, Renée," he said and his tone was pleading.

"You're very sweet, André," she hedged.

"And you will marry me?"

"I will consider it. I must think it over," was all the assurance she would give.

It was a scene that was to be repeated again and again, until she tormented him almost beyond endurance. He who had always slept the moment his head touched the pillow, now lay awake night after night tossing. He delayed his work, watching for her and timing his arrival in the house so as to meet her on the stairs or alone in a room. He snatched at every opportunity, and each time she added one more piece of fuel to the fire, playing with him, leading him on with passionate embraces, teasing him with visions of what the ultimate could be, seeming to be about to surrender and then denying him when his fever was at its highest.

All through the winter the game progressed, as Renée de Renault studied the situation around her, looking carefully over those in Montreal who flirted with her, weighing each possibility and then when the ice on the river broke, consented to be his wife. He had been quite prepared to have her insist upon a prolonged engagement but it seemed that once she had arrived at a decision, she no longer hesitated. Contrary to his expectations she consented to an early wedding and they set the day for May, following the Lenten and Easter season.

The wedding was a great event on the Seigneuries and everything was done to make it as festive as possible. Paul and Ann spent the night with Elise and Antoine, leaving early the following morning for Three Rivers where they would spend a few days with a married sister of Paul's whom they rarely saw now. It had been planned thus, so as to leave the newly-weds to themselves, since they had decided not to go to Quebec. This had really been André's decision and one to which it had not been easy to get Renée to agree. Though André would not have admitted it, even to himself, he was tired of the dissipations of the winter and the thought of continuing in Quebec for several months was disagreeable to him. He was forcing his nature to do something against which it revolted. Furthermore he felt it was time Renée should begin to understand how life was lived on a seigneury. He had hoped that they could have been married soon after Christmas and so still have several months of leisure before them. But because of Renée's procrastination this was now impossible.

On the morning following his wedding, André stood a long time by the river, looking out over the blue water and trying to work out, for his own satisfaction at least, some doubts which were troubling him. The consummation of his marriage the night before had been everything that he could have wished, everything that from his courtship he had been led to believe it would be. The woman he had taken as his wife had a deep, rich passion, with an experience that had made it idyllic. Yet it was this experience that now worried him, for he had found he was not the first who had enjoyed the richness of her passion. He kept turning it over in his mind and arguing with himself that she was nearly thirty years old and therefore he could not expect her to be as virginal as a young girl. He was quite well aware that in France, and even in the colony, women had lovers but he was jealous of these lovers. He was tormented by wondering how many lovers there had been and who they were. He kept telling himself that he should accept the satisfaction she had given him and ignore the rest.

Then there had been her attitude during the wedding feast. Towards the de Longueils, and the de Ramezays and others of the nobility she had been ingratiating, but towards the habitants her manner had been patronizing. Before the day was over André had felt a growing resentment. As usual the feast had culminated in dancing and singing around the open fires and André had suggested to Renée that, as was customary, they visit each group. But she had declined, covering her refusal, however, in such a way that he could not say anything. Looking deep into his eyes she had murmured seductively:

"Let us go away and be alone. We have waited so long. I want you."

No man in love could refuse such an invitation. Yet as he now looked over the Seigneuries, still untidy from last night's festivities, he wondered what the habitants had thought when they had not appeared. Would they feel slighted, or would they understand?

He thought it over with a lover's tolerance and told himself he must give her time to adjust herself. He went inside and ran into Mère Clarissa, who with her husband had for some years been their servants. She was coming down the stairs, a deep frown on her face, which faded as she saw André and turned into a smile. André was her favorite, and she gave him a pleasant: "Bon jour, Monsieur André."

"A very wonderful morning, Mère Clarissa," he replied gaily. "The happiest morning of my life. Marriage is wonderful, my dear."

"You shouldn't have wasted so many years then," she replied.

"Ah, but it was worth waiting for. Have you been up to my wonderful wife?"

"I'm just going to get Madame's hot chocolate," she replied. There was a slightly sarcastic note in the way in which she said the "Madame" but André was too much in love to notice it.

"Then she is awake. I must go up," he said and bounded up the stairs, bursting into the bedroom, his arms wide to gather up his wife. But before he could reach her she reproved him with:

"Really, André, must you rush into the room like a bull! Do please remember that you now have a wife and that she doesn't like her room besieged."

He stopped abruptly, looking very much like Paul-André used to look when he was reprimanded.

"I'm so sorry, darling. It was thoughtless of me. I shall have to improve my manners." With that he plomped onto the bed and drew her to him kissing her ardently and stopping fresh protests that were on the tip of her tongue. In a moment she pushed him away with a rather irritable:

"Please, André, not so rough. I'm tired. Surely you can understand that."

"But you look so lovely, darling."

Probably no one else would have thought so. The rouge which she had not removed the night before stood out in hard blotches and there were dark circles under her eyes. And her irritability made her mouth a hard line and her onyx eyes sharp.

"Mère Clarissa is bringing up your hot chocolate. Take your time drinking it and rest awhile."

"That's what I intend to do. I don't like getting up early in the morning."

"That's all right, darling. Get up when you want to."

"And, André, please have a bell rope put near the bed. I had to get up and shout several times before Clarissa came."

André looked up, rather puzzled and said: "Bell rope? Why, yes, of course. We've never had them." He could have added that none of the women in his family had ever had time to lie in bed. "I shall see about it. I'll have to go into Montreal and get a bell."

She was regarding his homespun clothes. "Surely you're not working today?"

"Only for a little while, just until you get up. There are so many things to do at this time of the year."

"Let the farmhands do it then," she said sharply.

He did not feel like having an argument, so replied: "By the time you are up I shall be all clean and dressed, darling."

Mère Clarissa came into the room. There was no smile on her face.

"Ah, here's your hot chocolate," André said and took it. He put it down on the table and when Mère Clarissa had gone out said: "One more kiss and then I'll leave you alone."

She gave it to him but he could not stir her to any warmth.

The argument which Andrè had avoided that morning, came up again in the evening as he and Renée sat before the fire after supper. He had only worked until dinner, by which time Renée was up and dressed. Then he had changed into broadcloth and had driven her into Montreal to shop.

With an idea of acquainting her with the many responsibilities of running a seigneury, he began talking to her of his plans for the new season that had just started. She listened patiently for a few moments and then said:

"But you're a seigneur, André."

"No I'm not, my father is," he replied shortly.

"Well, you're his heir and entitled to the same privileges."

"What privileges?"

"The privilege of not having to work like a farmhand."

"You don't understand, my dear," he explained. "In this colony seigneurs and habitants work side by side."

"Oh I don't know ..."

"But I *do* know," he told her firmly. "After all I have lived here all my life ..."

"That's just it. You have the farming habit and can't see that things have changed."

"Oh, is that so?" he said and gave her a half-smile. "Who gave you this interesting information?"

"The Chevalier de Breslau."

"And what does he know about it? If I recollect he has been here only a short time and anyway is a government official and not of the land."

"And just because he is a government official he is in a position to see the changes. You are so close to things that you are not able to observe. He told me that in the early days permission had been given to gentlemen to work without it being derogatory to their position but that nowadays gentlemen felt it was becoming derogatory."

"Very interesting, my dear," André replied and not without some sarcasm, "but I am afraid you have been misinformed. We might as well understand each other from the beginning. I come from a family of pioneers who have always worked the land and I shall continue to do as they have done. Maybe you should have considered this before you married me and have married this Chevalier de Breslau." The anger in his tone increased.

Renée looked at him and smiled. "Thank you. I refused him," she said. She noted the sharp look that came into André's face at the mention of another proposal. "Did you think you were the only one who wanted to marry me?" she asked tauntingly.

"Obviously not," he replied. "What I don't understand is why you chose me…"

"Obviously because I preferred you," she said and let her voice drop to a low tone. André's eyes softened. It was always to be this way with their arguments. She had only to give her eyes that smoldering look to have him at her feet.

"I am glad you preferred me," he said as he gathered her into his arms. "But if you preferred me you must accept me as I am," he added.

"We shall see," she said slowly.

# CHAPTER TWENTY-FOUR

S PRING changed into summer and André changed as imperceptibly as the season. His happy, carefree nature became tense and irritable—tense because of his desire to make his marriage happy, and irritable because he was aware of a growing antagonism in his family towards his wife. Whereas hitherto he had never found it necessary to analyse himself and watch what he did, he now was constantly introspective. He decided that his parents had spoiled him, for they had never found fault with him and now he so often seemed to be doing or saying the wrong thing. His manners were gauche, his dress untidy and he smelled of the barn. So Renée told him. Pondering over these things, all too frequently he left the work he was doing, to go back to the house to see whether everything was all right with Renée—usually to find that his trouble was unnecessary and appeared stupid. Then at night when he lay with his head cradled in her arms and she was so responsive to his love, all the doubts and worries of the day appeared needless. He was sure then that she loved him, mistaking intense passion for the warmth of love.

One of the things that worried him most was whether he was doing right in continuing to live at the Manor House. By custom, he should now have taken his portion of land and have built his own house. With the crowded condition of the Seigneury this would have been a disadvantage and it seemed rather unnecessary to build another house when there was so much room in the Manor House. In the evenings his mother and father always retired to the library, leaving the rest of the house to him and his wife. Often it was only at meal times that they all met.

Furthermore, despite all hints that André might give, or arguments that arose between them, Renée adhered to her idea that the wife of a seigneur should be a lady and live as one. She never appeared before noon and André could not see how they could run a house of their own this way. His mother was tactful about it and though she herself had probably been up since daylight, when Renée appeared she was always charming and gracious. Ann ignored Mère Clarissa's grumbles over having to answer the bell that had now been installed in the bedroom, and at times when Clarissa was in a bad mood and refused to take up the hot chocolate, she took it up herself.

When it came to the fruit season and the kitchen buzzed with activity, Ann did make a veiled suggestion to Renée that she should help.

"This is our busy time in the kitchen, my dear," she commented one noon as Renée made her appearance. "The men are bringing in the fruit. Are you fond of fruit?" she asked.

"Oh yes," Renée replied casually.

"It is so nice to have such quantities that we can preserve them for the winter. You must, of course, have put up plenty yourself…"

"I? Oh no! I have never done so. You forget that I was brought up in France…"

"No, I didn't forget it. I was also brought up there…" Ann answered.

"And did you preserve fruit then?" The tone was slightly sarcastic and Ann did not fail to notice it. She calmed her rising anger and said quietly, a patient smile on her face:

"Here women have to do many things, my dear, that they did not do in France."

"So I have observed," Renée replied and nothing more was said.

But that night, Renée had more to say to André. As they were preparing for bed she remarked: "Your mother certainly lowers herself by working in the kitchen."

André replied quietly: "My mother never lowers herself, Renée."

"That is a matter of opinion."

"Not the opinion of those who know her. My mother is too cultured a woman *ever* to lower herself. A cultured lady knows that she can go into the kitchen and help, particularly here, and yet retain her dignity."

"And you expect me to do those things?"

"If my mother can, I don't see why you can't."

"Because I don't intend to, André. As you once said to me, we might as well understand each other from the beginning. If you choose to work in the fields, then you must do so. But I shall not demean myself with menial tasks. I have never been used to it in France and ..."

"And neither had my mother. She was brought up in the highest circles ..."

"At the Court of Versailles! Am I never to cease hearing that!" Renée retorted angrily.

André ignored the remark and continued with what he was saying: "And when she became the wife of a Seigneur, she adapted herself to the life. After all, if a woman who lived in Paris can do these things surely you, who were a native of Brittany ..."

She ceased brushing her long hair and swung round to face him. "A Breton is as good as a Parisian. Don't you dare say such a thing again!"

"Then don't criticize my mother." André's equable temper was frayed these days. It was becoming as inflammable as his red hair indicated. "You should have considered these things before you married me, Renée. I told you what it would be like and I wish you had thought of it before you became my wife."

"It is too late now," she retorted.

Vicious words came to André's lips but he did not utter them. Angrily he turned away and climbed into bed, lying with his arms behind his head and staring up at the ceiling. Through her mirror Renée watched him. Though it pleased her to enslave him, she knew enough not to goad him too far. A half-smile played about her lips as she finished brushing her hair. She knew that she could easily make him forget his anger—she knew that he could not resist her however irritated he might be. She blew out the candle and nestled up to him. His anger faded.

It was a little less than three months later that Ann received a shock that she was never to forget. She was distributing the clean linen to each of the bedrooms. She knocked on the door of Renée's bedroom and receiving no answer presumed the room to be empty. She opened the door and then stood there, horrified by what she saw. Renée was hanging from the top of a cupboard door, stretching and jerking her body. At her feet a stool was overturned.

In a quick glance Ann took in the situation, realizing the intention behind her daughter-in-law's strange behavior. For some time she had had the suspicion that Renée might be pregnant but as neither André nor his wife had mentioned it, she kept her own counsel. Now she knew.

Quickly Renée slid to her feet and turned on her mother-in-law a look of such deadly hatred that Ann was startled. The two women faced each other, fury blazing from their dark eyes.

"How dare you do such a thing to my son?" Ann said, her voice vibrant with anger.

"What do you mean, Madame?" Never once had Renée addressed her other than formally.

"You know what I mean. I have suspected this for some time."

"So you came spying to find out," Renée sneered. "I despise people who spy!"

"And I despise women who destroy the life within them. Have you no religion as well as no regard for the man you married?"

"I would have more regard for you if you attended to your own business and did not not come into my room without knocking."

"I knocked but you did not answer. I thought you were out and was going to leave these." She tossed some clean linen on the bed.

"It's bad enough having to share a house with my husband's parents let alone having them watching me suspiciously all the time," Renée snapped.

Ann ignored the remark. Slowly she walked towards her daughter-in-law, her expression so menacing that Renée stepped back expecting Ann to strike her. But Ann kept her clenched fists by her sides. All the anger and hatred that she had felt for months now rose to the surface.

"Why did you marry my son?" she asked, the words seething through her teeth. Renée did not answer. "I'll tell you why you did," Ann continued, "because your peasant mind thought it would make you a great lady. You've done everything you can to destroy my son's happiness. It was a sad day for us when I invited you to become our guest."

With that she turned and left the room, before her control should break and she should give way to her desire to slap Renée.

A few days later the baby miscarried. Ann had told no one of the spectacle she had witnessed but she had to confess to Father Xavier that as she saw Renée writhing in pain she had wished she would die. She forced herself to assist only for André's sake and because she must be humane.

André was in the fields when it occurred and he came running when he learned that his wife had been taken ill. Renée had not told him that she was with child. When she had refused his attentions in the past weeks, he had put it down to her strange temperament, though secretly harboring the hope that some day soon she might have news for him.

Aunt Marie had been sent for and she and his mother were working over Renée when he rushed into the room.

"What has happened? She is ill?" he exclaimed, though the latter was quite evident.

His mother turned quickly and motioned him outside. "I will be with you in a moment, André. There is nothing that you can do. Leave us now," she said and he obeyed.

As soon as possible she went to him and explained as delicately as she could, trying to keep the bitterness out of her voice, bitterness that increased when she saw his distress.

"You're sure she is all right?" he asked several times. "Poor Renée. To think that I should have made her suffer like this!"

Ann turned away, trying to hide her hatred and contempt of the woman he pitied so. From that day on the house was divided. Ann never spoke to Renée except when politeness necessitated.

# CHAPTER TWENTY-FIVE

AFTER the death of her husband, Madame la Marquise de Vaudreuil returned to take up her residence in Montreal. At fifty-five she was a woman of handsome dignity and around her revolved the social life of the town. She had given the Marquis ten children, of whom there remained four sons and two daughters, both now married. All four sons had entered the army, though the second, Philippe-Antoine, had been destined by his father for the church. Philippe-Antoine, however, had no taste for a religious life and went to France and became a soldier. Of all the sons, the third, Pierre de Cavagnal, now twenty-nine, showed the most promise. The previous year he had been created Chevalier de Saint-Louis and would eventually occupy a position of great importance in the colony, though he was to end in disgrace.

The highlight of the winter season of 1727-1728 was the opening of the Chateau de Vaudreuil, commenced five years earlier by the Marquis. The erection of this magnificent edifice on a tract of land between the Rue St. Paul and the Rue Notre Dame added to the pride of Montreal. To celebrate its opening, Madame gave a grand ball to which all the nobility and seigneurs and the more important merchants were invited.

Antoine and Elise attended the ball with Jean-Baptiste. Ann-Marie and her husband also were there with a party from the de Ramezay Chateau. She was now expecting her first baby and it would have been difficult to say who were the more excited— the de Ramezays or the de Brievaux. She attended the ball but only as an observer which was a little irksome as she delighted in being in the center of things. Those from the de Courville Manor were, of course, invited but only André and Renée attended. Ann pleaded a headache at the last moment, which was an excuse as she had not intended to go although she would have enjoyed it. Because of the incident which had occurred, she preferred not to be in the same company as her daughter-in-law.

It would have sickened her had she seen Renée flaunting her charms to a cirle of men at the ball. She heard it later from Elise but made no comment. André had the first dance with his wife and then finding that all the rest were taken, he retired to the card-room. He was a poor dancer, as she made a point of telling him, and he therefore did not blame her for dancing with other men who could match her own grace. In the cardroom he found his old friend, the Sieur de la Vérendrye and immediately his boredom vanished.

"It seems to take a ball for us to meet!" La Vérendrye laughed as they clasped hands.

"*Sacré bleu!* What brings you here?" André asked.

"And I ask you the same question or have you now become a frequenter of the high life?"

"Meaning what?" André asked, a broad smile on his face.

"I hear you have married at last..."

"Yes and when you see my wife you will see how wise I was to wait..."

"I have seen her and met her," La Vérendrye said, jabbing André in the ribs.

"Oh, and where?"

La Vérendrye signalled with his head to the ballroom. "The Chavalier de Breslau introduced me. He had been dancing with her."

A frown flashed almost imperceptibly across André's face, but he covered it with a cheerful smile: "She is very popular. And as you know I am not much of a dancer. But we are wasting time.

Let us find some seats. I want to hear what you have been doing. How about the western journey?"

They pushed their way through the crowd of men standing around watching those at the card tables and found two seats over by the wall. There, fortified with glasses of brandy, they talked.

"The best I have been able to secure is command of the small trading post on Lac Nipigon ..." La Vérendrye said.

"North of Lac Superior?"

La Vérendrye nodded.

"But that's going to be very much out of the way, isn't it?" André asked.

La Vérendrye sighed and sipped his brandy slowly. "Yes, but it's something. I'm just rotting away in Three Rivers."

"When do you leave?"

"I don't know yet."

"And the western project is dead?"

La Vérendrye's face brightened a little. "I had thought so. When the Marquis de Vaudreuil died I lost my best connection with France. But Madame la Marquise told me yesterday that while she was in Quebec she spoke of the project to Governor de Beauharnois and that he seemed interested. She is using her influence with him."

"Then it may be revived?"

"Yes."

As La Vérendrye expounded upon new theories which he had developed for the discovery of the western ocean, the name of Madame la Marquise came in frequently. While he listened André wondered how many of the rumors regarding La Vérendrye and the Marquise were true. If they had any foundation then their discretion was to be applauded for they were never seen together.

"Madame la Marquise has always been very interested in your expedition to the west," André said hoping to lead La Vérendrye on. But he might have known better than to try. La Vérendrye was much too clever to be led into anything and André's was not a subtle nature.

"Yes, she has always been keenly interested. In fact, it was she rather than her husband who kept France's interest alive, though of course it was done through the Marquis. She was, as you must have known, always the power behind her husband." La Vérendrye smiled knowingly. He then changed the subject. "And you've given up the adventurous life and become a farmer?"

"Yes," André said slowly, "but the spirit is always there, Pierre."

"Of course. Men like you and me can't remain quiet for long."

"I have for over seven years now," André said and couldn't conceal the sigh in his voice.

"You'll break out again. I can tell it by your manner."

"If ever you get your expedition together, Pierre, come what may, I'll join you. I have dreamed of it too long, to be able to give up *that* idea."

"We've dreamed of it for years. If I were wealthy I'd arrange it myself. I *know*, André that there must be a vast country beyond here. And if we don't discover it, the English will. They're active now." He drained his brandy. His eyes were ablaze with eagerness and his hands fidgeted nervously.

"How about Madame la Marquise? She is wealthy isn't she?" André asked.

"Not sufficiently so for such a project. And then it isn't only the financial side. One must have support or at least belief in what one is doing. There is so much opposition."

They talked of it a long time until the cardroom had begun to empty and André had to seek Renée. He felt guilty because he had neglected her all the evening, though from the radiant look on her face, she had been employing her time well. On the way home he found it difficult to listen to her chatter of the ball, because his thoughts were flying westward and the old longing for the adventurous wilds was gnawing at him.

The Marquis de Beauharnois had not been long in showing that he was a Governor who did not intend to sit idly by. He studied the situation keenly and found many difficulties confronting him. The chains which held the two dogs at bay were growing weaker and some of the links threatened to give way at any moment. He tried to strengthen these links and one of his first moves was to start a correspondence with English Governor William Burnet at New York, relative to a fort and trading post which was being erected at Oswego on Lac Ontario with a view to diverting the Indian trade to Albany. The two Governors argued and threatened. The French dared not attack Oswego since it would undoubtedly be the match which would set a new war aflame between the two countries. Beauharnois, therefore, set to work to improve the French fort at Niagara, the key to the Great Lakes and one of the most strategic positions, since it closed all access to the Upper Lakes.

Niagara was, however, in the Iroquois territory and to provoke this savage tribe was more dangerous than any provocation of the English, since the English claimed that the Iroquois were their subjects and would come to their defense. Beauharnois despatched the Baron de Longueil to Onondaga, the seat of the Iroquois government, to obtain their permission to erect the fort at Niagara. No one was better known to the Indians than de Longueil who had on many former occasions used his eloquence to advantage with the tribes. At Onondaga he had a powerful ally in the person of an officer named Joncaire, who was the French agent among the Senecas, the division of the Iroquois nation nearest to Niagara. Joncaire had been adopted as an Iroquois and his influence among them was powerful. Governor Burnet had sent a message to the Senecas urging them to hinder the erection of the fort at Niagara and this they endeavored to do before they were persuaded by Joncaire that it would be to their advantage. Then they gave their consent and the work of the fort continued, making it one of the most important forts belonging to the French.

The two fierce dogs now had their teeth bared. Burnet strengthened Oswego and Beauharnois Niagara. But it was Oswego that became the center of the Indian trade while Niagara, despite its more favorable position, was comparatively slighted by the Western tribes.

At the same time another great danger threatened trade—the antagonistic and warlike Outagamies or Foxes, about whom Governor de Vaudreuil had repeatedly warned the colony, were again giving trouble. This tribe had its home on the Fox River of Green Bay,—named after them. Nearly all the tribes in the lake district were their hereditary enemies and on the slightest pretext the young men of the tribe would seek bloody revenge with a fury which their elders were powerless to restrain.

The only solution would have been to exterminate them but for this the French did not have the men or supplies. Time and again they had been crippled, which only increased their ferocity and hate. Governor de Beauharnois was averse to violent measures, realizing that unless they were completely successful, the life of every Frenchman in the west would be jeopardized. Nevertheless, the time had now arrived when something must be done and he began to lay careful plans for an attack within the near future. He was hampered in his plans by the Intendant, Dupuy, who, as had been suspected, was proving a very difficult official. One of his first demands had been for two armed men to be posted beside his pew in church, which even allowing for the ceremonial spirit of the day, was a demand which caused ridicule. He was constantly quarrelling with the Governor, and at this time sent a communication to Versailles in which he declared that de Beauharnois' intention to make war against the Foxes was only a pretext for spending the King's money and for enriching himself by buying up all the furs in the territory that would be traversed by the army.

The government of the colony was difficult enough without all these internal dissensions and the constant accusation levelled at the heads of all governors that they were trying to fill their own pockets. Despite all, however, de Beauharnois persisted in the measures that he thought right and began preparations for an expedition against the Foxes. Interest in the project increased when the *coureurs de bois* brought further disconcerting rumors to Montreal.

The ice broke on the river that year of 1728 about April 15th and a month later flotillas of canoes came down to Montreal bringing the *coureurs de bois* and their bales of pelts. As every year, the annual fair turned the town into a bedlam, with men drinking and trading, fighting and gambling. No women, except those who plied their trade, ventured into the town during this week. The taverns and wineshops did a thriving trade and the *coureurs de bois,* nearly as naked as their Indian friends, strutted about the streets, getting into fights and brawls and trying to filch the profits from their neighbors by gambling or robbery.

These men brought with them stories of the unrest in the territory of the Foxes; of onslaughts which this vicious tribe had made upon other of the northern tribes. Their reports coincided with orders which Governor de Longueil had received from the Governor-General to mobilize all the men he could in addition to the regular soldiers. The Sieur de Lignery arrived from Quebec, with power to command the expedition. Before the week of the Fair was ended, he had recruited many men from the *coureurs de bois,* for these intrepid men were invaluable to such an expedition. And among those recruited was André de Courville-Boissart. Despite Renée's objections he had gone into Montreal, unable to resist seeing some of his *coureur de bois* friends. He had met many and had been welcomed by them and returned that night far from sober. He was drunk enough to admit to himself what he had hitherto refused to do—that his marriage had been a mistake. He realized it as he approached his house. Not many times in his life had he come home inebriated and when he had there had been no one to reproach him. Now it would be different and he began to rebel, though the extent of his rebellion was to go to his old room to sleep so that he did not disturb his wife.

By the next morning the Seigneuries were abuzz with the news of the expedition and many of the habitants had been called to join. When André informed them that he had been called, the objections he had expected came from Renée.

His reply was unexpectedly terse. "In this colony, my dear, all men answer the call. That is why we have a militia and it is not a matter of choice, it is a matter of duty."

Later in the day, Jean-Baptiste de Brievaux stopped in to bid them goodbye. He was on his way to resume his duties at the Montreal garrison. He and Jean-Baptiste de Ramezay would both have to go and because of their military training would undoubtedly be put in charge of companies.

"I wish I were young enough to go," Paul said.

"You've had your share," Ann said quietly. She knew that Paul's remark was sincere although she suspected it was made for Renée's benefit.

"What about Antoine? Will he go?" Ann asked.

"I don't believe so, unless he volunteers."

"Then why do you have to go, André?" Renée asked quickly. "Antoine's the same age as you, isn't he?"

"But he's a seigneur and I'm a *coureur de bois,* or was. We are the most intrepid fighters, my dear, and also know more about Indians and the type of fighting that is required."

She did not answer. She gave André a penetrating glance. He had not been able to conceal that he was looking forward to the expedition.

And not only in Montreal was the call heard. Throughout the territory of the northern tribes, came the steady beat of the tom-tom and the Mohawks of Caughnawaga sat in council, with Paul-André witnessing for the first time a tribal preparation for war.

# CHAPTER TWENTY-SIX

O N THE 5th of June, 1728 a flotilla of birch-bark canoes carrying five hundred French soldiers and several hundred Indians set out from Montreal. With them went five canoes manned by *coureurs de bois* with André in charge. All along the route the banks of the river were lined with people, watching—as many of them had done so many times before—these men who were ready to risk their lives that the colony might continue to thrive. They watched until the last sound of the canoe-men's songs had died away in the distance. Then they went back to their work, many with heavy hearts and fears that their men might never return.

The light of dawn had not long broken through the darkness when they started but by the time they reached the de Courville and the de Brievaux seigneuries the sun was beginning to come up, shedding its radiance—and its heat—upon them. Mothers anxiously scanned the canoes for a last glimpse of their sons and wives of their husbands. To the surprise of Ann and Paul, Renée had come down to join them. They made no comment, except later to each other. André saw her and waved frantically, his face radiant with joy. He was leaving with mixed feelings, the joy of freedom now marred by his reluctance to leave his wife because of the attitude she had chosen to take during the preceding weeks.

Renée knew all the artifices of holding a man. She knew that had she nagged at him he would have been all the more pleased to get away. She took the opposite course, knowing that her power lay in her passionate nature which she exercised to the full. Every night she had come eagerly to his embrace and the day before he had left she had played her most important card.

The entire body of men had been ordered to report in Montreal by noon of the day before in order to get the company organized for the early morning start. André had breakfasted with his parents, Ann being scarcely able to refrain from comment when Renée did not join them on his last morning. André went upstairs to bid Renée goodbye and found her lying in bed with the curtains drawn back. She had laid the scene carefully. While he breakfasted she had removed the ravages of the night, dressed her hair so that it fell in long curls over each shoulder and had applied fresh rouge and powder. When he came in, she held out her arms to him and his heart leapt as he rushed to her embrace. Never once had she uttered the words, "I love you," nor at this time did she say, "I shall miss you," though he had uttered the phrases a dozen or more times. Now as he embraced her with a long ardent kiss she said in a low tone: "Draw the curtains, André."

For a moment he did not understand, until he looked into her eyes and saw that they were soft as black velvet. A half-smile played around her lips as she loosened her nightgown at the throat. Behind the seclusion of the drawn bed curtains, he once more floated into the world of ecstasy over which she held mastery. All other thoughts, all regrets and rebellions were thrust aside as she deluged him with her passion that seemed unbounded. Through a haze he heard the Angelus sound—the first time he had ever heard it in bed—and knew that he should by that time have been in Montreal. Yet in the dim light around them, she lay against the pillow relaxed and with the radiance that satisfied desire brings to a woman's face. Once more he drank from her soft yielding lips, caressing her body and never knowing that within her she was laughing and saying: "I'll make you sorry that you wished to leave me." He was. He could not tear himself away and again and again went back to drink from the tantalizing cup that she held to his lips. Now he wished that she would push him away as she had done oftentimes before but instead she lay there with lips half-parted, yielding to his slightest touch. With a wrench he tore himself from her, hastily dressed and hurried to the door, only to fall into the temptation of looking back and with that returning. She stroked his wavy hair and touched his lips with the tips of her fingers and once more he strained her to him. "Tell me to go, Renée, tell me!" he urged, but she only smiled. He staggered from the room in a daze.

That was the memory he took with him the morning he left and all the feelings she had stirred up in him returned as he saw her standing with his parents on the riverbank. He wanted to plunge into the water and swim to her. The song he had been singing died on his lips. Father Xavier who was in the same canoe watched him. The old man had a mind that was keenly observant. He had seen the struggle André had had with his marriage and as his father confessor knew many things.

Father Xavier had gone along with the expedition as chaplain at his own request. His services were welcomed, for his knowledge of the country they would traverse as well as his command of the Indian languages would be invaluable. Though nearing sixty his energy and powers of endurance were amazing and the fact that he travelled with the *coureurs de bois* instead of with the Sieur de Lignery was considered very broadminded, though actually it was his own preference because of his fondness for André.

The contingent took the famed route of the *coureurs de bois,* making portage over the Lachine Rapids and pausing at Caughnawaga to pick up six more canoes. As they approached, André strained his eyes to see whether Paul-André, now Ours-feu, was among the Mohawks lined up on the bank ready to leap into the waiting canoes. With the "disguise" that Ours-feu had now adopted it was difficult to recognize him, though from the bank Paul-André easily recognized his uncle's red hair. He set his face trying not to show the emotion he felt.

It had been hard these past days to hide his excitement for this was his first expedition with his Indian friends and he was proud that they had included him. For several days he had sat around the council fire, smoking the calumet adorned with the red feathers of war, marvelling at the preparations, listening to the Chiefs harangue the younger men and admiring the younger braves who one by one jumped up and in long speeches recited their various exploits. From such they would be chosen and Ours-feu longed for the day when he, too, could recite exploits of his own. Like them he had daubed his face with war paint so that no sign of fear should be noticeable on his countenance. He had stained his body with walnut juice so that now he seemed as dark as they. Only when the men climbed into their canoes was André sure that Ours-feu was among them for after one man jumped a brown dog.

They took the rugged route along the Ottawa River whose brown waters flowed for a time side by side with the blue of the St. Lawrence but did not deign to mingle. The Ottawa was wide and filled with rapids that necessitated many portages. Beyond, its banks were lined with dark impenetrable forests whose stern depths looked silent and forbidding. They passed through the territory of the Algonquins, traversed the two lakes of the Allumettes and then for twenty miles or more the river stretched before them straight and black, between mountain shores. At Lake Nipissing they were greeted by the friendly tribe of the Nipissings, the savage race which had given its name to the lake. Thence across the northern tip of the Georgian Bay they entered Lac Huron and skirting its northern border reached the fur traders' paradise—Michilimackinac. It was midsummer by the time they reached the trading post where they paused for supplies and further additions to their company.

For over half a century Michilimackinac had been the center of the western fur trade because of its strategic position which gave easy access for the Indians and traders from the north and west and those who came to it from Montreal. Many *coureurs de bois* had now made their permanent residence at the post, taking Indian squaws as wives, with or without the benefit of the Church. Here they lived lives of debauchery and licentiousness with every dwelling place a tavern and every tavern a brothel. The initial purpose of the settlement had been a mission, but neither the Church nor the military could exercise any authority over the lawless inhabitants. High up on a hill stood the fort, badly in need of repair. It looked down from its height upon the bark cabins of the Hurons and the clustered wigwams of the Ottawas. If the white man scorned the red man, the latter in turn despised the white man and not without good reason. Far from attempting to check the debaucheries, the officers of the garrison encouraged them and made use of the squaws who used the place as a resort. Officers and men alike were engaged in the fur trade and as long as he received a supply of brandy, the Indian gave no thought to whether the trader operated within the law. Here man made his own laws and there was little redress against wrongs. The Indian and the *eau de vie* did not make good companions and many a savage found that with his senses dulled by brandy, he had been robbed or tricked of all the furs for which he had endured a bitter winter. At intervals the Church had attempted to ban the sale of brandy to the Indian but on this subject the traders could argue effectively. Unless they traded brandy for furs, the savages took their pelts to the English and traded them for rum and without the fur trade the backbone of the colony was broken.

The arrival of the expedition set all the town ablaze with excitement. Indian girls rushed to the banks as the men pulled in the canoes and hung on to their arms offering themselves as companions as long as the men should remain there. It was all that the officers and leaders could do to keep any order among their men. The Sieur de Lignery and his officers made their way up to the fort, while the leaders among the Indians made arrangements for the setting up of their tents along the shores. The *coureurs de bois* knew their way about the town too well to need any direction. To them it was familiar territory. André left them to themselves with orders to report at dawn the following day. Before going into the town to greet his many friends he sought out Paul-André. He had hoped to be able to have a word with Jean-Baptiste to tell him he was certain Paul-André was with them, but Jean-Baptiste, now a lieutenant and de Ramezay with the rank of captain had both had to follow the Sieur de Lignery. Father Xavier excused himself and went up to the mission to visit with the priest who had taken his place there.

Paul-André saw his uncle as he approached and came to meet him. The sight of Paul-André with face and body striped with war paint and head shaved, except for the forelock which was black with bear grease, brought a shock that André could hardly conceal. It was hard to believe that this tall, lithe Indian before him was really his nephew. He seemed years older than fourteen, for the lines on his face had deepened with outdoor living and experience.

André looked up at him with a smile, and despite the changes which had brought a shock, he could not help feeling admiration for the boy.

"I was hoping that you might be coming along with us, Oursfeu," André said. He used the Indian name because he knew it would please him.

"It was a wonderful surprise to me, Uncle," Paul-André said. He spoke in French and André noticed how his voice had deepened. He was glad to find that he had not forgotten his native tongue. "I had not known that there would be *coureurs de bois* in the expedition and even if I had I would not have expected to see you among them."

"I am their leader as a matter of fact," André said with forgivable pride.

"Are you voyaging then once more?"

"No, this is my first expedition since I gave up the fur trade. I am a married man now ..."

"Oh!" Paul-André registered surprise. "To whom?" he asked.

"To a lady you never met. She arrived in Montreal about a year and a half ago to visit your grandparents. Her uncle was once a bondsman of my father's. I have been married a year now."

"Oh. And have I some cousins I know nothing about?"

André shook his head and said quickly: "Not yet." He changed the subject then and said. "Your brother is with us and also your brother-in-law—Ann-Marie's husband, young de Ramezay. You remember him?"

"Yes, of course."

"They're up at the fort. They're officers as you know. I wasn't able to catch Jean-Baptiste to tell him you were among us."

"You saw me as we took to the canoes?"

"No, I saw this." He pointed to the dog who walked at Paul-André's heels. "She's remained very faithful."

"She never leaves me. I don't know how she will fare on the trip—it's her first one and mine too. Oure is with us, in fact he's one of the leaders. Will you come and see him?"

"Presently. But first I would like to chat with you. Tell me about yourself. You're happy still?"

Paul-André immediately retired within himself. Not even with André did he want to discuss his life. "Yes," he said rather tersely, and then inquired after his mother.

"She is very well, Paul-André. Your sister will give us an addition to the family soon."

Paul-André nodded. "What about Jean-Baptiste? Has he married?"

"No, not yet. He will want to see you."

"Will he? I wonder."

Paul-André had to wonder for some time, for the officers remained up at the fort, having a ribald evening and André did not see Jean-Baptiste until they were ready to embark the next morning. Then there was only time to say: "Paul-André is with us, Jean-Baptiste."

André saw the expression change on Jean-Baptiste's face. "I wondered about it when I saw the Indians joining us at Caughnawaga. How is he?"

"Fine. You'll find him changed though. He seems much older."

Jean-Baptiste's eyes strayed to the far end of the long line of canoes, trying to catch a glimpse of a red head, not realizing how great a change he would find in his brother. "I'll see him at the first opportunity," he said. "Unfortunately, there isn't time now. Thank you for letting me know, Uncle."

The flotilla of canoes started off, the regulars leading the way and as they passed the Indians, Jean-Baptiste tried unsuccessfully to spot his brother. With the Indians who had joined them at Michilimackinac there were now over a thousand, as well as the five hundred soldiers and *coureurs de bois*. The long and impressive line of canoes paddled across the northern end of Lac Michigan until they reached the fort at the head of Green Bay, where they made camp and prepared for the final lap of their journey which would take them into the Outagamie or Fox territory.

Hardly was the camp set up than there was the first excitement as a Fox Indian and three Winnebagoes were captured and brought in. The Sieur de Lignery made short work of them by turning them over to his Indian allies to dispense with in their own manner. The savages prepared for a night of enjoyment. The four captives were tied to posts and put to slow torture. When Father Xavier saw what was about to happen he hastened to the commandant and lodged a protest. The Sieur de Lignery listened dispassionately and then said:

"Father, I understood you had had much experience among the savages."

"So I have and that is why I am making this protest." Father Xavier met the challenge.

"But surely you must know that it is customary to turn Indian captives over to their own people..."

"These are not their own people. They are opposing tribes..."

"How else do you expect me to keep our Indian allies content unless I follow their customs and it is always the custom in times of war to let them do as they please with captured savages."

"And you will allow them to proceed with this torture?"

De Lignery merely shrugged his shoulders and repeated: "It is the custom, Father."

By the time Father Xavier returned it was too late to save the unfortunate Indians. Red-hot ramrods were being thrust into their ears and noses. Hands and feet were slowly severed as well as other sensitive parts and these were stuck on top of the stake to which the victim was tied. At their feet, or what were now the stubs of their feet, slow fires were built and the miserable captives roasted alive, while their captors danced around them.

It was unfortunate that this should have occurred on the evening which was the first opportunity that Jean-Baptiste had of seeing his brother. Paul-André was standing on the outskirts of the group of Indians who were watching the tortures and was feeling nauseated at the sight yet not daring to show his feelings because Oure was standing beside him. He turned to look at Oure but his expression was inscrutable.

"An Indian custom?" he asked.

Oure nodded.

"And you approve of it?" he continued.

Oure slowly turned his eyes to Paul-André. "We are Christian Indians," he said.

"Then you disapprove of it?" he persisted.

"It has a purpose. Until you have seen such sights without being affected, you have had no test of your courage. That is the purpose."

Paul-André felt a touch on his arm and turned to see André beside him.

"Your brother would like to see you, Ours-feu," André said.

Paul-André was glad of the opportunity to get away and without a word followed his uncle.

Jean-Baptiste was in his tent. André spoke to the sentry who stood by to let them enter. Then he signalled to Paul-André to go in, but did not himself enter. He thought it better for the two brothers to meet alone.

Jean-Baptiste looked up from his writing, saw the Indian before him and did not recognize him. "Yes?" he inquired in the stern tone of an officer. Paul-André smiled and a look of horror slowly crept over Jean-Baptiste's face as he recognized that smile. His eyes roved over the shorn head with the forelock, to the yellow and red stripes on the face; down the painted body to the breech-clout and again to the face.

The smile faded from Paul-André's face under the scrutiny and when Jean-Baptiste's eyes went to his face a second time there was a set look on it that showed no emotion or recognition.

"*You're* not my brother!" Jean-Baptiste said, unable to believe that the man before him could be of his own flesh and blood. "No, you can't be."

He covered his face with his hands. When he looked up again Paul-André had gone.

# CHAPTER TWENTY-SEVEN

THE expedition continued its journey, crossing the Winnebago country and paddling up the Fox River till they saw the chief village of the Outagamies,—a tract of rising ground a little above the level of the bog. They had reached their destination and everyone was on the alert. The village of bark wigwams was without palisades or defenses of any kind and a strange stillness lay over it. Fearing an ambush, the Sieur de Lignery proceeded carefully. He ordered his Indians in as an advance, and with a war-whoop they descended upon the village, dashing into the wigwams and setting fire to them—but there was no response. As de Lignery had feared from the stillness, their enemies had eluded them. Somehow they had been apprized of the approach and all that were left in the deserted village were three squaws and an old man.

The troops were enraged and the four prisoners that night suffered tortures and death worse than the previous captives. The only revenge the attackers could take was to burn the village and destroy the crops. It was small satisfaction to leave desolation behind, knowing that the carefully planned expedition had failed. Dejectedly the troops returned to their canoes and prepared to go back to Michilimackinac.

As they landed on the shore of Lac Winnebago where they would camp for the night, they encountered half a dozen Indians who had been fishing. The Sieur de Lignery immediately gave orders for their pursuit. The savages made for the forest but before entering, turned and with bravado let loose six arrows which whined through the air and found six well directed marks. Four uniformed men and two savages fell to the ground. With a howl of rage the Indians went after them, among them Oure and also Ours-feu anxious for his first taste of battle. Everything was in an uproar with officers and leaders shouting commands that in a short while brought a return of order. De Lignery despatched a troop of regulars to follow up the Indians, believing that they might be the vanguard of the Foxes from the village. But the scouts returned bearing six scalps and reported that they were all they had been able to find.

Father Xavier administered to the wounded men, five of whom had already received the last rites and were beyond further care. The sixth lingered but died during the night. By the light of dawn Father Xavier read the burial service as the dead men were interred in hastily dug graves. Jean-Baptiste de Ramezay and André stood together—Paul-André apart, his face drawn and aged as they lowered his brother into the grave. When the sod had been replaced, he walked away and sat alone, not even André venturing to break in on his grief. André had heard from Jean-Baptiste an account of the unsatisfactory meeting between the two brothers. He had talked with Jean-Baptiste and had made him see that with Paul-André's sensitivity it was up to him to make the first advance and Jean-Baptiste had promised to do so before the expedition ended. Opportunities were few because of his responsibility as a leader but it had been his intention that night when they made their first camp, to see if he could not heal the breach. He had left it too long. Paul-André could not forget the look of horror in his brother's eyes as he had said: "You're not my brother!" As he sat there he fingered the knife which Jean-Baptiste had given him and which he always carried. It seemed a symbol of the severance of their brotherly love. Paul-André thought of his father, whom Jean-Baptiste had so much resembled. He had seen the likeness as he had stood before him in his tent that evening. Jean-Baptiste who was to have carried on as

Seigneur when his father passed. And now? Paul-André held his head, and tangled thoughts milled through his mind. Brun lay at his side, her face on his knee, sensing that something was wrong with her master.

At a distance André sat watching him. Presently he moved closer and sat down beside him, neither breaking the silence for a while. Then André said: "I, too, lost a brother—also a Jean-Baptiste. He was my only brother and the elder one. It changed my life, also, Paul-André." His use of Paul-André's real name had its significance and the boy realized it. "They will need you now." The boy said nothing. He knew that his uncle was right but he must work it out in his own way.

They lingered only a few hours at Michilimackinac on the return journey. André bid goodbye to the *coureurs de bois* who left the expedition at this point. At Caughnawaga, Paul-André left them. Few words had passed between him and his uncle who had no idea whether or not the boy would return to his home. That was a question he would be asked but would not be able to answer.

As they left Caughnawaga, Captain de Ramezay handed over his command to his lieutenant and joined André in his canoe. As he shot the Lachine Rapids, André was reminded of his last journey home as a *coureur de bois* when he had had the same distressing task of bringing news of death. He had encountered it so often he should have been familiar with it, but it was something to which few ever became accustomed.

By the time they reached Montreal the first October frost was on the ground and the colony was preparing for the winter season. He and de Ramezay pulled the canoe into the bank below the de Brievaux Seigneury. Ann-Marie was visiting her mother and when they saw the two men they hurried to the *galerie* to wait for them.

"Oh, I'm so glad he has returned before the baby came," Ann-Marie said.

"Jean-Baptiste isn't with them," Elise said and there was fear in her voice.

"He's probably farther behind," Ann-Marie said. "They're still coming down."

It was true that the bevy of canoes continued to stream by but those now passing were filled with Indians. Elise knew that the officers and regulars would be in the vanguard. Before André spoke she knew.

Ann-Marie was enveloped in her husband's arms, his joy at seeing his lovely wife when he had expected to have to wait until he reached Montreal, making him forget momentarily the sad news they brought. He saw André, with his arm linked in Elise's going into the house and knew that it was better to leave them together.

"Darling, I'm sorry to bring you a shock at a time like this," he said gently.

"My brother?"

"Yes. It is the more dreadful because it was an ambush and only he and five others were killed. We had no fighting."

"And it had to be Jean-Baptiste. Oh poor mother and father. I must go to them, darling." She reached up and kissed him, burying her face for a moment or two against his shoulder as she tried to blink back the tears. "Thank God you came back to me," she murmured. "We should have an heir, dear, in a very short time."

"Do be careful. I know how you must feel about your brother and I don't want to be selfish ..."

"I know, Jean-Baptiste. Would you want to go and tell grandmother and grandfather, while I go to mother?"

"Yes, of course."

André came out as Ann-Marie entered. "I am going to find your father, dear," he said.

"I'll go to mother, Uncle," she said. He smiled at her and thought how much softer approaching motherhood had made her.

Elise was sitting by the window, gazing out, her grief controlled as they had all had to learn to do. Ann-Marie went to her and together they mingled their sorrow.

When André had talked with Antoine and walked back with him to the house, he left him and went to his own home. He met his father and mother with de Ramezay coming to the de Brievaux Seigneury and embraced them affectionately.

"Renée is waiting for you, dear," his mother said.

He nodded and hurried on. His mother's remark, made in her deep, gentle voice, surprised him, for he had known that she did not like his wife. Perhaps things had improved while he had been away. In this respect he was right. From the day he had departed, Renée had changed her policy. To Ann's surprise on the day of departure, instead of returning to her room after her early rising, she had come into the kitchen and asked if there were anything she could do. Ann had been loading her arms with provisions for the storeroom and instead of the refusal which had come instantly to her lips, she had changed it and had accepted her help.

Renée's tactics had been well thought out. From the day that Ann had discovered her attempting to bring on the miscarriage, she had feared her. Beneath her offhand, superior manner, there had always been fear—the fear of the upstart for the genuine. With the fear there was envy, for in Ann she saw the woman she would have liked to have been. She envied her the surety of her good birth, the poise which came with cultured assurance. She knew that pretending to be a lady did not cover her own relative unimportance. Her own father had had only a smattering of good breeding, with the self-importance of a petty official in a small town far from Paris.

When Renée showed a desire to be more pleasant, Ann had smothered her dislike and had tried to meet her half way. She distrusted this new mood even more than she had distrusted her before but for André's sake she was determined to do all she could. Renée had even tried to be more friendly with the habitants and their wives and families, but her manner was always patronizing—the great lady from the Manor throwing them a little consideration and they resented it. The older men smoked their pipes and said little; the older women were silent. The younger men she disturbed by the same quality with which she held her husband. It showed itself in her walk, in every movement of her body, in the way that she looked at a man and occasionally in remarks which she intended for quick repartee.

During the journey André had regained much of his old love of freedom and the joy of adventure, but now it seemed good to have a wife waiting for him and to receive her embraces which four months of absence had made so keenly desirable. All the way home he had been wondering whether she would give him the news he so longed for—the news that she was again in the way of giving him a son. Though in this event he would have been denied the bliss which came to him that night, yet he would have been willing to forgo even this for such welcome news. He consoled himself with thoughts that there was the winter before them and many hours of leisure.

There was disappointment in Montreal at the failure of the expedition which now seemed to have been so superfluous. Those who had lost their lives did not even have the glory of having died in battle. Furthermore, the failure brought with it the contempt of the western tribes for their French allies who had failed to rid them of the menace of such bitter enemies. They were never to exterminate the Foxes who were as wily as the animal after which they had been named. Again and again expeditions were sent out attempting to humble them, but though they sometimes killed several hundred of them, the tribe scattered and in time increased. At the request of the French, the Hurons, Ottawas and Iroquois made war against them, burned their villages and chased them into the woods. From time to time came reports that at last they had been destroyed, but these were exaggerated and it was only scattered villages that were exterminated. The tribe continued to thrive, with new sons as brave and restless as their forefathers, until a century later they were still giving trouble under the leadership of a man whose name was to become legend—Chief Blackhawk.

# CHAPTER TWENTY-EIGHT

THE loss of Jean-Baptiste was one of the bitterest blows that Antoine had ever experienced and one from which he could not quickly recover. All his plans and ideas for the Seigneury had centered around this son who was to have taken over the management of it. Jean-Baptiste's interest in the Seigneury had always been so genuine and since he had been a little boy he had loved it with an intense passion. During these two years following his army training he and his father had worked side by side and many an improvement had been an idea originating with Jean-Baptiste. The two Seigneuries seemed fated not to have the eldest sons continue the heritage.

Because of her brother's death, Ann-Marie had decided not to return to the Chateau but to remain at the Manor House until the baby came. Radiant with coming motherhood, she was now hardly recognizable as the self-centered, egotistical girl who had brought them so many worries. There was no question that the incident with Ménard had curbed her emotional impetuosity. Her father had never mentioned it to her, but Elise had spoken to her at length about it. Perhaps it was that or perhaps it was the happiness that she had found with her husband. De Ramezay's career was showing promise. Governor de Longueil had taken a keen interest in this son of his old friend and was schooling him for future participation in the government. When he had gone to Onondaga regarding the argument over the building of the fort at Niagara he had taken de Ramezay with him. He had never forgotten that visit to the Iroquois. It was his first contact with the red man and he had studied de Longueil's attitude towards them. He had listened to the Governor's extremely long speeches to them and had learned that nothing impressed the Indian so much as rhetoric. He had observed their tribal customs, had smoked the calumet for the first time, and afterwards had asked the Baron many pertinent questions on points that he had not understood. Upon his return he had begun to learn some of the Indian languages and in this respect André helped him. During his leave following the expedition, he continued these linguistic studies with André. He knew that at the expiration of his leave, he was to be sent to the Hudson Bay region, possibly as Commandant of the fort there.

Madame de Ramezay also came to stay at the Manor House. She, who had lost so many of her children, could understand their grief and bring them comfort. Her excitement over the coming grandchild was contagious.

André came frequently and sometimes Renée accompanied him. Elise had not been able to be as tolerant as her mother and her initial dislike of Renée had never changed. She resented her treatment of her brother and more especially resented the fact that there was now a subject which she and André could not discuss freely.

It was not until some days after his return from the expedition that André told Elise Paul-André had been with them. A distressed look came into her face and it was a few moments before she said: "Tell me about him, André. How is he?" André had thought it over carefully before broaching the subject. After he had given her the details, he told of the unfortunate meeting between the two brothers.

"Is he so changed then?" she asked.

"He has adopted Indian methods of dress and customs," André said. He hesitated to describe Paul-André's appearance and only said: "He has grown tall and has matured, Elise. There is something very fine about him."

"And will he come back?" she asked anxiously.

"I believe he will, dear, but I don't know when. I don't believe he would want to come back as he is now."

"What do you mean by that?"

He hesitated. "Well, you know he covered his hair with bear grease and, well, it will have to grow back."

"You mean he wears it like an Indian?"

"Yes."

"Then you think he won't return here as an Indian?"

"That I don't know. I think that is what he is probably trying to decide."

"I'm sorry he and Jean-Baptiste never spoke again." She paused. When she looked up her eyes were bright with tears. "Oh André, everything seems to have gone wrong with my children! God seems to be punishing me."

"I don't believe so, dear. You will feel better when Ann-Marie gives you grandchildren," he said sympathetically.

"I suppose so. But…" she did not finish for the tears overflowed.

André was right. The arrival of Ann-Marie's baby brought new joy to the house and dispelled some of the sorrow. At midnight on November 1st, she gave birth to a fine, healthy boy whom they named Nicholas-Jean. The advent of a grandson alleviated some of Antoine's desolation about the future and he began to center his hopes in him. Rousing himself from his depression he suggested to Elise that they close the house for the winter and go to Quebec, since Charlotte-Marguerite had written them that she would enter the novitiate in January.

"We could be there for the ceremony, dear," he said.

"Oh Antoine, I had hoped we could!" Elise exclaimed. "I want this more than anything."

"Then we will certainly go. I must remain for St. Martin's day but we can leave any time after that. I'll go into Montreal tomorrow and make all the arrangements for sailing."

St. Martin's day, November 11th, was the official beginning of the winter season or, as some thought of it, the close of the farming season. Every year it was celebrated with much formality. It was the day when the habitants came to pay their *cens et rentes*—the meagre payment which each seigneur received from the tenants on his land. At such times the yards of the Manor Houses resembled a fair, with chickens, pigs and other livestock loudly voicing their protests, for much of the *cens et rentes* was paid in kind. Eggs, wheat and other produce were also used for payment. When the seigneur estimated his receipts against the prodigious quantity of breakfast and brandy which were consumed by the habitants at his expense on this morning, it was doubtful whether his profits amounted to very much.

On the de Brievaux Seigneury it did not take long, for there were only the five habitants and one was absent. Ménard was now away much of the time, though just what he did during these absences was a matter of speculation. He said that he went trapping but he never brought any pelts to the market in Montreal and when questioned replied tersely that he disposed of them in Michilimackinac. Antoine had scarcely spoken to him since the day he had fought him over Ann-Marie.

Paul and Ann joined Elise and Antoine for the trip to Quebec. It was Ann's suggestion and Paul readily acquiesced. It would leave André and Renée with the house to themselves and Ann hoped it would help André to adjust the difficulties of his marriage.

Madame de Ramezay also accompanied them so that she could visit her daughter, and at the same time see Governor de Beauharnois about the pension which she had not yet received from France.

On the day of the Novitiation, the families and friends of the novices gathered in the outer chapel to witness the ceremony. There were four others besides Charlotte-Marguerite entering the novitiate. The five groups sat silently waiting for the ceremony to begin, each engrossed in thoughts which vibrated through the small chapel. There were tears from some of the women—tears of mingled joy and sorrow. The men fidgeted or sat with features rigidly controlled. Paul de Courville-Boissart, seated between his wife and daughter, added another great moment to the annals of his long life. This grandchild was the first one of the family to bring blessing and honor by entering the Church.

As the five postulants came slowly down the aisle, accompanied by the Mother of Novices, Elise felt that she hardly dare breathe. Her eyes followed every movement of her beloved child, now, like the others dressed as a bride in white dress and veil. The thought crossed Elise's mind that it was strange Charlotte-Marguerite had been born with the straight unbecoming hair which it would give her no qualms to have cut, while Ann-Marie should have had the beautiful tresses.

Charlotte-Marguerite's replies to the questions asked by the Celebrant came clearly to their ears. There was no hesitation and obviously no doubt that she was now doing something which she had long desired. From the Mother of Novices the Celebrant took each habit and blessed it and then handed it to the novice. Holding their new raiment in their arms they retired, returning after a short interval clothed for their religious work. It was a dress of black serge falling in folds, with wide sleeves, and guimpe and bandeau of white linen. Around the waist was the black leather girdle—"the girdle of perpetual chastity,"—from which rosary and crucifix were suspended. A white veil covered the hair. This would be worn for the two years of novitiation and changed for a black veil when the perpetual vows were taken.

With the others she knelt before the altar, no longer Charlotte-Marguerite de Brievaux but now Sister Charlotte St. Joseph—the name having been selected as St. Joseph was the patron saint of New France. Holy Mass was celebrated and after receiving Holy Communion each novice pronounced her vows of Poverty, Obedience and Chastity. When at the end of the ceremony, the novices left the chapel, Elise caught sight of the expression on Sister Charlotte St. Joseph's face—the happiness of one who has now realized a dream. That radiant look remained firmly impressed on Elise's memory for all time.

# CHAPTER TWENTY-NINE

DESPITE the efforts he made, André found the long winter difficult. Recognizing the change in Renée's attitude, he renewed his efforts to make his marriage a success. Unfortunately he did not understand that the best way with a woman of her type was to be masterful. That was contrary to his nature. Instead, he acceded to her every request, even to going into Montreal for some of the entertainments, though they should have observed a period of mourning for Jean-Baptiste de Brievaux.

Madame de Vaudreuil gave occasional *soirées* and a few small parties, some of which André and Renée attended. There was, however, less entertainment that winter than during previous seasons because the de Ramezay Chateau was closed. Ann-Marie and her husband had left for the Hudson Bay region soon after the others had gone to Quebec. With her new baby the journey would be tiresome but she had insisted upon accompanying her husband as he would be away several years.

Renée's energy seemed unbounded as she skated and danced. Then it ended abruptly as one noon she fainted and André learned from Mère Clarissa that his wife was pregnant. When later he poured out his happiness to Renée, she smiled but without enthusiasm. She had known it for several weeks and wished that she could avoid it. Though Ann was away she did not dare to try to induce another miscarriage. Whether Mère Clarissa knew what had caused the previous one or whether it was merely intuition, she did not know. But she feared the keen eyes of the old woman, whose tones grew sharper as Renée expected to be constantly waited upon. André guarded her carefully, pandering to her every whim and not allowing her to exert herself in the least, for fear that he should again be disappointed.

That was the end of frivolity for the rest of the winter and Renée did not take it graciously. She was fretful and irritable. She hated pain and feared it, for she knew that at thirty-two child-bearing was not going to be easy for her. She had always prided herself on her figure and hated the distortion. She did not want children but would not have dared utter such a statement in a community where women bore them every year.

André liked nothing better than to talk of the coming child and to build his dreams, but he never found her responsive. And one day when he allowed his imagination to carry him away and began talking of the joy it would be to have several children around, she snapped at him sharply:

"Then you should have married earlier, André."

"Yes, I suppose I should have. I was letting my imagination run away with me," he replied apologetically.

The months dragged and he was restless because he was not happy. He would have liked to go hunting with the men but was afraid to leave Renée. Though several times Mère Clarissa snapped that she should take some exercise, Renée either ignored it or told her to mind her own business. All day long she lounged, many days never dressing beyond a wrapper over her nightdress and perpetually grumbling at André.

He walked every day over the Seigneury, visiting with the habitants and that gave him some relief. Excepting Aunt Marie, none of them visited at the Manor House and André noticed it. Hitherto there had never been a day during the winter and par-ticularly in the evenings, when the parlor had not welcomed the men and their wives who came to gossip and enjoy the Seigneur's hospitality. Even Aunt Marie called only occasionally and then only for André's sake. The few times she did come, Renée's grumblings and irritability so infuriated her that she could hardly hold her tongue.

Never before had André so welcomed the ice-break and the prospect of again being busy on the Seigneury. News had come by the postal system that the family would return by the first ship and on the morning of April 29th he rode over to the de Brievaux Seigneury to tell Madeleine that the ship was expected to weigh anchor about noon that day. He found her busy with preparations.

In a short while the table was laden with freshly baked bread and several large cakes. Over the fire hung a large iron kettle to which from time to time, she added handfuls of vegetables and herbs, for her soups were her pride. She added more wood to the large open fire so that it roared fiercely causing the young pig roasting on the spit to splutter and crackle. With the efficiency of years, Madeleine would stir the soup and turn the spit at the same time, and then hurry back to the table heaped with chickens from which she was plucking the feathered finery. Her red face glistened with the heat of the fire and she sang as she worked.

A tall young man stood for a while in the doorway watching her without her being aware of it. He passed his tongue over his lips and breathed in the wonderful aroma. In his arms he held a dog. He waited for Madeleine to turn but she went on plucking chickens, her broad back to him. He could wait no longer, he was so ravenously hungry.

"Hello, Madeleine," he said softly.

She swung round on the stool, almost overbalancing, stared a moment and then threw up her hands. "Merciful God!" she exclaimed, "where'd you come from?" The next moment she had enveloped both man and dog in a strong embrace, while tears of joy rolled down her red cheeks.

"My dog's sick, Madeleine," he said awkwardly.

"Eh? Oh the dog. Mother of God, he's been away five years and all he says is that his dog is sick! Why, boy, don't you know what it will mean to your father and mother to have you back?"

Paul-André sank wearily into the nearest chair.

"Poor lad, you're worn out," Madeleine prattled on. "What ails the dog?"

"She fell out of the canoe as we shot the Rapids and was badly tossed about. The rocks hurt her."

"Put her by the fire in that box. The warmth'll help her if she's had a good soaking."

Paul-André laid the dog in the box near the fire. Brun looked up and licked his hand, while her tail thumped.

"She's been with me all the time, Madeleine. She is such a friend."

"Of course. She'll be all right," she said.

Paul-André was eyeing the newly baked bread. His insides felt hollow.

"And you're probably starving. You always were hungry! Sit down and I'll get you something to eat."

She pushed the chickens aside and cleared a space for him. Paul-André took off his jacket and without further words began eating hungrily of the bread and bowl of soup she placed before him. He emptied the bowl twice, devouring a whole loaf of bread and a plate of meat, some of which he fed to Brun. Madeleine went on plucking chickens and watching him.

"Your father and mother are certainly going to be happy when they get back," she said.

"They're away?" His voice sounded his disappointment.

"But they'll be back today," she assured him. "They've been in Quebec all the winter. Your sister entered the novitiate this year..."

"Oh, Charlotte-Marguerite..."

"Ann-Marie has a son..."

"She has!"

"And your brother—but then of course you know that," she broke off abruptly. There was no change in his expression. His face was set. He's become very Indian, she thought.

Paul-André's eyes roved about the bright, clean kitchen with its well-scrubbed floor and shining pots. There was a warmth and a welcome in it.

"You say they'll be back today?" he asked after a lapse of silence.

"Some time this afternoon. Monsieur André has gone to meet them. Your grandparents went to Quebec too."

He nodded. The heat of the kitchen was making him drowsy. He stood up. Brun watched him inquiringly. "I'm going into the orchard, Madeleine. Don't tell them I'm back. I want to surprise them."

"Your old tree's still there," she said understandingly.

He nodded. He bent down to fondle Brun. "You stay here in the warm. It's better for you. I'll be back," he said. He turned to Madeleine. "Do you mind her there?" he asked.

"Of course not. I'll look after her," she said good-naturedly.

A feeling of nostalgia came over Paul-André as he looked over the Seigneury. He could see the habitants working in the fields. He did not want to talk to any of them yet. He darted around the back of the house and into the orchard. By his old tree he sat down and let his mind wander. The fresh smell of spring came to him. How he loved the outdoors! It was going to be very difficult to adjust himself again to the white man's way of living. Comfortable though the kitchen had been, yet in that short time he had begun to feel the confinement. And what would his father's attitude be? From the message he had sent him by Uncle André, he felt fairly sure that he would be welcomed, unless his father was angry that he had not returned after Jean-Baptiste's death. Would he be able to take his brother's place and work on the Seigneury as Jean-Baptiste had done? He loved the place. He had always loved it, yet could he curb his restlessness?

He thought of Oure and the freedom of their lives together. The friendship between them had become very deep, the more so because Oure had not been contemptuous over his return. He had made no comment; nor as they had parted at the foot of the Rapids, had there been disapproval in his attitude. "Remember you're a Mohawk," was all he had said.

Paul-André's thoughts travelled far as he sat there and then he fell asleep.

It was the middle of the afternoon before Antoine and Elise reached the Manor House. The habitants and their families hurried over to greet their Seigneur and his lady and there was the bustle and excitement of homecoming. Madeleine was impatient for them all to leave. She knew that Paul-André would not come in while there were others there. From the kitchen window she watched the orchard anxiously.

As later she helped Elise unpack, she saw the sad look in her eyes as she said: "It's so quiet with no children about." Madeleine kept her word to Paul-André and said nothing, yet could hardly contain herself. She wanted so much to tell Elise that these momentary tears would soon be dried.

After the last guest had left, Antoine sat on the *galerie* smoking his pipe and waiting for supper. How good it was to be back! He had enjoyed Quebec but the greatest part of going away was the joy of returning home again. In a couple of days it would be May Day—the day when the new season officially opened. There would be the usual celebration that took place each year. He fell to thinking of the speech that it was customary for the Seigneur to make to the habitants. He closed his eyes, wondering what he should say. They would expect news of Quebec of course. He was glad he would have that to talk about. It would save having to make it too personal. This was going to be a sad May Day without Jean-Baptiste beside him. Never once had it occurred to him that this beloved son would not survive him. Not even when he had gone away on the expedition had the thought crossed Antoine's mind that he would not return. He dozed, and as though to comfort him, Jean-Baptiste returned in his dreams. He was standing beside him and a soft expression came into Antoine's face as he heard Jean-Baptiste address him. Several times the word, "Father," was repeated until Antoine awoke with a start to hear the word actually spoken. He could not believe his ears and strained his eyes into the fading light, sure that he was still in a dream and that the figure standing there was part of the illusion.

"It is I, father. Am I welcome to come back?" the voice asked.

Antoine sprang from his chair and clasped Paul-André in his arms. "Oh my boy, my boy," he cried and kissed him repeatedly on both cheeks. It was a greater welcome than Paul-André had dared to dream. "I must call your mother."

Antoine grasped the door by the handle and flung it wide, shouting at the top of his voice: "Elise, Elise!"

She came running downstairs, alarmed by Antoine's shout. "What is it, Antoine! What is the matter?" she called. Then she saw a figure standing beside her husband in the dim light but could not recognize him. "Oh! Someone here?" she asked.

"Yes, dear, *someone*. Look closer," Antoine said.

Her mouth half opened and her eyes widened with expectation and then she was in Paul-André's arms and crying against his rough coat. "Oh, darling, darling! I can't believe it!" She lifted her wet face and looked up at him. "My little boy grown to a man! Come inside. I can't see you at all in this light. Antoine get candles quickly. Lots of them."

Antoine rushed to make a light and they both turned to look at their son. He stood regarding them with all his love reflected in his face. He felt ashamed that he had stayed away so long; ashamed that he had let a hurt penetrate so deeply. He held out his arms and looking at them both said simply: "Forgive me."

"There is nothing to forgive," they both said together.

"It is I who should ask that, Paul-André," Antoine said.

"Let us not talk of it. I am back now," Paul-André said.

"To stay?" Elise asked.

He nodded his head. With an arm around each of them, all the old doubts and fears were gone and as he kissed them both, he knew that he had been cleansed of all that had caused misunderstandings between them.

"How you have grown!" Elise exclaimed. "You are nearly as tall as your father now." She looked up at his hair, remembering what André had told her. Tight auburn curls covered his scalp and she smiled as she looked at them and ran her hand through them.

"You will be in time for the May Day festival," Antoine said.

"I timed it so," Paul-André told them. "It seemed an appropriate day to start afresh."

Elise threw her arms around him again and nestled her face closely against his shirt. "Oh darling! Is it really you?" she said and then added: "I have dreamed this moment over and over again."

Paul-André looked down at her red-gold hair and gently stroked its waves. Her eyes seemed more blue than green as she gazed up at him full of emotion. "How beautiful you are, Maman," he said and kissed her.

She smiled at his compliment. "And now we must have supper. You must be starving. I'll tell Madeleine, she'll be so excited." Before Paul-André could explain, she had bustled off to the kitchen.

As they sat at supper, Elise was too excited to eat. Madeleine set a steaming pot of pea soup on the white tablecloth and Elise helped Antoine and Paul-André to large bowls of it. She kept looking at her son, her eyes glistening with joy.

Paul-André took a spoonful and then exclaimed: "How good it is!" Instinctively he looked at the soup tureen, expecting to see a dark incrustation around the rim and perhaps some hairs adhering to it. He glanced into it and Elise remarked:

"There's plenty more, dear."

"Oh no, I haven't finished this yet," he said rather confused. "I was looking at it because it is so good." He did not explain that he had not been able to refrain, so used was he to seeing thick lumps of fat floating about inside. In all the years of his Indian life he had never been able to get used to that horrible Indian stewpot.

Paul-André finished two plates of the fricassee and washed it down with wine. Antoine had offered him brandy but he had declined with a smile.

"No brandy was allowed at Caughnawaga. It and the Indian temperament do not mix."

"Have some more wine, won't you?" Antoine asked, according Paul-André all the deference of an honored guest because he could not yet accustom himself to viewing this young man as his son.

"You look so much older, dear," his mother said.

He smiled and there was something wistful in the smile. "Outdoor life," he said rather crisply and she knew that he was not yet ready to talk about his experiences.

"Your Uncle André will be so delighted to know that you are back," she said.

"I'm anxious to see him and grandpère and grandmère."

"You haven't seen anyone yet?"

"No. I went to the orchard and frankly, I fell asleep. I wanted to see you first anyway."

Elise laid her hand over his. She still could not believe he was home again. She was so overcome at the unexpectedness of it that she found it hard to converse naturally. They told him about their visit to Quebec and about Charlotte-Marguerite and all about the family.

When it was time for bed, Elise went into his room. "It's all ready for you, dear. I've always kept it ready in case you came home." She went about touching things and turning down the bed. She opened the drawer where nightclothes lay and said: "You'll find all you want there."

Paul-André watched her, not showing any sign of what was passing through his mind. He put his arms around her as she said goodnight.

"You're sure I'll find you here in the morning?" she asked. "I'm so afraid it's a dream."

"I'll be here, Maman. I won't run away again. I'll be a good boy," he said.

He looked then like the little boy who had always been promising not to run away. She kissed him and tears left a wet mark on his cheek.

When the door had closed he stood looking around the room. How was he going to be able to sleep in this confinement! He went to the window and threw open the shutters, breathing in the night air. He stood there for several minutes. Then he went to the bed and pulled the curtains back as far as they would go. How had he ever been able to sleep with them tightly closed around him! He ran his hand over the spotless white sheets and felt the softness of the pillow. Slowly he took off his deerskins and then went to the drawer where his nightclothes lay. For four and a half years now he had slept in his clothes and he felt stupid in a nightshirt. He blew out the candle and climbed into bed. The softness of it was soothing to his tired body but he could not sleep. He tossed for a while and then got up and went to the window again. Outside all was so quiet and peaceful and it beckoned to him. Should he take a blanket and go and sleep in the orchard? He could not decide.

Then he heard a scratching at the door and remembered Brun. In the excitement he had forgotten her and felt guilty. He opened the door and she came in slowly. He felt more than ever remorseful at his neglect. He gathered her up in his arms and she licked his face. Then he pulled a blanket off the bed and laid it on the floor. He put Brun on it while he put his deerskin jacket over his nightclothes. Together they rolled in the blanket and slept.

# CHAPTER THIRTY

WHAT Antoine had expected would be one of his saddest May Days, turned out to be one of the happiest. It was so essentially a day when a Seigneur liked to have his family around him. The habitants had already welcomed Paul-André home, but this would be the real welcome.

As was the custom, a tall fir tree had been raised outside the Manor House, stripped of its bark and branches so that it gleamed white in the sunlight. At the top had been left a tuft of greenery known as the "bouquet" and from this extended a long rod painted red and surmounted with a green weather-cock adorned with a red ball. Strong wooden pegs had been driven into the trunk of the tree at regular intervals to facilitate climbing it.

Inside the house all preparations had been made. Madeleine had prepared many dishes for the breakfast and she and Elise had been up since dawn finishing the arrangements. They heard the signal gun and took their places in large armchairs placed so that they faced the entrance to the Manor House. Then the four habitants, also dressed in their best clothes, entered and in the same formal speech that was used every year, the eldest of them asked permission of the Seigneur to plant the Maypole before his threshold. Antoine de Brievaux replied in the customary formal manner and the men retired to inform those gathered outside that permission had been granted. Then all knelt in prayer, those inside the house kneeling before their chairs. Formerly this prayer had been one asking for protection during the day, for these occasions had frequently been chosen by the Indians for attack. Today it was a prayer of thanksgiving and the words flowed from Elise's heart to her lips and she knew that Antoine's prayer was the same.

There was another gunshot and then the deputation returned. Marcel Frenaux, the oldest of the habitants, carried a little greenish goblet about two inches high on a plate of *faïence*, while one of the others carried a flagon of brandy.

"Will our Seigneur honor us by coming and accepting the Maypole?" he asked.

"The honor will be mine, messieurs," Antoine answered.

"And would our Seigneur be pleased to wet the Maypole before he blackens it?" he asked, using the formal parlance.

Antoine bowed and accepted the goblet filled with brandy. "We will wet it together my friends," he said and at this signal Madeleine brought in other goblets which were filled with brandy. Antoine touched the goblets of the delegation and then emptied his own as they emptied theirs. Though the same procedure went on year after year and the words never varied, yet none of them ever tired of it. It was a solemn occasion, accepted with all its seriousness.

Antoine then took a musket that one of the delegation handed him and went outside, followed by Elise and Paul-André. At this signal a young boy clambered up the Maypole with the nimbleness of a squirrel. When he reached the top, he gave three twirls to the weather-cock, shouting "Long live the King! Long live the Seigneur!" The people cheered at the words. Then the boy climbed down, cutting off the pegs with a tomahawk as he descended.

Antoine came to the top of the steps of the Manor House, raised the musket and fired a blank charge, marring the whiteness of the Maypole. He handed the musket to Elise and she did the same. Then Paul-André followed. Each habitant and his family fired their muskets at the Maypole, for the more it was blackened the greater the honor to the Seigneur.

There was an echo in the distance as shots were heard from the de Courville Seigneury where the same ceremony was being performed. When the rattling fire was over, the people turned to their Seigneur who stood waiting on the top of the steps. They were immensely proud of him and all respected and loved him. They saw the happiness wreathed on his face. In a few well-chosen words he thanked them for their loyalty, for the way they had worked their land. Then with a broad smile he turned to Paul-André and back to them.

"And the joy of today is made complete by the return of our son, Paul-André, after four and a half years of fur trading. He will now take his place beside me." He put his arm across Paul-André's shoulders as the habitants all cheered lustily.

"Now will you join us at breakfast?" Antoine invited.

The party at the de Brievaux Manor was more intimate than that at the other Manor House where a much larger number of people sat down to breakfast. André had had a very unpleasant scene that morning with Renée who had refused to get up and participate in the ceremony. She insisted that she felt too nauseated and complained of the noise outside. It was seldom that André lost his temper but he had that morning. Her attitude was an insult to his father and he told her so. Also it put him in a very awkward position. On this day, of all days in the year, the entire family was expected to participate.

"You're utterly impossible," he had said to her and had slammed the door as he left.

When the signal gun was fired, however, Renée was seated beside him in an armchair. Instead of taking no notice when she came into the room, he turned to her and kissed her, his face expressing his gratitude. She received his kiss on her cheek.

The following Sunday Elise invited all the family to dinner after Mass, to welcome Paul-André home. It was a bright warm day and Paul and Ann walked together along the riverbank, but

André drove Renée in the *calèche* because of her condition. All the way she grumbled about the unevenness of the road which she said caused her distress. André half-listened. He would have much preferred to walk and his thoughts were more on Paul-André than on his wife.

At the junction of the two Seigneuries, they alighted and joined the rest of the family who were greeting the de Brievauxs. A moment or two later Aunt Marie and her family joined them and they all chatted for a while. No one had given Paul-André a more hearty welcome than Aunt Marie with whom he had spent the previous evening.

Father Xavier waited on the steps to greet his flock. Paul-André had been to see him the day before. The priest smiled warmly upon all of them, patting Paul-André on the back as he went by. The church was filled as they entered and when the two families were seated in their pews on either side of the aisle, the service began. Though the church was now five years old, every Sunday morning Mass brought renewed gratitude and happiness to Paul.

After Mass, when they all gathered at Elise's dinner table, Father Xavier was among them. Paul-André sat watching the family and feeling proud of them. Here was a heritage one could not deny and he must be sure that he didn't. He was sad inside, for that morning at daybreak he had buried Brun. He kept his sorrow to himself. No one could be expected to understand how he felt about this stray mongrel dog. She had come to him the day he ran away and had returned with him. Then, as though her work were finished, had quietly drifted away in her sleep. He had wakened that morning to find her stiff in his arms. He had buried her beneath his favorite tree in the orchard.

He started out of his reverie to find he was being questioned about Caughnawaga. He did not want to talk of his Indian adoption. He knew he could not expect it to be understood and it was something of which he was proud. He confined his remarks to his experiences in trapping and hunting. He and André entered into a discussion of these topics, while the others listened with interest and studied the prodigal son for whom the fatted calf had this day been killed. There remained so few of the characteristics of the small boy they had known, that all felt they must become reacquainted with him. Not only had the years matured him but his association with the red man had given him a definitely Indian appearance insofar as his features were concerned. This was not due to the cast of the features but to the expression that had now become habitual. He had acquired the Indian habit of half-closing his eyes and shielding them behind an inscrutable glance. His mouth was frequently set in a straight line as of one who intends to utter few words. They had also noticed this Indian trend in the way he now walked, placing his feet straight and moving soundlessly. Yet all were agreed that his experiences had developed him in a way that called for admiration. He had the woodsman's air of adventure, with the accompanying aura of mystery that made them all so interesting. Though the excitable, impulsive little boy was no longer there, a strength of character had taken its place.

Antoine found that he was closer to the man than he had been to the boy. On the day after Paul-André's return, they had gone over the Seigneury together. Antoine had pointed out the developments that had taken place in the past years and was particularly proud as he showed the fields of ginseng. He had forgotten that it was this product which had indirectly led to all the trouble between them. Paul-André had not, though he did not revive the memory with his father.

During the week, he sat alone often, particularly in the evenings, and neither Elise nor Antoine disturbed him when they saw him lost in his thoughts. They understood that the change would need much adjustment. Elise could never find out whether he slept in his bed or on the floor, for he was always up before she, and the bed was always rumpled. He worked hard with his father each day and this perhaps was the most difficult thing of all, for along with his Indian training, he had acquired their laziness. There had been work to do up at Caughnawaga and on some days they had worked hard, but mostly it was a leisurely life with no thought given to time.

Antoine watched him all the week, studying him and determined to understand him. On the following Saturday evening as they both sat outside smoking their pipes and waiting for supper, Antoine voiced some thoughts which had been maturing during the week. They had fallen into one of their long silences, which Antoine now broke.

"I don't want you to think, Paul-André, that you have to remain here indefinitely," he said. "What I mean is this. After the life you have led during your most impressionable years, a farmer's life will be irksome to you. I know from your Uncle André how much the woods call to a man who has once experienced their freedom. You have become an experienced fur trader and there is no reason why you shouldn't continue as such if you want to. I won't hold you. If you want to go away with the *coureurs de bois* or whomever you choose, please feel free to do so." Paul-André did not reply, though Antoine could see that he was listening intently. "Naturally I hope that when I am gone you will take my place, but until that time comes, there is no need for you to feel it is binding you," he added.

Paul-André looked up at his father. "Thank you, Father," he said. The words had a warmth that showed his appreciation.

This conversation with his father lifted a load from Paul-André's mind. Even in these few days home he had known that to remain on the Seigneury through endless summers and winters would be something which he would not be able to endure, particularly the long winters. Now that his father had offered him his freedom, it changed everything. He would look upon the summer as a respite and then make further plans later. Antoine had reason to be very glad that he had spoken, for in the ensuing weeks Paul-André acted very differently. Though he fell from habit into long silences, they were silences that were peaceful and not laden with struggling thoughts.

Paul sat in his office attending to his accounts, while André finished the work outdoors. Now that André was with him he did not work in the heat of the afternoon sun. Presently Mère Clarissa's husband, Pierre, came in to tell him that an Indian runner had come to the house and was asking for him.

"Where's he from?" Paul asked.

"I don't know, monsieur. Do you wish that I should ask?" Pierre inquired.

"No. Send him in." While he waited for the man he wondered what news he could be bringing. The Indian came in and without a word held out a letter to Paul.

"Where're you from?" Paul asked as he broke the seal.

"Me from Albany," the Indian replied.

"Albany!" It was almost a shout from Paul. Quickly he scanned the letter, while the Indian watched him fascinated. This custom of the white man of writing words on a piece of paper that others could read was always a matter of amazement to the red man. Paul stood up quickly, agitation on his face.

"Go to the kitchen and get food," he said to the Indian, leaving the man to find his own way, while he hurriedly sought Ann. She was in her room, lying down.

"What's the matter, dear?" she asked as she saw the disturbed expression of her husband's countenance. He sat down quickly as though his legs would not support him.

"Marguerite," he said. "They've been attacked by Indians and their house burned ..."

"Oh no!" Ann exclaimed.

"Eric has been seriously injured and she wants me to come to her and bring a priest ..."

"Albany is a long way. Could you get there in time if he's seriously injured?"

Paul began pacing the floor. Though forty years had passed since Marguerite's capture by the Indians, Paul knew that her dread of the savages had never lessened.

"But I must go to her, Ann. She wouldn't have sent for me unless it were serious. An Indian attack—you know what that must mean to her."

Ann had risen from the bed as he talked and was already marshalling her thoughts. "Of course, dear. You must go. Sit down and let us try to think clearly how it can be arranged. Maybe Father Xavier would go with you... May I see the letter?"

Paul handed it to her and she read it over carefully several times. It had evidently been written under great stress for the words were badly put together and the writing showed haste.

"You think Father Xavier would go?" Paul asked.

"I'm sure he would. But you two could not go alone. He is an old man and you would need help. You would have to go by canoe wouldn't you?"

"Most of the way..."

"And you haven't handled canoes much these past years."

"I can still handle a canoe well," Paul said with slightly hurt pride.

"I know that, dear, but it is a long journey."

"The Indian who brought the message will have to go back. He can help."

"One Indian and two old men..."

Paul tossed up his head and then despite the seriousness of the moment he smiled. Ann returned the smile and added: "I know you're not as old as Father Xavier; still you are fifty-eight, dear, and haven't the endurance you used to have. I wonder if André would go with you?"

Paul shrugged his shoulders.

"Go and call him and we'll all talk it over."

"All? You mean Madame too? She'll raise objections."

"Of course. But objections can be overruled," Ann said in a hard voice.

André came at his father's call and was told the news. "Of course I'll go, Father," he said. Paul left to find Father Xavier. Renée came at André's call.

"My dear, I have to go on a trip with my father. His twin sister has been attacked by Indians and her husband injured. She has asked us to come and bring a priest."

"Oh I'm sorry," Renée said and André was encouraged by her sympathetic manner. "Where do you have to go?"

"Albany..."

"Albany! But that's nearly to New York!"

"Yes, it's a long trip."

"But you'll be away months!" Her tone had no sympathy now.

"Not necessarily. Five or six weeks possibly," André said.

"Then it's absurd! I don't know what you are thinking of. I suppose you have quite forgotten that I am carrying your child?" she said caustically.

"No, Renée, I hadn't forgotten it. That won't be until about August and this is only May."

"And in the meantime I can take care of myself? Much you care what happens to me when you get a chance to go adventuring!"

"It is hardly in the nature of an adventure; it is a necessity. And there are plenty of people here who will give you every care. You will look after her, mother, won't you?"

"Of course," Ann said quietly.

"André, you can't go," Renée said and her tone was brittle. André looked at her and his face clouded with anger.

"My father needs me and I am accompanying him, Renée," he said decisively.

"Suppose you and I talk this over quietly, Renée," Ann said.

Renée shot her a look of anger. "This, Madame, is a matter for my husband and I ..." she said tartly.

Ann turned to go. "Wait, Mother," André said sharply. "You are mistaken, Renée, this is a family matter. In this family we all discuss our problems together. I know it is difficult for you to understand the life here, despite the fact that you have been here nearly three years. In a colony like this we all stand together and go to the help of those needing it. I am going with my father because he needs me and because you will be well taken care of in my absence."

He turned and walked from the room and out of the house. The look that Renée sent after him was so full of anger and hatred that Ann feared for the child she was carrying. She quietly left the room and went to the kitchen where with Clarissa's help she began assembling things for their journey.

# CHAPTER THIRTY-ONE

A T DAWN the following day they crossed by canoe to the opposite side of the river, stopping at the de Longueil Seigneury to obtain permission from the Governor to make the trip and also enlist his aid. They had learned the previous day that the Governor was at his Chateau and not at his house in Montreal and this had facilitated matters.

Father Xavier had willingly consented to go with them. Like many a priest who had come to this colony, he loved adventure and though he now went on an errand of mercy, he really welcomed the change. He had always tried to model his life upon that of the famous Father Dollier de Casson, the soldier-priest who for thirty years as Superior of the Seminary, had been the guiding spirit in Montreal.

On arrival they learned that the Baron de Longueil was still in bed and his servant seemed reluctant to disturb him, stating that the Governor was unwell.

"We're sorry to disturb him," Paul said, "but if possible would you tell him that the Sieur de Courville-Boissart is here and wishes to see him on urgent business. Otherwise we would not trouble him at this hour."

After a brief interval, the servant returned and said that the Governor would see them. Paul was shocked at the sight of the Baron. whom he had not seen for some time and who now seemed to have shrivelled. He was propped up in bed, a shawl over his nightshirt and a nightcap perched on his bald head. He smiled as they entered and gave them a warm welcome, but in a voice that was low and feeble. Paul hurried to the bed, while André and Father Xavier waited.

"Why, Excellency, I didn't know you were ill!" Paul said and apologized for their intrusion.

The Governor waved it aside. "I'm getting old, Paul, that's all. Seventy-three years next birthday you know."

"Yes, but ..." Paul began.

Again de Longueil waved aside his protests. "Just tired, that's all." He turned to greet the others.

Briefly Paul explained the need of their visit to Albany. "You remember my sister Marguerite?" he asked.

"Yes, the twin. Sorry to hear they have had trouble." He sighed. "Shall we ever keep this country peaceful?" It wasn't so much a question as a lament. "Albany? How're you going? Canoe?"

"If we can obtain one."

"They'll provide you with a good one at Chambly. Give my compliments to Major de Sabrevois or better I'll give you a letter to him. He'll take care of you."

"Major de Sabrevois? Is that the same man who went with Governor de Ramezay at the time of the Walker attack?" André asked.

"The same. You probably know him then ..."

"Yes, slightly. I was with that expedition."

"So you were ..."

"Though he probably wouldn't remember me. I was just one of many men on the expedition."

"Still it wouldn't hurt to remind him of it. We old soldiers like to meet men who have campaigned with us. He's getting along in years too. Fine man. He'll do everything he can to help you."

While they discussed the matter the Governor had been thinking. "While you're in Albany, I wish you would do something for me. This is a job for you, André. Your father will have plenty to do with family affairs."

"I shall be glad to do anything you wish, Excellency," André responded.

"We have been considerably disturbed by the amount of furs going to Albany instead of coming here. Try to find out, if you can, where the leakage is. You're a fur trader, or were, and should be able to learn something of what is going on."

"I should think I could, even if I have to pretend I am one of the men involved in it," André said and smiled.

"Don't get yourself too involved though," de Longueil warned.

"Perhaps I should have something to exonerate me in case I do. What I mean is, someone might later on say they saw me there and get me involved. I wouldn't want to get hanged for my trouble!"

"That is just what I am thinking," de Longueil said thoughtfully.

"Couldn't you give me a letter or something, Excellency?"

"I could. But that might fall into the wrong hands." He remained thoughtful for a few minutes. "I will incorporate it in the report I am sending in a few days to the Governor-General. Then it will be on record and you should have no trouble in explaining anything later."

"Of course you would know and could always vouch for me," André said.

De Longueil gave him a slow and rather sad smile. "But I might not be here at the time," he said. "The span of life nears its conclusion at my age and dead men cannot speak. No. We must have it in order." He shook the small handbell on the table beside him. When the servant appeared he said: "Send my secretary."

That night they arrived at Fort Chambly and were welcomed by the Commandant, who after satiating their ravenous appetites with a good supper, offered them the hospitality of the Fort for the night. It was such visits as these that broke the monotony of a Commandant's life at these out-of-the-way forts. He would have liked to have sat up late into the night talking with his visitors and it was with reluctance that he let them retire on account of their early start the next morning.

The canoe with which he provided them was a sturdy one. They loaded it with their provisions, augmented by several bottles of wine, meat and fruit with which Major de Sabrevois had provided them. He inquired as to whether they were well supplied with bullets and powder, checked the supply and agreed it was ample. With a hearty farewell from the Commandant and his officers, they started on their journey.

For twenty-four miles they followed the Richelieu River and then entered Lac Champlain. It was agreed that André was the most expert canoe-man among them, accustomed to traversing rapids and falls which they would encounter in number, and he became the leader.

All of them loved adventure and despite the critical purpose of their trip, their natures immediately responded to the thrill of the journey before them. André forgot his quarrel with Renée as the peace of his surroundings lightened his mood.

The weather was hot and became increasingly so. By midday the three of them had shed their shirts, feeling rather sorry for Father Xavier who must retain his serge soutane, though no word of discomfort came from him.

For several days they moved amidst the most beautiful scenery. The lake was over one hundred miles long, though when the number of turns and twists they must make to avoid currents and circumvent the many islands were considered, the distance was greater. They kept close to the western shore, where the country beyond was at first low-lying and covered with trees. Led by André they soon were voicing their thrill of freedom with the many canoe songs, in which Father Xavier joined. They swung their paddles to the rhythm of these songs.

Because they must make all possible speed, they continued their journey until the last vestige of daylight had gone. Then they pulled the canoe up on to the bank and prepared for the night. They were still in French territory and the danger was not so great as it would be later. For all that they made sure that their muskets were never far from their hands. Kanaktoue built a fire and they cooked their evening meal, which was washed down with a bottle of de Sabrevois' wine.

Kanaktoue made one remark, evidently to sound out the men with whom he was travelling. With a strange smile he inquired whether they had brought any *eau de vie*.

Paul shook his head and replied: "Brandy not good for Indian," and Kanaktoue did not ask the question again. Still it was enough to remind them that they must keep a close watch on the small supply of brandy that they had brought. They offered Kanaktoue some wine but he shook his head.

The following day they were off again immediately daylight showed and with each mile that they travelled the scenery became more beautiful and more rugged. Paul's mind went back to the days when he had been a *coureur de bois*. He had never become casual about the beauty of his surroundings as did most *coureurs de bois*. The sight of a waterfall or of rapids racing over rocky surface, always thrilled him. It sent his mind back to his earlier days and the many things that had happened. He thought of his own good fortune throughout his life; of the misfortunes of his sister Marguerite. As children they had been so close together, but now for many years they had been separated. He thought of Marguerite when she was a beautiful vivacious girl with red-gold hair, very much like his own daughter Elise. Marguerite who loved life but had not been very sensible about it. Of the illegitimate child she had had by the Comte de Favien; of the massacre at Lachine when the savages had murdered her child and had taken her prisoner; of her escape through the help of the English boy, Eric Walker, whom she had married many years later; of the interval before this marriage when she had married Charles Péchard, Paul's fur trading partner; of Charles' death at the hands of the Indians and the accidental death of their child; of Eric Walker's return to Montreal and her elopement with him. Only once since then had she visited Paul and that was many years ago. She had not repeated the visit, for her people had not accepted her because of her marriage to an Englishman. Paul wondered about her son, Henry, who had been taken prisoner during the Walker expedition and brought to Montreal where Paul had ransomed him. He thought now about this son and his wife Rosalind, who had seen her parents brutally killed by the Indians in a raid. Marguerite had made no mention of them in her note, but that might have been because of her haste. They had all been living together outside Albany and he wondered whether Henry and Rosalind might also have suffered in the raid.

Before the day was over the lake began to narrow and they knew they were getting to the end of it. By nightfall it had narrowed to less than four miles and they camped by a waterfall made by a small stream that emptied from Lac St. Sacrement (Lake George).

The next day proved to be the most disagreeable and arduous. After skirting Lac St. Sacrement they had to portage to the small river which would connect them with the Hudson. Their path lay through woods and swamps where the mosquitoes swarmed about them, biting into their flesh until the irritation was almost unendurable. Kanaktoue led the way, slapping his arms and legs and constantly exclaiming, "Sacré marangoins," mixing his own language with that of his companions. Carrying the canoe and the provisions was difficult and retarded their progress, but they either had to take it with them or lose more time by having to build another when they reached water again. Around his neck Father Xavier had fastened his skin bag containing his breviary and the sacramentals, leaving his hands free to assist in the carrying of the canoe.

They were approaching enemy territory and they divided the night into watches, though with the mosquitoes buzzing around them, none of them had much sleep. The next day they were all weary and disgruntled, comforted a little by Kanaktoue's assurance that soon they would reach an island where he had Indian friends who would supply them with a salve to keep the mosquitoes away. It was not only the mosquitoes that had troubled them during the night, but the wood-lice which swarmed over them.

Fortunately for the rest of the journey they would have the current with them, so that they could make better progress. At times it was shallow and very rapid and at others moving more slowly and very deep. It required constant attention, for the currents were treacherous and it took careful manipulation to get over the falls. All day long they encountered groups of rapids. The shores were covered with woods which they had to watch constantly for lurking enemies. That day they paddled with their muskets always across their knees. The river here was not more than two musketshots wide and though at this season the tribes were mostly interested in fishing, yet they dared not be over-confident. Several times during the day they passed boats containing Indians and held their speech while they passed them, waving in a friendly way and receiving a salute in return.

The next day they came to the island inhabited by Kanaktoue's Indian friends. They, too, were Mohawks and though at first they regarded the white men with suspicion, when they discovered they could speak their language, they accepted them on Kanaktoue's recommendation. At once he asked for some salve for their bites and the women brought it to them. Like most Indian remedies it was immediately effective.

They asked Kanaktoue about the Indians on the island and learned that they leased it from the Dutch. They lived by planting corn and several kinds of melons, though now their chief occupation was harpooning the sturgeon which they cut into long slices and hung to dry in the sunshine for winter food. Their houses were simple—four posts driven into the ground perpendicularly, over which they placed poles and made a roof of bark.

They had no walls. Their beds were deerskins spread upon the ground. In their haste the travellers had not provided themselves with presents for the Indians but they gave them some of their cotton shirts in return for the salve. With these the Indians were well content and added small articles made of skin and ornamented with porcupine quills.

The next and last day was the most comfortable for they were able to travel without their shirts, covering their bodies with the salve. However, if their bodies were now comfortable their noses were not, for all day they had to endure the vilest stench which came from rotting sturgeon on the banks. These were fish which had been wounded with the harpoon and had later died. The river was so filled with them that the dead ones lay in heaps on either bank, and as the river here was very narrow, there was no way of getting away from the odor. The water was clear and shallow and at times they could touch the bottom with their paddles. This meant an even more vigilant watch lest a sharp rock damage the canoe.

At midday they reached the Cohoes Falls and here it was necessary to bank their canoe while they investigated the falls, for their Indian friends had warned them that at this time of the year there was little water in the falls or in the river below, and had they shot them without investigation it might not only have wrecked the canoe but killed them. They found that the bed of the river immediately below the falls was quite dry except for a channel about fourteen feet wide and about a fathom deep. Furthermore it was filled with large rocks. A vapor rose from the falls like drizzling rain and they were soon soaked, but with the heat it was welcome.

Now came their most difficult task. How were they to get the canoe and themselves over these falls which were seventy-five feet high and nine hundred feet broad? Though in some places they were able to slide the canoe fairly easily, the greatest difficulty was to get a purchase for their moccasined feet. In some places the water had cut deep holes in the rock and these gave a fairly good hold. Kanaktoue went first, being the surest footed of them all, and André guided the other end, with Paul and Father Xavier at the sides. Up to now they had been glad of a heavy, strong canoe, but as they wrestled with it over the steep descent they wished it had been lighter. The persistency of inanimate objects infuriated them, as the boat seemed to become alive and insist upon going its own way, pulling them off balance, jerking away from their hands or hitting against their shins. Father Xavier had the most difficulty because of his long soutane, which though he had tucked it up about his waist, kept coming loose and interfering with his progress. It was this and the slipperiness of the river bed that caused the accident. Fortunately, they were not far from the bottom. In a flash it happened. Father Xavier was thrown forward and as he tried to retain his hold on the canoe he pulled Paul off his feet. André crouching from above held on with all his strength but the canoe shot forward with such force that he had to let go for fear of being hurled over the craggy surface. Only Kanaktoue retained his hold, slipping and sliding as the boat gained momentum and took him along with it. Valiantly he clung to it until they reached the flatter ground at the bottom and came to rest against a sharp boulder. Paul quickly recovered himself and so did André and they went to the help of Father Xavier who was rolling over and over unable to help himself as his soutane entangled him.

"Father! Are you hurt?" they both shouted. André finally managed to grab the loose robe and steady the priest. He sat up dazed, clutching at the skin bag around his neck. Blood streamed from a gash on the side of his head. He had ended up on a rock, his soutane up around his waist and his thin legs dangling over the side. He presented rather a grotesque figure, with his white hair flying. He ran his hand over his face, felt the sticky blood on his forehead and then as the daze passed, his face broke into a grin.

"Quite a tumble," he said.

"Your head is cut," Paul said solicitously. "Are you hurt anywhere else?"

"Now I really don't know," he said and felt his arms and legs. He made a grimace as he touched some tender spots. "Bruises, but no bones broken, I hope."

"Let us help you down," André said.

"You'll have to help me *up* first," he said as he saw his bare legs dangling. This was not so easy for the ground sloped around them, but after two ineffectual attempts he was on his feet. He was more shaken than he would have admitted and his uneven perch made it difficult for him to get a purchase with his feet. As he took out his handkerchief and wiped the blood from his face, they saw that his hand shook.

It was a problem to get him down to where Kanaktoue waited for them, for there was no place level enough for them to get either side of him. Holding on to him they pulled him off balance, until at his own suggestion it seemed better to let him scramble down by himself. This he did on all fours. André and Paul watched in case he should again lose his footing, at the same time having to watch their own.

"Well done," André said to Kanaktoue. The Indian pointed to the canoe. There was a deep gash in its side. André made a grimace and showed it to his father.

"We had better make camp," Paul said. "Where's a good place?" Then he turned to Father Xavier and asked: "Are you all right, Father? We'll make camp as soon as we find a good place."

Father Xavier nodded.

"Look after him, Father. Kanaktoue and I can manage the canoe," André said in an undertone. Paul nodded.

It took them another half hour before they were clear of the rocky falls and then they camped. They were all hungry and tired, but grateful that from the whirlpools at the foot of the falls they had no difficulty in catching their supper. This was left to

André and Kanaktoue, while Paul attended to Father Xavier, binding up his wound which fortunately proved to be only a light gash. The priest protested when they insisted that he rest; yet it was obvious that he needed it and was grateful for it. The fall had shaken him badly.

"I'm not the young man I used to be," was his apologetic remark as he lay back on the blanket Paul spread for him.

After supper they examined the canoe. The light was too far gone to start repairs, so they rolled in to their blankets and slept. They were not now many miles from Albany.

# CHAPTER THIRTY-TWO

NONE of them had been to Albany before and they eyed it with interest. Though now an English possession, it had been founded by the Dutch in 1614, at which time it had been called Beverwyck. In 1664, when it was surrendered to the English, they changed the name to Albany,—one of the titles of the Duke of York who later became James II of England. The Dutch bitterly resented the English occupation and the language was seldom heard, though they often imitated the English in their manner of dress.

Next to New York the town was the most wealthy in the province. It was situated on the slope of a hill along the western shore of the Hudson, with high mountains to the west. Like Montreal its long streets ran parallel to the river. The houses showed the innate Dutch neatness and cleanliness. Some were built partly of stone covered with shingles of white pine and some were roofed with tile brought from Holland.

There were no city gates but merely openings through which the people passed to and from the town. The main street ran between two churches—one English and one Dutch. Kanaktoue guided them along this main thoroughfare which was fairly broad and served as a market place. There was also a second market place in the town. To these the farmers brought their produce twice a week. The roadway was littered with filth that gave off a nauseating stench. This did not, however, appear to disturb those who crowded around the booths making their bi-weekly purchases. The unpleasantness was mainly due to the cattle who during the summer nights were left in the streets. This and the lack of any drainage were the causes, for, as in Montreal, the people emptied all their slops into the gutters outside their houses.

At the far end of the street, Kanaktoue turned to the right along a narrow cobbled road. Halfway along he stopped before a house and said: "Here." It was a neat house with shingles of white pine. The door in the center was flanked by seats on either side. Before knocking, Paul inquired:

"What arrangements did my sister make for paying you?"

"I go in now to get," the Indian replied.

Paul would have liked to have offered to pay him but he had no Dutch money. He turned and rapped on the door. After an interval it was opened by an elderly woman whose head was covered with a neat white cap. The expression on her face was stern, and disdain was added to it as she saw the priest and the men in the deerskins with bundles on their backs. Her expression embarrassed Paul and he wished that he had followed his first inclination and gone to a hostelry to change. But the clothes in the packs would have had to be pressed and he had wished to avoid unnecessary delay. Father Xavier's appearance was also incongruous with his mud-stained soutane and the half-healed scar on his forehead.

Making the best of the situation, Paul pulled off his cap and bowed in a manner that belied his dishevelled appearance. André did likewise. To their relief the expression on the lady's face relaxed. There was a further embarrassment for she was obviously Dutch and none of them knew the language. Paul therefore simply inquired: "Madame Walker?"

The lady's expression became more pleasant but she did not smile. She nodded and stood aside for them to enter. "After you, madame," Paul said in French and waited for her to precede them. Without a word she went ahead down a narrow hall, which seemed dim after the glare outside. She stopped before a door, knocked and opened it, signalling for them to enter. Paul stepped inside quietly and waited. A white-haired woman was seated at the window, a missile on her lap. In the corner was a bed on which lay a man apparently asleep.

The woman turned and when she saw Paul, jumped up and ran to him. Paul enveloped her in his arms as she cried: "Paul! Oh Paul!" That was all she could say, for sobs racked her. Gently he comforted her.

"Marguerite darling, it's all right now. We're here," he said. But the sobbing continued. André and Father Xavier waited quietly.

"Oh Paul, it is so dreadful," Marguerite said. "To think this should be the end of all our hopes." She looked towards the bed and together they walked over to it. Silently Paul looked at his brother-in-law lying so quietly that he seemed already to have passed to another world. His head was swathed in bandages and the face beneath was drawn with suffering and without a vestige of color.

"He is dying, Paul. There is no hope."

Paul tightened his arm around her as she was again shaken with sobs.

"I'm so glad you could get here," she said tearfully.

"And I have brought Father Xavier with me," he said.

She turned towards the two waiting men. Father Xavier came forward, his hands held out to her.

"Be comforted, child," he said and the gentle tone of his voice was soothing.

Marguerite grasped his hand and through her tears said: "Oh Father, we need you so."

"I am glad we have arrived in time," he said.

"You remember André, Marguerite?" her brother said.

She looked towards André and tried to smile as she said: "I would hardly remember him as he is now. He was only a little boy when last I saw him."

André came forward and kissed her. "I was unfortunately away, Aunt Marguerite, when you visited us."

"Yes. It is good of you all to come. I must get you some refreshment." She dried her eyes hurriedly and tried to pull herself together.

Paul asked: "Can we go somewhere dear, while you tell me all that has happened?"

"Mevrouw Ruysdael will let us use her parlor. They have been so good to us, Paul."

"Thank God for that," he answered.

"I will stay here while you have your talk," Father Xavier said.

"Thank you, Father," Marguerite said.

She went out with Paul and André. "Your Indian returned with us. I believe there is a matter of paying him, dear," Paul said. "I would have taken care of it but I have no Dutch currency. Have you money?"

"Oh yes. I will get some."

"Do you want me to take care of him, Aunt Marguerite?" André asked.

"Will you André?" She went back into the room again and fetched her purse. "He is quite honest. Pay him what he asks," she said and gave the purse to André.

"Did Mevrouw Ruysdael open the door to you?" Marguerite asked as she led the way to the kitchen.

"I presume so. An elderly lady, rather stern …"

"That would be she. She is stern but very kind."

"We have other clothes, Marguerite, but they will have to be pressed. We had an accident on the way and …"

"You weren't hurt!"

"Nothing much. Father Xavier cut his head as you probably noticed. I think Madame was rather horrified at our appearance. Will you explain to her? I don't know any Dutch."

"Of course. I will explain."

The kitchen into which she took him was spotless and shining. Marguerite introduced her brother formally and as he bowed she began to explain the situation. Paul noticed his sister's fluent Dutch. He stood politely by guessing by her gestures that she was apologizing for his appearance as he had asked her to do. Mevrouw Ruysdael listened to Marguerite and nodded and then said something in reply. Marguerite turned to Paul and said:

"Mevrouw Ruysdael says she will have your clothes pressed."

Paul bowed again to the Dutchwoman and said to his sister, "Please thank her. We would appreciate it, if it is not giving her too much trouble."

Marguerite translated what he had said. Mevrouw Ruysdael answered by a gesture instead of words. Paul had the impression that she had taken the refugees out of the kindness of her heart but against her principles.

Marguerite asked if they might use her parlor and received her consent. This room too was neat but severe in its furnishings. There was a large fireplace some six or eight feet wide, which at this time of the year was not being used. Above it was a shelf with teacups and other crockery. On either side of the fireplace were blue and white Dutch tiles with little figures on them. The floor was of wood and scrubbed very clean, with a few mats scattered about. The chairs also were of wood and like the rest of the furnishings, quite severe, so that one had to sit upright and be a little uncomfortable.

Paul drew two of them together and as they sat down took Marguerite's hand in his. She looked into his face and again her eyes filled with tears. When last they had met her hair had been prematurely white but she had not looked old. Now her face was wrinkled with age and worry. His own hair was now white so that the likeness between them was more apparent though not as much as it had been when they had both been red-heads. While his face was also wrinkled, yet they were more the deep lines of a man whose life has been spent out-of-doors. He was, moreover, as bronzed as an Indian while Marguerite was white and her cheeks were hollow.

"You've had a dreadful time, dear, I know," he said kindly. "I have always hoped that at last you would obtain peace."

"I had found peace, Paul—until this happened."

"Was it the usual kind of attack—surprise?"

She nodded. "It came at night. How we escaped I'll never know. We lived, as you know, about five miles out of Albany. I was always afraid, Paul, but wouldn't let them know. There were only eight houses and though they had built palisades, I never felt they would be much protection. They weren't. The savages came in the dark, as they always do, and built fires around the palisades and lighted them before we were aware of it. I don't know where the guards were. We were supposed to have men watching every night. I can't go into the details." She covered her face with her hands and cried again.

"Don't try to tell me now, dear. Eric was badly wounded?"

"Terribly. I don't know how he has lasted this long. He was slashed with a tomahawk. One of the other men came to his rescue and killed the savage and brought Eric out. It was a heroic gesture and the worst of it is that the man was killed trying to rescue some of the others. The soldiers came but too late. Our homes were all in ashes by that time and except for a handful of us who managed to get to the woods, everyone was killed."

"What about Henri and Rosalind?"

Paul saw her face cloud and was surprised when she said: "They were here in Albany. Mevrouw Ruysdael is a friend of theirs. That is how we happen to be here."

"Then they are both all right?"

"Yes." She looked up sharply into her brother's face as she said: "Oh Paul, it is dreadful. I am losing Henri. He is turning Protestant. I don't know what to do."

"Protestant?" he said rather lamely.

"You knew he had become a doctor? I wrote you about that."

"He always wanted to."

"Yes and he has done well. He is so clever. But he insists that a doctor must be of the same faith as his patients. That it is detrimental to him to be a Catholic in a community where there are no Catholics, or only a very few. We have argued about it so much. Perhaps Father Xavier can do something about it."

"Eric was a Protestant, of course, until he became converted when he married you," Paul remarked quietly.

"And so is Henri's wife," Marguerite said and her voice was hard.

"Rosalind? Yes, of course, I remember that."

"And they will bring the children up as Protestants too."

"I suppose so."

"What am I going to do Paul?"

"It is very unfortunate. Is Henri in Albany now?"

"Yes. He and Rosalind moved here shortly before the massacre. He had told me a few weeks before about his intention to change his faith and we had argued rather strenuously about it."

"You mean you had quarrelled?"

"Not badly. We just did not agree."

"How old is Henri now?"

"Thirty-four ..."

"Three years younger than André. At that age they have a definite mind of their own."

"Oh yes. But when he heard what had happened to us he came immediately and brought us here. He's such a wonderful boy, Paul. We stayed with them for a few days but they have such a tiny house and it is also his office, so then he made arrangements for us to come here. They don't really like us here because we are English, but they are very kind."

"Is there a Monsieur Ruysdael too?"

"*Mijnheer* Ruysdael," she corrected.

"Oh yes, of course."

"And you must address her as *Mevrouw* and not as Madame."

"I see. Yes. I'll remember that—Mevrouw." He turned the word awkwardly over his tongue. "What had we better do about accommodations?"

"You can stay here. It is a large house. Before I sent for you I had spoken to Mevrouw Ruysdael about it."

"That is very kind of her, but there are three of us. You probably only expected one."

"No, I expected that someone would come with you." She was silent a moment and then said quickly: "Paul, will you take me back with you when Eric … leaves me?"

This was the question Paul had expected and he knew what he would answer, though at the same time he wondered whether Marguerite had forgotten the unpleasant reception she had received on the Seigneury when she had visited him. Perhaps alone she would be accepted. It had really been her English husband to whom they had objected.

"Of course, dear," he said. "That was what I intended. You think there is no hope for Eric?"

She shook her head and again the tears streamed down her face. "Henri has been attending him and has done all that he can. He has been unconscious these past days. I was so fearful that he would go before you could get here with a priest. Perhaps we had better go back now and see what Father Xavier says we should do."

As she stood up she threw her arms around her brother's neck. "I am so relieved, Paul, that you are here. It was good of you to come. Ann did not mind?"

"You know Ann better than to ask such a question. By the way, André's married and expecting an heir."

"Oh, how lovely," she exclaimed.

"Well—yes," Paul said dubiously.

"You're not pleased about it?"

"He married a difficult woman. I'll tell you about it later."

They returned to the bedroom. Father Xavier had drawn a chair to the bed and was reading his breviary. He looked up as they entered and the smile on his kind old face was comforting.

A few minutes later, Henry came in. His face lighted up when he saw them and he hastened to greet them warmly. He had always been devoted to this uncle who had ransomed him in Montreal and had shown him the hospitality of his home during a whole winter. They also were very fond of him, for it had been due to his medical knowledge that Elise had been brought through a bad attack of smallpox without being badly scarred.

After greeting his Uncle Paul in the conventional French fashion of kissing him on both cheeks, he turned to André and greeted him. André had become a great favorite with him during his sojourn in Montreal. He spoke to him in English and André replied in the same language.

"So you haven't forgotten the lessons!" Henry exclaimed.

"And how about you?" André asked in French.

"By rights I should now reply to you in Dutch," Henry said in French.

"Then I should have to resort to the Indian language."

"Quite the linguists aren't we!" Henry exclaimed and laughed.

"Though it's not going to help me much here," André said. "I understand they frown on the English language."

"But it is used all the same."

While they were talking Henry had put his arm around his mother and turning to her he said: "I know how relieved you are now, dear. It was good of you to come, Uncle," he said turning to him.

"I am glad we could get here in time," Paul said. "I want you to meet Father Xavier." Because of what Marguerite had told him he half-expected Henry to be cold towards the priest, but he bowed respectfully and said:

"Thank you for coming, Father. My father needs you."

He went then to the bed and looked down at the man lying there so quiet. He lifted the white, thin hand and felt the pulse. He shook his head. "There doesn't seem to be any change. If you will all excuse me I will dress his wounds. There's so little I can do." A sigh escaped him.

"Can we help?" Paul asked.

"I'll need someone to help me lift him," Henry said.

Immediately he became the doctor. He drew back the bed-clothes and they saw the heavy bandages which covered Eric's body. "He was slashed on the shoulders by a tomahawk," Henry remarked as he gently took off the bandages and replaced them with fresh ones. The wounds were deep and though partially healed, gave off a terrible odor which revealed their unhealthy condition. "He lost so much blood before anything could be done for him," Henry said.

Marguerite was talking with Father Xavier and when Henry had completed his task, she turned to him and asked rather nervously: "Will you stay, Henri, while Father Xavier prays for your father?"

"Of course, Mother," he said gently. As he looked down at his mother, Paul thought how like his father he was. He had the same sharp pointed features and the same aesthetic quality which had been Eric's charm. His fair hair with the reddish tint had darkened and had grown thinner since Paul had last seen him. He wore no wig and had his hair dressed in Dutch fashion. He was tall and thin as Eric had been and it was evident that he was far more English than French.

"You do not think that he will regain consciousness?" Father Xavier asked him.

Henry shook his head. "I think it is very unlikely, Father," he replied.

"He did not make a confession?"

"We have no one to hear our confessions, Father," Marguerite said.

Father Xavier nodded that he understood and opened the skin bag which he had brought and set up a small altar on the table. "I will administer conditional absolution," he said.

# CHAPTER THIRTY-THREE

ANDRÉ sat at a table in an "ordinary" along the river front, drinking beer. He had purposely selected this tavern near the dock. On the way down he had wandered into one or two others nearer the market place but there he had been eyed suspiciously. Here no one took any notice of him; in fact he had not been seated very long before other *coureurs de bois* nodded to him in a friendly way as they came in. It was the melting pot of Albany. Every man was a law unto himself and as long as he stayed in this section, went unmolested and unquestioned.

As the tavern filled up other men seated themselves at André's table and he was soon in conversation with them. He spoke in English as did most of them, though many with the same accent as he.

"You Frenchman?" one man asked.

"And you?" André countered.

The man grinned as he put down his mug of beer and nodded his head.

"Where do you trade?" the man asked.

"Out of Michilimackinac," André answered vaguely.

"Several others here too," the man said.

"I recognized them," André lied. "Better market here," he added noncommittally.

"*Mon dieu,* yes!" the man said and spat on the floor. "You new here?" he asked.

André nodded. "Trying it out," he said.

"Bring in much?"

"Not this time. Came down for another reason. Have an aunt here whose husband's dying. Came with my father. He's also a trader."

They ordered more beer as other men joined them. André glanced around wondering whether there were any men whom he had met up at Michilimackinac.

"Any of the traders ever get caught coming here?" he asked.

"You must be new here!" a man said, "or you wouldn't ask that."

"I am. But why do you say that?"

The man who had spoken gave him a penetrating look.

"Why do you want to know?" the man asked suspiciously.

"Well, as I was telling our friend here a moment ago, I came down on account of an aunt whose husband is dying and am taking the opportunity of looking things over because this seems a much better market than Montreal."

"*Sacré bleu,* yes! But you're afraid you'll get caught, eh?"

"No, not afraid. Just curious."

"And cautious?"

"Naturally."

The man leaned over and the expression on his face was not altogether pleasant as he said: "The man isn't *living* who would betray any of us. Any informer is quickly disposed of."

A moment or two later he saw a face that seemed familiar to him but he could not place it.

"That man over there—isn't he from Michilimackinac?" he asked.

The men looked in the direction he indicated and as they did the man André had mentioned looked up. André thought he saw recognition on the man's countenance but he gave no outward sign of it.

"I don't know him. Do you, Ducroix?"

"I've seen him," the man addressed as Ducroix replied. "He's from Michilimackinac. Been coming here for quite a few years."

"I thought I recognized him. Do you know his name?"

"I don't. Do you?" Ducroix asked one of the other men.

The man looked over and said: "Ménard."

"Oh yes, now I remember him," André said. His discomfort grew. He had felt fairly sure that it was Ménard but his heavy beard had changed his appearance. This was getting too near home. He had not thought his investigations would carry right into his brother-in-law's Seigneury. He wondered whether Ménard had recognized him. He was sure he had.

As later he was leaving he had another encounter which sealed his dislike of the task he had undertaken. He was making his way through the crowded tavern to the door when a tall Indian loomed up in front of him.

"Why Oure!" he exclaimed speaking in the dialect. "You here!"

Oure's face was set and expressionless. Only his eyes showed his alarm. "Monsieur André! I am glad to see you," he said politely.

"Will you have a drink with me?" André invited.

"I was just leaving, monsieur."

"So was I. Let us leave together then," he said. He wanted to talk to Oure where there were not so many ears listening. Even though they spoke Mohawk dialect there were too many who understood it. Outside he said: "And are you now trading in Albany?" There was reproof in his tone.

"This is my first visit, monsieur."

"With furs?"

"Yes." Oure's tone was crisp.

"Your father with you?"

"No, monsieur, I came with friends."

"Finding it a better market?"

"Much better."

"And more dangerous. You know the penalty if you get caught?"

Oure did not reply.

"Your father knows you have come here?"

"No, monsieur. Are you trading here?" Oure asked hoping to divert the conversation.

"No. I am merely here on a visit with my father."

Oure made no comment. There was an awkward silence as they walked along.

"Paul-André would be glad to know I have seen you, but of course I cannot tell him," André said pointedly. As he spoke he looked sharply at Oure to indicate his meaning.

"How is he?" Oure asked.

"All right, when I left."

"He will remain now at his home?"

"Temporarily. His father is encouraging him to go into the fur trade. It is the life he likes and for which he is best suited. But he won't be trading in Albany so you won't meet." Again André let his eyes meet Oure's. His glance was steadily returned.

"It's none of my business, Oure," he went on, "but tampering with the law is dangerous. Think carefully before you come here again. I have been a trader for years. We break enough laws as it is." He looked steadily at the Indian who had now grown into a man and whom he had known since he was a very small boy. "Be careful," André warned as they parted.

He was worried. He had the greatest respect for Amrusus and did not like to see his son flaunting authority in this way. He hoped he had made it clear to Oure that he would not mention his having seen him, yet he felt very uncomfortable as he made his way to Henry's where he was to meet his father for dinner.

Paul had arrived at Henry's quite a little while before the appointed time for dinner because he hoped to have an opportunity of talking with his nephew. Rosalind admitted him, giving him a warm smile. Her courtship with Henry had begun in Paul's house during the winter when they had both remained there until the ice broke so that they could return home. In the intervening years she had grown into a round, plump woman with a serious face. She had been a serious child, suffering from the shock of having seen her father and mother dragged from their home and cruelly murdered. She herself had nearly suffered the same fate but had been rescued by Paul's elder son, Jean-Baptiste. The terrific shock had left her with little desire to smile or laugh. Her hair which had been long and golden was now rather faded and partially concealed beneath a white cap. Her clothes were also designed after those of the Dutch women. She was a quiet, determined woman and it was not long before Paul was able to understand why it was that Henry had decided to turn Protestant.

Rosalind called to her husband that his uncle had arrived and Henry hurried from his dispensary. "Ah, Uncle Paul! I'm glad you came early, it will give us time to have a chat before dinner. Would you care to come into my office?" he asked.

This was a large room off the parlor, intended for a bedroom but used by him as a dispensary.

Henry swept some books and papers off a chair and said: "Won't you sit down, Uncle? It's a bit untidy in here but I am so busy I am never able to get through everything to clear it up."

"You're happy you became a doctor?" Paul asked and gave him a broad smile.

"It has become my life, Uncle. You know how interested I always have been. But—we progress so slowly! It is a difficult profession and besides our inadequacy we have so many prejudices to combat."

"Such as what?"

"Well, many. Take smallpox for instance. That is something near to both our hearts."

"Yes, indeed," Paul agreed thinking how nearly he had lost Elise.

"By the way, before I go on with what I was going to say, has Elise much disfigurement from her illness?" Henry asked.

"Practically none. A few small marks on her face but they have faded very much since you last saw them."

Henry sighed. "We have so much to learn."

"Do you have many cases of smallpox here?"

"Continuously. And in Montreal?"

"Likewise continuously. Do you think we shall ever be able to check it?"

"Yes, if we can overcome prejudices. When I was in London in '21 I had the good fortune to meet Lady Mary Wortley Montagu who had recently returned from Turkey and had brought back the information that there smallpox is becoming practically unknown because of their practice of inoculation. Lady Mary had her own daughters inoculated with success and came back to England expecting to be heralded as a great discoverer, only to receive instead a great deal of censure."

"The same story of all who wish to advance new theories," Paul said sympathetically. "Is your friend Doctor Fitch still living?" This had been the man of advanced ideas who had been Henry's mentor and from whom he had learned enough of smallpox to save Elise's life.

"No, he died five years ago. Fortunately not before I had returned from England and had told him what I had learned there. I wish he could have lived to work with me on it."

"You have been successful, though—I mean in your profession generally."

Henry hesitated and said rather dubiously: "Yes. But there are two things against me—my advanced ideas and my religion." Paul was glad Henry brought up the latter subject. But Henry continued discussing professional prejudices.

"Another of our deadliest enemies is the number of women who die in childbirth. There is a growing belief among a few doctors that much of this death during childbirth is due to lack of knowledge on the part of the midwives, but just merely mention to any woman that a doctor should attend her at that time and she will have nothing more to do with you. The very idea of a man being near at such a time is loathesome to them." He slipped into silence as his thoughts wandered over the many prejudices he had to contend with and then with an effort to throw them off, said with a smile: "But I am talking too much profession, when we have other things to discuss. Mother told you I have become a Protestant?"

"Yes, she did, Henri," Paul said.

"I know I have hurt her dreadfully over this and I would not hurt her. You know that. But I have a life work to perform and have so many obstacles to combat in the actual work, that I feel I must eliminate others if I can. You knew that my father was originally a Protestant?"

"Oh yes."

"Fortunately I was able to talk the matter over with him thoroughly before he was injured. He agreed with me."

"I am glad you were able to do that," Paul said quickly.

"I am deeply grateful that I was." He leaned towards Paul earnestly. "I *must* do it, Uncle. There are too few doctors. I would find the same objections wherever I went—not only in Albany. I can't practice in the French colony because I am an Englishman. Don't you see that I have to adopt the religion of the community in which I practice?"

"Frankly, I do. I naturally regret that you have to change your faith—but I do see your difficulties."

"Believe me, Uncle, this has caused me a great deal of anxiety. I don't know what to do. I think and think, and always at the end I feel that God guided me to this work to help his suffering people. So long as we worship—so long as we believe in God—well, I don't quite know how to put it—the work that I am doing is of such vital importance to humanity and if by becoming a Protestant, I remove prejudices and can thereby save lives, surely I can't be committing a sin?"

"The only thing I can suggest is that you talk it over with Father Xavier. He is a very broadminded man. Of course, he won't agree with your changing your faith. You can hardly expect that."

"No, of course not. But I will talk with him. And then, Uncle, there is the question of Mother. Father will die; there is no hope of his recovery. She has had so many sufferings in her life and I am miserable when I think of adding to them."

"I think the best thing is for me to take her back with me, Henri."

"I had hoped that. But—it will mean our separation. It seems that she must always face separation. Yet for her to stay here without Father ..." He threw out his hands hopelessly. "It would mean so much unhappiness for her. Father protected her. She is a Frenchwoman among enemies."

"I understand that. I believe she will be happier back in her old home."

"Will they accept her?"

Paul thought for a moment. "There may be a few difficulties at first—but without her husband they will perhaps accept her after a time. Memories are short."

Rosalind put her head inside the door and announced that dinner was ready and that André had arrived.

"We will join you at once, dear," Henry told her. "What do you think of Rosalind now?" he asked as she left. "Remember what a timid little thing she was in Montreal. She is a wonderful wife."

"I'm sure she is," Paul replied.

As they entered the dining room two young boys were standing respectfully near the table. Paul saw their eyes quickly appraise this "foreign" uncle. He had changed from deerskins to the more formal broadcloth, which gave him an air of distinction, and that morning he had allowed a barber to do his hair in set curls with the back held in place by a neat bow.

"You haven't met our sons have you, Uncle?" Henry asked in French. "This is John." He turned to the taller boy who was very much like him. In English he said: "John—this is Uncle Paul."

As they shook hands Paul said in English, "How do you do, John?" That and a few other phrases were the extent of his knowledge of English and he wondered how they were going to manage at dinner.

"Very well, thank you, sir," the boy replied formally.

"And this is our younger boy, William," Henry said.

Paul greeted William, who gave him the same formal handshake and reply. Both boys were fair, with the blue eyes and sharp features of the Englishman.

All through dinner Paul was conscious of the intense English of these two boys and their well-guarded resentment of these French relatives. They spoke only when addressed and then in English, so that either their parents or André had to translate most of it for Paul. Never once did either of them address their uncle in any other manner than as "Sir." They warmed up a little to André whose fringed deerskins intrigued them and whose stories of Indians and the woods fascinated them.

Trying to relieve the tension a little, Paul asked John through André's interpretation what he was going to do with his life.

"I shall enter the army, sir," he said. "I shall be a guardsman."

André could hardly repress a smile as he translated for his father, for there was a little defiance in the boy's tone. The last part of the sentence was obviously intended to make it clear that it would be the English army he would enter.

"And you, William, are you going to be a soldier?" André inquired. William was only six years old. There had been an older son and a daughter between the two boys but both had died when only a few years old.

"No sir, I am going to be a doctor like my father," William replied.

André relayed this to Paul who nodded approval.

"We need many more doctors," Paul said. When André repeated it, young William raised his eyebrows and started to say:

*"We..."* but his mother silenced him.

Paul turned his attention to his dinner which was frugal compared with the dinners served in the French colony, because the Dutch did not believe in loading a table with food. His thoughts were tumbling over one another. He saw the Sword of Damocles hanging precipitously, threatening to cleave the family in two, with these nephews alien to him and growing up violently opposed to their French relatives—even resenting that there was such a strain in the family. It seemed hard to believe that these were his sister Marguerite's grandchildren. Charming, well-mannered and reserved—but so very different from Elise's warm-hearted children. He could see now how difficult things must have been for his sister with grandchildren who no doubt behaved exceedingly well but showed her only tolerance and no love.

# CHAPTER THIRTY-FOUR

THE journey back to Montreal was slow and more compli-cated. There was little conversation among them for each was engrossed with his own thoughts. Eric had lingered for nearly a week and then had succumbed without regaining consciousness.

With the loss of her beloved husband, Marguerite had lost that which was dearest to her. Though their married life had been fraught with many troubles because of their different nationali-ties, yet their love had been so deep that though they had not been able to overcome the difficulties, at least they had shared them together. Now she had no one to share them with her, for though she loved her brother and he was always understanding, yet naturally he could not feel the way Eric had. And to leave Henry behind had been the hardest cross she had yet had to bear, for she knew that she would probably never see him again. Though he had assured her he would write to her often and come to see her whenever possible, she knew that such statements could be little more than words. To get anyone to take a letter into the French territory was well nigh impossible most of the time, as she knew when she had tried to communicate with her brother. And the same applied to visiting; that was even more difficult. She knew she must try to reconcile herself to the loss of her son—but reconciliation in that respect was not possible. Always there would be a heaviness in her heart.

Paul's thoughts were also rather heavy. Though he was delighted to have his beloved sister back with him, yet he feared the difficulties that in all probability would have to be faced. All her life it seemed Marguerite had had to battle adverse opinion. There were few now who could actually remember her disgrace of having had a child out of wedlock, but the story had been passed down among the families. Some were more charitable and remembered her remarkable return from Indian capture, feeling that the sufferings which she had then endured, wiped out her sin—but these charitable minds were in the minority. Some had changed their viewpoint when she had eloped with an Englishman, even though it was this Englishman who had brought her safely out of Indian captivity.

With only three of them to man the canoe on the return journey, the task was harder, especially as most of the time they were going against the current. Father Xavier stalwartly did his share of the work every day and at night tried to ease Marguerite's troubled mind as he talked and prayed with her. Even he was sad on this journey for he felt he had failed. He had talked for a long time with Henry trying to persuade him to retain his faith. Henry had listened intently and respectfully to the priest's words and had thought them over carefully. Though with one line of thought, Father Xavier had to admit that Henry's arguments were sound, yet to have failed in keeping a son within the Church was something that no priest liked to admit.

André, with his usual good nature, kept them all going throughout the journey, though he, too, had his troubled thoughts. He had spoken to his father about the investigation he had made into the fur leakage and had also pointed out to him the difficult position in which it placed him. Paul agreed immediately that to jeopardize his reputation by becoming an informer was not what could be expected of him. "Give the Governor the information that there were many Frenchmen trading there but don't mention any specific names," had been Paul's advice. André had not mentioned even to him that Oure had been among those he had seen. He had mentioned Ménard and had asked his father whether he should say anything to Antoine. Paul had thought it over carefully and had decided that it would be best not to mention it, for the present at least.

When at last they reached Fort Chambly, Marguerite was so weak she could scarcely stand. Immediately the Commandant ordered a bed prepared for her and while the others supped with him, they exchanged news. This contained the distressing information that the Baron de Longueil had died on June 7th.

With the death of the Baron de Longueil passed the last of the great men who had pioneered in Montreal from its earliest days. Jean Bouillet de la Chassaigne, who succeeded him, was his brother-in-law, having married Marie-Ann de Longueil, the Baron's youngest sister. He was a man who had distinguished himself in the many wars which had involved the colony and for this he had been decorated with the coveted Cross of St. Louis. He was well-known in Montreal and liked, but would make no outstanding contributions as Governor.

"He's as old as de Longueil, isn't he?" André asked.

"The same age, I believe, or maybe a year younger Anyway he's well in his seventies," the Commandant replied.

"He was a fine officer," André observed. "I remember him at the time of the Nicolson attack."

"Yes, he's done fine work. He even impressed the English," the Commandant said with a smile. They looked at him questioningly. "You remember the row over the English fort at Oswego?" They nodded. "Governor de Beauharnois sent La Chassaigne as envoy to Governor Burnet in New York and I heard that Burnet was so impressed with his manner and diplomacy that he wrote Beauharnois to that effect."

"Still it didn't prevent their building the fort," Paul observed.

"No. And it will give us a lot more trouble yet."

"It will ruin our fur trade if we don't take some action," André said.

"You saw that in Albany?"

"It wouldn't take a very discerning man to note it," André said guardedly.

"Then we should build another fort without delay. Did you note the territory I mentioned to you when you were here before?" the Commandant asked.

"South of Lac Champlain, yes. We were to have reported our findings to Governor de Longueil. Wonder if La Chassaigne knows anything about the idea?" Paul said.

"I should say he undoubtedly would. He and de Longueil were quite close and have worked together for years."

"Then we must report to him." As he said it André felt relieved that he would now be able to give only a general report regarding the Albany fur trade. The Baron would have plied him with questions which might have been difficult to avoid answering. Perhaps La Chassaigne would not.

Ann was the first to see them arrive. She was seated at her bedroom window watching as she had done so often during the long weary weeks of their absence. She could not remember having spent a more unpleasant time because of the effort it took to be amiable with her daughter-in-law. She keenly resented Renée's attitude towards André and was angry that she had sent him off without having made up their quarrel. Renée had kept very much to herself and had grown more irritable as her time of confinement approached.

Where Renée was now, Ann did not know, though presumed she was in her bedroom. She hesitated a moment as to whether she should tell her the men were arriving, decided not to bother and ran downstairs and out to meet them. They were helping Marguerite out of the canoe and Ann turned to greet her. She quickly appraised the white, drawn face and the deep sadness in her eyes. "I am glad you have come to us, dear. We will take good care of you," she said kindly.

"Ann, dear," Marguerite said and her voice was feeble. "I have lost them all—both of them …"

"Oh darling! Not both of them?"

"Henry is alive but I have lost him," Marguerite said.

Ann glanced swiftly at Paul.

"We must get her into bed," he said. "She is worn out."

André and Paul were supporting her and in her excitement at seeing Marguerite, Ann had not yet greeted them. She kissed them both and then turned her attention again to Marguerite. Then she saw Father Xavier standing quietly behind them and greeted him.

"God bless you, my dear," he said. "We are all back safely."

"You must all be dreadfully tired. Won't you come up to the house, Father?"

"Thank you, no. I will go to my house. I need a change of clothes."

"I'll send Clarissa over to look after you," Ann said.

"Indeed no. You will need her. I shall be quite all right." He waved to them and started across the Seigneury but the arrival had been noted and out of every house people poured to greet their curé.

Renée had evidently seen the arrivals, too, for she was standing at the top of the steps as they approached. Ann turned to André and said:

"I can help Aunt Marguerite now," and took his place. He waited until they had gone into the house before he turned to greet his wife. She was now very large with child. He was not sure how he should greet her or how she would receive him. He looked into her face. A half-smile played about her full mouth and this was encouraging for of all the things that upset him it was to see her mouth set in a hard line.

"Hello, Renée, we are back," he said awkwardly.

"So I see. I am glad you have returned safely."

"Are you really?" he said and kissed her. She returned his kiss not warmly but at the same time not coldly.

"Who was that?" she asked nodding towards the house.

"Aunt Marguerite. Her husband died."

"Why has she come here?"

André looked at her sharply. "Why not?" he asked. "My father is her brother."

"Hasn't she a family of her own?"

"She has a son."

"Why didn't she remain with him?"

"Must we stand here discussing that matter now?" André said, controlling his rising anger. "Won't you come inside? I am very dirty and need a change of clothes."

"So I observe. But I would like to know about this aunt. Is she going to live here?"

"Of course. I just told you her husband died. Next to him my father is the nearest one to her. They are twins and have always been very devoted. Why do you ask a question like that?"

She turned away and walked into the house. André looked after her puzzled. Then he frowned. He was desperately tired and in no mood for an argument. Although Renée had not answered his question he was fairly sure he knew what was going on in her mind. He had even thought of it himself on the trip. With the child coming it was going to be awkward not having their own home. Perhaps he should speak to his father about it. But just now he was much too weary.

It was ten days after their return that the crisis occurred. Dawn was just breaking on the morning of July 9th, when André was jerked from sleep by the violent ringing of a bell, which he realized could only come from his wife's room. At the same time he heard her calling. Since his return he had been sleeping in the room next to hers, so as not to disturb her and to give her the privacy that she insisted upon. These ten days had been extremely difficult, for Renée constantly grumbled over having to have the child. She grumbled that she was past the age of child-bearing and André's patience had snapped as he told her she should have thought of that before she married him. Relations between them became more strained, though André continued to do everything he could to make her comfortable.

The moment he heard her calling he hurried into her room and found her writhing in agony on the bed. Her dark hair was a tangled mass, clinging to her forehead which was damp with perspiration. André leaned solicitously over the bed and asked:

"Darling, what is it?"

"Get help or I'll die," she groaned.

André hurried along the corridor to his mother's room and met her coming out, fully dressed. She had heard the bell and had immediately surmised the cause.

"Maman, she ..." André began.

"I know dear. Don't worry. I'll take care of things. Get dressed and hurry over to Aunt Marie's. I shall need her help."

Renée was calling again and Ann hurried to her room. This, she knew, was going to be a most difficult day. There had already been words and arguments between her and Renée and also between Renée and André because Renée had insisted that they should get a midwife from Montreal. She scorned the idea that the women of the Seigneury were much more capable than any midwife and had had constant experience with child-birthing. André had asked his mother whether he should accede to Renée's request and for once Ann had spoken sharply to him about his wife. Nothing more was said and now she prepared to take care of things. She tried to show a compassion she did not feel. She bathed Renée's forehead with cold water and made her as comfortable as she could.

It was fortunate that they had no way of knowing how difficult the day was going to be. When the sun set Renée was still in labor and there was nothing that the waiting women could do to help her. Elise had arrived earlier that morning and had taken the men over to her house and had given them their meals. But André was too restless to stay away from the house and he paced back and forth, jumping every time there was a scream of pain from upstairs. Renée was not one to control herself under such circumstances and to these women who had all borne so many children, it was irritating, yet as they watched her suffering their kindly hearts were sympathetic. They had all hoped and expected that the child would be born in the daylight which would have made their task much easier. As dusk fell, Ann collected all the candles she could and arranged them on the table ready to be brought closer as they would need them. The bed stood in an alcove and though they had drawn the bed curtains far back, the light was still poor.

Paul stayed with André all day. During the afternoon he had suggested that they work and this had relieved the situation to some extent. They had now had supper, most of which André had left untouched and both the men sat outside smoking their pipes. Paul tried to keep up a conversation but André could not keep his mind on what they were saying and so they ceased trying to talk. Then Father Xavier appeared and his jovial presence helped.

"I'll just go inside a moment and speak to your mother," Father Xavier said.

"She's upstairs with Renée," André said. "Do you want me to call her?"

"No, no. Clarissa can do that."

The priest went inside and sought out Clarissa in the kitchen. Her worried face lit up when she saw him. "Oh Father, I am so glad you are here. Things are bad," she said.

"Bad, Clarissa?" he asked and smiled gently.

"She's getting very weak. I don't think she will survive."

A look of alarm crossed Father Xavier's face. He covered his anxiety by saying: "Oh come now, Clarissa, you are over-anxious."

"No, Father. I have seen too many of them at these times."

Father Xavier stroked his chin thoughtfully. "Would it be convenient to tell Madame that I am here?"

"Yes, Father, immediately. She will be relieved I know."

Father Xavier waited below while Clarissa hurried upstairs and took Ann's place while she came down to speak with him. He held out both hands to her. Her face was drawn and tired and she was weary with the intensity of the heat and her anxiety.

"Bless you, Father, for coming," she said as she placed both her hands in his. "We are going to need you, I'm afraid."

Father Xavier's blue eyes widened. "You mean what Clarissa told me was correct?"

"I don't know what she told you, Father, but the situation is critical. She has had a terrible struggle all day and is getting very weak."

"I see. Then I had better be prepared. I will return to my house and fetch my burse."

"Can you do it without letting André know? I don't want to alarm him…"

"Yes. It would be better not to do that."

"Pierre could fetch it for you, couldn't he?"

"Well, yes. I can tell him where to find it. I always have everything ready."

"I'll call him."

"No, don't you bother. He is in the kitchen. I will find him myself. Meanwhile, child, we must all pray. God be with you."

After giving Pierre instructions, Father Xavier returned to join the men outside. He was very thoughtful. He had come over at the end of his nightly rounds, expecting that there would be little that he could do at such a time and now was concerned to find that matters were taking a critical turn. From upstairs came agonized cries, more prolonged and more frequent. Andrés nerves were near to a breaking point but he calmed down as Father Xavier began to talk quietly.

Ann, Elise, Aunt Marie and Clarissa stood around the bed trying in every way to help the struggling woman. The birth had begun but it was not normal and they began to fear not only for the life of the mother but for the child. She was indescribably tortured. They had fastened a large towel to the foot of the bed but she was too weak to pull on it and help herself. At last it came, not catapulting head first into the world as it was expected to do but thrusting its way feet first and with knees bent. Renée gave a long, heartbreaking cry and lost consciousness.

Quickly the women worked. Then the men downstairs heard another cry, which after their long wait brought joy to them. It was the lusty cry of André's son. André leapt to his feet and bounded up the stairs two at a time, hesitated and called through the door asking if he could come in.

"Not yet, André," his mother called. "Is Father Xavier with you?"

"He's downstairs."

"Get him will you?" she said.

"Er … oh!" she heard him exclaim and then he hurried away.

Swiftly they cleaned up and put the room in order. Ann held the hartshorn to Renée's nose and presently she stirred. Her face was ashen and beads of perspiration stood out on her forehead. Gently Ann wiped them away and spoke to her, calling her name. Her eyelids fluttered.

"I'll take the baby into your room," Aunt Marie said.

Ann nodded.

Outside Aunt Marie met André and Father Xavier and showed them the infant. André's face lit up as he gazed at his child.

"Your son, André," Aunt Marie said.

"My son!" he whispered. "My own son! Oh, Aunt Marie isn't he wonderful!"

She smiled at him.

"How is Renée? May I go in now?"

"Yes," she said and hurried away with the baby, after giving Father Xavier a significant glance that made him hurry into the room.

The joy that had wreathed André's face faded as he looked at his wife lying so still on the bed.

"Is she asleep mother?" he asked.

Ann put her arm around him. "She has had a very bad time, dear. She is very ill."

"You mean ... Had I better go for a doctor?"

"She needs Father Xavier more, dear ..."

"She's not going to ... Oh no! Not after giving me a son." He hurried to the bed and knelt down. "Renée," he called softly. She opened her eyes and recognized him, but the look she gave him had no gentleness or love in it. She turned from him and the words she said sounded like, "Go away." Her voice was so low and muffled that André was not sure. He looked up and met his mother's eyes.

"Let us leave Father Xavier alone with her," she said softly.

Elise took André's arm and led him dazed from the room. They went into the room he had been occupying. "Elise, I don't understand. What has gone wrong? You have had babies—you were all right. Is it because she was past the age?"

"Whatever gave you that idea, André?" she asked.

"She said so. She said she was too old to have children. It is all my fault."

"It isn't at all, André," Elise's voice was sharp.

"I know you dislike her, Elise," he said, "but ..."

"I don't dislike her, dear. I was perhaps a little prejudiced because of her likeness to Gaston. I know that wasn't fair. But André if she told you she was too old to have children that wasn't true. You mustn't think that."

"Then why did she have so much trouble? Why is she so ill?"

Before Elise could answer, Ann came in quietly. Her large black eyes were pools of anxiety as she went to her son. "André dear, Father Xavier has summoned us all to Renée's room. He...will administer the last rites."

"Oh mother..." he leaned his face for a moment against her shoulder as she strained him to her.

"Take courage, darling," she whispered.

They all gathered in the room. Renée had been able to make her confession and now received the Last Sacrament. At two o'clock in the morning Ann gently drew the sheet up and covered her face. André stumbled from the room. Elise followed him and together they walked up and down the riverbank. At first he was silent; then he opened his heart telling her of all the problems that had worried him during his married life, all the things that so often he had wanted to talk over with her; asking her for an explanation of the failure of his marriage. Then only did Elise tell him what her mother had confided to her—the cause of Renée's miscarriage which undoubtedly was the reason she had now lost her life in giving birth to his son. He knew that she was trying to make him see that it was not his fault, but it would take time before he could reconcile his own conscience.

"And now my son will never know his mother," he said distressed. "That is going to be so difficult."

"Antoine surmounted that difficulty, dear," Elise said quietly.

André looked at her quickly and found consolation from her words.

Dawn was breaking in the sky as they parted on the steps of her house. He clung to her a little as she kissed him. Then he walked to the church and within the cool quiet of its atmosphere, peace began to come to him.

# CHAPTER THIRTY-FIVE

ANDRÉ named his son Philip Rénault de Courville-Boissart—the Philip in memory of Uncle Philip. Though little Philip was never to know his mother, he did not lack for motherly love and attention, for from the onset Ann and Marguerite vied with each other in caring for him. And to the devotion of his grandmother and great-aunt was joined the constant attention of his aunt Elise, to say nothing of the other women on the Seigneury, with Aunt Marie in the foreground. A woman from the Seigneury had been secured as wet nurse and day by day he grew into a sturdy boy.

It was a few days after the christening that Paul spoke to André of a matter which he and Ann had discussed in detail the night before. Since Renée's death, André had been quiet and brooding as he tried to overcome the shock. On this evening while the womenfolk attended to Philip's last feeding, he and his father sat in the library, enjoying their pipes. They had finished supper and Paul had put a flagon of brandy on the table between them.

"André, why don't you take Paul-André with you and go into the woods this winter?" he suggested.

André looked up at his father rather sharply and puffed thoughtfully at his pipe.

"You knew Antoine had suggested to Paul-André that he become a voyageur?" Paul went on. He used the term "voyageur" advisedly, this having now replaced the former name, "*coureur de bois*" which had acquired such a disreputable reputation. The new name identified a life of adventure, and could mean fur trapping or exploring.

"Yes, Paul-André has spoken to me about it," André said. He continued to smoke silently and then looked at his father with eyes that were haggard with worry. "I have to do something, Father. This ... this situation has left my nerves on edge." He ran his hand quickly through his hair. "I don't understand it. I look around the Seigneury, I see Elise with Antoine and Ann-Marie with her husband—they have found happiness. Why was my marriage such a failure and such a tragedy?"

"That's a hard question to answer, my son. But I don't believe it was your fault."

"But it must have been my fault to some extent. I suppose it's just that I'm not suited to marriage."

"From what I saw you did everything to make your wife happy. But ..." he leaned forward and put his hand on André's knee, "is there any use in brooding over what has passed? You can't do anything about it now. It is over. And I am sure you tried your best. Try to forget it, André. I believe if you had a season of trapping you would feel better for it."

"But what about Philip?"

"He is woman's work for a year or so. You would be leaving him in good hands." Paul's leathery face creased into a smile as he said: "It is a long while since I have seen your mother so eagerly occupied. Bless her. It reminds me of the days when you children were small."

For the rest of the evening they discussed plans for the trip and André went to bed with a lighter heart than he had had for some time.

Paul-André was delighted with his uncle's suggestion, yet there was hesitation in his manner.

"Have you spoken to my father?" he asked.

"Not yet. But he will agree, I'm sure," André said.

"Yes, I know that. He has left me perfectly free. But it doesn't seem quite fair to leave him just at haymaking time."

André smiled. This was a new Paul-André, showing a serious interest in the Seigneury.

"We would not leave until after harvesting. I, too, have the Seigneury to consider."

"Yes, of course. After harvesting? That would be fine."

"About the middle or end of August would be plenty of time. Perhaps we might be able to get Amrusus and Oure to join us."

Paul-André's face lighted up. He drew thoughtfully on the pipe that he now smoked constantly. His face was tanned from exposure to the sun and his mass of auburn hair was in its usual state of untidiness. He wore no shirt and his skin was deeply bronzed, emphasizing his Indian appearance, which became accentuated as he stood with his eyes squinted in the direction of Caughnawaga.

"If they haven't already left for the woods by the time we reach Caughnawaga," he said.

"We'll send them word. There's bound to be a canoe going that way."

"That would be well. I would like to have them go with us."

The thought of seeing his friends again so soon filled Paul-André with delight. He had enjoyed the summer, feeling a new understanding with his father and deepening that which he had always had with his mother. Yet as he had thought of the coming winter he had wondered what he would do with himself during the long months. Now the problem had a solution.

They did not, however, leave until the end of September as Amrusus sent word he could not be ready before then. On the morning of their departure, André stood looking down at his son lying asleep in his cradle. He still found it difficult to believe that he had a son of his own. A tremendous gratitude flooded him as he thought of it, gratitude to the woman who had given him this son. He thought then only of the happy hours they had spent together in this same room. And tears pushed at his eyes as he remembered Renée. He knelt by the cradle and prayed for the soul that had departed and for the new life that was beginning. When he stood up, he watched his infant son musingly. What would he be like when he grew up? Would he look like Renée? Would he some day go out into the woods with him, or would he be content to be a farmer, or would he choose the more active life of a soldier?

"My son," he said half-aloud and the words sounded strange yet very wonderful to him.

They stayed nearly a week at Caughnawaga. Paul-André was greeted warmly by all his friends there. Oure's mother smiled slyly as she greeted him—a smile which seemed to say, "I knew you would return," but she made no comment. It seemed to him that he had been away much more than five months. His life at home was so different; so much went to make up each day, that he felt that much more than a season must have passed.

André had half-expected to find that Oure was not at Caughnawaga and wondered when he had returned from Albany. He made no comment. While André related to Amrusus his journey to Albany with his father, Oure's face was set.

"Many traders going there," Amrusus said.

"So I observed," André replied. "I think though we can find a good enough market in Montreal."

"No trading with English. Against the law," Amrusus remarked. "We no tamper with law."

André still could not be sure whether Amrusus had found out about Oure's digression and there was no opportunity to speak alone to Oure. He left the matter where it was for the present.

They left their smaller canoe at Caughnawaga and used a sturdy one that Amrusus had just finished. This time their voyage would be different, for instead of merely trading with the trappers as André had done in the past, they themselves would

do the trapping. Amrusus was well-experienced in this and
Oure nearly as proficient as his father. André had often watched
but had never before participated in the actual trapping to any
great extent and he eagerly welcomed Amrusus' suggestions.
Paul-André was also eager. During his years at Caughnawaga he
had been on many such expeditions with Amrusus and he was
pleased that he would now have an opportunity of showing his
uncle how much he had learned in the years he had spent with
the Indians.

Beaver trapping did not begin until November when the
animals' fur was thickest. The most numerous beaver colonies
were along the Ottawa and French Rivers and they travelled in
this direction, making their way without hurry so as to gain full
enjoyment from the trip.

André realized more than ever that he should never have
given up this life. Even its hardships, with the deep snow and
the intense cold brought an exhilaration that no freedom-loving
nature could be denied. He forgot the anxieties and problems
that had weighed so heavily on him in the past years and every
night as they rolled into their blankets around the campfire, he
was far happier than he could ever be lying in a soft bed.

Beaver was hunted in several ways but Amrusus used only
two—the trench and the trap. In both André had to be schooled
and laughed when Paul-André reversed the position and became
his teacher. When they had scouted and discovered the beaver
tracks, they made a trap shaped like a figure four, with small
pieces of freshly cut green wood as bait. Many of these were
placed at intervals and then left, for the trap would take care of its
victim. The moment the animal attempted to nibble on the soft
wood it loved so much, a heavy log fell on it and broke its back.

The other method required more care, yet brought a greater
excitement. It was easy to learn, though the trapper had to
exercise patience and time his movements perfectly. They were
camped along the bank of a frozen river. Amrusus selected four

places where the ice was four to five inches thick and with his axe cut an opening. Each of them kept watch at an opening, waiting for the beaver who would seek out this space so that he could breathe more freely. The animals gave the hunters good warning of their approach, for they created such a commotion in the water with their heavy breathing that they could be heard when quite a distance away. Around the hole had been placed broken reeds and soon two forepaws would appear and an inquisitive snout. Immediately one of the paws was siezed and the animal thrown on the ice. A swift blow on the head completed the task.

Before the season ended in April they had so many bales of pelts that they could not handle any more. They had to work in relays getting them to the sled which had replaced their canoe. They would take turns standing guard over the bundles while the others made the portage.

They had agreed to go on to Michilimackinac before returning home, as with the exception of Paul-André, they all had friends there. They could have disposed of their pelts at Michilimackinac but had agreed that the Montreal market would bring a better price.

After more than six months in the forest they welcomed the diversion of the town. Indian squaws rushed to meet them as they landed but they pushed them away good-naturedly. The two white men made their way to *Le Castor* while Amrusus and Oure went to the Indian section to visit their own friends.

André pushed open the door of the tavern and they entered a large room which was thick with smoke and odorous with fumes of brandy and beer. He paused a moment and looked around to see who was there and immediately a tall figure jumped up from a table and came towards him with a loud clatter.

"Le Roux! Am I glad to see you! Again we meet unexpectedly and most opportunely." La Vérendrye clapped him on the back.

André greeted his friend warmly. "Don't tell me you have found the Western Ocean?" he chided.

"I'm not far off this time. Come and sit down. I must talk to you."

"This is my nephew, Paul-André," André introduced.

La Vérendrye appraised the tall youth before him. "Your nephew? He looks more like your son."

Paul-André smiled, the slow smile of an Indian. He had heard of the Sieur de la Vérendrye and was delighted to meet him.

"That's not surprising. His mother and I are twins," André replied.

"Indeed." La Vérendrye held out a hand to Paul-André and his grip was strong and friendly. "I am delighted to meet you, my boy. Are you a fur trapper too?" he asked.

"He's more than that. He's an adopted Indian. He lived with them for over four years at Caughnawaga."

"Did he indeed," La Vérendrye replied and his tone of interest pleased Paul-André. "We can use you, Paul-André." Then turning to André he said: "I really believe we can soon start on our quest, André. I have some very exciting information."

"I'm anxious to hear it."

"First let us have some drinks. What will it be? Brandy?"

"Yes. Beer for you Paul-André?"

"Please."

La Vérendrye called for the drinks and then said: "But before I begin, tell me what you are doing in Michilimackinac."

"I was about to ask you the same question."

La Vérendrye smiled, a broad frank smile that was appealing. "I asked first. Am I to assume that you have gone back to trading?"

"Yes and we've just come back from a very successful winter of trapping beaver."

"Good. I thought you'd not remain at home long. What did your wife say about your leaving? Make a fuss?"

André paused a moment before replying. "I lost my wife, Pierre. She died giving birth to my son."

"Oh, pardon me, my friend, for being so gauche. I am so sorry."

"You would not know."

"And the son?"

"Thriving."

"Fine. I have four boys you know and what fine lads they are!"

"They're growing up now I suppose?"

"Indeed yes. The eldest is sixteen and they range down to twelve, so you see they are all men now. How old's this boy?" he asked turning to Paul-André.

André let him answer for himself.

"Sixteen? You'd make a good companion for my boys on the trip," La Vérendrye commented.

"Your boys would join you?" André asked.

"They've thought of nothing else since they were old enough to think for themselves at all. The youngest wouldn't go yet. He's going to Quebec to study mathematics and drawing so that he can draw maps of the territory for me."

"And you really have some news of the Ocean? I presume it is this that brought you to Michilimackinac?"

"Yes and no. I come here frequently for supplies. And to break the monotony. Life in a small trading post is very dull. Still, had it not been for that post I wouldn't have gathered the information I have." He drained his brandy and called for another before leaning across the table eagerly. "It was through a missionary that I learned what I have. A Father Gonner who has lived for a long while among the Sioux. From them he has found out that a great river flows straight towards the setting sun. I've always felt that there was another river like the St. Lawrence that would take us to the Ocean."

"And where is the source of this river?"

"Well, they at first thought that it was in the region of Lac Superior but now it seems it is a little farther on." He leaned closer and lowered his voice. "I have been assured that Lac Ouinipigon (Winnipeg) drains into the river that leads to the Western Ocean."

"Lac Ouinipigon? That's beyond Lac Superior."

"Yes. The Indians assured Father Gonner that the water ebbed and flowed and a river does not do that. Of course one has to discount much that the Indians say. They are all liars and make up stories just to please the white man. Still thinking it over carefully and, as I say, discounting much of what they said, my belief is that this river that flows towards the setting sun connects with Lac Ouinipigon on the one side and with the Western Ocean on the other."

"And how are you going to find out?"

"Father Gonner has gone to Quebec to lay his information before the Governor. I have given him a letter to the Governor asking for my release from the trading post at Nipigon next spring. Then I will go myself and see the Governor and get him to equip our expedition."

"You think he will help you?"

"Who, the Governor? I have reason to believe that he is interested. I have not met him myself but from what Madame de Vaudreuil told me he is even more interested than her late husband. André, we *must* find that Western Ocean. Think what it would mean to France. We would then know our way practically across the world or at least from ocean to ocean across this continent. And we must get ahead of the English in this matter. I have learned from several sources that they are actively engaged in sending out expeditions to find this Ocean. We *must* get there first."

André looked at his nephew. His eyes were alight with excitement.

"Would you permit me to ask a question?" Paul-André said politely.

"Of course, my boy. As many as you like."

"This... Western Ocean. What is it? I suppose I am very ignorant..."

"Not at all. It's a fair question. We have reason to believe, in fact we know, that to the west is another ocean. Just as the Atlantic Ocean is on the eastern shore and connects us by sea with France, the Western Ocean would connect us with China and other countries. We do know that the Spaniards have found it and inhabit the western shore. The question is, how far is it from here? How many leagues would we have to travel to reach it? And what kind of territory would we have to traverse? The Indians maintain that the country is level, without mountains, but that I do not believe. If we can discover this river that leads to the sea, it would be our best means of travel, since otherwise we would have to go on foot. From my knowledge of the waterways here, we would undoubtedly encounter rapids and many portages and we may have to climb mountains. It will not be easy but it will be so worthwhile." La Vérendrye drained his glass and then resumed. "Your uncle and I have been talking of it for years. This is the first real hope we have had of seeing it materialize. Many men have already devoted their lives to the search. You have heard of the Sieur du Lhut?"

"Oh yes, monsieur," Paul-André replied.

"He died trying to find this ocean. Then there were Marquette, Radission and many others. Someday it will be discovered and I hope by a Frenchman."

"If the French government will only give support," André said doubtfully.

La Vérendrye nodded thoughtfully. His steel-blue eyes were ablaze with excitement, but his tone was wistful as he said: "If they only will. We can but try. I have dreamed of it so many years. I shall not give up easily."

"I'm with you, Pierre. I always have been. And I know that Paul-André asks nothing more than to become an explorer."

"It would be a privilege to be allowed to join you, monsieur," Paul-André said enthusiastically.

"With my sons and you two I would have good men to start out with. Nothing can be done until spring. I shall devote the winter to trying to find out more from the Indians who come to Nipigon."

"When do you return to Nipigon?" André asked.

"In a couple of days or so. And you?"

"We'll remain about that long …"

"Then let us enjoy ourselves. I've no doubt after a winter in the woods you'll want a little light entertainment," he said with a sly smile. "What about you, Paul-André? Ever have a squaw?"

# CHAPTER THIRTY-SIX

THE month of May was always the most stimulating of the entire year, for with its arrival everything sprang to life. Winter snows had been washed away by the rains and the young green shoots of the fruit trees responded to the warmth of the sun. Narcissus and violets began to bloom and the wild strawberries showed their flowers. The traditional Maypole ceremony began the month and by the middle the spring sowing was finished. As it ended, the wild cherry, plum and apple were in bloom, and the voyageurs began to return from their winter trek. Throughout each day the air resounded with their songs as flotilla after flotilla of canoes made their way to the Montreal fur market. The workers in the fields waved gaily to them and picking up the songs went on singing as they worked.

As soon as the first bevy of canoes was sighted, Ann or Marguerite sat outside constantly, holding little Philip and humming the voyageurs' songs to him. This was the picture that André saw as he pulled the heavily laden canoe up on to the bank. His heart pounded with excitement. He had thought of this moment for days and had only stopped briefly to leave Paul-André at his home and greet Elise.

He shouted a greeting to his mother, for it was she who watched on this day. With long strides he covered the distance to the house and bounded up the steps.

He enveloped her and the baby in his arms, kissing her warmly. Then he looked down at his infant son, still scarcely able to believe that he was his. Ann put the baby into his arms. Two black eyes blinked at him and then the small mouth parted in a smile.

"He's smiling!" André said and smiled back at his son. He buried his face against the baby's cheek and a small fist came up and grabbed a handful of red hair. What his remark was no one could have interpreted but it was a sound that seemed to convey approval.

"Why you little rogue you can almost talk!" André exclaimed.

"A lot of sounds but none very clear yet," Ann said smiling. "But it won't be long before he will talk and walk."

"When can I teach him to handle a gun?" André asked.

"Guns! That's all you men can talk about," Ann chaffed.

"You'd like to handle a gun wouldn't you young man?" André asked and was rewarded with a large smile that showed two small teeth.

"And you have teeth too!" he exclaimed.

"He's going to be like you," his mother said.

"He is? How can you tell?"

Ann laughed. "How can I tell! I have eyes, dear. See the shape of his features and I do believe he will have auburn hair like Elise's children. It won't be as red as yours but it will have a red-dish tinge." She ruffled the straggly hair and little Philip cooed at her and held out his arms to be taken.

Ann lifted him back into her arms. "He's getting heavy," she said.

"You shouldn't be carrying him about," André said with some concern.

"Why not?" she asked archly. André looked at his mother intently. He had always thought her wonderful and now with her grey hair and radiant expression, she looked even more so.

"Maman, you're very beautiful today," he said earnestly.

"Spend your time admiring your son, dear, and not his old grandmother," she said. There was a pleased smile on her face.

André put his arm around her and kissed her. "You'll never be old," he said as they went inside.

Paul came hurrying in and they exchanged warm greetings. Then Aunt Marguerite joined them. André gave them a rather disjointed account of the trip because his attention was constantly diverted by his son, who had a magnetic fascination for him.

"He'll soon be a year old," he remarked. "One whole year of life, my little one, and so much before you."

Ann watched him and was content. The old carefree André had come back, with the strained look gone. She and Marguerite vied with each other in giving him an account of his son's behavior during his absence.

The Sieur de la Vérendrye arrived in Montreal about the middle of June and at André's invitation came to visit at the de Courville Manor. After dinner Paul and Antoine as well as Paul-André, discussed the Western Sea project with him and it was Antoine who made the suggestion which was subsequently to be adopted after La Vérendrye's visit with Governor de Beauharnois.

"If the government will not finance you, why not make an arrangement with the merchants and some of the seigneurs in Montreal?" was Antoine's suggestion.

La Vérendrye turned his eyes steadily upon the speaker. They had all met him occasionally before but this was the first opportunity they had of becoming better acquainted with him. Like André, they were immediately impressed by him and fully in accord with his ideas. "I had thought of that as a last resource, monsieur. Do you think they would be interested?" he asked.

"If it is profitable to them," Antoine replied.

"And only if it is," Paul added. "I doubt whether you will find any interested simply because of discovering new territory."

"That I hardly expect, monsieur," La Vérendrye replied.

"Do you think there *is* profit to be made out of such a venture?" Paul inquired.

La Vérendrye gave him an odd smile. "You'll hardly believe me, monsieur, when I say I have scarcely thought of it in those terms. Perhaps I am too much of an idealist. My one thought has been to find a way across from ocean to ocean. I see the profit that there would be in *that*."

"But it takes money to carry out such a project or at least the equivalent of money—supplies, food, presents," Paul said.

"Yes—so much of all of them," La Vérendrye said rather sadly, because whenever he thought of it, it seemed so stupendous. "I have always entertained the foolish hope that the government would meet the expenses ..."

"And if they won't?" Antoine asked.

"Then, monsieur, your suggestion is the only recourse I have. Undoubtedly the territory will be rich in furs and these must be the means of meeting expenses. I must give up being idealistic and realize that there are few men who are interested in discovery merely for its own sake."

"There are a few of us—but unfortunately only a few, monsieur. Personally I admire your unselfish ideals and I know my family feels the same," Paul said. "André has always wanted to explore. Even when he was a little boy he continually plagued me with questions as to where the river went."

"Always," André agreed. "And now that I have discovered where it does go, I want to know what is beyond and further beyond."

"And he has filled my son with the same eagerness," Antoine chided. "May I say, monsieur, that while I have never had this urge to explore, I am fully in accord with it and will pledge two hundred livres towards the enterprise."

La Vérendrye's face lighted up. "That is most generous of you, monsieur," he exclaimed.

"And I will add another two hundred," Paul said.

"And I also," André said.

"And I would like to contribute the same," Paul-André added.

"Let me see," Paul said practically. "That will be eight hundred livres between us. Why don't we make it two hundred and fifty each—one thousand altogether?"

They all readily agreed. La Vérendrye listened in silence, overcome at this enthusiasm for his venture. Then quietly he said: "Thank you, messieurs. Your confidence will not be misplaced."

At La Vérendrye's invitation, André accompanied him to Quebec to see de Beauharnois, stopping on the way at La Vérendrye's home at Three Rivers. André had visited Three Rivers occasionally but this was the first time he had met La Vérendrye's family. His wife, the former Marie-Anne du Sable, to whom he had been married for eighteen years, was a quiet woman who had resigned herself to being wedded to a man who was seldom at home. Their manner towards each other was formal. This André found rather strange, accustomed as he was to his own warm-hearted parents. That La Vérendrye was a hero to his sons was evident from the first moment of their arrival. Eagerly they plied him with questions as to the imminence of the proposed expedition to the West. The boys all took after their father, with the same sharp features and eagerness of expression. To André's surprise, he was now introduced to a daughter, a young girl of six whom La Vérendrye had not mentioned, though from his fondness of her this appeared to have been an unintentional oversight. Marie-Catherine, it was obvious, was the joy of her mother's heart, and this was not surprising when for twelve years Madame had been surrounded only by males.

They were a jolly, noisy family whose entire interest centered on the stories and experiences that their father had to relate. For supper that night they were joined by Pierre's widowed sister, Marie Renée, and her son Christophe Dufrost de la Jemeraye, a young man of twenty-two who was also eager to be part of the expedition. André was impressed with this nephew who was a man of strong character, with the same instinct for leadership as his uncle. Meeting this family, increased André's keenness for the expedition, even though it would mean his being away from home for perhaps many years.

The two men who waited upon the Governor-General a week later looked very different from the men clad in deerskins who had discussed the project over the tavern table in Michilimackinac. They were now dressed in well-tailored clothes, with flowered waistcoats, carefully dressed hair and swords at their sides. It was only their rugged faces and hardened hands that showed they were not accustomed to wearing formal clothes.

Governor de Beauharnois received them cordially and ordered brandy for them while he entered into a lengthy discussion of the proposed journey. Neither of them had met the sixty-year-old Governor before but the reports they had received of him from others were sustained. Over forty years service in the Navy had given him a much broader outlook than those who spent their lives within the shadow of Versailles. He had shown an understanding of the people of the colony and enjoyed rugged men like the two now before him. He had read every word of La Vérendrye's reports carefully, had weighed the matter and had forwarded them to France with strong recommendations. The results he had obtained had, however, not been very encouraging.

He took out his snuff box, applied a pinch delicately to each nostril, sneezed, cleared his throat and continued the discussion.

"I had hoped by this time, monsieur," he said to La Vérendrye, "to have more encouraging news for you." He paused to see what effect his words had on the explorer.

La Vérendrye smiled. "I have learned not to expect too much, Excellency," he replied.

"It is as well. To speak frankly, I cannot understand their attitude, but then ..." he threw out his hands in a gesture of despair, "who has ever been able to understand it? I am ready to admit that not knowing the colonies they cannot always realize the importance of these explorations but you would think that when I have impressed upon them how much it would mean to the Mother Country, they would at least give me credit for knowing what I am talking about. Unfortunately, as you no doubt know, these matters rest in the hands of the Comte de Maurepas, the Minister in Charge of Colonial Affairs—not that he knows anything at all about Colonial affairs!" He laughed and there was exasperation in the laugh. "I don't know whether you gentlemen know anything of His Highness the Comte de Maurepas?"

La Vérendrye and André both replied in the negative.

"Well, since you are going to be helped or hindered by this gentleman, I will tell you about him—but you must never quote me or I might lose my head for treason."

"Of course not, Excellency," they both replied together.

The Marquis rose from his chair and walked about to ease the irritation which contemplation of de Maurepas always incurred. "Because he is the grandson of the late Chancellor Pontchartrain of worthy memory, this young man has been closely associated with the Court since he was about eleven or twelve years old. I have met him several times." The expression on his face indicated that that had not been a pleasure. "He is flighty, frivolous and pleasure-loving, with an aptitude for writing witty epigrams and facetious verses. These attributes apparently make good ministers, at least in the eyes of those who arrange governments. As you already know, our illustrious King Louis XV has not inherited his grandfather's interest in the colonies. He is only twenty years old and so we must be patient. Perhaps as he grows older he will develop more interest—though not with ministers like de Maurepas to advise him. With such men, alas, rests the fate of the French empire."

He stopped and said abruptly: "Some more brandy, gentlemen." He filled their glasses and while they sipped it, he sat down again at his desk and fingered the letters that lay thereon. "I have told you this to give you some idea of the difficulties that lay before me—and before you," he continued. "The most encouragement I can give you, is that His Majesty has expressed interest in the explorations you propose. They always express interest!" The last words were said with disdain. "But that is as far as it goes. Oh, yes, they are interested but they won't do anything to further the project. Unfortunately, Father Charlevoix, whom I had hoped would aid us, has been of little help. He has urged that the—let me see just how does he put it." He hunted through the letters before him and said: "Yes, here it is. 'The discovery of the Western Sea is a matter which should be carried through continuously and without a stop'. Yes, that is hopeful advice but he, too, er … has the lack of foresight to say that no money should be expended upon it. Do you know Father Charlevoix?"

"We both met him when he was here some ten years ago," La Vérendrye informed him. "I had thought he would support us."

"So had I," de Beauharnois said dryly. "Well now, to get to the point and stop haggling and grumbling. You have His Majesty's permission to proceed with your explorations but not one sou will he appropriate to the cause." He leaned forward and snapped the last sentence out. "He makes one concession—you are to be granted a monopoly on all furs obtained in the region you explore. And—you must establish trading posts all along the way."

The Marquis leaned back ready for the explosion which he knew would come.

"But, Excellency, that will retard our progress and take us years!" La Vérendrye exclaimed.

"I know. I have written them that again and again. The same answer comes back."

"I have already secured the services of several fine men to act as my lieutenants and with perhaps twenty or thirty men whom I could hire to go with us, strong trustworthy men, we could make much better progress than having to stop and establish forts," La Vérendrye said despondently.

"Don't think I don't feel for you La Vérendrye. I do. I know your unselfishness and that your only desire is to make this discovery because of what it will mean to this colony. But you cannot make petty men understand such an idea. Because they themselves in such a position would make capital out of it, they suspect other men of doing the same."

"I will not give up the idea, Excellency. If France will not support me, then I shall have to go to those who will."

De Beauharnois' expression sharpened. "You mean, monsieur?" he asked guardedly.

"I used the word France when I should have said if the *government* of France will not support me," La Vérendrye corrected. "It sounded as though I meant I would go to the English ..."

The Marquis laughed. "You startled me for a moment," he admitted.

"I am a Frenchman, Excellency, and shall always be one. But that thought does bring to my mind that if we don't proceed with this idea and *promptly,* the English will get ahead of us."

"I know. I know. I have mentioned that in my despatches, too. All I can do, monsieur, is to urge you to proceed as quickly as you can and to rest assured I will not cease to argue your cause from every possible angle. One thing I have decided and have already informed de Maurepas—I shall appropriate from our funds here the sum of two thousand livres to help you in the purchase of presents for the tribes."

"Thank you, Excellency. I am grateful for whatever help I can obtain. I have another idea, suggested by Monsieur de Courville-Boissart's brother-in-law." He glanced at André as he made the statement. "That is that we make an arrangement with the merchants in Montreal. If they will agree to let me have periodical supplies we will repay them with the peltries we receive in trade from the Indians."

"Excellent, excellent," the Marquis agreed.

"Monsieur André's family and my sons and nephew are willing to invest in the project."

De Beauharnois turned to André. "Your family are pioneers are they not?"

"Yes, Excellency. We have been in Montreal since 1653..."

"Splendid! Fur traders?"

"Some of us. I have spent several years at it; my nephew also—he will go with us too. My father spent some years in the woods and his grandfather before him."

"Then you will all be excellent men to accompany our intrepid explorer." He rose and held out his hand to La Vérendrye "I regret that I cannot do more for you. But I shall not give up trying. God go with you."

Though they were disappointed, yet they were not greatly so, for neither of them had expected much. And the sincerity of the support of the Marquis de Beauharnois encouraged them.

# CHAPTER THIRTY-SEVEN

BY THE time La Vérendrye had concluded his negotiations with the Montreal merchants, winter had again *set* in and the expedition had to be postponed until the spring. The merchants had driven a hard bargain, and because he had no other alternative La Vérendrye had to accept their terms. Without a continuous flow of supplies he was helpless and only the merchants could furnish these supplies. His arrangements concluded, he returned to Three Rivers for the winter and those on the Seigneuries settled into months of idleness that were, however, quite acceptable with the prospect of several years absence facing some of them when spring came.

It was one of the happiest winters that they had known with all members of the families at home. Ann-Marie and her husband had returned and divided their time between her home arid the Chateau. She was expecting another child. She brought little Nicholas-Jean, now two years old, over to play with Philip and again there was the sound of childish voices to gladden their hearts.

It was six years since Paul-André had spent a winter at home. Probably it was the projected expedition that made him more content or perhaps it was because he was older, but he found that the winter months no longer dragged. With his father and the habitants of the Seigneury, he joined those of the de Courville Seigneury on hunting expeditions from which they brought home bear and venison for the winter store cupboards. Then there were trees to be hewn and cut into logs, for fires must be kept constantly alight during these sub-zero months. This was healthy, hardy work that kept the men in condition during the leisure months.

But it was not all work, though the men hardly considered these chores as work. There were the sleighing and skating parties that neighbor shared with neighbor and which were conducive to romance. As André had in his younger years, so now Paul-André with his tousled auburn hair and dreamy eyes excited the hearts of the young girls. He was shy and despite all the efforts of his parents, avoided the opposite sex and preferred men's company. The men chided him and reminded him that he would have to pay a fine if he did not marry by the time he was twenty.

"I have four years yet," he would reply good-naturedly and leave the matter there.

André's chief interest naturally centered in his son. Though he had for many years looked forward to exploring, yet now he had considerable misgivings about going away. He was much torn between his two loves. Never before had he so wanted to settle down and watch the son who changed day by day. His fondness for children which had been apparent with Elise's family, was intensified in his own. Nothing delighted him more than to see Philip's eyes light up when he came in or to have arms extended in an invitation to be picked up. "I don't want him to forget me while I am away," he would say frequently, or "If I'm with him all the time now, he's more likely to remember me," and his mother would assure him that they would keep his memory alive no matter how long he was away.

Of all of them, perhaps Aunt Marguerite was the happiest. It had taken her many months to recover from the shock of her husband's death, and the previous winter she had taken little part in the festivities. But gradually the love she had always had for her native home had healed her wounds. This had been aided by the attitude of those on the Seigneuries and also by the receipt of some letters from Henry. The French habitant was naturally warmhearted and hospitable, in contrast to the colder natures of the English and Dutch with whom she had had to associate during the years of her marriage. There were a few who remembered her as a light-hearted girl who had been the favorite of the Seigneury, and those few took her back to their hearts and forgave her for having married an Englishman. To most of them she was a comparative stranger and they accepted her as a charming, white-haired lady of nearly sixty who was the twin of their Seigneur to whom they were devoted. Aunt Marie was her champion even as she had been during the prior visit with Eric when there had been so many difficulties. There was always much work for women to do and when she wasn't helping Ann with little Philip, she was assisting with a birthing or caring for those who were ailing. And above all, her greatest joy was having a church to which she could go every day, and she and Father Xavier became the closest of friends.

They were all concerned over Father Xavier. From his rugged experience on the trip to Albany he had sustained a hacking cough that grew steadily worse with the severe winter weather. Yet all the naggings and persuasions could not keep him indoors when he was needed, and his short, rotund figure could be seen tramping through the snows almost every day. Several of the habitants' wives spoke to Paul, but he could not influence the aging priest to take care of himself. Paul sent him over a supply of brandy and urged him to take some whenever he returned from a cold trip. Exasperated, Aunt Marie closed up her own house and went to live at the curé's home as his housekeeper. Her care and brusque nagging brought about an improvement and at least she could see to it that he was warmly clothed when he went out and well fed when he came in.

In the town itself there was the usual entertainment and gaiety. The noblesse gave balls and *soupers* and occasionally those on the seigneuries harnessed the horses to the sleighs and went into town. Governor de la Chassaigne and his wife gave the customary formal entertainments. Madame de Ramezay gave a supper to celebrate the birth of her second grandchild—a girl whom they named after her. Madame la Marquise de Vaudreuil gave several balls and *petits soupers,* some of which they attended. Of all the entertainments those at the Chateau de Vaudreuil were the gayest.

At one of the balls the Sieur de la Vérendrye was present, starting again the rumors that had always linked his name with that of the Marquise. The fact that he was accompanied by his eldest son, Jean-Baptiste, did not lessen the rumors. They were both guests at the Chateau de Vaudreuil. He was in Montreal, he said, to conclude arrangements for the expedition that would shortly get under way. But though curious eyes might watch, they could detect nothing. La Vérendrye danced the first dance with his hostess and once again during the evening. The remainder of the time he was equally attentive to the other ladies. At forty-five he was still a striking man, with a strong athletic figure and a careless audacity that women loved.

The winter closed on an unpleasant note. Early in April, Governor de la Chassaigne sent for Antoine and also André. When they were seated he informed them that Georges Ménard had been arrested with five other men for trading with the English in Albany.

"As you are aware," Governor de la Chassaigne said, directing his remark to André, "we have for some time known that many of our furs were going to Albany. It was largely upon your report, André, that we acted."

"But I hope I shall not be involved, Excellency," André said quickly. "As I told you upon my return from Albany, I do not wish to appear as an informer ..."

"Oh no, no," the Governor said suavely, as he casually applied a pinch of snuff to each nostril.

"Especially as Ménard is a habitant on my brother-in-law's Seigneury," André continued.

"That is understood," de la Chassaigne said. "Of course, Monsieur de Brievaux, we shall have to call upon you for testimony since this man is one of your habitants."

"Yes, I suppose so," Antoine said reluctantly. "He has always given me trouble. You have definite evidence that Ménard is involved?"

André opened his mouth to speak but decided against it. He would tell Antoine later.

"Quite definite. Furthermore he was the leader. The other five men worked under him," the Governor stated.

"Oh. Then it is serious," Antoine replied.

"Very serious. We must stop these leakages to the English and I intend to make an example of these men."

The trial was hastened so that André could be present. Ménard knew that he was trapped and fought with every weapon he had. He knew that he could not be exonerated but with the viciousness of his nature, was not going to pay the penalty without others having to suffer too. The small courtroom was filled to capacity each day and many of the spectators were *coureurs de bois*. Therefore, when Ménard accused André of having informed on him after seeing him in Albany, there was a hard look on the faces of all the woodsmen.

"That is a lie!" André protested. "It is true that I saw Ménard while I was in Albany but no one except my father knows this. I did not even tell my brother-in-law on whose Seigneury Ménard is a habitant. If your Honor will ask them you will find that it is so." Even as he made the remark André realized that it was a poor substantiation of his statement, since members of his own family would hardly deny his words. "Even better, ask his Excellency the Governor to whom I made my report and he will tell you that I stated then—and he has it in writing—that I had seen many Frenchmen trading in Albany but I *mentioned no names whatsoever*." André looked directly at the *coureurs de bois* in the room as he emphatically made the statement.

Fortunately he had always been popular with the woodsmen and few of them knew Ménard.

"We accept your statement, Monsieur de Courville-

Antoine was next called upon to give his testimony regarding Ménard. All the habitants of his Seigneury were present to corroborate the statements he would make in regard to Ménard's neglect of his land, his laziness and his frequent recourse to the brandy bottle.

Ménard listened slumped in his chair, glowering. When he was asked whether he had any reply to make to the statements of his Seigneur, an ugly smile took the place of the frown.

"The Seigneur has been waiting a long time to get his revenge," he said slowly.

"Would you please explain that statement?" the avocat asked.

"Gladly. Ask him how he got that scar over his right eye," Ménard sneered.

Antoine blanched as he realized what was coming.

The counsel turned to Antoine. "Would you care to answer the question, Seigneur?" he asked.

"The matter is entirely irrelevant," Antoine replied coldly. Then in an undertone he spoke quickly to the avocat who referred the matter to the Judge, speaking to him so that those in the room could not hear.

The Judge turned a sharp eye upon the prisoner. "Being vindictive will not free you from the charge, Ménard, and what you evidently intended to say has nothing to do with the case."

"This colony is run for the aristocrats and the sooner the people here realize it the better," Ménard shouted. "Men like me and you," he pointed to the *coureurs de bois,* "have no chance against them. When they want us out of the way they trump up any charge against us. The Seigneur has been determined to rid himself of me ever since the day he found me making love to his daughter. Ask him why he rushed her off to a convent and then married her in such a hurry," he sneered.

Antoine's face was livid with rage. "You dirty rat!" he growled and his clenched fists moved so that for a moment it looked as though he were going to strike the prisoner. Then he calmed himself and turned to the courtroom. "Half-truths are worse than whole truths. Therefore, your Honor, I will clarify what has been said. Not only has this man always neglected his land but, as other habitants on my Seigneury can testify, they have always had to watch over their women where he was concerned. His own wife left him for reasons that are known to all. This man attempted to seduce one of my daughters but fortunately I discovered it in time and the small scar on my forehead, which he has indicated, was the result of the fight we had. Naturally any father would keep such a matter to himself and not involve the name of his daughter. Make of that what you wish," he concluded with disgust and sat down.

The town immediately became alive with gossip, providing as the trial had, chatter for both tavern and drawing room. When the court adjourned, André went directly to Dillon's Tavern determined to face his critics if there were any. His appearance caused a momentary cessation in the buzz of conversation, which was at once resumed, though in most cases with a change of topic. He stood in the doorway a moment, his eyes carefully surveying the faces turned to him. It was seldom that anyone saw André de Courville-Boissart with a set, hard expression such as he now wore.

"Le Roux, come and join us," a man's voice shouted and the tension in the air broke. André looked in the direction of the voice and saw a number of voyageurs seated at a table. Immediately his face broke into its customary grin and his good humor returned as several whom he passed on his way to the table gave him a friendly slap on the back. Louis Dillon himself came over to the table and held out his hand to André. For many long years Louis had been the friend of the *coureurs de bois,* back to the days when his tavern had been only one room and had not grown to its present grandeur as a hostelry.

"Glad you came over, André," he said, then turning to those at the table and others who had gathered around he said: "I knew this boy's great-grandfather, Old Pierre. And we all know his father, the Sieur de Courville-Boissart. I remember your father when he came here the first time with Old Pierre. That was when he was starting out as a *coureur de bois* with that rogue Charles Péchard. It goes a long way back, men, and there is no finer blood in Montreal than runs in this boy's veins." Though André was now thirty-eight he was still a boy to Louis Dillion who was nearing eighty. Louis raised his glass. "I give you Le Roux Boissart, our comrade and one of the finest voyageurs in Montreal."

It seemed to André that the whole tavern rang with the response to the toast, and the misgivings which he had had when he entered were dispelled. In response he related the whole story to them; his journey to Albany, its reason and the Governor's request. He told of seeing Ménard and they knew he spoke the truth when he told them he had not even mentioned it to Antoine de Brievaux.

"My father was the only one who knew," he concluded.

While this was going on at the Tavern, Jean-Baptiste de Ramezay was galloping towards the Chateau. Throwing the reins to a lackey he strode into the house and went in search of his wife. She was in her bedroom, a maid informed him, and without a thought to etiquette, he pushed open the door and strode in. She was feeding Marie-Charlotte and exclaimed angrily at his abrupt entrance. Quickly she snatched a shawl and covered her breast. Though he had seen them bared many times it was under different circumstances and the peculiar quirks of etiquette made that different from when she was feeding her child.

"Jean-Baptiste! What are you thinking about? Leave the room immediately!" she exclaimed angrily. He had made her jump so that the baby began to voice protests. By the time she had soothed her, Jean-Baptiste had left.

It proved to Ann-Marie's advantage, for by the time she saw her husband again his anger had cooled to some degree. She purposely kept him waiting, lingering over her dressing and not coming down until it was time for dinner. At the Chateau they dined at a more fashionable hour. Jean-Baptiste had only time to apologize to her before Madame and his three sisters joined them. When later they retired to their own suite, Ann-Marie turned and faced him.

"Well, what was all the anger and excitement?" she asked.

He regarded her steadily for a moment and wished she had not looked so beautiful. Her thick auburn hair was arranged over each shoulder in long curls, as she always wore it when they were at home. At twenty she had a poise and maturity beyond her years. Knowing that her husband was angry over something that was presumably connected with her, she had put on one of her most becoming dresses, which, though simple, nevertheless enhanced her charms.

Looking at her Jean-Baptiste's anger faded and he would have preferred taking her in his arms. Then, remembering the cause of his anger was that she had been in another man's arms, his quick temper returned and he said abruptly:

"Why did you never tell me about this man Ménard?"

He saw her color drain from her face and this made him still more angry. But her voice was quite controlled as she said: "Ménard? You mean the man who is on trial?"

"Who else would I mean?"

"What about him?" she hedged.

"That is what I am asking you!"

"I don't understand."

"Yes, you do, and I want the truth. Stop asking foolish questions so that you can think up some trumpery story." For some reason that she could not herself have explained she half-smiled and Jean-Baptiste's combustible temper broke its bonds. They were standing before the fire, and seizing her by the shoulders, he gave her a shake. It was a habit of his that had always infuriated her, for this was not their first argument or quarrel.

"I demand an answer, Ann-Marie, and the truth. Why did you not tell me Ménard had been your lover?"

"My lover! Don't be a fool! And take your hands off my shoulders. You are hurting me."

But instead he gripped her shoulders until his powerful fingers dug into her flesh.

"Haven't I warned you times enough about your behavior? I expect to be Governor of this town some day and I will not have my name ruined by my wife—if it is not already ruined. All over town tonight they will be talking about you and Ménard ..."

"It's a lie!"

"Then go and ask your father. Tell him I'm sending you back to him because I don't want a ... strumpet for a wife."

With that he strode into their adjoining bedroom, slamming the door. Ann-Marie stood there bewildered. She had not been out that day and had not heard what had occurred at the trial. "Ask your father." What had he meant? She must find out. But first she had to straighten out her own mind. How had this scandal been renewed? Obviously something had been exposed at the trial. The thought angered her. She had always been ashamed of her behavior with Ménard. In recent years she had forgotten it. And now it had somehow been revived. She stared thoughtfully into the fire and felt degraded. Somehow she must preserve her dignity with her husband. Hitherto their quarrels over men had rather amused her, for she liked to keep him jealous and when they made up he was always so lovable. Theirs had not been a marriage of solicitude and understanding. Both had natures that were tempestuous, yet it was this that had made their love so exciting.

Jean-Baptiste stood before the window in the bedroom looking out towards the town where gallows were probably being erected for the men condemned that morning. He was trying to control his surging anger. Always after they had quarrelled it was he who went to her and asked forgiveness. But this time, he told himself, he would not. He would be firm. He had given in to her too many times, because he loved her so deeply and was afraid of losing her to some other man. He had no doubts about her fidelity. She was provocative and seductive, but she was always honest and he knew that in their other quarrels she spoke the truth when she insisted that her flirtations were harmless. And was she to blame? She was so beautiful that men could not resist her. He had felt sorry for the men. There had been the young ensign at the post at Hudson Bay who had fallen so deeply in love with her that de Ramezay had had to arrange his transfer. And there had been other men there too, older men as well, who had made fools of themselves over her. And since their return to Montreal and the winter season of entertainment, there was scarcely a day that *billets-doux* were not delivered to the Chateau. Ann-Marie would laugh over them and hand them to him to read. After every ball she was deluged with them, all from men who considered marriage as merely a convenience and expected she would do the same.

His thoughts ceased abruptly as he heard the door open. He did not turn. Her arms came round his waist. Still he did not move. She sidled around, lifting his arm up across her shoulders. He tried to be well-controlled but it was difficult.

"I'm sorry, Jean-Baptiste," she said and his control broke. Both arms went around her and he held her to him tightly, forgetting that he had been angry and hungrily pressing his lips to hers.

"Let me tell you about it," she said when the ecstasy momentarily passed.

He did not then want to speak of it but it had to be done. With ease he lifted her and sinking into the nearest chair, held her on his lap.

"All right, the confession," he said and smiled gently.

Briefly she told him what had happened that day at Ménard's house, concluding with the remark: "I thought then that all women had lovers before they married ..."

"And did you?" he asked.

"You were my first lover. You know that." She buried her face against his neck and again emotion flooded them as they sat there without candlelight and only a pale streak of moonlight illuminating the room.

"And I'm still your lover and always will be darling," he said and drew her to him hungrily. The feel of his lips sent passion surging through her. It was a night such as only lovers know as with each waking from blissful sleep, they turned again to each other and renewed their profound desire.

The next morning when she had attended to her duties as a mother and had given Marie-Charlotte her breakfast, Jean-Baptiste came to the door and tapped. She was sipping her hot chocolate, her long tresses making a shawl around her shoulders. She put down the cup and held out her arms to him. With his head lying on her shoulder, she spoke again of the matter of Ménard.

"Darling, have I really disgraced you?" she asked.

"It will die down, dear. Your father and I can handle the men, but ..." he smiled broadly as he added, "you will have to handle the women. They love gossip of this kind."

"I can handle them," she said determinedly and there was a glint in her eyes.

"I'm sure you can," he said and smiled again. "Ménard meets his fate this morning."

"This morning! Oh dear, how awful! He will be hanged?"

"Yes."

She covered her eyes a moment. These public hangings were such a horrible sight.

"I shan't go out today then," she said. "I can't feel sorry for him. He was such a vile man. Still, it's an awful end."

"He deserved it from all accounts."

Ménard and the five men with him were condemned and the town shuddered at the gruesomeness of it. First they were broken on the wheel and then hanged, their distorted bodies dangling from the gallows for several days. Then they were burned in the public square, a warning to all who dared to trade with the enemy.

A few weeks afterwards, Jean-Baptiste de Ramezay left Montreal with a small force of thirty men who under the leadership of the Sieur de la Fresnière journeyed down the Richelieu River and across Lac Champlain to establish a fort at Pointe de la Chevelure (Crown Point as it was later called). This was the French answer to the English fort at Oswego and the result of the report Paul and André had brought back with them from Albany. Situated at a strategic point at the far end of Lac Champlain, Fort Frédéric, as it was named, guarded the approach to the St. Lawrence River. By this step, the French established a policy which was indirectly to lead to war some ten years hence.

# CHAPTER THIRTY-EIGHT

O N A warm day in June of the year 1731, the long projected expedition in search of the Western Ocean set out from Montreal. The flotilla of canoes laden with supplies and presents for the Indian tribes, was an impressive sight. La Vérendrye had chosen to use small canoes, each manned by four men, as these were more easily handled over the portages. He had organized his company well, hiring thirty experienced men. Each canoe was in charge of those he called his lieutenants—André, Paul-Andrè, his nephew Christophe de la Jemeraye and his eldest son, Jean-Baptiste. André was virtually the second in command, though he insisted upon dividing this honor with La Jemeraye who, though only twenty-three was an experienced voyageur and a favorite with his uncle.

All Montreal, it seemed, was out to watch the flotilla leave. La Vérendrye, standing in the first canoe, was very proud as he waved to those on the shores. After years of dreaming, he was about to realize his ambition. He was not starting out as he had wished and planned, but he hoped to overcome the handicaps which had been forced upon him. Much was the discussion and much the doubt among those who watched the expedition leave. La Salle and Du Lhut had failed and so had De Soto and Ponce de Leon. Wasn't it a hopeless task? Wasn't this desire to discover more territory rather futile? Hadn't they already more land than they could care for and cultivate? Why couldn't these men stay at home and help develop Montreal and its surrounding territory? No, these more lethargic natures could not understand the intensive urge that surged through the minds of men like La Vérendrye.

La Vérendrye had hired only men who were accustomed to the rigors of the wilderness. Even before they reached Michilimackinac he found that this advantage could also prove a definite disadvantage. The route they were taking at the onset was familiar territory to all voyageurs and every night when they encamped there were arguments, for every man had his own ideas as to the vantage points for stopping on the journey and was not willing to accept the decision of the leaders. Sharp words passed and La Vérendrye had to enforce a rigid discipline and insist that the men carry out the orders relayed by his lieutenants. It did not make a good beginning. La Vérendrye liked to have harmony and cooperation among those with him and not have to force his men to obey.

Therefore when six weeks later they reached Michilimackinac he would have preferred not to stop. But he had to replenish his supplies and also pick up Father Mesaiger who would be their chaplain and missionary. Even without these necessities for stopping, he would have had no alternative. Michilimackinac was the last point of civilization—if such it could be called—and he would never have been able to get his men to consent to pass it by.

The town was wild, packed with fur traders preparing for their winter treks. As the Indian women swarmed to the shore to greet them, La Vérendrye looked significantly at his lieutenants and said: "Do your best. We are in for trouble. We'll leave as soon as possible."

The men were told to report at dawn the following day though La Vérendrye knew they would not get started anywhere near that time. It would take a lot of rounding up before they were all accounted for.

He and his lieutenants went at once to the merchants to barter for supplies. When their business was concluded they went to *Le Castor* for refreshment. Paul-André now had his real baptism.

When last he had been at Michilimackinac with his uncle it had been off-season and comparatively quiet. Now the sights he saw were nauseating. Men behaved worse than beasts, rolling drunk in the gutters, raping women in the taverns or the streets and constantly engaging in fights. Frequently he and André had forcibly to disentangle themselves from the squaws who hung on to them and this had to be done carefully, for should a squaw get hurt, she would shout abuse so loudly that in a moment they would have had a fight on their hands with some drunken white or half breed who chose to champion the cause.

When finally two days later they started out again, two men were missing and one dead, knifed in a brawl. Several of the others were so sodden with brandy as to be useless in the canoes and others were nursing injuries of which they constantly complained when made to work. La Vérendrye was experienced with men of this type and counted it lucky that the casualties were not heavier. He merely shrugged his shoulders, knowing that there would be no more towns from then on. In a couple of days the men would have straightened themselves out.

In this he was correct and for the next several weeks all went well. They skirted across Lac Superior and by the end of August reached Grand Portage. This was the end of the familiar territory to the voyageurs and now La Vérendrye experienced real difficulties with the men he had hired. Many of them had been bribed by those in Montreal and these successfully played upon the superstitious fears of their comrades with vivid stories of the fiend-infested regions that lay farther west. La Vérendrye was faced with mutiny. The majority of the men refused to continue so late in the season and insisted that they remain at Kaministikwia for the winter. This was a small trading post that Du Lhut had established years before at the mouth of the river of the same name, on the north shore of Lac Superior.

There were only two methods open to La Vérendrye to get his men to continue—persuasion or armed force. The latter was out of the question for sooner or later it would have reacted against him and perhaps have led to his murder as it had with La Salle. He tried the former and was partially successful. Some of the men agreed to continue with La Jemeraye, while La Vérendrye was forced to spend the winter with the remaining mutineers at Kaministikwia.

Paul-André and La Vérendrye's son, Pierre, went with La Jemeraye and they made their way over difficult terrain to Rainy Lake. It took months of heavy travelling that required great fortitude, through a seemingly endless chain of small rivers and lakes, some of which were so shallow that the canoes had to be dragged for miles over insect-infested swamps. There were innumerable portages that made the going still more difficult. At Rainy Lake, La Jemeraye established the first fort and named it Fort Pierre in honor of La Vérendrye.

Their efforts were rewarded, for when La Jemeraye and his men rejoined La Vérendrye in the spring of 1732 they brought with them the first cargo of peltries to be sent to the Montreal partners.

The entire force returned to Fort Pierre in the spring. It was a beautiful spot, standing in a meadow surrounded by a grove of oaks at the foot of a series of rapids near where Rainy Lake discharged its waters into the river of the same name. Here La Vérendrye left some of his mutinous men to look after the post and trade with the Indians, while he pushed forward, descending the Rainy River to the Lac des Bois, or Lake of the Woods.

Crossing to the western shore of the Lake, he established another fort—Fort St. Charles, named in honor of Governor Charles de Beauharnois. It was situated amidst the most beautiful scenery that nature could provide. Not only did the Lake collect the waters from the Rainy River on the east, through which it connected with Lac Superior, but also those of the Ouinipigon River on the northwest where it discharged its waters into Lac Ouinipigon, forming a strategic route later to be known as the

"Northwest Angle." Here he was to suffer his first great disappointment as he discovered that the Indians assurance that the Western Ocean flowed from Lac Ouinipigon was a myth.

The fort was a typical one with a post in the center from which waved the French flag. It was protected by a strong stockade, with bastions at each corner. Within were four buildings—rough cabins constructed of logs and clay and covered with bark. These constituted the Commandant's house, the missionary's house, the church and the main house for the remainder of the force.

Here they were to remain for two years! Lack of cooperation from Montreal and the stupidity of government officials in France prevented the voyage of discovery from progressing. It was what La Vérendrye had foreseen and feared but had hoped to overcome.

On a spring day in 1734 he contemplated the situation with a deep frown on his face. In his hand was a letter which he had just received. He had already read it several times but read it again to see if there could not be at least one ray of hope to be gleaned from it. He threw it down and resting his head in his hands gave way momentarily to the despair that overwhelmed him.

He was still sitting thus when André came in, paused when he saw his leader's dejection but at the invitation of La Vérendrye pulled up a roughly hewn wooden chair and sat down.

"Bad news?" André asked.

Pierre de la Vérendrye looked towards him. His blue eyes were very tired and his long, thin face appeared lengthened by his distress.

"The same thing," he said in answer to André's question. "I just don't understand it, André, that's all. Listen to this." He took up the paper before him. "It is from the Governor who quotes from a letter he has received from the Comte de Maurepas. There is the usual preamble and then he goes on to say, 'His Majesty has observed with pleasure the details of all that occurred in the course of the Sieur de la Vérendrye's journey; he has approved of his conduct with relation to the different tribes he saw; and was particularly pleased at the zeal he displayed in complying with the request made by the Crees to let them have his son to go to war with them. Such a mark of confidence will secure him the attachment of those savages.' " La Vérendrye paused and looked up at André with an ironical smile playing about his mouth. "Up to that point I was very encouraged. But now listen to the last part. 'His Majesty, however, is still indisposed to incur any expense in connection with this enterprise, in which it seems very likely the parties concerned will sustain no loss.' Note that! *'The parties concerned will sustain no loss'! Sacré dieu* and we are already in debt for 43,000 livres! Oh yes, he approves of the zeal I am showing in devoting myself to the work. How kind of him! It isn't soft words we want, it is their support, support in money or supplies so that we can carry on. Approves of my zeal! *Sacré diable!"*

He threw down the paper and getting up abruptly began to pace back and forth across the narrow floor. "What is wrong with these people, André? Or am I just mad? Can't they understand what this route to the Western Ocean would mean to France?"

André shook his head. "If so many of those with you here can't understand your purpose, how can we expect those far away in France to do so?" he said.

La Vérendrye swung round facing André and his blue eyes were blazing. "But I shall succeed despite their foolishness. I have dreamed of this for too many years to give up easily." He stopped and gazed out of the window. "I know, André, that one day we shall climb to the top of a mountain and shall see the Western Ocean stretching before us." He looked up at the sky enviously watching a flock of birds that soared over the fort. "If only man could fly," André heard him remark, "If only God had fitted us with the same advantage as these winged creatures. Then instead of plodding along on the ground we could see over the mountains. My feathered friends, what can you see up there? Is it the ocean not too far distant? If only I could fly like you," he said again.

He fell into silence and André knew him too well to interrupt. He took out his pipe and lit it, leaving La Vérendrye to cogitate upon the vast schemes seething through his brain. These three years with La Vérendrye had taught André much. He had always liked him; now having worked side by side with him, that liking had grown to admiration and devotion because of the man's indomitable courage and resourcefulness and his unselfish devotion to an ideal. Furthermore, he had discovered in him a rare quality—that of making friends. This was not only with the white man but with the Indian. In the name of France he had welcomed the red men to the fort, surprising them with the treatment accorded them. This contrasted vastly with what they received from the English who always regarded them as savages and treated them as such. La Vérendrye treated them as human beings and often as comrades and because of this the tribes assured him they much preferred to trade with the French.

It was this that was now worrying him. He turned again to André. "The canoes brought no supplies," he said in a flat voice.

"So I heard," André said sympathetically.

"What am I going to do, André? Here I have been insisting to the Indians that they bring us all their furs, warning them not to trade with the English and now, when they come I shall have nothing to offer them in exchange. What will they think of the friendship that I have assured them we have for them, when they come and I have no supplies? Of course they must go again to the English and they will say Frenchmen are liars. They have to have supplies on which to live."

"Do you know why no supplies came?"

"We haven't sent the merchants enough peltries. I have letters here full of vilification." His head sank into his hands again. "They'll never understand." He stood up again and paced the floor. "I'll have to go to Montreal. There's no other way. We have to have supplies. I must go and make some arrangements, though God knows what more I can offer the merchants. The men will starve if we don't get some help. There isn't enough fish and game to feed us all the time ..."

"And the wild oats are a failure ..."

"Perhaps if I go to Montreal I can find some way out of the difficulty."

"It would seem to be the only thing to do," André agreed.

There was a commotion outside and La Vérendrye went to the window to investigate. The next moment he fairly leapt across the room shouting: "There's Jean-Baptiste!"

André followed him to the door and watched smiling as La Vérendrye hugged his tall son and kissed him on both cheeks. "Well, there's one worry less for him," André thought.

Men were pouring into the yard welcoming their returned comrade, while six Indian chiefs stood by regarding a little contemptuously this strange display of emotion by their white friends.

Early the previous autumn over six hundred Crees had arrived at the fort, singing their war song and informing La Vérendrye that in order to protect themselves and preserve their dignity they must go on the warpath against the Sioux. They asked his permission, though at the same time warning him they would not be responsible for what might ensue if he refused. They tempered their demand, however, with a compromise—if he would let his eldest son go with them they would do exactly as he directed. This was one of the hardest decisions La Vérendrye had had to make. Though he had made friends with the Crees and Assinboines he was too wise to trust them too much. Yet if he refused to let his son go with them they would brand him and all Frenchmen as cowards. He had talked it over with his lieutenants who were all agreed he should accede to the savages request and this opinion was supported by Jean-Baptiste himself.

He had a courage equal to his father's and the same strength of character. Never had La Vérendrye been so proud as when he had watched this son of twenty-one years march away, the only white man among hundreds of savages. And now Jean-Baptiste was back and unharmed.

La Vérendrye produced the last flagon of brandy which he had been hoarding against necessity but which he now felt should be used to celebrate his son's return. As he filled the mugs, he gave his son the news, unsatisfactory as it was. La Jemeraye and Pierre, he told him were at Fort Pierre. Jean-Baptiste's own account had little in it that was of importance. In fact the expedition had proved futile. He had been made a Chief according to the rules of the savages and had been treated with the greatest respect and kindness. The two opposing tribes had, however, not attacked each other and he had thought it unnecessary to proceed any farther and had returned with the six chiefs. *But the Sioux had learned that the son of the Sieur de la Vérendrye had been with their enemies.*

The next day custom necessitated that La Vérendrye and his lieutenants receive the Chiefs in formal council. Paul-André had been assigned a most important task—that of chief interpreter for the expedition. With his aptitude for languages, he had soon mastered the Cree dialect. André had learned it too, but he was not as fluent. Now, as they all assembled, Paul-André took his place beside La Vérendrye and prepared to translate for him.

At the head of the circle, La Vérendrye set an example to all the white men with him. He had a natural dignity and an appearance of fearlessness that never failed to impress the red men. His boredom with the long council meeting was well-concealed beneath an expression of assumed interest and never for a moment did he let it change.

An Assinboine chief had been talking for a long while and then he began to tell of the representatives of a tribe they had met on their wanderings.

"He says they are called Ouachipouennes," Paul-André said.

"Repeat that name," La Vérendrye said.

"Ouachipouennes," Paul-André repeated slowly, looking towards the Indian chief to see if he had said it correctly.

La Vérendrye considered it thoughtfully. "That's a new name," he said.

Paul-André addressed a question to the Chief and then said: "He says it means *Sioux-who-live-underground* but I can't get any further explanation from him."

"Question him further," La Vérendrye directed.

The Chief babbled on and then Paul-André said: "He says they are tall, white in color, with hair that is light, chestnut, or sometimes black. They talk and sing like Frenchmen and they build their houses very like ours."

"Ask him where is the home of this tribe," he said.

Paul-André repeated the question to the Chief, and waited for his answer. "He says about three hundred leagues or so from here. He also adds that he has spoken to them of us and that they sent a message to you saying that they greatly desire to be our friends and begs that you will send someone to visit them."

"Tell him that we shall do so at the earliest possible opportunity," La Vérendrye said and while Paul-André relayed the remark, La Vérendrye turned to his men and said eagerly. "If they are white in color and these men think they are descended from the French, perhaps... perhaps it could be that they are descended from the Spaniards. At any rate, they should know where the Spaniards are and from that we can find the Ocean. Our goal comes in sight."

The Chiefs finished and La Vérendrye must now reply to them, of necessity making his speech long to conform with their ideas. Again it must all be interpreted, for though La Vérendrye had learned much of the language, he had been too busy to become really proficient.

"My children," he began. "In the name of the Great White Father across the ocean I welcome you. As I have told you often before, the French are the most powerful nation in the world and there is no land unknown to them. The Great White Father whose mouthpiece I am and whom we all obey, loves you as his children and if you obey him he will give to you all that you need." He paused a moment while Paul-André finished his translation and in that pause studied the copper-colored faces turned towards him. In the warmth of the spring day they were clad only in breech-clouts and moccasins. La Vérendrye had a genuine admiration for these men whose tall, muscular bodies showed their strength and whose faces were so serious and stern and in many cases quite handsome with the determined lines that showed their character. With the right guidance and understanding there could be no better friends.

"I want you, my children," he continued, "to think seriously of the benefit it is to you to have Frenchmen among you, at whose establishments you find all the things you require throughout the year. We permit you to come within our forts to trade; we do not, as the English do, insist that you remain outside and thrust the goods to you through a window, obliging you to take what they give you whether good or bad. We allow you to choose what you want in trade. We buy your meat, your wild oats, your bark, gum and roots. You make great profit out of us, but you must also make some return to us. You cannot come here empty-handed as you often do. You must bring us your peltries so that we in turn can live. It is not fair to us nor to the Great White Father to take what we have to offer and then go to the English with your furs. Any man among you who does this, will not be permitted to enter our forts ever again. I repeat to you, you must not come here empty-handed. You must be more industrious. You must hunt all the winter and you must bring us more furs."

Again he paused to let Paul-André finish translating and to watch the effect of his words. He saw the men opposite him nodding as they heard Paul-André's translation and knew with satisfaction that they had understood the urgency of his words. Paul-André was a good interpreter. He did not merely translate the words but he put the emphasis where it was needed and he now repeated several times his leader's insistence that they must have more furs.

"I am preparing to return to Montreal in order that I may procure for you the further supplies that you need. Our storehouse is getting low. By the time you again return to us we shall be well-stocked but we shall not give to you unless you bring the peltries that we need. In my absence my son who accompanied you on your recent expedition and in whom you have shown such confidence, will be in charge here. I place in you the same confidence that you have placed in him and shall look to you to serve him and protect him and his men until my return."

For a long time he had to continue talking to them. It did not matter that he repeated what he had said before as long as he talked a long while.

All except the red men were exhausted and weary when the speeches were over. The presents in the center were then distributed and then the stewpot was brought out, for without this pot there could be no lasting friendship. La Vérendrye and his lieutenants retired to his house to eat their own meal.

# CHAPTER THIRTY-NINE

I N THE absent years not many outward changes had taken place in Montreal. To André it seemed as though time had stood still as on the morning of August 25, 1734, he jumped out of the canoe and waved La Vérendrye and the others on towards town. It was scarcely an hour since dawn yet already the fields were busy with workers, for the wheat was ripe and harvesting in full swing. The sun's rays beat down on them, heralding a day that would bring sweltering heat.

André stood for a moment absorbing the beauty and the peace, and then hurried up the steps. He could have asked for no greater welcome, for his small son was sliding down the balustrade and with a whoop rushed to him, shouting, "Mon père."

André swept him up in his arms and held him aloft, his eyes gleaming with pride that this sturdy youngster was his own flesh and blood. "Why, you young rogue, you talk!" he exclaimed.

"Of course he talks," a voice behind him said and André turned to see Mère Clarissa whose red face beamed a welcome.

"Mère Clarissa!" he shouted and lowering Philip gave her a large hug and kiss. "Where's the family?"

"The Sieur is outside somewhere. Madame is upstairs ..."

"Not up yet!"

"It's early ..."

Mère Clarissa had tried to hide the hesitation before answering but André had noticed it.

"Isn't she well?" he asked anxiously.

"Oh yes. She just needs more rest."

"Shall I go up and see her?"

"I don't know whether she's awake yet."

"I'll go and see."

"Me too," Philip demanded, hanging on to his father's arm.

"All right, but we must not make a noise," André said. He swung Philip astride his shoulders and mounted the stairs. At the door he lowered him, motioning for him to remain quiet. He tapped lightly and then opened the door. The bedcurtains were drawn back and his mother lay with her eyes closed. He had never thought of his mother in terms of age and now it came as a shock to him to see her face so deeply lined. Her grey hair was spread over the pillow. As he watched, she gave a heavy sigh and passed a hand wearily over her eyes. Then opening them, saw him and sat up quickly, the tiredness leaving her face as it broke into a smile. "Andrè, darling!" she exclaimed and held out her arms. Swiftly he crossed the room and was enveloped in her arms, letting his head rest for a moment or two on her bosom. When he looked up tears were streaming down her face.

"Why, maman, tears from you!" he chided.

She brushed them away with the back of her hand and smiled through glistening eyes. "I'm getting to be a foolish old woman. But you have been away so long."

Philip had climbed on to the bed determined to get his share of the attention. He wriggled himself up beside his grandmother, who encircled him with her other arm and kissed him.

"Now I have both my boys," she said proudly and hugged them.

"He isn't a boy, he's a man," Philip objected.

"He used to be my little boy," Ann said laughing, "but he's a very big one now." She studied the strong, leathery face that was looking so intently at her. It was hard to think that he had ever been a little boy like Philip. "And now he has a beard that makes him look very fierce," she said and laughed again.

"How have you been, Maman?" André asked and his tone was anxious.

"I've been very well, dear," she lied. "I would have been up had I known you were arriving. I'm getting lazy. It's been a busy season. We've had quite a lot of sickness and so many new babies on the Seigneury."

"You do too much," he said.

A light tap on the door admitted Aunt Marguerite.

"I thought I heard a familiar voice!" she exclaimed and André went to greet her. She looked over André's shoulder as he embraced her and Ann shot her a warning glance.

"How fine you look, André," Aunt Marguerite said proudly. "And how delighted we are to have you back."

Philip was lying beside his grandmother, his head resting against her chest. "This is where I sleep when I'm sick," he said steering the conversation back to himself.

"When you're sick!" André exclaimed. "Has he been ill?"

"No," his mother said reassuringly. "Only a cold or two and then he likes to be with me."

"I cut my hand once and had it all tied up," Philip protested. "I have a scar too." He proudly showed a cut about a quarter of an inch long.

"Well, that *is* a scar!" André said.

"Now run along all of you and I will dress," Ann said.

"I'll go and find Father," André said.

"No, no!" Philip scrambled off the bed. "I want you." The dark eyes he turned to his father were Renée's and his expression just like hers when she had wanted her own way.

"But don't you want me to see Grandfather?" André asked.

"Yes, but not now. I want you."

"Your father will be coming in for breakfast soon. Let Philip have these first moments," Ann said indulgently.

André looked at his son, a broad smile on his face. "All right, young man, where do you want me?"

"Downstairs." The lower lip which had been pushed out petulantly, receded as he gained his own way. He grasped his father's hand and began pulling him. Laughing, but obviously enjoying it, André waved to his mother and aunt and followed his son.

Yelling with delight Philip raced into the library where his toys were strewn all over the floor. André sat down to watch him as he went from one toy to another and then came and climbed into his father's lap.

"Grandpère says you are a great ex... ex... pawrer," he said.

"Explorer," Andrè corrected.

"Ex-plorer," Philip echoed "and that you have been among Indians and have been looking for the sea."

Andrè smiled at the description. "That's right."

"And you've been away three years and two months..."

"Have I now! Who told you that?"

"Grandmère. And Tante Marguerite said you are a very brave man..."

"Did she! Well, well."

Philip was fingering the fringed seams of his father's trousers. "What are these for?" he inquired.

"Well, mainly for decoration. All voyageurs wear trousers like these and jackets too when it isn't so warm. Do you know what this is made of?" Andrè asked pointing to the trousers.

Philip shook his head.

"It is deerskin. Do you know what a deer is?"

Philip shook his head again.

"I'll have to take you into the forest this winter and show you. It is a wild animal and has a skin like this. Any time you see a man dressed like this you'll know he is a fur trapper," he explained.

"What's a fur trapper?"

"A man who traps fur-bearing animals. You said you knew bears—they have a thick fur coat which men take to make into coats and rugs..."

Philip studied his father's clothes thoughtfully. "It isn't as nice as Uncle Jean-Baptiste's uniform," he commented.

"Uncle Jean-Baptiste is a soldier and an officer."

"Why aren't you a soldier?"

"Well, men here are usually one of three things. They're farmers like Grandpère, or soldiers like Uncle Jean-Baptiste or voyageurs, explorers, fur trappers—that's about the same thing—just as I am. Do you understand that?"

"Yes. You're an ex-plorer, Uncle Jean-Baptiste a soldier and Grandpère's a farmer. And where's my present?"

André dug into the bundle and pulled out a small pair of moccasins trimmed with beads and porcupine quills. "An Indian made these especially for you."

"An Indian!" Philip grabbed them, his eyes wide with delight. He squatted on the floor and began putting them on.

"They're a little large but you'll grow into them. Grandmère will fix them so that you can wear them."

"Of course she will." Ann's voice came from the doorway. Now that she was dressed and her hair done up, she did not look as old. There was a flush on her cheeks that André did not realize came from a light application of rouge.

"Breakfast is ready, dear. You're undoubtedly famished. And here's Father."

Paul hurried in, his leathery face wrinkled with delight, as he kissed his son on both cheeks and then held him back to look at him. He nodded approvingly.

"Delighted to have you back, son. Did you bring us an ocean?"

"I'm afraid not, Father. We ran into difficulties."

"To be expected."

"Unfortunately they were not only territorial. The merchants cut off our supplies..."

"So I heard. There's been a lot of talk around the town. You can't make them understand..."

"That's what we came back for, but I'm afraid Pierre's going to have a difficult task. It's been most disheartening, though we made some progress."

"I'm most anxious to hear it all," his father said.

"Come and have breakfast first. You'll have plenty of time to talk," Ann said.

As they sat down Mère Clarissa came in with platters piled with meat and freshly baked bread. Platter after platter followed until the table was heaped with all kinds of appetizing food. Ann did not eat much. She was too excited over André's return and more intent upon seeing that his plate was well filled.

If his mother looked older, Aunt Marguerite did not. Back again among those she loved, she had lost the strained look that had marred her appearance for many years and now had a serenity that had restored her looks. André discovered the reason for the change in her when he asked about Henry and found that she had heard from him quite frequently.

"I don't know how he manages to get the letters through but he does," she said.

"The new post road helps," Paul said. "You didn't know that we now have a post road all the way to Quebec?" he said to André.

"You mean they actually have done something more than talk about it?" André exclaimed.

"Thanks to Beauharnois."

"He's a fine Governor."

"Indeed he is. Did you know Governor de la Chassaigne died?" Paul asked.

"No, when?"

"Last winter."

"Who's Governor now?"

"De Beaucourt—former Governor of Three Rivers. And Pierre de Vaudreuil is now Governor of Three Rivers."

"Back to the old families, eh?"

"Yes, though Pierre hasn't his father's qualities," Paul said.

"It doesn't seem so," André agreed.

"Did Paul-André come back with you?" Ann asked.

"No. Pierre offered him the opportunity but he said he would stay. He really is needed there. He's doing splendid work. He's our interpreter."

"Good," Paul remarked.

Philip was feeling left out of the conversation and this he didn't like. "Who's Paul-André?" he asked.

"Why, darling, you know who Paul-André is!" his grandmother said.

"Who is he?" he insisted.

"Aunt Elise's son. Don't you remember?"

"Why does he have two names?" he went on, addressing the question to his father and not answering his grandmother.

"Paul-André?" André said. "Well, you see, his mother loved two people very much—Grandfather Paul and me, so she gave her son both names."

"Didn't you love two people very much when you named me?" Philip asked.

André grinned. "I loved so many people, Philip, I had to choose just one or you would have had too many names. So I named you after Uncle Philip whom I loved very much."

"Whose Uncle Philip?"

"Uncle Philip was your great-aunt Marie's husband."

"Isn't he any more?"

"He was killed by the Indians some years ago when he and I were away together."

"What Indians?" Philip persisted but his grandmother leaned over and told him to eat his breakfast.

"I'll tell you all about them later," André said. Then turning to them asked: "What news is there?"

"You just mentioned Aunt Marie. We have a big surprise for you. She has married again," his mother told him.

"Aunt Marie! When? To whom?" André asked excitedly.

"To a Monsieur Henri Roberval. He took over Ménard's land."

"Well, and I suppose had no wife so Aunt Marie…"

"Wait a moment and I'll tell you," Ann said. "It wasn't quite like that. There was a Madame Roberval and five children when they came here. But soon after, Madame—she was such a sweet woman too—became ill and died. Marie, as you would expect, nursed her all through the illness. Bless Marie, she's always there when people need her. You knew she had been housekeeping for Father Xavier?"

"Yes that was before I left."

"Our saddest news is that he died last winter…" Paul said quietly.

"Father Xavier! Oh no! Oh I am sorry. He seemed to be failing when I left."

"Yes, he gradually became weaker but he would not give in. He went the way he would have asked. They found him early one morning before the altar."

"I'm glad it was like that. We shall miss him," André said sadly.

"We have. Father Sebastien, however, is making good progress. He is younger and more reserved than Father Xavier, slower to make friends, but we are all growing to like him," Paul said.

"He came from the Seminary?"

Paul nodded. "He's been a missionary many years. Born in France of course, but has a good understanding of the colony."

"I must call on him later. I am sorry not to have seen Father Xavier again."

"Yes. Well to finish telling you about Aunt Marie," Ann resumed. "After Father Xavier died she returned to her own home. Henri Roberval had become much attached to her and so he asked her to marry him and mother his children."

"You sound very pleased about it, so I presume everyone approves," André said.

"Yes, we do. It is wonderful for her. Henri pulled down Ménard's old shack and built a very comfortable house. Marie's Philip has her house now as his son, Jean, has married and so it saved having to build another house for him."

"Mon Dieu! So many changes. I must go over and call on Madame Roberval."

"She will be eager to see you."

"How is Elise? Well?"

"Very. She and Antoine went to Quebec when Charlotte-Marguerite took her perpetual vows. They are very happy…"

"And you have another great-nephew," Aunt Marguerite interjected.

"Oh? Ann-Marie?"

"Yes—she has another son."

"Splendid. Was there any more trouble over the Ménard affair?" André asked.

His mother shook her head but made no more comment as a small boy was listening too carefully. "Ann-Marie has developed wonderfully," she said. "We have such good times with her and the children. She brings them over frequently to play with Philip."

"Who?" Philip inquired.

"Nicholas-Jean and Charlotte-Marie."

"I can beat Nicholas even if he is older," Philip said defiantly.

"Beat him at what?" André asked.

"Everything. I can run faster and anyway he always cries."

"Not often, Philip," Ann reproved.

"I'm much stronger too. And I'm almost as tall as he is."

André smiled. It was obvious to him that his son had inherited many of Renée's qualities. Also that he was being very much spoiled.

"Ann-Marie and the children are staying at Elise's now. Jean-Baptiste is away on a mission."

"Oh then I'll see them all together. I believe I'll go over and see them now."

"I want to come too," Philip demanded.

"All right, young man, come along," his father agreed.

André gave Antoine and Elise all the details of the years of voyaging. They were proud that Paul-André had become so valuable to the expedition, though this did not compensate them for his long absence.

"I do wish he had come back with you, André," Elise said sadly. "It is such a long time and now it will probably be years more. These absences are so difficult."

"I know, dear," André sympathized.

"The boy will always be a wanderer," Antoine remarked. "Perhaps eventually he will have had enough."

Elise smiled at her husband. His tone was now so different from what it had been in regard to Paul-André.

She did not say any more and though for the rest of the winter they all enjoyed having André with them, whenever they were all gathered together, Elise's thoughts were with her absent son.

From Elise, André had learned the truth about their mother's health. "Don't say anything to her about it," she warned him. "She may tell you herself, though I don't think so. She will be all right as long as she does not do too much."

With André's return Ann rallied and during the winter seemed to regain much of her former strength. She laughingly promised André that when spring came she would leave most of the work to others.

"I shan't be here to see that you keep the promise," he chided her. She only smiled and reiterated her promise.

May Day came around again with the customary preparations for the ceremony. But for the first time in eighty years the ceremony did not take place on the de Courville Seigneury. Paul came down dressed formally as always on these occasions and told his sister that Ann would be down in a few minutes. Marguerite went into the kitchen to see that all was ready.

The signal shot outside announced that the habitants were ready.

"I'll go up and tell Ann," Marguerite said.

She hurried upstairs to her sister-in-law's room. "Ann dear, they're all ready," she said as she entered. "We're…" She stopped abruptly thinking the room empty. Then she saw Ann lying fully dressed on the bed. "Ann!" she called sharply and went to her. There was no reply and even before she leaned over to listen for a heartbeat she had a premonition of what she would discover.

She ran to the door and then steadied herself. She must break this to her brother gently. Trying to control her voice she called down to him.

"Paul, will you come up." The words would hardly come she was shaking so.

He came out of the parlor and looked up the stairs. "You called, Marguerite?" he asked.

"Yes, Paul. Er, come up will you?"

He hurried up the stairs saying: "Isn't Ann well?"

Marguerite waited for him to reach the top, bracing herself to appear calm. She put her hands on his shoulders and said gently: "Paul, she has left us."

"What do you mean?" he asked and did not wait for an answer but dashed into the bedroom. He looked around frantically and saw her lying on the bed. "Ann, what is it?" he said and lifted the hand that lay limply over the side. It was soft and warm to his touch. "Ann dear," he repeated and then turned wild-eyed to Marguerite. Her hands covered her face and she was weeping. He looked again at the bed and then dropped to his knees, covering the hand he held with kisses. "Ann, Ann," he called frightened and then again hysterically: "Ann!" He covered his face with his hands and moaned. "No no! No, Ann, you can't leave me. Ann come back! Marguerite! André!"

André rushed into the room and took in the scene. He stood by the bed gazing, unbelieving, at the still form of his beloved mother.

"What has happened? Should I get a doctor?"

Marguerite put her arm across his shoulders? "She's beyond doctor's help, André. She's left us."

He looked from one face to another, incredulous. "It can't be," he said. "Perhaps she's only fainted. I'll fetch a doctor."

But Marguerite was right. Ann *had* left them. About her mouth played a half smile—a smile of peace. She who had always been so serene in life was serene in death.

# CHAPTER FORTY

ANN'S death cast a pall over the entire Seigneury, for no one had been more beloved. Paul looked all of his sixty-four years now and could not rouse himself from the shock. For forty-four years his beloved Ann had been his wife and he could not believe that she was no longer there beside him. Having Marguerite with him helped, for next to Ann she was closer to him than anyone.

When in June, La Vérendrye was ready again to set out, accompanied now by his youngest son, Louis-Joseph, André was in a quandary. His father urged him to go, yet he still hesitated on account of Philip. He talked it over with Elise and Antoine and his sister assured him that she would give her undivided attention to Philip and that he would be brought up with Ann-Marie's children. Still André felt he was shirking his responsibilities.

"I'll return with Pierre and see how things are and then come back," he assured them.

Much of his desire for adventure had gone. He was now forty-three and felt he could leave the task of exploring to younger men. What weighed his decision was the fear that he would be disappointing Pierre by giving up the expedition at this juncture. La Vérendrye needed his support for he had not fared well with the merchants. Not only had they refused him further supplies, but had threatened to bring suit against him because they had not received sufficient peltries to cover their initial investment. Governor de Beauharnois' continued support was the only comfort and at his suggestion La Vérendrye agreed to lease the forts he had established to certain merchants for a period of three years. Thus he renounced all hope of being able to reimburse himself or his friends from the profits obtained from these trading posts. But he had either to agree to this suggestion or give up the expedition.

It took them three months to reach Fort St. Charles where they found the men almost destitute of supplies. Furthermore the wild oat crop had again been a failure as the waters rose and flooded it.

The most encouraging news was that La Jemeraye had pushed forward during his uncle's absence and had established another fort on the west bank of the Red River. This they named Fort Maurepas. It meant progress but it also meant a further depletion of supplies, for the amount they had brought with them did not go very far when distributed among all the forts.

They settled into a winter of hardship, having to rely mainly on what food the forests yielded. The spring began badly. On the 4th of the following June, Paul-André and La Vérendrye's two younger sons arrived from Maurepas with the news that Christophe de la Jemeraye had died during the winter. With his death La Vérendrye lost one of his ablest and most trustworthy leaders.

André's decision to retire from the expedition came about in a different way than he had anticipated. Fort Maurepas had not been included in the bargain La Vérendrye had made with the merchants, since it was not at that time established. He decided to take the furs that had been brought from there and send them to Michilimackinac so that they could exchange them for supplies. On June 8, 1736 two canoes set out, one in charge of La Vérendrye's eldest son, Jean-Baptiste, and the other under André. Father Mesaiger, the missionary, went with them as he was in ill health and wished to return to Michilimackinac. He travelled in the first canoe with Jean-Baptiste and two other men, while Paul-André and two more were with André.

The progress was slow on the first day as they travelled against the current. When the light began to fade, Jean-Baptiste signalled to André that they were preparing to land for the night. They paddled on for a while looking for a suitable spot. At the bend of the river, Jean-Baptiste espied a good place and headed the canoe towards it. Well-trained and experienced, he paused before making a landing, studied the selected place and let his eye roam from tree to tree and then satisfied, prepared to land. The air was still as they pulled the canoe up on to the bank, but the next moment it was rent with the wild yells of Indians who suddenly appeared from seemingly nowhere and swooped down before any of them could grab a musket.

André and his men rounded the bend at that moment. Immediately they shipped their paddles and grasped their muskets. Four shots rang out simultaneously, and three hit their marks as three savages fell to the ground. Only then did the savages see the second canoe and before the men could reload, a shower of arrows pinged through the air, one lodging in André's left arm. He went overboard capsizing the canoe as he did so and throwing the other men into the water. More savages swarmed out of the forest, racing along the riverbank and aiming their deadly arrows. The strong current carried the men away from their enemies—and the boat out of their reach. All were, fortunately, good swimmers and while the other two kept under water and went after the canoe, Paul-André gave his attention to his uncle. He grabbed hold of him and headed into the current, pulling him towards where the men had managed to right the canoe. Arrows continued to whine through the air but they were now out of range.

Other savages were pushing out Jean-Baptiste's canoe preparing to follow them. Paul-André left André in the bottom of the boat and turned to grasp a paddle but the men had only been able to retrieve two. With all their might they rowed, two men against four strong savages in pursuit. All their muskets had been lost when they capsized. No one spoke. They knew the river well but to have taken refuge in any of the hiding places would probably have been certain death, for undoubtedly the savages were as familiar with them as they were.

Only the darkness saved them, or else their pursuers gave up to return to the sport which the four prisoners would provide. Still the men dared not stop, even when there was no sound to indicate pursuit. Indians were adept at paddling silently. All night they continued, risking the dangers that lurked all around them.

All Paul-André had been able to do for André was to tie his sash under the armpit to cut off the flow of blood. This he had learned from the Caughnawaga Indians. The arrow had completely pierced André's upper arm and there it had to be left until they reached the fort. André was moaning and delirious as they carried him in.

Briefly they told La Vérendrye what had happened. He took the news without flinching, what he suffered showing in his eyes. Then he turned his attention to André. Unfortunately, there was no doctor at the fort. Paul-André had once assisted Amrusus with an amputation while they were on a hunting trip and he spoke to La Vérendrye about it.

"I have seen Indians do it, monsieur, and I could try it. At least I could make the attempt. It might save him."

La Vérendrye's face was drawn as he watched his friend groaning in agony. "Try it," he said tensely. "What help do you need?"

"First we must take off the arm. Have we brandy?"

La Vérendrye fetched a flagon.

"Give him all he can take," Paul-André said to one of the men. "I'll need some irons and a pot of boiling pitch …"

"What kind of irons?" one of the men asked.

"Any kind that will get red-hot. Ramrods will do if we have nothing else. I'll need several men to help me."

Volunteers were not wanting. When the pot of pitch was boiling they stood around ready to assist. Paul-André took a swig of the brandy himself and told the men to keep giving his uncle all he could take. "Hold his legs and sit on his chest," he said abruptly.

Then bracing himself he took a hatchet and severed the arm. A terrifying scream came from the injured man and he shuddered into unconsciousness. Paul-André gave him a quick anxious glance not sure whether he had died or only fainted. There was no time to pause and find out. With set face he called for the ramrods, heated to a glowing red. He dipped one into the pitch, looked at the bloody stump, braced himself and covered it with the pitch. There was a convulsive movement of the body but no sound. Several times Paul-André applied the pitch until the entire wound was covered. Then he bound it up.

In a voice that seemed to him far away, he told them to watch André and if he recovered consciousness to give him more brandy. Then he went outside and vomited, leaning against the side of the building for support. La Vérendrye had watched it all and he now came outside and put his arm across Paul-André's shoulders.

"Well done, boy," he said.

"We don't know yet. He may be dead," Paul-André said tensely and walked away. He had to be alone and he stayed away from the fort all day. Never had he thought that to hear a man raving would be a welcome sound but it was to him as he returned and knew that his uncle had not succumbed to the drastic operation.

For weeks he lay weak and delirious but the stump began to take on a more healthy appearance and though Paul-André could not give him back his arm, he had at least preserved his life.

La Vérendrye faced the sorrow of having now lost his eldest son as well as his nephew, and having his best friend incapacitated. The horror of what they found when the search party went out to look for the captives was beyond description. It was said that this was the Sioux revenge for La Vérendrye having let his son go with the Crees to war against them. Whatever it was, they had used all their devilishness in revenge. The four bodies, including that of Father Mesaiger, lay in a row, headless. Jean-Baptiste had been subjected to the worst torture. His back was scored with knife cuts, a stake thrust into his side and his scalped head lay on a beaver robe not far from the body. The savages had trimmed his body with leggings and armpieces of porcupine. The bodies were gathered up and brought back for burial in the Fort.

La Vérendrye was bowed down with grief that for a few days he could not hide. The Crees came and wanted to go out at once and revenge the death of his son but this he would not allow. He was short of powder and ball and a tribal war would only have added to his troubles as well as preventing the Indians hunting during the winter and this was so essential to him. In the depths of his sorrow and despair, for the first time he showed signs of giving up the venture.

"No, Father, you cannot give up now," his sons insisted and Paul-André echoed the statement. "The expedition must go on. We must find these Ouachipouennes and reach our goal. Let us go on."

Looking up at the four young men before him, strong and fearless, he felt ashamed of his momentary weakness. His face relaxed into a tired smile, and he said quietly: "We will carry on."

Paul-André brought his uncle home the following spring. They came down with La Vérendrye who must again negotiate for further supplies. Paul-André would stay only a few weeks and then rejoin the expedition. André's adventuring days were finished. During long months of illness he had lost so much weight that his clothes hung upon him and he was also suffering acutely from the bloody flux.

As before, it was Philip who first saw his father but not until André had been watching him silently for a few moments. He had walked slowly up from the riverbank towards where his young son was kneeling on the chest of a fairhaired boy and pummelling him in the side.

"Come on, fight," he was shouting to his cousin.

"Let me go," Nicholas cried and the words ended in a whimper.

Philip began pounding again.

"Philip," his father said quietly. Philip looked up, saw his father and his face flushed.

"Mon père!" he shouted and ran to him. Nicholas took advantage of the respite and scrambling to his feet, ran away.

André was too tired and ill to remonstrate with his son. In the two years that he had been away, Philip had grown tall and no longer seemed a little boy. He was staring wide-eyed at his father's empty sleeve.

"Give me some help, son," André said.

Immediately Philip sprang to his side and leaning on his son's shoulder André slowly mounted the steps.

# CHAPTER FORTY-ONE

I T WAS not until November of 1738—a year and a half after André had left the expedition, that La Vérendrye finally made contact with the fabulous tribe of which he had been hearing for many years. Accompanied by two of his sons and Paul-André, and with twenty picked men and an equal number of Indians as guides, he made what was later to be regarded as a memorable journey across the plains to an Indian village on the Missouri River where the Heart River joins it. On the way he established another fort—Fort La Reine—on the Assiniboine River, west of Lac Ouinipigon, where later the town of Portage La Prairie was to rise.

When he reached the Indian village, he found that the tribe which the other savages had called the Ouachipouennes, were really the Mandans—a tribe entirely different in appearance and customs from any he had encountered. Unfortunately for La Vérendrye, bad luck still thwarted him and he was able to learn little from them at this time as the Cree whom he had hired as interpreter deserted to pursue an Assiniboine woman of whom he had become enamoured and took all the presents with him. They were, therefore, reduced to signs and gestures which proved quite inadequate and had no gifts to give to the Indians.

La Vérendrye's misfortune proved eventually to be Paul-André's good fortune. It was decided that two men should be left behind to winter with the Mandans and learn their language, while La Vérendrye and the rest returned to Fort La Reine.

Paul-André was the natural choice for this task and with him remained young François de la Vérendrye.

After the departure of their leader and his men, Paul-André and François settled down to a study which was to prove of immense interest, particularly to Paul-André, who having lived among Indians before, now discovered that this was to be an unparalleled experience, bringing contrasts that amazed him. The first thing that he noticed was the cleanliness and orderliness of this race which contrasted with the filth and squalor of the Mohawks at Caughnawaga. Their village was arranged in streets and squares, all kept very clean. The houses looked like a collection of large molehills, for they were circular in appearance, made of earth with a smooth coating of clay on the top, pounded down until it was flat. It was here on this flat top that most of the inhabitants had gathered to watch the entry of the Frenchmen into the village. Later when he had time to make detailed investigations, Paul-André found that every house had a foundation at least two feet underground and this, with the cellars where food was stored for the winter, was undoubtedly the reason the Assiniboines had called them "the Sioux who live underground." Also, as he studied the language, he learned why the Assiniboines had called them Ouachipouennes, for the Mandan word for white man was *ouachi* or waci.

The interior of the houses was likewise different, though as with other tribes, there was a central excavation for the fireplace. Around this were grouped seats made of small willows supported as a sort of sofa and covered with buffalo robes. To the left began a range of beds. Each house served a family or circle of family connections according to its dimensions. Instead of the dirty shelves on which he had slept with the Mohawks, Paul-André now saw beds which, while unique in themselves, nevertheless furnished the maximum of comfort. They resembled tombs or large boxes. Four posts supported them with a base or mattress about a foot from the ground, comprised of poles lashed from one side to the other and covered with a green buffalo hide, stretched on wet and allowed to dry. This formed a springy foundation. Around the sides and across the top, hides were stretched with a small opening in one side through which to enter. The interior was filled with buffalo robes, making it so soft and warm that at first neither of the white men could sleep, accustomed as they had become to sleeping on the hard ground.

Neatness and cleanliness predominated. Between each bed, posts were set provided with pegs and from these were suspended the arms and accoutrements of the warriors and a skin bag into which were packed personal possessions.

There was, too, none of the dilatoriness that they had seen among most of the other tribes. These people were considered the best husbandmen among the red men and raised corn, maize, beans, pumpkins and squashes in vast quantity. The girls and women were never allowed to be idle. They must gather in the fuel for the fires, help with the cultivating, and dress and embroider the buffalo robes, which formed such an important part of their dress as well as their furnishings. They made glass beads for their embroidery, from a secret known to only a few and these they dyed with colors which they themselves made—red from the buffalo-berries; black from sunflowers and yellow from a kind of moss which came from the Rocky Mountains.

These people loved feasts and ceremonies which were frequent and for which they dressed in the most lavish and barbarous manner. As with other red men, youth grew to manhood with the one idea that true dignity and glory came only to the one who could fringe his belt with the scalps of his enemies. The ceremonies through which the young men proved their strength and courage were accompanied by the most vile tortures and customs. The men kept fit through indulgence in many sports and every day there was the game of the stick and the rolling ring, archery practice, horse-racing on the prairie and incessant games of chance.

If the dwellings and customs of these people amazed the white men, this was nothing compared with what they discovered in their personal appearance. As the Assiniboines had told them, the Mandans were practically white, and certainly were half-breeds of some description. When the men had mastered the language, they heard the astounding story of their origin—a story relayed to them by the Chief himself, who guarded it as his special prerogative, insisting that it had been handed down from father to son from the original progenitors of the race. The story he told appeared logical, as something must certainly account for their difference from other tribes. Many hundred moons ago, he told them, a party of people from Wales had landed near the mouth of the Mississippi. (White men later set the date as 1170 and the place of landing about where Florida stands.) The Welsh explorers became involved with hostile tribes and were never heard of again. But from them had descended this tribe of half-breeds, retaining through the ages so many of their characteristics. (Later this hypothesis was supported by a likeness between the Welsh and Mandan languages; their physical peculiarities and their type of fortification).

Whether the Chief's story was true or imagined, it was obvious that these people had somewhere acquired the white man's characteristics. Instead of the aquiline nose found in most tribes, theirs was thin and straight and the cheekbones were less prominent. The eyes were long and narrow, raised and contracted a little at the inner corner, and, amazingly enough, their color was hazel, blue or grey. And instead of the course black hair of the Indian, theirs was brown, or frequently grey, the latter predominating even in the children and young girls. Some had long fair hair which was soft and fine. In fact, every shade of hair could be seen except red, which made Paul-André with his auburn hair particularly interesting to them.

The two white men were treated with every courtesy and always accorded places of honor at meal times and at ceremonies.

For the first time they hunted buffalo, a dangerous sport which put both of them on their mettle.

Probably of all the amazing things that they now discovered, the most astonishing was to find that these people *began each day with a bath*. Paul-André and François found that they were expected to do the same, and of course complied, though it seemed to both of them that this was carrying cleanliness to rather an absurd degree. After bathing, the body was carefully oiled with castoreum, a custom which the white men declined. Few of the Mandan men wore any clothes, not even a breech-clout. Their only covering in winter, was a buffalo robe carelessly thrown over them. The women wore more but not much more.

This bathing habit almost led Paul-André into trouble. Both the men had been given complete freedom of the village and as they learned the language, they began to feel quite at home with their new friends. One morning when the weather was warmer, Paul-André took a stroll along the river, enjoying its beauty and the peace which it brought. Suddenly and without any warning, two savages leapt towards him brandishing knives and making all manner of hostile gestures. He fell back a pace or two, calling to them in Mandan but still they came at him with the points of their knives extended towards him. Though alarmed he stood his ground, smiling in what he hoped was a friendly fashion, and with the palms of his hands turned upward to show he had no weapon and was a friend.

"Go back," one of them shouted.

"Is this forbidden territory?" he asked in their language.

"Yes, forbidden. Go. Women."

At the last word he raised his eyebrows, curious. He did not move and they lunged dangerously towards him.

"Peace," he said not able to think of any other word in Mandan at that moment. "Explain so that I don't make the same mistake again. I wish no harm."

Both men were tall and of splendid physique as were most of the Mandan men. Their hair was brown and descended below their shoulders, for, again contrary to most Indian tribes, these Mandans did not shave their heads. They were, in fact, very proud of their long hair, which they wore in a number of plaits, glued and matted with red-earth. Only now did Paul-André see that in addition to the two men who had jumped at him, there were also others stationed at intervals on a circle of rising ground. He looked up at the other figures silently watching him and then at the two men before him.

"Explain please," he repeated. "I would learn your customs."

Realizing now that his intrusion had been unintentional one of them explained.

"Women bathing, private. We guard so not disturbed."

"Oh!" Paul-André said and could not prevent the smile that came over his face. "Oh I apologize. I did not understand. Do they always bathe here?"

"Special reserve. Go away. Forbidden."

Making the best apology he could Paul-André retired. Further questioning revealed that this special cove some distance from the village was reserved as a resort for the women where they could perform their morning ablutions undisturbed. He learned, too, that both sexes were excellent swimmers and could easily cross the Missouri.

That Paul-André should here fall in love was something that he least expected. Having always given little attention to women, he had continued to think little about them, except to study them as a part of the life of the village. He became accustomed to seeing them with breasts bared and nothing but a small apron about a hand's breadth wide covering the more intimate part of their bodies. A few wore deerskin dresses but whether this was because they were more modest or because they happened to have the dresses, he did not know. From the first, François had been more disturbed than he. In fact, Paul-André was certain that he was sharing a buffalo robe with more than one of them. Virtue, he learned, was held in high esteem but rather scarce. François chided him for his celibacy but Paul-André only smiled good-naturedly.

Then it happened. She was sitting on a hillock a short way from the village combing long fair tresses that reached below her waist. She was crooning as she sat there and looking out over the blue waters of the river. For a moment as he accidentally came upon her, Paul-André was afraid that he had again wandered into forbidden territory, for it was obvious that she had just bathed.

He stopped suddenly when he saw her and would have turned back in the direction he had come. But something suddenly happened to him. His heart began to pound so rapidly that his breath could not keep up with it and his legs seemed weak and shaky. She was sitting sideways to him, her shapely legs stretched before her. She did not appear to see him standing rooted there, or at least he did not think she had. To add to his disturbed emotions, she suddenly raised her arms above her head, showing beautifully curved breasts that were extended invitingly. Then in an ecstasy of delight and freedom she rolled over on the soft green turf. Paul-André had heard men talking of the disturbance that occurred within them at the sight of a naked woman but he had never before experienced it. Now he wanted to rush towards her and gather that enticing body into his arms.

As she rolled over she saw him but did not scramble to her feet and run away as he expected. Had she done so perhaps he would have run after her. Instead she looked up at him and laughed, and it was the sound of music. A pair of blue eyes twinkled at him. With a graceful movement she sat up, flipped her long thick hair over each shoulder so that it partially covered her breasts and then smiled again.

With difficulty Paul-André found his tongue and stammered an apology.

"You are one of the white men," she said and her voice matched the softness of her laugh.

"Yes," he said nervously. "I am Paul-André or Ours-feu as the Indians call me."

"Ours-feu? What language is that?"

"Mohawk. I lived with them several years." He did not know why he told her this. It was the first thing that came to his mind.

"You lived with Indians?" Her voice was deep with interest. "Come here and tell me." She patted the ground beside her and he stepped forward and sat down.

He had always thought of Indian women as squaws, treated as less than nothing by their men and expected to do all the work. Even among the Mandans he had seen the same thing. But this girl had such remarkable poise.

"I am Kikidacoc," she said.

"Kikidacoc," he repeated. It was the Mandan word for laugh.

"Yes. I like to laugh," she said and rippled mirthfully. The sound disturbed him. "And your name—what is it? The Indian name."

"Ours-feu," he repeated.

"And what does it mean?"

Paul-André smiled. "In my language—fire-bear, fiery-bear." He tried to find the right Mandan words to explain it. He touched his auburn hair to denote the "fiery" but was not sure that she understood.

"I have seen you in the village. Chief Harrata is my father."

Paul-André raised his eyebrows in surprise. Chief Harrata he had heard had many wives, for polygamy was permitted, though many men were content with one wife. He had not known that the Chief had a daughter like this.

"You remain with us?" she asked.

"Not much longer. I was left here with my friend to learn the language."

"Your friend, yes," she smiled and added: "He likes Mandan women."

This confirmed what Paul-André had suspected and he knew there was no blame to be attached to François. He could have done the same.

Looking at her Paul-André's disturbance continued. She was wearing only the customary breechclout and her body was beautifully shaped.

"You are beautiful," he found himself saying.

She smiled and went on oiling her hair. Paul-André wished she would not spoil it with oil. It looked so fair and soft, with the parting painted red.

"You have lovely hair," he said and she smiled again archly.

"Yours is the wonderful hair," she said.

"Mine!" he exclaimed and put his hand up to it.

"We never have red hair among us," she said.

"Mine isn't really red. You should see my uncle's and my mother's. They are really red."

"Yours is red compared with ours. I would like to touch it."

Smiling Paul-André bent his head to her and she ran her hands through its thick waves, laughing as she did so. What then possessed Paul-André he did not know, but he could no longer control his emotions and seizing her in his arms he pulled her to him and kissed her. He had expected an outburst of rage; none came. Instead she lay back in his arms, her blue eyes a deeper color and a smile on her lips. He became bold and closed one hand gently over her breast, cupping it in his hand, fascinated. He had never touched a woman this way before. His only experience in all his twenty-four years had been the one time at Michilimackinac, when rather than show his ignorance, he had lain with a squaw and had found the experience nauseating. This was so different. Her body smelled sweet of some perfume and her olive skin was soft and silky. He bent again and crushed her to him, and when she encouraged him by twining her arms around his neck, he was carried away beyond all control. Nor did he any longer want to control the delicious ecstasy that came to him.

# CHAPTER FORTY-TWO

PAUL-ANDRÉ did not return to the village. He went into the forest and remained there all day. He lay so quietly, his face in the thick leaves beneath the trees, that small animals stopped to look at him and then scurried away frightened. With his emotions spent, he was now appalled at what he had done. His blood ran hot with shame. He had taken a beautiful, unprotected girl and had seduced her—and that girl, the daughter of the Chief. In horror as he reviewed his behavior, he expected any moment to have a party of stalwart braves come after him and drag him back to the village, there to be subjected to all kinds of humiliations and perhaps driven from the village, if they did not put him to death. For hours he tormented himself with remorse.

Then his confusion began to clear and he reviewed things more sanely. What was the code of morals among these people? Had he really seduced her? Had she not willingly come to his embrace and encouraged him so that he had lost all sense of what he was doing? And had it not brought them moments of supreme delight? Back to him rushed thoughts of her graceful olive-skinned body and his blood began to pound. Could he really be in love? Was this how it affected men? He had seen her for only a few brief moments, yet he longed for her again. He wanted her for his own. He rolled on the ground in the agony that these thoughts engendered. Ought he to marry her now after what had happened? Could he marry an Indian girl? Somehow he did not think of her as Indian, as a savage, untamed though she obviously was. What would his parents say if he came home married to a native girl? Then into his mind rushed the memory of her deep blue eyes with their long lashes that rested so enticingly on her cheeks when she lay with her eyes closed; of her long mane of fair hair into which he had twined his hands; of her beautifully shaped body... He brought his thoughts to an abrupt stop. He must cease thinking of her physical attributes. Each time such thoughts drained him of all his strength.

What was he to do now? She had left him, murmuring that she would be there again on the morrow. What were her thoughts about it? Was it to be a clandestine affair, kept secret from the village? Was she now at this very moment regretting it all and hating him bitterly? Was she wanton? She had certainly offered herself with complete abandon. Yet he knew that she was not wanton, for slight though his experience with women had been, he knew enough from the talk he had heard among men, to know that her body had been virginal until that morning.

He thought of François. It was obviously known that François consorted with the women and no one had reproved him. Had not the Chief himself offered them women? Paul-André bristled. He did not want other men having Kikidacoc. He had been the first; he wanted her for himself. He wanted her... He buried his face deep into the earth, smelling its freshness, digging his fingers deep into the leaves—and wanting her.

It was nearly dark when he returned to the village. The dismal wailing of the women from the adjacent cemetery, smote his ears and made him feel more disturbed. Every evening there was this wailing as women paid tribute to the dead—lying on scaffolds away from the reach of the wolves. Though these people appeared more civilized, their strange customs and beliefs were many. The thought of these worried Paul-André as all night he tossed on his buffalo robe.

The next morning he came again to their place of rendezvous. He was weary from his sleepless night but again he leapt to life as he saw her. This time she had on a soft deerskin dress and he took this as an indication that she had no intention of allowing a recurrence of yesterday. He half-expected her to give him a cool smile. Instead it was radiant and she greeted him merrily.

He sat down in silence. There was so much he wanted to say. Even in his own language it would have been difficult—in Mandan it seemed impossible. He looked at her and his impression of yesterday was increased. The expression in his eyes must have mirrored his thoughts, for she put her hand over his and said softly: "Unhappy?"

He shook his head and tried to smile. He hunted for words. "You—angry—yesterday?"

A flood of words answered him and he could not follow all. It was evident that she was surprised at his question and was protesting.

He changed it around. "You—happy—yesterday?"

To this she agreed. He relaxed and with some of the tension gone he was able to remember her language better. "Marry me—be my wife?" he asked.

She pressed her hand against her throat and her eyes glittered. "You want to marry me? You remain here always?"

He shook his head. "No. You would come with me to my country—to Montreal."

"Montreal?" She turned the word slowly over her tongue. "Where?"

"Where is it? Many leagues from here."

"You live in big village?" she asked.

Mixing French and Mandan, sometimes able to find a flow of words and at others completely lost for adequate interpretation, he tried to explain his home and where he lived.

"Would your father let you come?" he asked.

"My father?" Her tone was slightly disdainful. "It is my mother who would have to consent. My father has twelve other daughters and twenty-one sons. He has had many wives. He would never miss me."

"But I would have to ask his permission to marry you?"

"It is the custom."

"What other customs are there relating to obtaining a wife?" All of this she could not understand because again he had to mix the two languages. "How get consent to marry?" he asked.

"You could buy me," she said and seemed to find it amusing. Her merry laugh rang out.

"Oh no!" Paul-André protested.

"Give presents to father."

He looked at her in despair. "I have no presents here," he said. He sat thoughtfully. "Perhaps I can find some way."

Her hand rested again on his and she asked, her face quite serious: "Why you want marry me? Because yesterday?"

He looked steadily at her asking himself the same question. Why did he suddenly want marriage and with an Indian? Wasn't he ignorantly rushing into something? Wasn't he confusing the physical? Wasn't he foolish to burden himself with a woman? Shouldn't he go away and think it over? This last thought disturbed him. He didn't want to let her go.

While these thoughts raced through his mind, he had continued staring at her and she had not moved under his scrutiny. She was more serious than yesterday and again he realized her strength and poise. He drew her to him and kissed her, at first gently and then with an onrush of passion. She would have come to him again wholly but with an effort of control that was difficult, he gently put her away from him and said: "Not until we are married."

Stumbling over their words they agreed on what they should do and later that day Paul-André sought an interview with Chief Harrata, whose name meant Grey Wolf. Paul-André had seen and talked to him frequently. He had seen him dressed elaborately for ceremonials, wearing the buffalo horns on each side of his head, showing that he was a man who had gained great renown. He had treated the two *waci* with great respect and attention and now received Paul-André very cordially. When rather haltingly Paul-André stated his request, he saw a look of surprise in the old man's eyes but it was quickly concealed. As Kikidacoc had asked so her father said: "You remain here?"

Paul-André shook his head.

"No I take her to my home."

The old man moved his dry, wrinkled lips over his toothless gums and ruminated.

Paul-André had brought with him a buffalo robe which he had received after one of the hunts and which he prized, hoping to take it home with him. Now he had decided to sacrifice it. One of the women had embroidered it and it was very beautiful. With the Mandans, buffalo was a means of exchange as beaver was in Montreal. Paul-André ceremoniously laid it at the feet of the old man. Apparently this had been what was lacking, for his small eyes lighted up and without further ado, he said: "She is yours."

Paul-André returned to his hut. He and François, after the first month, had succeeded in getting a small dome-like house to themselves. He found François sprawled on the bed. He would rather have been alone for he was still dazed over what he was doing and was not helped when having told his companion, he raged at him for a fool. He ran the gamut of what would happen, of the reception she would receive in Montreal, what his family would think when he brought home a squaw.

"She is not a squaw!" Paul-André protested angrily.

"All Indian women are squaws, you fool," François retorted.

They conversed, of course, in French and it was as well. There was a sound outside and going to the door, they found Kikidacoc placing cooked corn before their door.

"For you," she said to Paul-André and went away.

He turned expecting derision from François; instead he was staring at the receding figure with eyes dilated.

"Is that she?" he asked.

"Yes," Paul-André replied looking at him defiantly.

"I have never seen her before," François said.

"Perhaps it's as well," Paul-André retorted.

François smiled. "She's beautiful," he agreed. Paul-André did not reply.

For three days Kikidacoc brought cooked corn to his door, a sign that they were betrothed. Paul-André did not see her during these days. He was then informed that he could go to her father's house and claim her as his wife. Seeing how things were, François moved out and left them the hut. They were to leave in a few weeks anyway.

There were many things that Paul-André had yet to talk over with Kikidacoc—a name which he later abbreviated to Kiki. There was the serious matter of religion. The words Roman Catholic could not be translated into Mandan and it was difficult at this stage to explain to her all that his religion meant. Also, that though they were married according to her customs, they would not really be married until a priest had united them.

She listened very seriously to all that he said and without hesitation assured him that she would follow his instructions.

Paul-André's conscience was not quite at peace as he took her to him, feeling that they were not yet properly married. But this he soon forgot as passion dulled his senses. Whatever might come of his action, he knew that above all, he had found a mate whose caresses brought him an infinite peace.

When Paul-André and François arrived back at Fort La Reine in September they found La Vérendrye had been very ill. In a letter to Beauharnois he had written: "It would be impossible to suffer more than I do. It seems that nothing but death can release me from such miseries." Governor Beauharnois had continued his efforts with the French government for more support for La Vérendrye's expedition but could obtain no satisfaction.

The report that Paul-André and François brought back was only faintly encouraging. The Mandans knew nothing of the

Western Ocean and the only encouragement was their mention of a tribe which sometimes visited them and spoke "of a distant country towards the sunset where white men live in houses built of bricks and stones." The Mandans had promised to lead them to this tribe whose home "bordered on a great lake whose waters were unfit to drink."

One of the first things that Paul-André did upon returning to the fort was to ask the priest to marry them according to the tenets of his religion. Fortunately a Father Aneault had now joined them. As Paul-André had expected, he came in for some censure both from La Vérendrye and from the priest, though in both cases this became tempered when they saw Kikidacoc. Paul-André began teaching her French at once and she proved adept. At his request she studied their religion with Father Aneault during the winter and before they again left the fort she was accepted into the church.

Paul-André had no regrets over his marriage. Indian girls were well-trained domestically and Kikidacoc looked after her man as he had never before been attended. At their first, and a few subsequent meetings, he had thought her frivolous and light, and perhaps she was then, but with her marriage she immediately changed, giving deep consideration to her responsibilities. Paul-André tried to explain to her the different status of a French woman and an Indian. Despite all his talking, however, she still continued to fetch and carry for him and only after considerable argument would she sit and eat with him.

He realized how many French customs he must teach her before taking her home, but he delayed until the time of return should be nearer. As La Vérendrye was returning to Montreal, he sent letters to his mother and Uncle André, but did not mention his marriage and also asked La Vérendrye not to say anything. "It isn't that I'm ashamed at all, monsieur," he explained "but they will understand better when they see her." La Vérendrye respected his confidence.

La Vérendrye was too ill to continue the expedition but his sons and Paul-André were still full of enthusiasm. In the spring they started out again, a small but determined party of men and one woman, for Kikidacoc would not be left behind. Paul-André remonstrated with her, pointing out that the journey would undoubtedly be hard for men and therefore impossible for a woman; moreover, that she was with child and could not possibly go.

With an inscrutable expression she listened to him and then merely replied: "I go. Indian girls always tend their men."

Paul-André argued, at first persuasively and then angrily, but she had a stubbornness that was adamantine. He could have ordered her to remain behind, but he felt reasonably sure that she still would have followed after him.

For three more years the intrepid explorers doggedly pursued their way. After another visit to the Mandans, during which time Kikidacoc gave birth to twin boys, they set out again, but this time provided with good horses. Kikidacoc went along too and the men did not grumble as they had at first. They had soon discovered the qualities of the woman with them. She remained in the background when important business was being discussed and came forward when needed, which proved to be more often as the journey proceeded and they had dealings with Indian tribes, for in addition to her own native language, they found she also knew smatterings of other dialects and, what was of prime importance, she was more skilled than they in the universal sign language. She cooked for them and tended them when they were sick, always going about each task quietly and efficiently. With her babies strapped to her back she kept up with them, having an energy that equalled and sometimes surpassed theirs.

Their general course was west-southwest, with the Black Hills at a distance on their left and the Upper Missouri on their right. For weeks on end they encountered no human beings across the barren plains, the only sign of life being the game that was abundant. Deer sprang from the tall grass surrounding the rivers, buffalo tramped by in ponderous columns and the inquisitive antelope stopped to gaze at them and then darted away as fleet as the breeze. They saw elks and moutain-sheep and at night the wolves and coyotes disturbed their sleep.

They crossed the Little Missouri River and climbed the Powder River Mountains, hoping to meet the Horse Indians who were credited with knowing the direction to the Western Ocean, and it was hoped would guide them. When after many months they did contact the tribe they found them in a state of terror, most of their people having recently been destroyed by the powerful Snakes or Shoshones.

Again disappointment. The Horse Indians had no personal knowledge of the Western Sea nor where it lay. They said, however, they knew of a tribe which traded with the Spaniards. Though doubting this information, the party set out again, with some of the Horse Indians as guides. After proceeding southwest for several days they came to the village of the Bow Indians, one of the branches of the Western Sioux who predominated in this region. As they had expected, this tribe likewise had no knowledge of what they sought. They admitted they had heard of it from Snake prisoners but nothing would have induced them to go near the Snakes, who were their mortal enemies.

The explorers had now come as far as the Bighorn Range of the Rocky Mountains. Pierre de la Vérendrye wanted to go on but he could obtain no guides for fear of the Snake Indians and if the party went on alone it would have meant a certain and disastrous encounter with this hostile tribe. With longing eyes they gazed up at the snowcapped peaks of the Rockies, certain that if they could only reach the summit they would see the Ocean, never dreaming that more than eight hundred miles of mountains and forests still lay between them and their objective.

Their supplies and presents were practically exhausted and their Indian friends were anxious to get back to their villages, so there was no alternative but to return.

The year was now 1743. They had not found the Western Ocean but they had discovered the Rocky Mountains or at least part of them to which the name rightly belongs. With no support from their government and at considerable expense to themselves, reckoned not only in money but in health, they had explored a vast region hitherto unknown, had diverted a considerable portion of the lucrative fur trade from the English to the French and had established six forts. Sixty-two years later, two men of a newly established nation were to follow this route laid out by La Vérendrye and his sons and followers and were to find the Western or Pacific Ocean. But they set out free of encumbrances, supported to the fullest extent by their government and with the finest equipment.

And what credit did La Vérendrye receive? The Comte de Maurepas wrote to Governor de Beauharnois. "I fail to find anything satisfactory in the progress La Vérendrye has made or anything to justify his carrying on the enterprise inasmuch as it is obvious that the route he has laid down will never lead to the discovery of the Western Sea." De Beauharnois wrote back indignantly to the Minister and again the reply was: "La Vérendrye has been solely occupied with his own affairs for many years and has rendered no service to the country." Permission to proceed further was withheld and given instead to another man—the Sieur de Noyelles.

# CHAPTER FORTY-THREE

B Y 1743 the families of the two Manor Houses had for four years been enjoying added prestige of being related to the Governor of Montreal, for in 1739 Jean-Baptiste Nicholas Roch de Ramezay had been appointed Governor to replace de Beaucourt who had unexpectedly resigned. Jean-Baptiste was the youngest Governor that Montreal had had, being only thirty-one years old. His appointment was popular, for he had already made a brilliant reputation as a soldier, and further, the name of de Ramezay was held in high esteem because of his father. With a beautiful and popular wife to support him he stood at the height of his career and the Chateau again became the center of many brilliant entertainments. Unfortunately these had in the past year been curtailed by the death of Marie-Charlotte de Ramezay, who had died the previous July. Madame's kindness and thoughtfulness to so many during her husband's régime had never been forgotten and though in later years straitened circumstances had prevented her dispensing such lavish hospitality, nevertheless she had always been ready to give what help and comfort she could.

In 1740 war had broken out in Europe over the Austrian Succession. This matter, so remote from the colonies, was nevertheless the cause that once again set the English and French at each others throats. For many years both nations in the New World had been looking for an excuse to attack each other but had had to content themselves with border raids, carried out by the savage tribes incited by one side or the other.

Those on the seigneuries throughout the colonies paid little heed to these war rumblings and would have continued to ignore them had they not been brought more forcibly home to them.

One evening, early in the spring of 1743, Paul and Marguerite sat at supper with André and Philip. They were just finishing when Pierre Boissart burst in upon them. As *capitaine de milice* he had been into Montreal to gather the weekly report to present to the people on the following Sunday morning. He was a little out of breath for he had ridden hard, and his eyes were wild with excitement. They all turned at his abrupt entrance. He stopped just inside the dining room and without preliminary greeting stated dramatically: "War has been declared with England."

Silence greeted the announcement. Then Paul said quietly: "That is official, Pierre?"

"Yes, Uncle. I have here a copy of the proclamation that the Governor is having placed all over town." He handed the paper to Paul who read it in silence and then handed it to André.

"I have been afraid of this for some time," Paul said and his sigh was heavy.

"Shall I announce it at once, Uncle, or wait until Sunday?"

Paul could see that Pierre was eager to have the privilege of telling the news to the habitants. "Yes, Pierre, proceed," he said.

Around the table they were silent after Pierre's departure. Paul and Marguerite were too full of their own ominous thoughts to be able to speak. It was young Philip who broke the silence.

"I had better report at once, Father," he said and rose. He was now fourteen and wore the uniform of an ensign.

"I suppose you should," André replied and rose also. "I will come with you while you saddle your horse."

Philip kissed his grandfather and Aunt Marguerite and he and his father went out. André watched him mount and ride away. Then he stood for awhile on the steps thinking. War—and his son in the midst of it. He looked at the empty sleeve of his coat. He would be little use now to fight, except perhaps to defend himself or others with a sword. At least they had spared him his sword arm, even if he could not handle a gun. "Thank God Philip is a good swordsman," he thought. He had himself taught his son, stressing the fact that any man who carried a sword must be more than proficient in its use. It seemed to him unbelievable that his son could now be old enough to be a soldier. In these last half dozen years he had grown up so fast, changing rapidly from a little boy to a school boy and then to a man, with already two years of army training back of him. He had just come home on leave, having been stationed for some time at Niagara. André thought of him and was proud, yet not without misgivings. He had not been an easy boy to raise, possibly because he had been spoiled in his early years. He had so much of his mother's wilfulness in him. Yet André secretly admired the fiery qualities in his son. As he had grown he had become handsome and dashing, with little regard for others, and, as he had done as a child, always getting his own way. He had fought every boy on the Seigneury of his own age, and some younger or older, and had usually come out victorious. With his dark smoldering eyes, inherited from the Renault side of the family, he had kept every young female heart fluttering. Although André did not know it, he had scarcely donned his ensign's uniform when he had gone to the lower end of town with an older ensign and had tested his manhood with a half-breed girl. She had laughed at his ignorance and had accepted his pay with scorn, but this he had never mentioned to anyone, but had bragged to his fellow officers about where he had been. With his fine physique, handsome looks and dashing quality he was going to be involved in many conquests as he grew older.

Inside the house, Paul and Marguerite continued to sit at the table. Marguerite covered her eyes with one hand, trying not to let Paul see that they were filled with tears. But he saw and laid a hand gently over hers. He knew that she was thinking as he was. The last letter she had had from Henry had told them that John had recently been promoted to Lieutenant in the English Guards. What they had always feared had now happened. If this declaration of war was to become serious, then Paul's grandson would be wearing the blue uniform and Marguerite's grandson would be wearing the red. Cousin would be fighting cousin.

Marguerite looked up and her glistening eyes met those of her brother. "Oh Paul!" she cried and the tears burst their bonds. He went round to her and white head mingled with white head.

"I never thought it would come to this, Paul. Oh Eric!" she sobbed.

André came in and saw them and quietly went up to his room. Over the Seigneury came the sound of the church bell, summoning the people to where Pierre Boissart stood on the church steps, a lantern in his hand, waiting to tell them the cause of the alarm.

The following morning everything appeared to be the same as the people went about their work, though thoughts were all centered upon the same subject.

A tallish man, tanned and muscular, dressed in fringed deerskins, jumped from a canoe and pulled it up on to the riverbank. After him climbed two small boys. The woman with him needed no help, though he put out a hand to steady her. She looked up at him and smiled and he returned the smile, looking towards the Manor House.

"My home, Kiki," he said, "and yours."

She gazed with awe at the large house with the tall pointed roof and the gabled windows. It was so different from the low domed houses she was accustomed to seeing. Her fear was mirrored on her face, so that he said gently: "Don't be afraid. You will soon become accustomed to it."

Together they walked towards it, she holding on to her sons with each hand. As they neared the house she fell back a step or two, walking as she felt was right, slightly behind her husband.

Paul-André paused to let her catch up with him but still she was behind him when they stopped.

He turned and said: "There's mother."

Elise had seen them approaching and hurried on to the *galerie*. Her heart contracted as she saw the woman behind him, for a papoose was strapped to her back and by her walk it was obvious that she was Indian. For the moment Elise thought that she would strangle, her heart pounded so hard—pounded with excitement at seeing her son again after eight years and with the fear that now clutched her. The thing that she had always dreaded had happened. She knew that voyageurs often consorted with Indian women—but for her son to bring one home. In the swift moments that passed as they approached the house she suffered the gamut of every emotion.

But as she walked to meet them and then felt her son's strong sinewy arms around her, crushing her to him and kissing her, she forgot all but her delight in seeing him again. As she looked into his strange amber eyes they were the same eyes which when he was a little boy had asked her for understanding. She mustered all the understanding she possessed as he put his arm around her and turned her towards where Kiki stood, eyes to the ground, waiting to be noticed.

"Maman, I want you to meet my wife," he said and his words were crisp and clear. She felt the pride and the defiance in them. "Kiki—my mother, Madame de Brievaux."

Kiki raised her eyes and Elise was startled at their blueness. The long fair hair had been carefully twisted into a large knot at the nape of her neck. Elise was sure that she must be a native woman, yet was bewildered.

She smiled at her and held out both hands. "Welcome home, Kiki..." She hesitated on the name. "It is Kiki isn't it?" She turned to Paul-André with the question.

"Kikidacoc really but I call her Kiki. It is Mandan for *laugh*," he said.

"I see." She did not know whether Indian women kissed but she leaned forward and embraced the girl on both cheeks. The blue eyes smiled their thanks.

As they talked, a curly red head kept peeping from behind Kiki's skirts, first one side and then the other. Paul-André spoke sharply and then the red head became not one but two, as two small boys, identically alike, stepped forward together.

Elise's eyes opened wide with surprise and then her face broke into a delighted smile as she looked from them to her son and then back again at them.

"Paul-André! Twin boys!" she exclaimed and crouching down, hugged them to her, one in each arm. "Oh Paul-André, you have brought back my twin boys!"

"Yes, mother," he said quietly. He had already told Kiki the story of the disastrous accident and he smiled at her over his mother's head.

"Oh darlings, how I shall love you! What are your names?"

"I'm Paul," one answered.

"I'm André," the other answered.

"Paul and André. How wonderful! And I'm your grandmother."

They smiled rather shyly. They had round chubby faces in which there was no trace of Indian, except in the peculiar shape of their eyes which, like their mother's, were long and narrow and raised at the inner corner.

"Come inside," Elise said and then noticed the baby strapped to Kiki's shoulders. "Oh, I have missed this one," she said. She went round back and looked at the small sleeping infant. Straggling fair hair covered her head.

"She's our daughter," Paul-André said, "and her name's Elise."

"After me?" Elise said.

She looked at the tiny sleeping granddaughter and her eyes filled with tears.

"Come along," she said and led the way in, a small grandson holding either hand.

Inside Kiki cast furtive glances around the large room with such strange furniture. The two boys started to run from one place to another but Paul-André said something to them in Mandan and they immediately returned to their mother's side. Elise noticed all this but made no comment.

There was an awkward silence for a moment. Then Elise said: "I must call your father." But as she started to leave Paul-André held her arm.

"I would like to tell father myself, Maman," he said quietly.

"Oh—would you?" she said and their anxious eyes met. She did hope that this was not going to make another breach between father and son. "Just as you like, dear. Would your—would Kiki like to go upstairs? I did not know you were coming but your old room is ready—it is always ready as you know. Er—you must be hungry. I—er—I'll see about breakfast."

"I'll take Kiki and the children upstairs and then see father," Paul-André said.

"Is there anything you want for the baby?" she asked Kiki.

"No thank you, madame," Kiki replied politely. Elise noticed the soft musical quality of her voice and that she spoke in French. She was dreadfully puzzled over her.

Paul-André led the way upstairs, followed by his family. He threw open the bedroom door and motioned to them to go in. He had already explained to Kiki how the white man lived and slept but of course the mental pictures she had conjured up from his description were not anything like what she now saw. She stood inside the room and surveyed it with awe. She walked to the huge four-poster bed and looked at it. Timidly she ran her hand lightly over the white sheets and touched the pillow and as it yielded to her touch drew her hand back quickly. She looked up at her husband who was smiling as he watched her.

"So soft," she said and then: "Where are the sides? Won't we fall out?"

Paul-André drew the curtains around the bed. "Really much the same. You enter here at the side in the same way. Only we don't have buffalo robes."

She nodded and then let her eyes travel around the room.

The two boys were running quietly from chair to chair. Again Paul-André spoke to them in the dialect and they stopped abruptly. He called them both to him, crouching down and putting an arm around each.

"You're going to find many things different," he said speaking this time in French. "I have told you that. You must remember what I tell you and do *exactly* as I tell you, so that your grandmother and grandfather will like you and understand you. Now, to begin, we do not sit on the floor but on chairs. Watch what I do and do exactly the same. It won't be difficult after the first time. Now—watch how I sit down on a chair. You will have to pull yourselves up because you are small. Now watch."

He went to a chair and sat down. "Now, each of you do the same."

It was difficult because of their shortness but they managed it fairly well and of course began to swing their legs. "No—keep your legs still and don't kick the chair." They obeyed. Paul-André looked across the room and saw Kiki imitating what he had done, sitting down in an armchair, with her hands and arms resting demurely on the arms of the chair but with her legs wide apart as he had done! He smiled at her and walking over gently pressed her knees together. "Ladies must always sit in chairs with their legs together, dear," he said. She looked so distressed that he bent and kissed her.

Again he turned to the boys. "Now something very important. I want you to be sure to greet Grandfather properly. When I say: 'Father, this is Paul and this is André.' what do you do?"

Both small boys gave a jerky bow that brought a smile to their father's face. "Hmmm. Fairly good. And if Grandfather holds out his hand like this—what do you do?" He extended his hand and both boys grabbed it. "No, that isn't good. One at a time. And just lay yours in Grandfather's—don't grab it." They tried again and the second attempt was more successful.

"And this is what I do, monsieur, isn't it?" Kiki asked, a little archly. She put a hand on each side of her skirt and dropped a curtsey. Paul-André had to laugh but not at her. He had taught her this some time ago and it had always intrigued her. He knew that it would astonish his parents. As he laughed he bowed to her, and raising her from the curtsey, kissed her hand.

"Very charming, madame," he said and they both laughed. But the laugh was brief. Suddenly she ran to him and clung there. "I'm afraid, Ours-feu, awfully afraid."

"They will be kind and understanding. Don't be afraid," he said and kissed her. He felt defiant. Let anyone dare to make her afraid or despise her! She was as good as any of them and more beautiful than most.

"I must go to my father now," he said.

"I will feed baby," she said. "And ..."

There was a knock at the door and Madeleine came in carrying a large pitcher of water, her face full of curiosity.

"Ah Madeleine, how glad I am to see you!" he said and hugged her as he took the pitcher of water from her. With his arm still around her he said: "Madeleine—this is my wife, Madame Kikidacoc and these are my sons Paul and André." Madeleine's eyes were wide with astonishment as "Madame Kikidacoc" sank to the floor in a curtsey. Paul-André started but said nothing. Probably because of his embrace, Kiki evidently had not realized that Madeleine was their servant or if she had would not have known what to do. In imitation the two boys bowed, so that Madeleine's mouth opened wide.

"Well I ... bon jour," she said, looked at Paul-André and saw that his eyes were dancing and then hurried from the room. When she had left he did not tell Kiki that she had made a mistake.

"Who is she?" she asked.

He replied casually: "She looks after us all, dear."

Downstairs, Elise stood for several minutes in the center of the room, her confused thoughts tumbling over each other. She wished she could run and warn Antoine, yet she knew that it was best for Paul-André to do it himself. She passed her hand over her eyes, terribly concerned that again there might be a separation between father and son. Suppose he would not accept them? Antoine, for all the years that he had been a Seigneur, still had so much of the French aristocrat in him. And what effect was this going to have upon other people? Having been exalted by their daughter becoming the lady of first importance in Montreal, would they now be degraded by the marriage of their son and heir? Would Ann-Marie accept her? She was so proud and happy over Jean-Baptiste's appointment. "Oh dear! oh dear!" Elise murmured and offered a silent prayer for understanding and guidance. Then she went into the kitchen and told Madeleine to prepare extra breakfast. Briefly she explained, pouring some of her troubled thoughts out to the old servant.

When Paul-André came down again, Elise was standing by the window. She had seen Antoine over by the barn. She turned as he entered and said as cheerfully as she could: "Are they quite comfortable? We shall have to see about beds for the boys."

Paul-André put his arm around her and kissed her. "Thank you, Maman, for being so kind to her. I know it was a shock to you."

"Is she Indian?" she asked quietly, trying to make her voice sound natural.

"Mandan Indian. They are a tribe quite different from others. I will tell you all about it in detail later. But they are a fine race. Her father was their Chief. And they are much more civilized than other Indians."

"But her hair—it is so fair and her eyes are blue."

"Strange isn't it? They don't have the characteristics of Indians at all. Of course—they do live differently from us." He put his arm around his mother again and said anxiously: "You will help her, Maman, won't you?"

"Of course, dear," she said quickly. "In every way I can."

"I have explained several things to her. She still has much to learn but she learns quickly. With your help she will soon behave the way—er—white women do."

"I understand, dear," Elise said kindly.

"I will find Father, now," he said and kissed her.

"He's over by the barn," she said.

She turned to the window and watched anxiously as he strode towards the barn. She could hear her heart pounding. For all her concern she felt a swell of pride that the broad shouldered man striding across to the barn was her son. He looked so manly and strong. Antoine came out from the barn, saw a man approaching and then as he recognized him, rushed toward him. Elise watched them embrace each other; watched Antoine slapping him proudly on the back and saw the hurried interchange of words of greeting. As an interpreter Paul-André had so long utilized the sign language that now he talked with his hands as well as his tongue. Elise could follow the conversation. She saw Antoine's face light up and both of them look towards the house. "Now he is telling him he has brought back a wife," Elise said to herself. Then she saw a heavy frown on her husband's face and her heart began to pound again. His face was stern and heavy. She saw Paul-André put his hand up to his hair and then run it down way below his waist. "He's telling him about her long fair hair," she thought. She saw him touch his eyes. "And she has the deepest blue eyes," she could imagine him saying. Then he held his hands a few feet from the ground, one each side of him and she knew he was telling Antoine about the twins. The twins! Her heart leapt with joy. Her boy had given her back her red-headed twins. That alone was a joy not to be overlooked. Paul-André was talking very fast and at last she saw Antoine's face relax and then break into a smile.

"Don't judge, Father, until you have seen her," Paul-André was saying though his mother could not hear this. "She is a proud daughter of a proud race."

The two men came towards the house and Antoine's arm was across his son's shoulders. Tears welled up in Elise's eyes—tears of thankfulness. At least Antoine was not angry, or was not showing it, and somehow she knew that when he saw Kiki he would not be any more angry than she was.

www.ingramcontent.com/pod-product-compliance
Lightning Source LLC
Chambersburg PA
CBHW022241020726
47496CB00004B/1014